BOSTON BLUES SERIES

Coach Me

MOLLIE GOINS

To my Grammy who said the smut was good, but please have an FMC that doesn't curse so much.

Boston Blues Starting Roster
Bold - mentions in story

- Zane Mickels #01 | 2B
- Dante Newport #02 | CF
- **Adam Reyer #04 | C**
- **Mateo Keener #07 | SS**
- Keaton Locke #08 | LF
- **Tripp Pierce #11 | 3B**
- Wesley Nelson #18 | DP
- **Will Anderson #24 | P**
- **Beck Daines #36 | 1B**
- Grayson Nash #45 | RF

General Manager: Jim Olsson | Pitching Coach: Dex Larsen | Team photographer: Callie Reyer | Shannon Carlton: Team Secretary

For the full 26 man roster and teams in their division, please see molliegoins.com

Author Note

Coach Me is overall a low angst, feel good story, and while I feel it's safe for me to say this ends on an HEA, minor spoilers will be mentioned below.

It is important to me to note pregnancy in books. Some of my characters will end with babies, some will not, each one will look different. Dex and Lucie are a story that ends with a pregnancy involved. If you wish to conclude Dex and Lucie's story at the end of chapter 46, I wholeheartedly understand. You can rest assured they have a happy life together.

Thank you for reading Coach Me. Please see the Dick-tionary chapters with explicit content.

Dick-tionary

Listen, I'm not here to judge, so whether you're here to find those spicy chapters *wink wink* or skip over them, I'm so happy you're about to spend time with Dex and Lucie!

Explicit content is mentioned throughout the book. Coach Me is intended for a mature audience only. Chapters of high sexual content are listed below.

Chapter 29

Chapter 30

Chapter 31

Chapter 40

Contents

Chapter 1
Dex

"A hundred and two miles per hour." Will whistles, reading off the speed of the pitch I just threw. "Damn, Larsen, I knew you still had it in you."

"I'm your coach; there shouldn't have even been a doubt." I roll my shoulders back. I can already feel the muscles aching. Not warming up before throwing a pitch like that will definitely call for some ice tonight, but my kid was taunting me and my best pitcher wasn't helping.

"Dad, that was so totally awesome!" Miles yells as he races to me. "You threw faster than Will did!"

"By one mile per hour!" Will tosses a ball in the bucket. "Give me another chance, kid."

I laugh and shake my head. "I could throw a lot faster and you know it, Anderson. Remember, you're here because I retired."

Will gives me a cocky grin. He's holding back a jab— whether it's a glory days or old man joke, I'm not sure. Despite the shift in our teammate dynamic, I like Will. A player had to take my slot on the roster, and I can't say I hate it's been filled by someone who can throw as well as he can.

Miles pulls on my arm. "Dad, does this mean I could learn to throw as fast as you?"

Kneeling down so I can be eye level with my son, I say my next words with so much confidence. "I know you can, and I can't wait to see it happen."

Miles's eyes light up. "Good, because if I could throw as fast as you, maybe Callie will marry me."

I snort out a laugh as Will yells, "Hey!" then scoops Miles up and flips him upside down. "Little man, I thought we talked about this. Callie is *my* girlfriend."

"Not for long," Miles sputters out between giggles as Will starts to spin him around.

Leave it to my son to tell our new star pitcher that he's going to steal his girlfriend. It isn't exactly what I expected to happen when my boss said I could bring Miles to work every day.

I thought maybe he'd latch on to me or one of the players. He's been around the team enough growing up that most of the guys aren't exactly strangers, but Miles is only five, so, honestly, I expected him to get bored with all this pretty quickly. However, being around the team this much has done nothing but bring my boy to life.

Not to mention, gaining more than enough confidence to bat out of his league, considering Callie is our twenty-something team photographer.

I watch as Will flips Miles back around onto his feet. Will's hands land on Miles's shoulders as he tries to steady him. The moment Miles finds his footing he lunges at Will and tackles him to the ground.

Invisible strings tug at my heart with the sound of

Miles's laughter. Despite his world being completely turned upside down this year, he's here laughing.

"Oh my, what's going on here?" Callie chuckles as she appears beside me.

"I believe it's a fight for your honor." I tilt my head as Miles continues to wrestle Will. It doesn't last long, though. The moment Miles registers that Callie's here, he's off Will in a flash.

"Callie!" He beams, bouncing in front of her. "I kicked Will's ass!"

For all that's holy, did he really just say that?

"Miles! Where did you learn that word?"

Miles digs his little foot into the turf. "I don't know."

Yeah, right. Hell, feeling a little less grateful for this new arrangement now.

"Well, at least you know he's not a snitch." Will rests his hands on Miles's slouched shoulders. "Oh, come on, Dex. What'd you expect the kid to hear being around a bunch of baseball players? Let's be honest, he could have said a lot worse. He *does* spend a lot of time with Callie."

Callie swats at Will's arm. "Now who's the snitch."

"Jesus," I mutter. I suppose he's right, everyone here doesn't know how to keep their mouths free of curses, no matter how hard I try. Kneeling down to eye level again, I look at my son. "Miles, 'ass' is an adult word. You're not in trouble, but now you know that you don't need to say it anymore. Next time there will be a consequence."

Miles scrunches his nose as he digs his foot deeper into the turf. "Okay, Daddy. I won't say it again."

"There, all is well!" Callie claps her hands. "What were you guys doing anyway? I was editing away when I caught a glimpse of the time and realized practice ended nearly half an hour ago."

The spark comes back to Miles's eyes. "I asked Daddy to throw a ball like he used to do, but then Will said he couldn't. That wasn't true because he threw *faster* than Will did."

"Oh, he did now?" Callie chuckles.

"By one mile per hour," Will tacks on, but that small detail doesn't register with Miles.

"One day, I'm going to throw as fast as him so we can get married, Callie!"

Callie quirks an eyebrow. "Hmm, so throwing a ball is a marriage proposal now?"

If I hadn't been looking at Will, I would have missed the small glint that appeared in his eyes. Man's gone for Callie, so I have a feeling Miles just gave his competition the best idea.

Will shakes Miles's shoulders lightly. "Miles, I appreciate your game, but I've got to get Callie home. I'll warn you now, if you do steal her away, the girl gets hangry."

Callie crosses her arms then shrugs. "Eh, we're not all perfect."

"I think you are." Miles launches at Callie, hugging her waist.

Damn, my kid's smooth.

"I'm in for so much trouble when he gets older, aren't I?"

"I think so." Callie gives a pouty smile as she embraces Miles's hug.

Will watches with amusement for a moment before reaching for Miles's shoulders again. "Shi—Geez, Casanova. You're giving me a run for my money."

Miles looks up at Will with a smirk, "It's all a part of the plan."

"You guys go, we'll lock up." I tug Miles to me before Will has to take him outside for all his attempts at Callie.

"Thanks, Dex." Callie waves on their way out. "Bye, Miles!"

"Bye, Callie!" he hollers back with a huge smile.

When the door shuts, I squeeze Miles's shoulders. "Come on, bud, why don't you grab that ball over there and we can head home."

"Okay, Dad!"

Miles zooms over to the left side of the field to grab the ball, calling out what he was doing as if he were actually playing in a real ball game. "Larsen makes a diving catch... and he gets the ball!"

I chuckle to myself as he does a victory dance and continues on with his imaginary glory. After making sure all the equipment is locked up, I call for my MVP and wait for him to race out in the hall before turning off the big stadium lights in the training arena.

"Dad," Miles starts with an inquisitive tone. *Oh great, these are always interesting.* "Is Mommy coming home for dinner tonight?"

Fuck. Someone stab me in the heart. It'd fucking hurt less.

"No, bud, she's not." The pure ache in my chest threatens to fill me with rage. Miles's questions about his mom's sudden departure have happened less and less over these past few months, but they kill me every time. "If you want, we can try to call her before you go to bed?"

Miles purses his lips, but tears don't come—and for that I'm thankful. As much as I don't want to see my ex-wife, if

Miles wants to see her, I'd drive my sorryass all the way across town to her condo if it meant making him happy.

"Okay, yeah, I want to call her." Miles looks down at the ground for a brief moment, then, as if he put springs in his shoes, he bounces all the way to the front door.

Oh, to have that mental recovery time. I may not have been too heartbroken when Kate asked for a divorce last year, but seeing the effect it's had on Miles...that fucking kills me.

It's been six months since our divorce was finalized. It had to have gone down as one of the easiest divorce filings ever, I'm sure of it. Kate and I were never really this major love match; we were casually dating for a couple of months while she was in law school. Neither of us was really looking for anything serious, but that all changed when the double pink lines showed up on that stick.

We were careless and neither of us handled the shock of it all very well. Getting married shotgun-style was our first mistake. I'm man enough to own that it was more my fault than hers. My mom put a lot of pressure on us, and while I knew deep down that we weren't in love, I let that pressure push me too.

I can't fault Kate for not wanting to stay together, but her not wanting more than a weekend a month with Miles grates at my willpower. I know kids weren't a part of her plan, and I respected that in the beginning. Having Miles was completely her choice—after that was where I started fucking up and talking about marriage.

I can't say what would have been better in the long run, but I do know that Miles is just a kid. He didn't ask for any of this. I'm trying my best to atone for all that Kate and I have put him through, even if I can't help but feel like I'm failing at it. I am trying.

Miles rams into the front door of the facility with a giggle. "I beat you!"

I let the smile on my son's face pull me from my somber thoughts. "I didn't know we were racing. That's not very fair."

Miles pushes off the door and bounces at my feet. "What is it you say, Dad? Don't be a sad loser?"

I let out an amused huff. "You mean sore loser."

"Same thing."

I push open the door and Miles jumps across the threshold. "I guess you're not technically wrong, but still, if you want to race, you need to let the other person know it's a race."

Miles hums before wiping around to me. "Okay, so can we race now?"

I tug at the door to make sure it's locked, then scan the parking lot for any potential moving vehicles but considering we're the last ones here, it's only us in the lot.

"Alright, first one to the car gets to pick what I cook for dinner tonight."

Miles doesn't miss a beat. "Can it be ice cream?!"

Okay, I should have expected that. Miles has been fighting me on meals for a few months now. Some days it's worse than others, but I can't help but feel like this is a result of the divorce. Another point for the failing dad scoreboard.

"That could be the dessert of choice, but real food has to go with it."

"Alright." Miles flicks his eyes to the sky as if the term "real food" offends him.

I shake his shoulder. "Come on, you count us down."

Miles jumps around to face the parking lot and gets into his ready-to-run stance. "Okay, one...two...three...go!"

Chapter 2
Lucie

"Okay, everyone, line up!" I announce loudly to my class as I hit the small chimes by the door. I watch as each student scrambles from their desk to grab their backpack and races to the front.

Their sweet little minds are so ready to be out of this place and start their summer break. I get it, I do, but it hits me as each kid makes their way in line—I did it. My first year as a teacher, I crafted each of these little beautiful minds.

The squeals of excitement grow louder as each child files into the line. I see little hands start to high-five and hug, but they're kids, so the joy can get out of hand quickly. I hit my chime again.

"Eyes and ears..."

All the kids turn their heads to face me and say, "Looking and listening."

"You all did so amazing this year, each and every one of you should be proud of yourselves." A small tug pulls at my heart. *Okay, Lucie, don't cry, these children will judge you.*

Taking a deep breath, I start again. "Let's do our end-of-day affirmations for the last time, but we have a new one this time, okay?"

Cheers erupt in the sweetest voices, and I can't bring myself to care about the volume.

"I am smart," I say.

"I am smart," they repeat.

"I am kind to others and myself."

"I am kind to others and myself."

"I am important."

"I am important."

I smile, as it normally ends there, but now I get to add, "I am going into second grade."

"I am going into second grade!" they yell.

Happy tears prick my eyes as I grip the door handle of my classroom.

After walking my kids out for the last time this school year, I hold strong every time each student asks for one last hug.

I can't even begin to explain this high as I collapse into my desk chair. I did it. I taught. All that money my brother poured into my degrees is paying off. My dream job, and if I dare say, I killed it.

At that, I feel my phone buzz on my desk.

Will Cannot Leave This Group Chat

REAGAN

Excuse me, Miss Anderson, it's summer break! Get your ass out of that building.

Quit checking my location, it's creepy!

WILL

We'll be at Mom's for dinner at 6.

REAGAN

Creepy…Loving…such a thin line. Just ask Callie, I'm sure she knows the feeling with Will.

WILL

Don't push it. I'll leave this fucking chat…again.

CALLIE

Don't let him fool you, he totally laughed at his phone a second ago.

REAGAN

We all know he secretly loves the family chat. Lucie, why has your little sim not moved? You're supposed to be leaving that hellhole!

Okay someone's being dramatic.

WILL

You're surprised?

REAGAN

I'm not dramatic… I just think she should leave school already. It's her summer break!

Can't I just enjoy the fact that I finished my first year as a teacher for 2 seconds?

REAGAN

No, get your ass to Mom's and celebrate like a normal person. I'm making celebratory cocktails all with funny names for YOU! And Julie's about to slave in Mom's kitchen.

CALLIE

Will and I have to head to the stadium for a
bit, but I've got the nonalcoholic mixers
ready, Rea. Congrats on being a badass
teacher, Luce! See you guys later!

I smile at my phone, rereading Callie's message for a moment before my sister's face pops up on my screen.

"Hello," I answer with a sigh.

"Why aren't you moving?" she huffs. "Your little Sim should be chugging along on the highway right now, but it's still sitting in the building."

"Jeez, Rea, you have got to chill with the location checking. I'm about to get my stuff and head out." I turn in my chair to click on my computer screen for one last quick look at my school email. "You're still good to come back with me Monday to get the turtle tank for the summer, right?"

"Yeah, yeah, I'll come help get those two assholes," my sister grumbles. She's never been much of an animal person, especially reptiles. "What time again?"

When my email finally pulls up, I see I have a message from my principal. The subject reads: Monday Meeting.

I frown and put my phone between my ear and shoulder. "Um, hold on."

Opening the email, I see that it's sent only to me, which feels odd. My eyes quickly scan over the message and my frown only deepens. "Mrs. Riggets sent me an email requesting a meeting Monday morning." A pit forms in my stomach. "That's weird, isn't it?"

"She's your boss, right?" Reagan asks.

Scanning the email again, I try to find any hint of wording that could bring my stress meter from skyrocketing. "Technically. She's one of them, at least."

"I'm sure it's nothing, probably just an end-of-first-year check-in. I'm staying at Julie's place on Sunday, but I'll meet you there and wait in your classroom until it's over."

I snort a small laugh. "You could work on getting the turtles loaded while I have the meeting."

I can see the horror on my sister's face. "Fat chance. You're lucky I'm letting those slimy things stay in our apartment to begin with."

"Mmm, that's not how I recall that conversation going. I believe you said, 'over my dead body will those turtles stay here,' and Will overruled you."

"Semantics," Reagan huffs.

"What do you have against Pip and Pop, huh? They're just turtles." I put my phone on speaker so I can type a reply to my principal letting her know I'll be there.

"I'm your sister, you know the answer to this. I am a plant person—my entire being is my floral shop. Give me flowers, ferns, vines, anything. Don't give me animals. And honestly, don't give me a lot of people either."

Hitting send on my reply, I snort. "And yet, you're going to be living with two turtles for the whole summer. Can I feed them some of your clover?"

"Not in this lifetime." Reagan pauses for a second. "Your Sim still hasn't moved. Lucie Jo Anderson, come on!"

Sighing, I click off my computer and reach for my bag. "Okay, okay. Goodness, does Julie let you boss her around like this? I just wanted one moment to take this classroom in."

"One, of course she does, she loves me. And two, you've had all year to do that. Not to mention, you'll be back in two months. Your sister, however, will take your Teacher's Aid shot if you don't hurry up."

"Teacher's Aid?" Goodness, I can only imagine what sort of concoction Reagan's mixed up.

"Yeah, it's got Fireball and—"

"Okay," I cut her off as I stand from my chair. "I can already see the hangover tomorrow. Tell me any more, and I might bail on you."

Reagan's chuckle holds a hint of an evil tone. "My sweet angel baby sister would never. Now hurry up. If I don't see your Sim on the highway in five minutes, I'll come get you myself."

"*Hmph*" is all I manage back. I know my sister doesn't mean her sweet talk in a condescending way, but the whole Everyone Loves Lucie bit my siblings do isn't my favorite. "I'm walking out now, so you can relax. Go boss your girlfriend around in the kitchen, I'll be there by the time she kicks you out for being annoying."

"That means you've got a solid fifteen minutes at best. Drive safe. Love you."

"Love you too," I sing softly before hanging up.

I grab my bag and head to the door. Reaching for the light switch, I turn around to take one more look and let out a deep breath.

I did it.

"Oh my goodness. Julie, that meal was amazing." I slide down my chair and place my hands on my belly. "Best teacher appreciation meal ever."

Our celebratory dinners at our mom's house have only gotten better over the years, especially since Reagan started seeing Julie. With her officially finished with culinary school in Boston, she's back in Rowley, and we are definitely benefiting from it.

Reagan had several teacher-themed cocktails, and her chef girlfriend cooked a meal that was perfectly on theme. Teacher's Pet Pot Pie with apple tarts for dessert.

"Yeah, I think it's soaked up all the Teacher's Aid shots Rea gave us as we walked in the door." Callie pushes her empty plate forward and follows my movement of sliding down in her chair.

"Oh don't be such a lightweight, Cals. I have one more specialty." Reagan shoots up from her seat, and we all groan. "Oh, come on!"

Julie reaches for my sister's hand. "How about you make me one of the cocktails, but give everyone else the option. We still have plenty of non-alcoholic mixers."

I can practically see the softness wash over Reagan. I might have a special connection with my sister, but no one has ever gotten through to her like Julie.

"Fine, I'll allow it. Other than Lucie, of course, hers has to be alcohol."

"Hey, why me?" I hiccup, but she ignores me as she gets everyone else's preferences.

"Callie? Mom?" Reagan asks, leaving Will out because he doesn't drink at all.

"I'll do the cocktail, Rea, but light pour." Our mom sends Reagan a pointed look for emphasis, but I highly doubt Reagan cares.

"Mocktail me." Callie rests her head on my brother's shoulder, and he smiles down at her.

Then, as Reagan pulls Julie to her with a silent request for help, this ill feeling takes over me.

Huh, maybe I do need the alcoholic drink with seeing my siblings so happy with their significant others—it doesn't normally come with this pang of jealousy, though. Maybe it's just all the feelings of finishing my first year of teaching, heightening everything around me...

Maybe I don't need the alcohol.

"So, Lucie, what are your summer plans?" Callie asks.

"I'm not quite sure, the gym in town posted something about needing some extra hands for their summer programs. I thought about heading over after my meeting on Monday to see if they still need volunteers."

"There's no harm in taking a break for the summer, Luce," Will says, sounding like his typical dad-like self.

Will might try to stick to being an older brother primarily, but after our dad walked out Will took on both roles— whether he meant to or not. To Reagan and me, he's both— he has the respect of both.

"Okay, okay," Reagan announces as she and Julie walk back in with a tray full of drinks. "This one is a little different. It's a martini with vodka and triple sec—lemonade and orange juice for the mocktails—then cranberry juice, lime, and red sugar for the rim. Oh, and cranberries on a toothpick."

"Ooo, fancy." Our mom laughs. "Did you give this one a funny name too?"

"I did." Reagan blushes for a moment and tucks her head down as she passes the drinks out.

Will and I notice the shift in her demeanor immediately. No matter how I define the relationship with my siblings or the age difference between us, I always joke that we have some sort of...spidey-sense—eh, triplet-sense. We can read each other like a book, pretty much.

Will lifts an eyebrow in silent question toward me, but I have no clue why Reagan seems nervous all of a sudden. I give him a small shrug and take my drink from Julie.

When the drinks are all passed out, Reagan takes a deep breath and raises her glass. "This one is called 'Reagan and Julie are moving to Boston'!"

Mom and Callie process the name first while I'm frozen on my first sip.

"What? That's so exciting!" Callie beams. "We'll be living in the same city!"

Mom chips in next. "Reagan, this is wonderful news! Did Julie get the job at that restaurant?"

I can hear the happiness around me, but my thoughts are stilled. Restaurant? Moving to Boston...an hour away...not living with me in our apartment? Reagan never even hinted at the idea of moving to me. I can feel Will's eyes on me—studying. The concern he had for Reagan's mood shift is now directed at me.

You know that 'we can read each other like a book' thing? Yeah, Will's the best at it, and if I don't snap out of it, I know he'll try to fix it.

Not that there's anything to fix. I'm just...surprised? Shocked? I don't know what I'm feeling.

I take a deep breath and plaster a huge smile on my face. "This is so exciting, I'm so happy for you two!" My voice turns squeaky at the last part—okay, dial it back. "When... where?" I choke out. I'm failing so bad at acting normal right now.

"What's the plan for Boston?" Will asks. "Trying to decide how excited I am...Julie's cooking is a plus, but Reagan's a different story." Reagan gives Will a pointed look, but he doesn't falter. "Mine and Callie's place is scheduled visits only by the way."

Callie smacks his arm. "It is not. You are always welcome."

Reagan crinkles her nose. "I think we'll send a text first. But we won't be there for a couple of months. Julie starts as a chef at Zenith at the beginning of August."

Reagan looks at me with this gleam in her eyes as she clears her throat.

The room goes dead silent...or, well, to me it feels like it's silent. Deep down, I'm so happy for my sister, but I'm feeling a little blindsided. My siblings are my best friends, and while I know Reagan and I weren't going to be roommates forever, I did not see this coming.

I know the love her and Julie have for each other, and I don't have a right to be upset about that. It's more the idea of ending this era with my sister. I'm like 10 percent sad right now...okay, 20 percent...I'm mostly shocked. Okay—25 percent upset, *max*.

"Rea, this is so great. Really, I'm so happy for the both of you."

Reagan exhales and her shoulders fall to their normal level. "I'll have to keep Stigma's storefront until the end of this year with my lease agreement, but this way I have plenty of time to transition the business over while still holding my clientele here."

Reagan's shoulders tense again. "And our apartment won't be ready until mid-July. There's still time for me to slowly move out, and we still have a few weeks of being roommates, Luce."

"That's perfect," I breathe out as I force a smile to my lips.

At least when she moves out in the next couple of months, I can throw myself back into the school year. It might seem silly now, but I already miss my sister.

I look to Will next because I know I have to say something so I won't get a pep talk from him before the night ends. "I think I might take that break then."

Chapter 3
Dex

"Dad, what city are we going to again?" Miles asks from his car seat in the back.

"Atlanta," I huff out. I swear I've been nothing but a broken record this morning. Repeating where we're going and the time it'll take for us to get there. I had to tell Miles at least five times to brush his teeth. Three times to find his blanket that he wants to take on the plane. And then answered where we are going at least ten more times.

"Riiight, but not Atlantis because that city is underwater, right?"

"Right."

"Dad, how did Atlantis go underwater?" Miles asks, completely oblivious to the stress radiating off of me.

"I don't know, bud." Normally, I would do my best to come up with some sort of educated or fun answer, but today it's just not in me to do something for a made-up city.

I got shit sleep last night. After dinner Miles wanted to call his mom, and like usual it took three tries before we got her to answer, and then she only talked to Miles for five minutes before she was ready to hang up. That alone had my frustration high, but then the texts I got following the call made me bubble over into rage.

KATE

If you want to call me every night then we need to work out a scheduled time and put it in our agreement. I can't just talk whenever you want.

It's one thing that she threw in the "you"—like I'm using our son to talk to her when that couldn't be further from the truth—but then to expect her son to only call her during scheduled hours pisses me the fuck off. Maybe one day Miles won't want to talk to her every day, but he's only five. He didn't ask for any of this bullshit—he just wants to talk to his mother.

What Miles also didn't ask for was this sour mood of mine that's carried throughout the morning. Like I tell Miles when he wakes up grumpy, I woke up on the wrong side of the bed—and then it's gone downhill.

With each passing minute, I feel like I am the most unprepared father ever. Clothes I needed clean for this week were still wet in the wash because I forgot to move them over to the dryer. Miles's shoes all disappeared. Well, that's not technically true. I found several shoes but it took me a solid fifteen minutes to find a single pair that matched. After that, I realized every fucking to-go cup we have was loaded into the dishwasher...but guess who forgot to start it last night?

We barely made it out the door on time and when we got down to the lobby, I nearly ran right into the delivery guy and spilled every drop of my coffee...because my usual to-go cup was in the dishwasher.

"Dad, do you think that Atlanta picked its name because of Atlantis?"

Sighing, I try to roll my bad mood off. "I don't think so, but maybe we can look it up on the plane."

"Yeah, let's do it!" I glance back at Miles in the rearview mirror and a smile comes to his face. "I bet I'm right."

Well, that smile definitely helps.

I glance back at the time on the dash. I'm going to be pushing it, but I really fucking need a cup of coffee and the shit they have on the team plane is not going to cover it with the morning I'm having.

When I make it to the coffee shop on the next block, I see an open parking spot and consider it a damn sign. Hopping out immediately, I round my truck.

"What are we doing here? I thought we were getting on the airplane," Miles says as I get him out.

"We are, but unless we want to see Daddy bite some baseball players' heads off today, we're going to run in and I'm going to grab a cup of coffee."

Miles giggles. "That's silly. You can't bite someone's head off. You're not a dinosaur, Daddy."

I let out an amused *hmph*. "Some of the players might disagree with you on that."

I carry Miles inside because I know damn well that he'll walk as if there's not a care in the world.

When we walk in the door, Miles wiggles incessantly. "Put me downnnnn. I don't want to be carried right now."

Oh, to be five.

I let out a sigh of relief when I see that there's only one other person in line. Maybe my morning's turning around.

"Okay, but stay close." I set Miles down next to me. "Do you want anything? A juice? Fruit cup?"

Miles hums while he places his finger on his chin.

Oh, dear Lord, help me.

Miles is still humming when the girl in front of me steps over to the side.

When the barista smiles, signaling it's our turn, I step up and immediately place our order. "I'll have a large cup of whatever house drip you have and a small orange juice."

"But I want a fruit cup!" Miles whines at a very unnecessary volume.

Oh, I love my child. I love my child.

"And a fruit cup," I add as I exhale a deep breath.

"Can do!" The barista eyes me closer, then raises her eyebrows. "You're Dex Larsen, right? With the Boston Blues?"

Hell, I can hear every bit of her true intentions in her tone. After several years in the major leagues I can spot the cleat chasers pretty quickly.

I pull out a twenty and set it on the counter. "Yeah, that's me. I'm sorry, but we're in a bit of a hurry, so you can keep the change."

"Oh, of course." She giggles in an overly high-pitched tone as she scribbles what I know has to be her number on my coffee cup. "Our house coffee is over to the side. I can bring the orange juice and fruit cup over for the little man."

I simply nod back at her as I take my cup, but really, I'm debating how big of a meltdown Miles will have if we leave before she gets that opportunity. I don't want to come off like an ass, even in these situations, but I hate when they use Miles as a way to get to me.

"Come on," I say to Miles as I head over to the side so I can make my drink. I just want to get our stuff and get out of here.

"Dad, why can't I have coffee?"

"Because you don't need it. Trust me, you have more than enough energy."

The woman who was in front of us earlier steps to the side where the creamers are, and I step right up. Perfect, I just need this and Miles's stuff and we can be on our way.

"But how does coffee not make you a dinosaur?" Miles asks with the genuine curiosity of any child.

The blonde next to me tries to stifle her laugh. Her laugh is much lighter than the barista's, and I'm tempted to look her way, but I don't have the time.

"It just does. Trust me, one day you'll understand, son." I place my cup under the tap and turn the handle up. The coffee pours into my cup for exactly three seconds before it stops.

"Hell no, seriously?" I snap under my breath. I try the nozzle again but nothing. "Great, this is just great."

"Here," a feminine voice says as a full cup of coffee is set in front of me. "I'm not in a hurry. I can wait for them to refill."

"I don't think—" I start to argue but when I look at the woman in front of me, I stop. She's beautiful. Long blonde hair, with bright blue eyes—hell, everything about her screams bright. She's got on a light yellow sundress that fits her too damn well.

The minor drawback is that she has to be several years younger than me, but, damn, she's stunning.

"Really, I don't mind. I haven't put any sugar or cream in it yet. I know you're in a hurry, so please, take it."

I check my watch for the time. Fuck, would it make me a huge dick for actually taking this girl's coffee?

"Here you are, sweets." The cleat chaser of a barista comes up with a smirk that isn't nearly as bright as the blonde's next to me. She hands over Miles's stuff and takes one look at the girl next to me. Her smile falters for a moment before snapping back. "Be sure to use that number on the cup." She turns to Miles next—because they all think he's their in. "Bye, cutie."

"I'm not cutie," Miles grumbles. "My name is Miles."

Blondie and I both snort small laughs, and when I meet her eyes she pulls her lips into a thin smile. I really like that smile. I also really like her laugh. Fuck, and this yellow dress she's wearing—

"I think I'm going to take your cup, actually."

She quirks up an eyebrow. "Are you sure? You can pour it into your cup if you want."

Ah, so she's got jokes too.

"You know, I'm good on that." I hand Miles his fruit cup, then reach for a lid to put on her cup.

"Need any cream or sugar?" she asks, turning away from me to look at the variety in front of her. "There's regular cream, hazelnut—"

"Two sugars would be great, please."

"Got ya," she says plainly. There's no flirty tone with this girl, no sideways or up and down looks. In a way, it's refreshing. I almost want to say she doesn't even know who I am. Which is so fucking nice.

But, then again, I think I want this girl to flirt. I want to hear her laugh again. I want to change my fucking favorite color to whatever yellow she's wearing right now.

When she turns back, I'm so damn tempted to ask for her name, but she doesn't spare me a glance. She holds out the sugars to Miles. "Think you can handle these, Miles?"

He nods eagerly as he takes them from her hand. "I can handle it."

Her bright smile comes back, but she doesn't look at me. She simply takes my cup with the phone number that's going 100 percent unused. "I'm going to let someone know they need more coffee. You guys have a good day, don't want to be late."

She finally sends me one quick smile. I should stop her, I want to stop her—but she's right, we're about to be so fucking late.

We pull into our parking spot at the terminal for the Blues chartered plane just minutes before we're supposed to take off. I know I have zero time to spare, but I twist my coffee cup around and around in search of Blondie's name but it's nowhere to be found. Fuck.

"Okay, bud, you can unbuckle and I'll be back there in a second."

"Okie!" Miles cheers.

Rounding the back of my truck, I start to pull out our bags when our team's first baseman, Beck, comes up.

"Cutting it close, Larsen," he says with a chuckle.

"Way to state the obvious, asshole."

I've played with Beck for the last seven years. The man is probably one of the nicest people you will ever meet, but I really didn't need that sentence today. I'm not one to cut these flights close. I hate being late—even as a player I was always fifteen minutes early.

"Ah, so Dad's in a bad mood, got it." Beck snatches Miles's duffle bag from my hands. "I'll take the bags while you get the nice version of you."

I try again to push all of my frustration out with a deep breath and mutter a "thanks" to Beck.

This morning has felt like a damn roller coaster, and now I'm kicking myself for not at least getting that girl's name. Yeah, she seemed young but it felt like the first normal interaction I've had with a woman since the divorce. The first time I've actually been interested in a girl in years, actually.

I know it's silly to even entertain the idea of dating—I'm stretched thin as it is. But part of me kind of feels like there was an opportunity missed from that interaction.

Rounding the side of my truck, I pull open the passenger door, and Miles launches at me. "Yay, we're going to the fake Atlantis!"

Miles's arms squeeze tight around my neck. Those deep breaths did shit for me earlier, but this? This helps more than anything.

I somehow get to carry Miles across the tarmac and to the stairs with him holding on tight, but the moment my foot steps on the plane, he wiggles out of my arms.

"I can walk now, Dad," Miles says, and I swear he puffs his chest out a bit. Between that and the change from "Daddy" to "Dad," I already know who my Casanova is thinking of.

We round the corner of the team's chartered jet, and it takes Miles two seconds flat to find Callie.

"Callie!" He bounces down the aisle. "Good morning."

"Good morning, Miles." Callie beams.

I can feel a full plan of wooing coming on, and while I hate to cramp my kid's style, we need to take our seats.

"Hey, bud, come on." I wave him back when his little head turns around. "We have to get buckled up."

"But, Daaaad," Miles groans out.

Callie and half of the players around us try to hide their laughs.

"Way to be a mood killer, Dex," Beck says, coming up behind me.

"Yeah, let the kid work his magic," Tripp, our third baseman, chimes in.

Callie's brother Adam comes to Miles's defense next. "Just give the kid five minutes so Will can remember he's not nearly as smooth as he thinks he is."

"Hey, whose side are you on?" Will snaps.

"Miles's," the guys all say in unison.

I bring my hands to my forehead. I've got a fucking headache.

Miles giggles happily and while in this moment I'm glad I have such a good group of guys that love my son, they aren't fucking helping.

"Okay, okay, no need to stress Dex out anymore," Callie says to the guys before looking back at Miles. "Listen, I love our talks, but it's time for us to get seated. How about when we get to the stadium we sneak some ice cream into the photo outpost?"

"Promise?" Miles tilts his head to the side.

Callie crosses an X over her heart. "Promise, kiddo, but you gotta take your seat for me."

The groan Miles lets out is a lot less annoyed-sounding than the one I usually get, but at least I can always count on Callie to help me out.

When Miles turns around to come back to our seats, I mouth a *"thank you"* to Callie.

Miles gives me the silent treatment during takeoff. Considering he's been on an extreme number of plane rides since birth, they're really like nothing to him now. But despite what he thinks, he's five, not twenty-five, so the appeal of the silent treatment wears off pretty fast.

"Dad, how do planes fly?"

Well, while thinking about how to answer Miles's original question, he's asked me at least three more.

"And why do we call them planes? Why do we have to stay buckled in a car but not in a plane? Where do the number ones and twos go while we are in the air?"

You know, if you would have told me that one of the main things you do as a parent is make shit up to answer your child's million fucking questions, I may not have completely believed you. I mean, how much time could it possibly take, right?

Our team's general manager—my boss—Jim Olsson chuckles in the seat across from us. "So many excellent questions. I can't wait to hear your dad's answers."

Shit, me too. I feel like I can only confidently answer one of these questions. This may come as a shock to my five-year-old, but as a newly retired MLB pitcher I don't know shit about the hows and whys of planes.

"Well, bud, why don't we look up the answers and see what we can learn about planes."

After pulling up a couple of articles, I read through them enough to bore Miles with factual answers. Turns out, my ways of learning aren't exactly keen on my child, so eventually I pull out his small Spiderman headphones and turn on some video with the title saying something about kids and airplane education.

"Well, Dex, you did your best." Olsson chuckles softly. "Granted, I think I missed the part about where our number ones and twos go? Can you repeat that part for me?"

Shaking my head, I look back at Miles to make sure his headphones are on good. "Respectfully, sir, fuck off."

While it might seem crass to speak to my boss that way,

I've worked with Olsson for years. He coached me for over half of my career—mentored really. When I informed the Blues of my retirement plan, Olsson was just a coach, but the moment he became one of the top staff with the team, he called me up with an offer I couldn't say no to.

"Oh, come on, Larsen, the kid's curiosity is what makes him so great. Have you taken even a second to watch him talk to the team? With Callie? He asks insightful questions and is eager to learn. This wasn't exactly where I meant for this conversation to go, but have you found anyone to help when he starts school this fall?"

Sighing, I run my hand over my face. "No, I haven't."

"Look, I swore to you Miles would always be welcome at every turn during this season. This is not me saying he's not been great, but the stress of doing everything on your own is starting to show."

"Gee, thanks. And here I was thinking I was handling this change pretty well."

Is that why Blondie didn't spare me a glance? Is it that obvious that I'm running on fumes?

Olsson snorts. "You are. I'm just saying, it's hard being a single parent. Believe me, my daughter is grown now, but I was on my own through the teen years—just thinking about it and I feel like I could use a nap."

I huff a laugh. "A nap sounds fucking amazing."

"Have you talked to Kate again? Is she still hellbent on not helping?"

I shoot another quick glance at my son to make sure he doesn't have any reaction to his mother's name.

"I'm not getting into all of that with him around. In short, yes, she's still hellbent. I mean, let's face it, she wasn't exactly flexible when we were together, so now it's just flat out no. Her one weekend only."

One weekend a month and she's stuck to it.

The time away from him is hell for me. I can't even begin to understand how she does it, but I told myself no matter how angry she makes me, I'd never badmouth Miles's mother in front of him.

Sighing, I glance at Miles again to make sure nothing's changed and keep my voice low. "My mom said she could start helping take care of him again now that she's feeling better after her double knee replacement, but I can't put all the traveling and responsibility on her again.

"Then on top of that, he won't be able to travel because of school and with this schedule we have...fuck, I'd only be home about a week out of the month. It was hard enough with him only able to travel half of the time when Kate and I were together, but now...I can't do that—I just can't."

In truth, I didn't want this retirement. Despite being thirty-six, I felt like I was still at the height of my career. The years with Miles growing up were tough. Kate hated the baseball schedule and rarely wanted to travel to away games, but with my mom's help, we made it work.

But with factors coming into play—from the divorce to Miles needing to start school and all the details in between— retirement seemed like the only option.

It was probably selfish of me to take this job knowing everything I had to retire for would catch back up to me, but when Olsson made the offer and said it would come with the flexibility of Miles being my plus one to everything—and I mean every practice, event, meeting, game, you name it—I couldn't find a way to say no.

"I get it." Olsson shrugs. "Have you thought about home-schooling?"

Thought of it? It's my only fucking option with the amount of traveling we do. The thought of finding someone to accommodate our schedule on top of that is also stressing me the fuck out.

I guess Olsson is right—it is starting to show. I get short-tempered with the guys easier than I used to, and I'm practically taking advantage of our team photographer and doubling her as my onsite nanny. Callie's been a saint through this whole process, but at this point, I should be adding to her salary.

"It's my only real option, honestly. The main issue is that I can't find anyone who wants to be both the nanny and the teacher. I've had countless applications come through from obvious cleat chasers. I can't even begin to tell you the amount of 'because I loved watching you play baseball' and 'I've always wanted to be a step-mom' that have been written as qualifications. Besides those immediate toss-outs, the most qualified homeschool teachers declined the offer as soon as they saw our schedule."

Olsson laughs at my misery. "It's not for everyone. It'll work out, Dex. You've got the summer to figure things out. In the meantime, you can still bring Miles everywhere we go." Olsson crosses his ankle over his knee and flips open one of his sports magazines. "But I'd also say you owe Callie some of those teas that Will is always getting delivered for her. I know she loves helping, but you're getting free labor out of my photographer."

All I can manage is a nod before Olsson looks down to read whatever article he opened up to. With a sigh, I turn back to Miles and watch as he smiles and giggles at the grown man in suspenders dancing in front of an airplane.

I don't shove screens in his face often, but sometimes it's necessary. Especially when Miles's second home is about to be this fucking plane. There's only so much to do in the air, I suppose.

Looking at my son, he's thoroughly entranced so I do my best to relax and pull myself out of this bad mood. I hadn't really thought about being a dad and now a single dad. I just feel like I'm fucking everything up.

Chapter 4
Lucie

I'm what?!

"We're so sorry to have to do this, Miss Anderson. You've been an amazing educator this past year, but unfortunately, due to budget cuts...we're going to have to let you go."

Let go—aka fired. Jobless. Not good enough for them to find extra room in the budget for. This is absolute bull.

I stare back at Mrs. Riggets. She seems as though she hates doing this as much as I hate hearing it. Figures our jerk of a superintendent isn't here, I'm sure I was on the top of his list for these cuts. I make one small suggestion for how to make the pick-up line more effective and suddenly I'm "too good" for this school.

Swallowing down my emotions, I clear my throat. "Um, how many are getting cut?"

Mrs. Riggets looks down at her folded hands. "Just one." She sighs. "You were the last hired, my dear. My hands are tied."

Just one? Just me?

I can feel the tears pricking in my eyes. Oh my goodness, don't you dare start crying. Everything will be fine.

"Again, I want to express my deepest regards. You truly are a great educator. You'll have until the end of the week to get everything that belongs to you out of your classroom." Mrs. Riggets extends a piece of paper. "A recommendation from me. I wish the best for you, Miss Anderson. I do hope it helps."

I take the letter with shaky hands as I try to swallow down my emotions enough to speak. "I-I, um—thank you. I enjoyed working here, despite..." I trail off because there's no point in dragging this on. I've officially been canned from my first job. After all this money my brother spent on my education—for what? Fired. Ugh, I've never been one to curse, but this might make me start.

Walking out of the office, I feel a total of five inches tall. Someone please just come out and crush me—finish the freaking job.

My hands tremble the entire walk to my classroom. The strength to even open the door feels lost to me. Fired. What is up with this week? First, my sister is leaving me and now I've been fired from the job I wholeheartedly loved.

When I step into my...soon-to-be former classroom, Reagan's spinning around slowly in my desk chair.

"Hey, whose phone number is written on your—" Reagan starts, but stops as she turns to me. "Luce, what happened? You're white as a sheet."

"I...I—" God, I can't even say it out loud. Voicing it makes it feel too real, but then voicing it to my successful florist of a sister who runs her business like it's child's play— the word that comes to mind isn't fired, it's failure.

"Okay, Lucie, you're scaring me. What happened?" My

sister takes me by my shoulders and forces me to sit in one of the child-sized computer chairs. "You know you can tell me anything."

"I just got fired." The words tumble out first, and the tears quickly follow. "They said due to budget cuts they have to let me go."

I try to pull back my emotions as quickly as I can, but I feel so defeated.

"Oh, Luce," my sister coos as she runs her hands up and down my arms. "I'm so sorry. I know how much this job meant to you."

"It meant everything to me, Rea." I push up from my chair, wiping my hands repeatedly on my cheeks. Being a teacher is my passion. The one clear thing I know about myself. I love these kids. I love watching them learn new things and watching their confidence grow with the things that I can teach them.

I've never understood the Everyone Loves Lucie bit when it comes to anywhere outside of the classroom. Outside of these four walls, I feel like the most boring person in the world.

I can't think of any hobbies that I have to help distract me from this. I have zero dating life because I chronically get ghosted. The things that define me are my siblings and being a teacher.

Christ, I really felt like a failure telling Reagan...but telling Will...I think I'm going to have a panic attack.

"How am I supposed to tell Will?" I whisper on a shaky breath.

Reagan's eyebrows crease. "What do you mean?"

"How am I supposed to tell him, after all that money he paid for my degree, that I just got fired! Reagan, Will pays for so much of my stuff already. All I had to do was keep my job, but now I've let him down!"

Reagan places her hands on my shoulders again with a small shake this time. "Okay, I know you're feeling a lot of emotions right now, but that one is just wrong. Lucie, I know this is a lot to process and, fuck, being fired sucks—"

"How would you know?" I yell and immediately regret it. "I'm sorry. I just—"

Reagan chuckles lightly. "Don't be, I liked it. You almost sounded like me for a minute there. I didn't realize your voice could sound so angry."

I huff, only a quarter tempted to smile at her attempt to make me feel better.

"I do know for a fact that Will won't be angry when you tell him. The disappointed father act isn't his stitch either. He may try to help fix the situation by making a donation to the school's budget because he's also a millionaire!"

She has a good point there. Not that I'll allow him to, even if the idea does sound appealing.

Reagan forces me back in my chair. "Sit back down for a minute and breathe. I may not know what it's like to be fired, but I've accepted Will's money just the same as you. So, have your pity party. Be sad about losing the job you loved, but then let's pull it together. I'm not trying to rub salt in your wound, but better things are out there for you, Luce. Maybe this is your opportunity to find them. You have time to find a new job too. It sucks, yes, but you have some time to figure it out at least."

I let my sister's words fully process in my head. I know she's right, even if the only real feeling I want to feel right now is sadness.

I let out an exasperated breath. "I know you're right, but

I want to wallow for a bit. We have until Friday to clean out my stuff. Can we just get the turtles and go home?"

Reagan scrunches her nose. "Right...the turtles. No chance they'll bring back sad memories and you choose to re-home them?"

The laugh sputters out of me. "Don't even start with me. You tell me you're moving an hour away from me, and now I've been fired from my lifelong dream job. We're taking the turtles, and if you're not careful, I'll guilt trip you into holding one."

Reagan blinks her eyes with her nose still scrunched. "Okay, the emotions are okay to feel, but now you're being dramatic. That's not fucking happening."

I let out a *hmph*. "Touché."

"So, is it okay now for me to ask whose number is on your coffee cup?"

I shake my head. "A barista's, but before you get too excited, I swapped coffee cups with Dex Larsen."

Reagan's mouth gapes as she hits my shoulder. "I know, in light of the new development, I can see why that took the backseat. But, as your sister, you mean you didn't immediately tell me about a run-in with the extremely yummy pitcher, Dex Larsen?!"

"It's Coach now, remember. Ya know, our brother's coach?" The extremely yummy part doesn't need correcting because that's an absolute fact. With his deep brown skin and espresso-colored eyes, I knew I had to keep my glances at him under control or I might have started blushing at every word out of his mouth.

Reagan cocks her eyebrow. "You mean your total baseball dream guy?"

Sure, I find him attractive, but "dream guy" sounds a tad

dramatic coming out of Reagan's mouth. In the family-first of it all, Will will always be my favorite baseball player, but it's also kind of a lie and Reagan knows that.

I've always been a fan of the Blues in general, but everyone's got a favorite player on their team and Dex was mine. He was their best pitcher by far, and again was super yummy to watch as he would strike people out consistently.

"I mean, a player I enjoyed watching. Don't make it weird. He didn't even realize who I was." Even if I deep down kind of wish he did.

Reagan gives me a small nod. "Probably for the best. His retirement was why Will got traded, right?"

I shrug. "Pretty much. Not to mention newly divorced."

I don't know the full details of the divorce; it seemed to be so non-problematic that the tabloids only ran one story about it, and then it was just over. The only other information I have is the snippets I get from Callie when she talks about Miles hanging out with her during the games.

I'm not about to claim I know Dex in any shape or form, but I know the Blues. I know Dex's career and stats. He's in the top two for fastest left-handed pitchers in the league. And not for nothing—I know baseball, yes, but I'm also just a girl, so yeah, I have also noticed that Dex's hair is a little more grown out than it used to be.

During the season, you'd always see him with a crisp fade, and his dark curls weren't too short but neat on the top. But when he was standing right in front of me at the coffee shop, I could definitely tell it was longer than any other time I've seen over the years of watching him play.

Don't get me wrong, he's still beyond gorgeous, it just seems out of character for him.

Then again, I don't know Dex. I know him as a baseball

player, maybe this is him as a coach and a single dad. But with how he responded to the barista's blatant come-ons, paired with all of the things mentioned already, he just screamed unavailable. I'm not exactly sure flirting is in my DNA to begin with, but between the flashing "don't hit on me" signals and the rush they were in, I kept my eyes on him to a minimum and simply offered him my coffee.

Reagan holds out her hand to pull me back up. "Well, just chalk that up to a small bright side in your day. It's not like you really need a man right now anyway."

I can only manage a hummed response. Rather easy for her to say, considering she's so in love and doesn't even entertain men to begin with.

I take a look around my room. "I mostly need you to help me with my turtles, Rea."

Reagan rolls her eyes but then hooks are arm around my shoulder. "Okay, okay, we're not moving on from the turtles. I'll come help clean out your classroom this week too."

Chapter 5
Lucie

Fake Powerpuff Girls Meets Shego Crossover

You have got to be kidding me. I stare at my sister's message in the girls' group chat at the entrance gate of Blues Stadium. She's got to be joking. She's the one who forced me out here to begin with.

I wanted to stay in bed, maybe venture to the bath at most because my back is still hurting from cleaning out my classroom all this past week...all by myself, mind you. Decorating my classroom didn't feel so labor-intensive, but taking it all down was a nightmare. Reagan's little "I'll help" was apparently forgotten the moment she walked out the door.

REAGAN

You have every right to be mad at me, but I can't make it. Julie and I found a place that might work for the new Stigma location but they can only do a walk-through right now.

Jensen! Can you meet Lucie at the stadium so I don't come off as the loser sister?

Don't call for backup. YOU were supposed to meet me here!

JENSEN

Sorry, I just left the shop, and I'm clocking in at the wine bar at 5.

CALLIE

Jen, you're going to work yourself to death! Luce, I'll meet you at concessions!

At least someone loves me.

REAGAN

I do love you!! You needed to get out of the house anyway. Fresh air and baseball pants will do you some good!

JENSEN

I feel like I've missed some info here, but Luce can fill me in at our mani-pedi tomorrow!

Don't worry if you don't show up, I've been stood up THREE times this week!

REAGAN

I said I was sorry!! I swear I'll make it up to you!

I shove my phone in my back pocket. I should have known something would come up. Reagan has had things come up all week. On our sister lunch date, she stood me up because she forgot about some floral arrangements she needed to make for a client. Helping clean out my classroom slipped her mind because she was helping clean out Julie's apartment.

I get it, those are things she needed to do, but it was the forgetting me part that hurt the most. She didn't call or text me a heads-up on those changes in plans, so yeah, it made my sour mood a little more bitter. And then she messaged, begging me to meet her at tonight's game. I caved, thinking I'd at least get some sister time out of it.

She knows it's like an hour drive here and back to Rowley. She knows I really only came all the way down here to spend time with her.

My phone vibrates in my pocket again. I'm half tempted to ignore it and send Reagan's apologies to voicemail, but when I see it's Jensen calling, I answer.

"Hey," I say with a sigh.

"I'm quitting my job; I miss all the drama! What's going on?"

At that, I chuckle. I only met Jensen through Callie a couple of months ago, but with us being the same age and sharing a reluctance to give up our self-care of a good mani-pedi, it's fair to say she's my only friend who didn't come from Will or Reagan.

Granted, Callie introduced us which does link back to Will, technically...but that's a minor detail.

"Ugh, Reagan invited me to the Blues game tonight for sister time and has now bailed on me," I grumble as I join the first concession line I see. "She's stood me up three times this week, Jen."

"What! Did she have any kind of excuse?"

"She did, but not one she told me until after I was already there waiting on her." I sigh and take a step forward in the line. "I'm being a bad sister...I know she has reasons, but—"

"You're not a bad sister, Lucie. You've had a really shitty week, and her bailing isn't cool. Why don't you come to Winedown? You can vent while you drink! First one's on the house."

"Tempting, but I'm already here. I'll see if I can sneak into the photo outpost with Callie instead of sitting alone."

I step to the front of the line and hold my phone away from my ear to order a Diet Coke and a hotdog.

Jensen laughs as I bring the phone back to my ear. "Dinner of champions."

"Hey, it beats your dinner which is usually an energy drink and a protein bar."

Jensen snorts again. "You got me there. Alright, well, if you change your mind, you know where to find me. I'll see you tomorrow for sure."

I hum as the guy hands over my stuff, and I mouth a "thank you" to him before stepping over to the nearest bench.

"I'm used to being stood up at this point, so I'm not going to hold my breath."

"Girl, you know I'd rather die than miss my nail appointment. You're the bonus."

"I'll take that as a compliment." I smile, even though she can't see me. It's nice having Jensen as my bonus, even if she does work herself to the bone.

After saying bye, my stomach growls. I didn't realize how hungry I was until the teenager handed over my hotdog.

It could be a nostalgia thing or maybe it's just that I've

learned to love them, considering we practically grew up on concession food, but there's no better hotdog in my opinion.

With my first big bite, I hear Callie. "Hey, Lucie!"

I can only wave at her and her usual game-day shadow. Miles trails along behind her and part of me wonders if he remembers me from the coffee shop. Not that it would really matter, it doesn't change anything.

I'm still chewing when she and Miles reach me because I apparently took a much bigger bite than I thought. "Hey, I have a huge favor to ask."

I hold my finger up as I try to chew faster while also not choking.

Miles giggles. "Good job chewing with your mouth closed. Sometimes my dad gets upset when I don't."

I give Miles a soft smile as I hold back my laugh so I can finally swallow. "It's good manners. Your dad is teaching you right."

Miles shrugs. "I guess so, but sometimes it's hard to remember."

Callie snorts a laugh. "Sometimes you just have to get what you need to say off your chest, kiddo."

"While still trying to remember to listen to your dad."

"Yeah, yeah." Callie waves off my addition in your typical fun-aunt style. "I, however, have a predicament. Shannon just messaged me that our snooty first pitch guest is a major diva and wants more photos taken for PR. I hate to do this, but Dex is in a meeting...could Miles hang out with you in the stands?"

I glance back and forth from Miles to Callie. Of course I would love to help, but... "Would Dex be okay with that?"

"As much as I respect Dex as a father, my hands are tied. I trust you more than anyone else here. Bringing him to the photos isn't an option, and—" Callie places her hands over Miles's ears— "Dex has been hella stressed this past week. Dude needs a break."

"Hey, Cal-lie." Miles drags out her name as he attempts to wiggle out of her hands. "I want to stay with you. I thought I was a good helper?"

Callie kneels in front of him. "Oh, bud, you're the best helper! You know I love having you help, but sometimes it's just not possible. I promise you can come to the photo cave when the game starts if you want. But trust me when I say that Lucie is major fun! Did you know she's a teacher who had turtles in her classroom?"

Miles's eyes go wide. "Turtles?!"

My heart aches a little at the mention of my classroom, but I know Callie didn't mean it that way. When I called to tell Will about my...termination, he did exactly what Reagan thought he would—offer to make a huge donation to the school.

As tempting as the idea was, I'm getting spoiled by my brother, and if adding Callie to our family has shown me anything, it's that compared to her, I can't do jack on my own —and that has to change.

Starting with a job that doesn't come from my brother's wallet, and expanding into ways I can be more independent. Maybe Reagan abandoning me is a good thing. Let's have this be the first act in figuring out who I really am.

First up, doing this game by myself, or well, with Miles partially, at least. Baby steps, I suppose.

"I think we can have a good time together," I tell Miles. "I know Callie is awesome, but I would love some company."

"Are you here all by yourself?" Miles quirks an eyebrow.

"Yep!" I force some confidence. "If you want to go back

with your dad or Callie once the game starts, I'll take you straight to them, but I wouldn't mind having someone to help me understand the game."

The last line is a major lie. I know baseball like the back of my hand—the Blues, specifically—but I've gathered Miles likes to be a helper, so I'll lean into it.

Callie gives me a knowing grin. "That would be so nice of you to do, Miles."

And with that, Miles couldn't be more onboard. "Okay! Let's do it!" Miles cheers.

"You're a lifesaver!" Callie gives me a quick hug, then looks at Miles. "Best behaviors?"

"The bestest." Miles nods.

I chuckle lightly and hold out my hand for Miles. "Perfect, let's go find our seats so Callie can get going."

"Okay," Miles agrees as he takes my hand. "You know... you look really familiar. What is your name again?"

Chapter 6
Dex

"Okay, I think that just about covers it." Olsson taps on his desk. "Let's take a beat and I'll meet you guys in the dugout."

Thank fuck. I get why we have pregame meetings to an extent, but honestly, with the day I'm having, I just need a break. Five minutes tops where I'm not dealing with anything related to baseball or dealing with the repercussions of taking this damn job.

On top of having another close call on being late this morning, my mother called me asking a million and one questions about things I don't have answers to.

What school am I going to put Miles in? Why haven't I decided what school? Didn't I know that the sign-ups were most likely already closed? And about fifteen more, but when I kept answering "I don't know," she hit me with, "Well, these are all questions stemming from your actions—time to make some decisions."

I thought that was going to be her final blow of a question, but then she hit me with, "When should I move in?"

After hanging up with her, I knew I could answer that

question confidently—she was not moving in with me. The rest she's going to have to give me a little bit of grace on. I still have the summer to find someone.

I just hope I haven't pushed the limit of Olsson's "bring Miles, the team will help" offer too hard already.

Walking down the hall, I'm tempted to steal a twenty-minute power nap in my office, but I know I need to check on Miles. Walking down the hall, I get the flash of red that is Callie racing down the hall, but I don't see Miles with her.

"Hey, Cals," I call before she gets out of earshot.

Callie whips around with a smile. "Hey, Dex, what's up?"

"I don't mean for this to come off real dick-ish because I know you're working, but I have to ask...where's my son?"

Callie chuckles. "I gave him to a group of drunken ball fans, is that not okay?" Sarcasm laces her tone. "He's with Lucie. Relax. Have I ever left Miles with anyone unsafe?"

"First, not funny. Second, I'm still dealing with the repercussions of the time you left Miles with Tripp and Beck —and third, who the hell is Lucie?"

Callie huffs. "Tripp and Beck are like giant children, how was I supposed to know they'd teach Miles how to catcall whistle? And I left him with Lucie, because I had to—"

"Callie, I don't know who Lucie is! You left my son with a stranger!" The outburst surprises both me and Callie.

Fuck. That's uncalled for, especially with how much Callie's helped over this season. My stress might be at an all-time high, but I shouldn't have let it get the better of me. "I'm sorry. I didn't mean to talk to you like that. I just—"

Callie's face softens for a moment despite my gruffness.

"Dex, it's fine. Lucie is—oh my word! Why didn't I think of this sooner?" Callie grabs my arm, her eyes wide.

Fucking hell. *She helps me with my son for free. She helps me with my son for free.*

"Alright, what's going on here?" Will's voice comes up from behind me. "My girl's got wild eyes going on right now. I'm a little afraid of what that look on her face means."

Callie gives him a pointed glare. "I always have excellent ideas. This one especially."

"For fuck's sake, Callie, my son. Who the hell is Lucie?"

"Lucie? My Lucie?" Will asks.

His Lucie? Isn't it his Callie?

A smile creeps up Callie's face as Will mutters some curses.

"My sister is not becoming his nanny."

"Hold on, no one said anything about your sister or a nanny. I just want to know who has my kid."

Callie crosses her arms over her chest. "Lucie is Will's sister, who just so happens to have a degree in early childhood education and currently needs a job. Being a nanny could be worked in, because, let's face it, you need one. How does a traveling homeschool teacher and nanny sound?"

Well, shit, Callie might be on to something.

"She has a degree? Like a real degree? How old is she?"

"She just turned twenty-four," Callie exclaims while Will hangs his head with a shake.

"And she has her master's...I should know it's real since I've paid for it all," he mutters.

Master's...okay, she's definitely qualified—overqualified, really—albeit a little younger than I would have thought about hiring, but I'm borderline desperate on this whole nanny-homeschool situation.

"I told you I have excellent ideas!" Callie hits my shoulder. "Don't get me wrong, I love having Miles around, but during some games we're all running around like crazy and I hate having to pass him off to whoever's closest. I know you feel the same."

I bring the palm of my hand to my forehead, applying pressure as Callie's words rattle around in my head. This could work. If she's Will's sister, she should be familiar with how our schedules work...I think, at least. I know Will is new to the team and all, but the fact that I didn't know Lucie was his sister reminds me that I don't know her at all.

"Okay, I know you're right, but the point of my original question of 'Who's Lucie?' still holds a lot of weight."

"Fair." Callie shrugs. "But she's the first real candidate you've had in a long time. Especially for both positions. Come on, Will, back me up."

Will glances back and forth between his girlfriend and me, his coach, several times before he lets out a breath. "Yeah, I want no part of this conversation, actually."

"Will—" Callie starts to protest, but Will cuts her off with a quick kiss to the forehead.

"Sorry, Beck's calling for me. Got to go."

"Mmm," Callie hums with anger before sighing as Will takes off down the hallway.

"Not exactly what I would want to see out of my nanny's brother," I joke, then instantly regret it when the fire lights in Callie's eyes again. "I'm not saying I'm on board with your plan, Cals. I still don't know this person."

Callie holds her hands up in defense but then her phone digs in her pocket. "Look, I'm just saying it's an idea. I have to get to Shannon before she has an aneurysm over these first pitch photos. Lucie texted me that they're sitting in Will's reserved seats, fourth row back from the pitcher's mound. For today, why don't you just go check on him?"

I glance at my watch. I've got some time to spare, and while I do trust Callie, I really don't feel comfortable handing Miles off without even meeting the person. In fact, the more I think about it, the less confident in the plan I feel. I know I need someone to help, but there's this fear I don't understand that comes with it.

"Fine, but don't get your feelings hurt if I take him to the dugout with me."

Callie rolls her eyes. "Oh, yeah. Will's sister is already five beers deep," she says with a snark as she pats my shoulder before walking away.

"Not funny, Cals," I grit out.

"Who said I was joking?" Callie hollers over her shoulder.

"For fuck's sake."

Weaving through the crowd of people, I keep my head low and move as quickly as possible. Venturing into the crowd as a coach is one thing, but as the newly retired pitcher, I usually get stopped a lot.

"Dad! Dad, look! It's Dex Larsen!" I hear what sounds like the voice of a little boy ahead of me.

The 'no eye contact and keep moving' method usually works, but I've clearly got a soft spot for the kid fans. When I spot the kid tugging on his dad's shirt, jumping up and down unable to contain himself with excitement, I know I have to stop.

Kneeling in front of him, I swear the kid stops breathing for a second as he grips the ball in his hand with a huge smile on his face.

"Hi there, want me to sign your ball?"

The kid nods his head aggressively before looking up to his dad for late permission. The dad and I chuckle at the same time. Yep, I know how that goes.

After signing one ball, a small crowd of kids makes their way up to me. Some with genuine excitement, and some I know are only getting an autograph for their parental figure.

I finally make it to the reserved rows behind the mound. Heading down the first set of stairs, I scan the rows and spot Miles right away, but then almost just as quickly, I notice the blonde next to him. Not just any blonde, though—*the* gorgeous blonde from the coffee shop. My Blondie.

What the fuck? This can't be Will's sister—she would have said something. She should have said something. I had wanted to know her name that day. Hell, if Miles wasn't with me and we weren't rushing out the door, I would have asked her for her number.

Shit, if this is her, that means Blondie here is twelve years younger than me. I could tell she was younger in the coffee shop, but I wouldn't have guessed there was that much of an age difference.

Maybe this is a friend of Will's sister, and Lucie's just at the concessions or in the bathroom—not *her*.

Miles seems completely entranced as she speaks to him, but that's not entirely surprising since I apparently have a ladies' man on my hands. Then again, I can't blame him on this one. Blondie seems to shine just as brightly today as she did last week.

That definitely feels like a thought I shouldn't entertain until I know for sure that this isn't Will's sister. The hope that she isn't also seems like something I shouldn't entertain given my situation, but it's there.

Walking toward them, she looks my way. Her piercing

blue eyes land on me, and it's as if the light around her intensifies. Hell, she seems like sunshine in human form.

Fuck, maybe I should go ahead and nip this in the bud and bring Miles to the dugout with me. Even if she's not Lucie, I just thought this girl had a light to her...she definitely can't be my nanny or even friends with my nanny.

"Dad! What are you doing up here?" Miles exclaims, as if it is unbelievable that I came to see him.

"Hey, bud, I came to check on you," I say as I reach them. I squat at the end of the row so we can be eye level. "I ran into Callie and noticed she was missing her shadow."

Miles sends his eyes up, looking at the sky. I guess I should be grateful he hasn't quite mastered the eye roll yet, but the implication of annoyance is thick on his face. "Miss Shannon said I couldn't be at the first throw, so I'm sitting with Lucie. We met her at the coffee shop, remember?"

The string of curses that go through my head at Miles's words is stupid.

Of course, this is Lucie. Of course Miles remembers her from the coffee shop. Dammit, dammit, dammit.

I clear my throat as I force myself to look at her. "Yeah, I remember. I'm Dex," I rasp out. I don't extend my hand to shake and I hope she doesn't either. Why didn't she say anything? Maybe she didn't realize who I was?

"She knows who you are, Dad," Miles drawls.

What the fuck? There goes that thought almost immediately.

Is it weird to feel a little betrayed right now? Why I feel that way is probably a road I shouldn't go down, but damn it, why didn't she say she knew who I was?

Lucie's eyes flash wide and pink blushes her cheeks as she quickly turns to Miles. "Well, I know *of* your dad, I don't exactly know him. Plus, Callie most likely told your dad that I'm Will's little sister, and while he knows Callie and knows that she wouldn't leave you with someone unsafe, he doesn't know me."

That's for damn sure, and now the only thing I need to know about her is that she is indeed Will's much younger sister. Consider this door closed and locked tight.

Clearing my throat again, I keep my focus on the reason I came here—to check on Miles. "I'm about to go to the dugout if you want to come with me?"

Miles chews on his lip for a moment, but then exclaims, "But I'm having fun with Lucie, can I stay with her, *pleeeease*?"

Miles looks back and forth between me and Lucie, his eyes big and pleading. Damn it, why her? What did I do to be put in this situation? The first real candidate I've had in months is both my player's little sister and the girl who captured my attention in one go.

While I'm too busy kicking myself, Lucie speaks up. "I'm having a lot of fun with you too, Miles. I'm happy to have you stay with me, but it could also be really fun in the dugout with your dad. Or even...what did you call it? The photo cave with Callie after the first pitch photos are done."

"But I'd rather stay with you!" Miles whines.

Fucking hell. Great, now I either get to be the bad guy who forces my son to the dugout or the guy who swallows his fucking pride so his kid can have some fun.

"You're sure he can sit with you?" My question comes out in a more clipped tone than I intend, but who cares. The door for nanny has been shut.

Lucie finally looks back at me, her blue eyes softening despite my harshness. "It's okay with me. I'm not sure if

Callie told you, but I have my degree in childhood education. I'm also certified in CPR and know the Heimlich Maneuver."

Is she trying to impress me right now? Is she thinking this is some sort of trial run or something? It wouldn't surprise me to find out that Callie told her all about me needing a nanny and homeschool teacher. I should have fucking known her gesture at the coffee shop was disingenuous.

"Man, really gunning for the job, aren't you?"

"Job?" Lucie's eyebrows pull together as she frowns. "The job of keeping Miles safe during the game? Sure...but, um, if you're uncomfortable with him sitting with me, I understand."

Miles turns to me and places his hands on my shoulders. "Daddy, I'm having fun and I really want to stay with Lucie for this game. I'm happy you came to see me, but it's okay for you to go to work now."

"Oh, is it now?" Gee, kick me while I'm down, kid.

I spare another glance at Lucie but she doesn't meet my eyes. She simply smiles at Miles. I think she's okay with me leaving too, and that's a weird feeling to process—they both are okay with me not being here. Miles leaving me for Callie never made me feel this weird ache in my chest, but somehow this is different and I don't like it. I think I want to stay here and talk to her more. Fuck.

"Alright. I'll give your name to our security team. If you need me, don't hesitate to come to the dugout."

Lucie finally looks at me and gives me a curt nod. Why did it have to be her?

I turn to Miles. "And you, behave, please."

"Okie, see you later!" Miles beams, all too happy to have me leave and not cramp his style.

Chapter 7
Lucie

Well, Dex Larsen sure is a prickly man. I could feel tension radiating off him at the coffee shop, but I just assumed it was because of the obvious cleat chaser and being in a hurry.

But now I think I just got a little bit of the same attitude he gave that barista. Surely he doesn't think that was my intention...yeah, he's hot, but I wasn't trying to hit on him. I really wanted to help.

Maybe it isn't me, per se. Will being traded to the Blues was a little bittersweet, considering the only reason the trade even happened was because of Dex's retirement after last season. As happy as it makes me to have my brother close and playing on my favorite team, I'm not entirely convinced that Dex's retirement was the choice he wanted to make.

Maybe that's the reason for his prickliness—finding out I'm Will's sister. I probably should have told him at the coffee shop who I was, but I mean, cut me a little slack. I may not have been hitting on him, but I was definitely fangirling in my head.

"Lucie, I have a question." Miles's inquisitive tone is so sweet.

"Shoot," I say, angling my body toward him. The announcer starts introducing the first pitch, but Miles deserves all of my attention.

"Do you like being a teacher?"

Oof, it's a little salt in the unhealed wound, but Miles doesn't know that, nor does he need to.

"I do. Being a teacher is what I'm meant to do."

Miles cocks his head to the side. "It is? What am I meant to do?"

"Well, that's up to you. You get to decide what you want to be when you grow up. As you get older, you'll learn more about yourself and that decision will be much easier."

Miles looks out to the field, his eyes searching. "Do you think I'm meant to be a pitcher like my dad?"

"Maybe. Trying is really the only way to find out." I follow Miles's gaze just to see Dex walk onto the field. He pulls his ball cap on his head and crosses his muscular arms over his chest as the general manager starts talking to him.

It feels a tad wrong to ogle him after our interaction. I'm a weird mixture of trying to decide how to feel about what just happened and how I really can't blame a single cleat chaser when the player is as good looking as Dex—when they're single...which Dex is.

I blink rapidly, pulling myself out of that twisting haze. I'm watching his son, and his fun energy could be exactly what I need to perk up my sour mood—not lusting over his hot dad.

"So, you think you want to be a pitcher? What about the other positions?"

Miles wiggles in his seat, then looks up at me. "No,

pitcher only. That way I can be just like my dad, and then Callie will love me too."

Ah yes, I've heard all about this little crush Miles has from Callie and my brother.

"Is that so? You know...Callie really loves homemade gifts. That might help too."

"She does?" Miles's eyes light up and he quickly leans over to give me a hug. "Thank you, Lucie!"

Invisible strings pull at my heart as I place an arm around Miles. "You're welcome. If I think of anything else, I'll let you know."

Miles sits back up as the crowd cheers at the first pitch. "Don't worry, I won't tell Will you told me."

Now I chuckle. I probably shouldn't be aiding in this crush of Miles's, but he's so precious about it. I'll let my brother be the bad guy because I know there's no way he's letting Callie go, no matter who tries.

"If that's the deal, then I've got some stuff on Will too."

"Oh yeah, like what?" Miles gives me a mischievous smile.

"Has he ever mentioned why he rides a motorcycle?"

For the entirety of the game, Miles talks to me about everything under the sun. We talk about Will and Callie for a bit—my childhood stories about Will definitely put me at the top of Miles's favorite list.

But then it changes into questions about the sky and why the clouds always look different. Commentary on the plays that Miles actually pays attention to comes in very heavy detail, and when he doesn't know something, he makes an elaborate story up anyway.

He tells me jokes, and I follow up with funny stories that my siblings got me caught up in growing up. With each inning, I forget all about the past week. There's no loss of job mentioned or the abandonment by my sister. I don't think I even check my phone, I'm having such a great time.

Now, with the game ending, a small pit forms in my stomach at the idea of talking to Dex again. Maybe Callie will meet me instead.

I walk Miles to the team's family waiting room. He skips along happily until we spot Dex coming down the hall. Welp, there goes that hope.

I assumed I'd have Miles hanging out with me for at least a few minutes before Dex made his way out and I could prepare myself more, but I guess not. Based on the speed he's walking toward us, I can't decide if it's spurred by missing his kid or not trusting me to bring him back.

"Dad!" Miles takes off down the hall, meeting Dex half-way, and it's just as bad for my kid-loving heart as it is for my ovaries when Dex scoops him up. Maybe it will be less awkward this time...

"Hey, buddy, did you have a good time?" Dex asks.

"The *best* time." Miles beams and my heart nearly explodes.

"I had a really great time with you too, Miles," I say as I reach them. Dex looks my way for a moment, but I do what I did earlier—focus on Miles. "Thank you for keeping me company."

"Can you come to tomorrow's game?" Miles asks. "Maybe you could sit with me and Callie in the photo cave."

Goodness, my heart. "Oh, I would love to, but unfortunately, I have plans tomorrow. Rain check?"

Miles purses his lips. "I don't think it's supposed to rain tomorrow, Lucie. Remember we talked about the clouds."

"She means she'll sit with you another time." Dex lets

out a low, amused chuckle that immediately puts some of my anxieties to rest.

That's a good sign, right? Even though it's a very contained laugh, it's enough to make me want to hear it again.

"Oh." Miles's face drops and he wiggles out of his dad's hold. "That's okay."

Ow, now that hurts.

I kneel in front of Miles so we're eye level. "No sad faces. How about I come to the game on Friday? I promise to have some new embarrassing Will stories for you to use against him."

"Yes!" Miles flings himself at me, his arms tightening around my neck. I nearly fall back on my butt when I feel two strong hands on my back.

"Whoa, easy Miles," Dex grunts out as his hands guide me back up and linger for a moment as I steady myself.

I flash him a grateful look as he continues to hold me firm, but I don't hold his eyes for long, or else I swear my face will turn ten shades of red.

Miles relents his grasp and takes a step back with a giggle. "Sorry, Lucie. I didn't mean to."

Dex's hands leave my back the moment Miles lets go as well. It's both disappointing and relieving at the same time.

I stand up quickly and tuck my hair behind my ears. "It's okay, Miles. I'm excited to sit with you, too."

"Hey, Miles!" Callie calls, walking down the hallway to join our little party. "I was just coming to check on you and Lucie."

"Callie!" Miles hollers, and I know we have now completely lost his interest. He bounces off to meet her halfway.

"And just like that, I'm chopped liver," I mumble with amusement.

An annoyed grunt comes from Dex that I don't know how to take. I rock on my feet for a moment, unsure of what to do next. Miles is fully consumed by Callie's presence right now and, really, watching him talk to her is just as enjoyable, but this weird vibe is radiating off Dex. I don't know if I'm just supposed to slowly walk away, go talk to Callie, or stay put.

Is this one of those weird things that comes with meeting your favorite player? They always say never meet your heroes, but I didn't expect it to be this awkward. I've only ever heard good things about Dex's fan interactions.

"Well, I guess—" I start.

"If you aren't going to come to the game Friday, go ahead and let me know so I can prepare Miles," Dex snaps in a hushed tone.

This time I have to face him, because what the heck does that mean? "I said I would come, so I'll be there. I wouldn't tell Miles I'm going to do something and not do it."

Dex's words ruminate in my head and it rubs me the wrong way. I may have forgotten my bad week for a moment, but I'm not about to let someone insinuate that I would purposefully do something to make a child upset. Even if they are a super hot baseball player I've always enjoyed watching.

I stare into Dex's eyes. I know the irritation is showing on my face, but I still keep my voice low so Miles doesn't hear. "If you have a problem with us sitting together, then I'll tell him I can't make it, but otherwise, the only plan I have on Friday is to come to the game and sit with Miles."

A weird expression comes over Dex's face. It's just as unreadable as everything else about him right now.

"You'd tell him you couldn't make it even though I said no?"

Didn't I just say that? "Yeah, I'm not going to villainize you as a father. What good would blaming you do?"

Dex raises his eyebrows in what I can't decide is surprise or admiration —maybe both— but it quickly disappears. "You didn't mention you were Will's sister at the coffee shop."

Ah, so it *is* about me being Will's sister.

"It didn't seem relevant. You were in a hurry—I wanted to help. Me being Will's sister didn't change that."

Dex grunts an aggravated *humph*.

"What's going on here?" Callie asks as she and Miles come back over to us.

"Nothing." Dex takes a small step back as if the two feet between us weren't enough. "I have to get back to the locker room. Miles, are you coming with me for the team meeting or hanging out with Callie?"

Callie, not me.

Miles looks back and forth between us all before jumping closer to his dad. "I want to do the meeting, but Callie, are you leaving with Lucie?"

"Nope, I still have some stuff to sort out here." Aka, she's waiting on Will but doesn't want to rub it in Miles's face. "How about you go with your dad, and you come say bye before you leave?"

"Okie!" Miles dashes to me for a quick hug, but then yells, "Bye, Lucie, I'll see you Friday" as he runs down the hall.

I chuckle and call after him, "Bye, Miles." I don't

mention anything about Friday because of Dex's weird reaction, but when I force a glance his way, he just gives a small nod and walks off.

Callie watches as Dex walks down the hall and whips to me when he gets out of earshot. "What was that about? Did he offer you the job?"

What is this job? Dex said something snarky about it earlier too.

"I don't know anything about a job. I just said I would hang out with Miles at the game on Friday, and he got all weird, acting like I was just getting Miles's hopes up to just crush him by not showing up."

Callie snorts a laugh. "Christ, no wonder he can't find a nanny. He's scaring them all away."

"Nanny? Callie, please tell me you didn't tell him I wanted to be his nanny!" Oh my gosh, no wonder he got all weird when I told him my qualifications.

I cringe at the memory...I was just trying to make him feel better, but ended up coming off as a show-off.

"Not just nanny...traveling homeschool teacher as well."

I smack her arm like I would my own sister. "Callie!"

"What? It's a good idea! I stand by that." Callie crosses her arms. "Tell me, how's applying for other teaching jobs going?"

Crap. I should have known Reagan would tell Will about my complete and utter lack of motivation to apply to other schools this week.

"I haven't started yet."

"Exactly. I'm not sorry because it's a win-win situation. You get a great job that involves hanging out with and eventually teaching an adorable kid. And Dex can finally stop stressing about finding someone who knows how demanding this schedule is."

I chew on my bottom lip. She's not wrong. I haven't ever thought about homeschooling before; the idea of a classroom full of kids and learning seemed the most exciting. But Miles is so cute and polite, curious too. When I think back on the game, he asked so many questions.

Miles is a smart kid. He's both inquisitive and observant—being his teacher does feel like it would be just as fulfilling as a classroom full of kids. Maybe even more considering I can give him 100 percent of my effort and attention.

The nanny part doesn't turn me off of the idea either. I have spent countless hours working at the daycare at our local gym over the summers through college.

"Okay, I'm not saying you're wrong. I can't say I would necessarily turn down the job, but I don't think Dex is too keen on your idea either."

Callie places her hand over her heart. "I think we both know I can be rather convincing."

"You're going to bring it up to him until he caves, aren't you?"

"Yep," Callie says, popping the *p*.

"I can't change your mind either?"

"Nope!"

Chapter 8
Dex

"I'm just saying, why not look at today's game as a trial run?"

I couldn't decide if I wanted Lucie to show up to today's game or not. I've been back and forth on it all week. The way I'm leaning really changes every time Callie brings it up. And if there's one thing about our photographer...she talks a lot.

"A baseball game isn't exactly the place to have a trial run for a homeschool teacher, Callie."

I stand off to the side of the bullpen as our pitchers finish up, and while I'm pretty sure Callie is supposed to be getting pictures right now, she's bugging me.

"Oh, come on, Dex. You know this is a good idea. Lucie's qualified to be Miles's homeschool teacher, overqualified to be the nanny, and—"

"And she knows the schedule. You've mentioned all of this already."

I don't want to dismiss Callie, but she's been on this topic all week. I know she has good points. On paper, Lucie is perfect for the job, but I can't pull the trigger. No matter how many positives Callie adds to the scale, the weight of our interactions combined with the number of times I found myself looking over at Lucie during the game earlier this week, outweighs it by a ton.

Her warm smile when she interacted with my son had me tempted to leave the dugout to sit with them countless times. He had all of her fucking attention, and I'm the shitty father who just wanted a second of it for myself.

"And yet, you still haven't offered her the job."

I toss one of the baseballs from my back pocket into the bucket next to us, then pick it up to carry to the dugout. Callie naturally follows.

"Didn't you say she thought I was an ass and didn't want the job? Gee, I wonder why I haven't offered her a raise with the offer?" I say over my shoulder.

"Okay, I may have been paraphrasing the whole 'you're an ass' part. Lucie doesn't cuss anyway—"

I tilt my head back again. "She doesn't?"

"No, she doesn't. See? Added perk number one million."

Fucking hell, she's relentless. "Cals—"

"She might not have called you an ass, but she did feel like you didn't like her. She didn't know anything about the job until after either. Think about that Dex, she wanted to hang out with Miles tonight without even knowing she could get paid for it."

Well, I guess her thinking I didn't like her was kind of my intention, even if it's the furthest thing from the truth.

I drop the bucket of balls by the dugout and run my hands over my face just as Will starts to walk up after finishing his pregame warm-up.

"Please take her away," I beg.

Will holds his hands up in surrender. "I already told you

guys, I'm not touching this conversation with a ten-foot pole."

"Much to my annoyance," Callie mumbles.

Adam comes up behind Will, clapping him on the shoulder. "Oh, come on, Anderson, pick a side. Girlfriend or coach?"

Will gives him a blank stare. "No. No, I won't be doing that."

I can't help it, coach or not, I don't think I'll ever not be able to cut up with the guys. "And why not? As your coach, I'm curious. I'm sure your girlfriend is too."

"Yeah, Will." Callie crosses her arms. "I'm curious."

Will gives Callie a playful smirk. "Right, right. Let me explain, I like having a very beautiful girlfriend. I like having a sister who is happy and not stressed out. I like having a coach who isn't an asshole—most of the time—and has a really cute kid, despite all his attempts at stealing said beautiful girlfriend. Now, I want to keep all these things, and if I get involved and something goes wrong, I will lose one, if not all of them. So I'm going to let you guys make the decision, and I'll support whatever you decide."

"You say that now. Wait until some player starts dating your sister." Adam pins Will with a glare.

Not that he actually cares about Will dating Callie, and really I don't think Will would care with Lucie, the whole pot-meet-kettle saying, but when I think about Lucie dating another player...

"That's not happening," I say, much to my shock—and horror.

Will cuts up an eyebrow for a moment. He better not question me on it, because I can't explain why I said that out loud either.

"Well, Lucie's a capable adult, so like I said, I'm not getting involved. If she wants to work with your surly ass, then that's her choice."

Callie swings her head toward me. "It can be her choice if Dex would offer her the damn job."

For all that's holy, I've got a fucking headache. I give Will a pointed glare, and he knows I've reached my limit on this topic for right now.

"Come on, Blaze, let's drop it with Dex for a bit."

As Will pulls Callie away, she starts her argument. "But—"

"I know, you can still talk to me about it," Will says, cutting her off.

Adam shakes his hand and claps me on the shoulder. "She'll be back."

"Well-fucking-aware."

With a sigh, I look out to the outfield where Miles is goofing off with some of the guys shagging balls during hitting warm-ups. As a batter hits one ball, Beck throws Miles a grounder off to the side so he's out of harm's way but can still feel included.

This team has been so great to Miles—they've helped more than they'll even know. I don't want him to lose days like this where he gets to be active and a part of the Blues' family.

The only way I can ensure that will happen is if I get a nanny and a homeschool teacher who can travel with us.

"Fucking hell," I grumble to no one.

I knew the idea of this job was too good to be true. As much as the team has helped with Miles's confidence, I made a selfish fucking decision and it seems like the one person who might be able to help is my pitcher's little sister.

His really pretty, much younger sister.

My phone dings just as that thought enters my brain, thankfully giving me an out as to why those details should matter when considering Lucie as my kid's nanny. I pull out my phone and give one more glance at Beck playing with Miles. It's almost too hard to look away with the huge smile on Miles's face.

And boy, do I not almost have immediate regret when I read the message from my ex-wife.

KATE

I know it's my weekend with Miles, but I'm going to have to reschedule. I have a huge case on Monday. I really can't be distracted right now.

I grind my molars.

You know what? Fuck it.

Chapter 9
Lucie

Weaving through the stadium, I stop by the concession stand for the ever classic Diet Coke and a hotdog. I texted Callie that I would be in Will's reserved seats if she needed to bring Miles to me, but I'm not holding my breath over it actually happening.

I told myself that whether Miles came to sit with me or not, I was going to enjoy this game—all by myself. I didn't invite Reagan, and when Jensen offered to try to get someone to pick up her shift for today, I told her not to worry about it.

With much reflection on my predicament over this week, I've decided that while I may not exactly be afraid to be alone, I don't know who I am well enough to even know my own company.

My whole family goes on and on about how I'm the one sibling everyone likes. The "angel sister," as Reagan says, but after the said reflection, all I can see in those comments is that I'm the boring one, the one who hides behind her siblings' personalities. Not to mention the one who's too reliant on her siblings.

All week, I worked on a list of things I want to work on this year. I'm sure I'll add more stuff to it, but for now it's a start. I want to try to venture out by myself more, or at least without my siblings. Have a day where I don't say no to myself and find a hobby I enjoy. I also want to try to be a little more spontaneous and do more things that scare me— i.e., coming to this game even if that means I'll be completely by myself.

Plopping my butt in my seat, I exhale any anxieties I'm harboring about my new plan. This will be good for me. I've allowed myself to be a supporting character long enough. It's time I actually be my own main character—now just to figure out what that role even is.

"Lucie!" Miles hollers as he hops up each stair to get to me while Callie trails behind him.

He looks so much like his dad with his deep brown eyes and dark curly hair. The faint freckles on his nose and cheeks must come from his mom, but when Miles gives me a smile, it's all I can do not to see a smaller, happier version of Dex.

"Hey, Miles! You coming to hang out with me?" I ask with a smile.

"Yes!" Miles jumps and plops down into the seat next to me. "How are your turtles? Did you bring them with you?"

My smile comes with a small chuckle. "Sorry, no turtles at Blues Stadium, I fear that might be a rule. But they're good. I've been looking forward to hearing all about what you've been doing this week. I heard there was quite the shutout at the last game."

Miles's eyes go wide. "Oh, Lucie, you missed it! It was so cool! Dad said he's played a couple of games like that too, but I don't remember."

I definitely do.

Callie chuckles as she ruffles his hair. "Alright, before you get on a classic Callie ramble with Lucie, I'm going to get to my spot. You're good here?"

Miles looks from me to Callie. "Yes, I'm good. I'll miss you a little bit, but I want to sit with Lucie for the game."

Callie and I both chuckle at that. "I want to sit with you too, Miles, but if you change your mind and want to see Callie or your dad, let me know."

Miles bobs his head up and down with a sharp nod. "Okay, I don't think I will but maybe."

I chuckle. "Either way is fine. I like you sitting with me, but I can't read your mind, so if you want to leave, I promise it's okay."

"Boy, I wish I could read people's minds," Callie says. "Or maybe not, I'd rather not know if Will ever wants me to actually stop talking."

"Something tells me that's not what he's thinking, but—"

"I never want you to stop talking, Callie," Miles cuts me off, not wanting to miss his opportunity.

"I know, bud, and you're the best for it." Callie squats in front of Miles and holds up her hand for a high five. "You gonna behave?"

"Always." Miles smacks his little hand against Callie's. "I'll see you after the game?"

"Find you after, Hotshot." Callie turns to me next. "I'm still working on our other little thing by the way. Someone's being stubborn."

"I'm not holding my breath, Cals, don't worry about it." I've got my new plan and new motivations—whether I work for Dex or not.

Callie stands back up with a shrug. "Eh, I'll waste my breath until he caves."

"Go to work." I shoo her off with a wave of my hand, and Miles laughs.

"Yeah, go to work, Callie," Miles mocks, but when he sees Callie's jaw drop, he adds, "That way I can start missing you!"

Callie's lips turn up for a smile. "Yeah, yeah, you two have fun!"

With Callie now headed to her spot, I adjust in my seat to face Miles. "So, tell me all about the games I missed."

Miles beams. "Okay, but it's a lot so you need to pay attention. Beck and Mateo had three double plays. *Three*, Lucie. Then Tripp did a bunch of bunts last game, which I think are really cool. It's almost like a trick because you could never tell when he was going to do it again."

I nod along at his excitement. Some of his recaps might be a little stretched considering I watched all of this week's games on TV, but I hope these guys realize what a hype man they have in Miles.

After the game ends, I walk a wired Miles to the family waiting area. I fully anticipate Dex meeting me halfway like he did last time.

Callie may claim that her *talk until he caves* is full proof, but with the glares I got during the game, I'm not so sure. I welcomed Miles's nonstop commentary on the games because it felt like every change in inning, I could feel Dex's eyes on us. As if we would have just vanished into thin air, or I'd have Miles chugging beers with me.

"Do you think you can come to one of the games next week?" Miles asks as he bounces down the hall. "I'm supposed to go to my mommy's house tonight so I won't be at the game tomorrow. But then Daddy picks me up two sleeps later."

"Oh, that sounds like a lot of fun, Miles, but I'm pretty sure you guys are hopping on a plane to Phoenix for the next week of games."

Miles comes to an abrupt halt and turns to me. "So, does that mean you're rain checking?"

I chuckle softly. "Yeah, I'll have to rain check, but maybe another home game."

"I guess that's okay." Miles's shoulders sag for a moment but then he bounces back.

My heart breaks a little at seeing his pout, and really, I'd like to lie to myself and think Miles won't even remember me over the next two weeks, so it doesn't seem like I've left him for so long, but I don't think that's going to happen.

"Oh wait, Miles," I call as he bounces right past the waiting area. "I think we should wait for your dad in here."

Miles turns around and tilts his head. "Oh no, let's go to the locker room! I'm allowed in there, Lucie, I promise!"

"I'm not so sure I am." I chuckle.

Miles looks completely flabbergasted at my words. "Of course you are! Come on!"

"Miles, I don't think—" But it doesn't matter what I say because he's already halfway down the hall. Welp.

When I finally catch up to the little speedster, I thankfully stop him before he races inside. "Okay, you gotta wait on me, bud."

"Sorry." Miles giggles. "I think I just want to see my dad real quick and then we can go back."

I contemplate, looking at the door for a moment. Surely Miles is allowed to go into the locker room...I mean, his dad is a coach, and hey, I'm not actually his nanny.

"Okay, deal, but I'm waiting out here."

Miles sends his eyes to the ceiling. "You can come with me, Lu-cieee. It's okay, I promise!"

Gah, he's so precious it's hard to argue, but this is very non-negotiable.

"Right here." I point to the ground. "I promise I won't leave."

"Okay, if you say so." Miles shrugs before bursting through the door.

Goodness, he's quite the rascal.

Unsure of how long Miles will actually be in there, I pull out my phone to see our girls' group chat blowing up.

Fake PowerPuff Girls Meets Shego Crossover

JENSEN

So are you the nanny yet?

CALLIE

Not from my lack of trying.

REAGAN

Have I mentioned this seems like a very ill-planned idea? Lucie liked watching Dex as a player, doesn't mean he needs to be her boss.

JENSEN

Sorry, your vote is null and void.

CALLIE

We're currently taking zero criticisms on this plan. Thank you for your input.

REAGAN

middle finger emojis

JENSEN

picture of her flipping off the camera

CALLIE

picture of her flipping off the camera

You all are insane.

"Lucie." Dex clears his throat, and I jump at the sound. "Sorry, didn't realize you were easily startled."

"What—sorry. I just wasn't paying attention." I look around for Miles because he's always a welcome distraction. "Is Miles good in there? He told me it was okay."

Dex crosses his arms and with his biceps filling out his uniform a little too well, the sleeves ride up to show the tips of his tattoos. Hmm, yep, those are nice additions to this man's already gorgeous arms.

"He's fine, but I need to talk to you," Dex grunts out, pulling me from my daze.

For Christ's sake, maybe Reagan is right; this is a bad idea. Based on Dex's tone, I feel this job option is about to get the final nail in the coffin.

I fiddle with the hem of my brother's fan jersey. "Um, yeah, what's up?"

"So, I imagine Callie's told you enough that I don't really need to beat around the bush. I need a nanny and someone to teach Miles. Do you want to do it?"

Wait, what?

I let out a small huff in disbelief, but that seems to come off wrong to Dex.

"If you don't, just tell me because I really can't afford to have someone half out right out the gate."

Goodness, why is this man so sour around me? I feel like Will would be complaining about him as a coach a whole lot more if he treated the guys this way.

I straighten my spine. Nonetheless, this is an opportunity, and with my newfound plan to be my own main character, I'm going to need a job.

"Your enthusiasm really sells it, but I'm qualified, and I know I can do a good job."

"Alright," Dex breathes out. "When can you start?"

"I'm agreeing that I can do the job, Dex. I do have some questions first."

Dex sighs as he takes a small step back. For what reason I don't know, but as he uncrosses his arms, he holds a hand for me to start. "That's fair. I might not have all my answers ready, but fire away."

"I'm assuming I'll be traveling with you to away games, what about home games? I live an hour outside of Boston, so it may take me some time to find a place, but I could crash—"

Dex holds up his hand again, only this time to stop me. "I need a live-in nanny, Lucie. I have a spare bedroom, it's yours if that doesn't make you change your mind?"

"Oh—" Considering I was just lusting over this man's arms, the ill-planned comment comes back in my head.

"If you—"

"That's fine," I cut him off. No, no more second-guessing myself or letting my siblings have input. I know they want what's best, but I have to start doing stuff on my own.

"What about days off? I know this schedule is very

demanding, and my hours will be pretty much nonstop, but when it's possible, I want to still have time for myself."

"Done," Dex agrees. "What else?"

"Pay?"

"Name a number."

I narrow my eyes at him. "Just like that? Just name a number and that's what you're paying me."

Dex's mouth dares to turn up into a small smirk. "I thought Callie would have made my desperation pretty clear. Yes, Lucie, just like that. Anything else?"

Oh, I don't know! Goodness, he put me on the spot.

"Maybe...this is the weirdest job interview I've ever had, so I'm a little caught off guard."

Dex shakes his head. "You're right. Shit, I'm sorry. I can give you my number so if you think of any questions, you can text me."

I take a moment before answering to contemplate this decision one final time, but when Dex runs his hands over his face, I see it. I see a dad who's looking, albeit still gorgeous, but also tired and stressed out.

I think Dex needs me to take this job just as much as I need it.

"I mean it, Lucie, any questions. I want you to ask," Dex states calmly. "If you decide it's not going to work, then okay, no worries...but if you do want it, then can you start tomorrow? Miles's mom was going to get him, but she canceled last minute and—"

I shuffle on my feet for a moment, but then stand straighter. "Okay, I'll do it. I'll be your nanny."

Chapter 10
Dex

Hiring regret isn't exactly a thing I thought I would have to deal with. Regrets on plays I've made over the years? Sure. Questionable life choices? Just look at the divorce papers.

But the immediate hiring regret I feel when the ray of sunshine that is Lucie Anderson walks through my office this morning is at the top of the list.

"Good morning," she beams as she knocks on the open door to my office.

It's eight in the fucking morning. I get that the sun is up, but I fear she shines brighter. Her long blonde hair falls over her shoulders, and while she wears simple black leggings and a slightly oversized Blues T-shirt, she looks every bit of...off-fucking-limits.

I give her a curt nod to the chair. When she sits down she takes a sip of some weird green-looking drink.

"What the hell is that?"

Lucie tilts her head, looking at the drink. "A coconut green juice. I wasn't sure about the order, but, eh, it tastes a lot better than it sounds...and looks." She shrugs before taking another sip.

"You mean you just randomly ordered a green juice?"

Hell, have I hired a health nut? I'm struggling to get Miles to eat as is.

"Relax, Dex, I'm not going to be forcing green juice on you." Lucie chuckles. "I've never had one, so I thought I'd try it."

"Well, if you could get Miles on that train, that would be great because he's been fighting me on food for months now."

Lucie takes another sip of her drink and nods. "Got it, I'll see what I can do. Where is the hotshot anyway?"

"Beck took him for a ride on one of the team's razors. I thought our conversation might go a little smoother without the many interruptions."

Lucie messaged me one question last night: what time do you need me at the stadium? I know I practically ambushed her with the offer yesterday, and with the instant hiring regret gnawing on my brain right now, I think offering one more out might be fair...just not sure if I'm offering it for me or for her.

"Look, if you want to back out of this, I get it—"

"I don't," Lucie cuts me off. "Dex, I get that this is a lot, but I do want this job. And I asked Callie for your team email, so my official pay request is in your inbox. My business-minded sister has drilled into my head that everything needs a paper trail, and a text felt a little informal."

"Kind of like my interview?" The dry joke tumbles out of me.

Lucie's face softens with a hint of a smile on her face. "Yeah, kind of like your interview."

This was a horrible idea and I'm putting her smile as reason number one.

Clearing my throat, I shuffle in my chair. Who am I kidding? Between her age and the fact that she's one of my player's sisters, those are the only things that need to be on my list.

"Okay, I know this is fast-paced, so stop me when you have questions. We're leaving for Phoenix on Sunday night. I'll have the team assistant, Shannon, send over the full schedule and itineraries for the team. You can also move some stuff in tomorrow before we leave."

"Sounds good. Anything I need to know about Miles, like allergies, medical things to watch for?"

"No, Miles is pretty healthy, despite wanting to fight me on every meal of the day that doesn't involve sweets."

"Can't fault him for that, I love a sweet treat." Lucie chuckles and tucks her hair behind her ears. "Like you said, we're going at an extremely fast pace. I know getting a routine will come. I looked into some of the requirements for homeschooling last night, but we have some time there so I thought we could talk about that later, but is there anything else I need to know?"

That Olsson's "no fraternizing rule" might be lax, but mine's not.

"In the paperwork Shannon will give you, she has a list of all the emergency contacts and my schedule specifically. Miles can pretty much go anywhere in the stadium, but some meetings and events aren't exactly the best times for him to be running around."

"Got it." Lucie nods again, but then her eyes light up. "Oh, I forgot to ask what you thought about turtles?"

What the fuck? "Turtles?"

"Yeah, I had turtles in my classroom. They're a hit with the kids, so I thought Miles might like them too since I'll technically also be his teacher."

"No, no turtles." I shake my head. She's lost her mind.

Or maybe I have, because when her shoulders drop and she nibbles on her bottom lip, I ask, "With the schedule we have, who's going to feed them? They'd starve."

Lucie straightens back up. "So my turtles are actually old enough that they only need to eat every few days, and I have an automatic feeder that I would use on our longer breaks. They come home during the summer, but ya know, things have changed."

I don't need turtles in my penthouse. No matter how pretty Lucie is. I. Don't. Need. Turtles.

"Also, Callie might have already mentioned to Miles that I have turtles."

"Fucking Callie." I run my hand over my face. I can't seriously be considering this. "Can I think on it?"

That seemingly innocent smile dares Lucie's lips again. "Yeah, of course."

"Anything else I need to think about? So far, you've come in with green juice and turtles."

Lucie snorts an adorable laugh, it sounds so warm and easy—I want to hear it again already. Yep, that's reason number two on my list.

Lucie looks at me. "Remember when you said you were desperate?"

I'm so fucking desperate.

"Lucie!" Miles exclaims as he bursts through the doorway. "Are you really going to be my teacher? Daddy said that you were going to talk about it."

Miles is practically hanging off the arm of Lucie's chair,

talking ninety miles a minute. When Beck finally makes his way in my office, Lucie doesn't even spare him a glance because she's giving all her attention to Miles.

"It looks like it. That is, if you're okay with it?"

Miles nods his head eagerly. "Oh yeah, I'd love for you to be my teacher! And my nanny. Oh! Does this mean we get your turtles in our classroom?"

I'm going to kill Callie.

When I open my mouth to tell my son that I'm thinking about it, Lucie speaks first. "I'm not quite sure yet. I might let some other students have my turtles, but either way, I promise we'll still have a fun time learning. Plus, we get to have a traveling classroom which is so cool, don't ya think?"

"So cool!"

Miles doesn't even flinch at the idea that he might not get to see Lucie's turtles—but internally, I do. Lucie responded to that so effortlessly, and what gets me the most is that she didn't once put the blame on me and my hesitations.

She could and probably should have. It is on me, really, but that's not what she said. She made it sound so good that Miles didn't even mind the idea that we might not have them and put zero of the well-deserved fault on me.

Finally pushing off from Lucie's chair, Miles moves to the edge of my desk.

"Dad, are you done talking now? Can I show Lucie around the stadium?"

"Yes, you can, but can you do me a huge favor and take Lucie by Miss Shannon's office first? She has some papers for her."

Miles crinkles his nose. "Do I have to? Miss Shannon's kind of grumpy."

Beck chuckles as he leans against my door frame. "So that's the kid version of she's kind of a bit—"

"Okay," Lucie cuts him off. "Miles, I would love for you to take me around the stadium. It doesn't matter if Shannon's grumpy, her mood doesn't affect ours."

"I guess, but she's still not very fun."

Miles very much has a point. Our team assistant isn't exactly the easiest to get along with, but she does her job. "Just a quick stop in there and Lucie will be with you for the rest of the day."

"Awesome!" Miles yells. "Can we still come see you sometimes, though?"

"Of course you can, just have Lucie text me to find out where I'm at, okay?"

Miles whips his head to Lucie then back to me. "Okay, we'll probably do that later. We have a very busy day today."

"Oh, well...squeeze me in where you can, please," I mock softly.

Another small laugh comes from Lucie as she stands, placing her hand on Miles's shoulder. "I'm sure there's extra time in there somewhere." Lucie looks to me next. "I'll keep you updated."

I nod. "Please."

Lucie's pink lips turn up slightly, but then she turns back to Miles. "So, should we get started?"

Miles beams like he's on cloud nine. "Yes!"

"Dex is really throwing you in head first, isn't he, Lucie?" Beck says as they leave my office. I knew that fucker wouldn't be able to keep his mouth shut.

Lucie waves her hand. "I'm sure there's a baseball pun in there somewhere, Beck. I'll let you think about it. For now, I've got a tour to get to."

Without another glance back at either myself or Beck, Lucie follows Miles right out.

"So, I see you hired a nanny," Beck teases. The cocky prick has that stupid cheesy smile on his face that he uses on all of the reporters.

"Don't start."

"What? I was just stating—"

Please. I know this fucker too well. "Beck, we've been friends for six years—don't start."

Beck takes the seat Lucie just vacated and holds his hands up in surrender. "Fine, fine. I'll drop it...for now. I think we all know the romantic in me won't let it go. Don't think I didn't see your eyes watch her as she walked away."

Why am I friends with him again? "The romantic in you has no place here. Lucie's my employee now."

"Oh, but when you say it like that, it only makes it sound so much hotter."

"Get out of my office."

I turn in my chair to check for the email from said employee. Scanning her email, it's written out so professionally. Her pay request definitely seems like she's lowballing, but I'll just add to it later when I actually have time to read this email thoroughly.

I'll admit, Lucie may be twelve years younger than me, but it sure as shit doesn't feel like it.

"I think someone else is grumpy too." Beck stands from the chair and raids the mini fridge in my office for water. "You coming for a morning workout?"

"Yeah, I'm coming." Pushing my chair back, Beck tosses me a water as I round my desk.

"Let's go. It'll help you work out some sexual frustration."

Chapter 11
Lucie

Well, I officially have a job. And a new place to live. My turtles, on the other hand, their situation is still up in the air. Dex may not have freaked out like Reagan did when I brought up the topic, but he definitely didn't love the idea.

It would hurt a little bit to give my babies away, but this job will be good for me, I can just feel it. Turtles or not. Creating makeshift travel classrooms for Miles will be tricky, yes, but the challenge feels good.

I feel good.

"Come on, Lucie. Don't be a slowpoke. Shannon's office is down this hall." Miles waves his hand over his shoulder as he starts to skip.

"I'm coming. You're just so fast, I can't keep up."

"That's what my dad says too! I must be really fast." Miles comes to an abrupt halt and whips around to me. "Can we race?"

"Race?" I laugh.

Miles jumps up and down. "Yeah, a race! My dad says

it's unfair to start a race with someone without letting them know about it. So, can we? Can we race?"

"Alright, let's do it."

Miles jumps next to me as he gets into his starting position. Now I'm not an overly competitive person, Reagan and Will definitely are, but that doesn't mean I'm not going to push Miles a little.

"Am I counting us down or are you?" I ask Miles, mimicking his stance.

"Me!" The small mischievous laugh that bubbles out of Miles tells me everything I need to know about his countdown. "One-two-three-go!"

Miles takes off, and for a moment I let him get ahead, but after a few steps I catch back up to him.

"Wh—hey!" Miles giggles.

I'm not actually running by any means, but I can tell he's not giving it his all, so I get a little bit ahead of him.

I look back because the giggles from Miles have stopped, and now there's nothing but pure determination on his face. That's much better.

Miles pushes himself a little harder, but it's not until he reaches me that I start to slow down.

I won't always let Miles win, but there's a give and take here, especially when we're unevenly matched. Sometimes letting them win helps build their confidence, and really, I want to build that confidence with me. Crushing his heart on my very first day doesn't necessarily seem like the best tactic, but I want him to know he's going to have to give it his all every time.

"Yes, I win!" Miles cheers when he passes the first office door we come across. When his victory dance starts, I have zero regrets about letting him beat me.

My head tilts back with a laugh when he starts to fake victory cheers from a crowd, but it's all quickly dashed when the office door swings open.

"What's going on out here?" Shannon snaps, but when she sees Miles, she opts for a softer, still annoyed tone. "Oh, hi, Miles."

"Hi, Shann-onnn." Miles's odd emphasis paired with his mocking tone has me fighting a laugh.

I've heard enough about Shannon to know that Beck's choice of word is probably accurate but since I've never been one to cuss, Miles's grump comment works. The bright side is I don't think my job will involve her too much. Turning a day at the field where we avoid Shannon entirely might even be a game we start playing.

Stepping behind Miles, I place my hands on his shoulders to remind him I'm here with him now. "Hi, I'm Lucie. We're here to get some paperwork Dex said you would have."

Shannon nods with a tight smirk. "Yes, Dex said he hired someone. You're one of Will's sisters, right?"

"Yep, the youngest."

"That part is obvious, dear."

Oof, okay. Callie said her strategy with Shannon was just to smile through it. Seeing the sour look on Shannon's face now, I get it. I can see genuine happy smiles being the most annoying thing to this grumpy woman.

"If we could get the papers, we'll be out of your hair."

Shannon hums. "Right, let me go get them. Olsson's on an important phone call, and I don't want any unprofessional noises interrupting him."

My only response is to make my smile bigger. When her

heels click and she disappears around the wall of her office, Miles turns his head back to me.

"What'd I tell ya, Lucie? She's grumpy."

I nearly choke on my laugh as I bring my finger up to tell Miles to be quiet. "That was a good one, but what did I tell you? It doesn't change our happiness unless we allow it."

Miles shrugs his shoulders, and after a moment Shannon comes back into the hall with a manilla envelope in hand. "Here you go."

"Thank you." Taking the envelope, I have a strange feeling as if one of my students had just handed me their homework, but they know something's wrong and they want to see if they can get away with it.

Pulling up the tab, I pull out the papers as Shannon huffs, "It's all in there."

Having a grumpy attitude isn't my style usually, even if that's sometimes the only way to combat it, but I'll be working a lot with Shannon. So, like Callie, I'll smile through it.

"Oh, I'm sure it is. I'm quite the planner, though. Blame it on the teacher's heart, but I just want to make sure the papers Dex mentioned are all in here. I'd hate to have to come bother you again."

Shannon lets out another sigh as she taps her heel.

Okay, what all did Dex say? Game schedule? Check. Plane itinerary? Check. Emergency contacts? Check. There are a few extras: a map with red marks I can only assume mean "don't go there," a roster of the guys, and, for some reason, a copy of Callie's schedule. I guess, just in case, since she's the other person here that Miles is the most comfortable with, but I'm missing Dex's schedule.

"Um, it looks like I need a copy of Dex's schedule, and we're good to go."

"What do you need his schedule for?"

Happy thoughts, Luce, happy smiles.

"Oh, Dex mentioned I would have it. Also, he mentioned Miles could go pretty much anywhere in the stadium, but I noticed a bunch of red marks on this map, so I was curious—"

"Not everywhere. Some areas need to remain kid free, and as far as Dex's schedule goes, it wasn't on the list of things he requested. If you need anything, I'm sure Callie can handle it."

Miles tilts his head back to me.

"Callie does know a lot. Probably even more than some other people." Miles's eyes look up to the sky as if to really set in his sarcasm. Yep, the kid definitely has been spending a lot of time with Callie, that's for sure.

I force down my laugh, because I know this is one of the prime examples of not needing to encourage the snarky attitude... even if he does have a point.

Shannon scoffs. "If that's all, I think we're set here."

"Right, I'll get with Dex on his schedule. Thanks for everything else," I chime and nudge Miles to head as far away from this woman as possible.

We make it halfway before Miles jumps around and begins walking backward. "First up on our tour, the gym!"

"Alright, Mr. Tour Guide, lead the way!"

Miles jumps back around to skip down the hallway again. Clearly taking my suggestion to not let Shannon's sour mood rub off on us.

When we walk past Dex's office, I may dare a peek to see

if he's still in there. I need to ask him about his schedule anyway, but his office is empty.

As Miles skips on, I pull out my phone to text him. I mean, he is the one who mentioned I would get it, right? Or is texting him about it too weird? It's not exactly an urgent thing, I guess. And worst comes to worst, Callie, I'm sure knows enough of the daily routines to help me out if I need.

"Come on, Lucie! It's right here!" Miles jumps as he reaches his hands high as if he could hit the hanging sign that talks about Lyfe Fitness providing their workout equipment.

"Oh, so close!" I chuckle.

"I know!" Miles boasts.

I gotta give it to the kid—he's got confidence.

When we reach the door, Miles grips onto the handle tightly as he leans his whole body back with a grunt.

"Need some help there?"

"No, Dad says we always get the door for girls. It's polite!" Miles grunts again, putting all his five-year-old strength into the door but it doesn't budge.

I'm not sure what I love more here, really—the fact that Dex is instilling these sweet mannerisms into his son now, or the fact that Miles so clearly wants to be just like his dad. He can put it on winning over Callie, but from my point of view there's more to it than that.

When the door still hasn't opened, I look around to find a small keypad on the side.

"Miles, I love the effort, but I think we might need the code first."

Miles drops his hands from the handle and catches himself before falling to his butt. "Oh yeah, I forgot."

I chuckle. "That's okay. Do you happen to know the code?"

Miles frowns. "No, I can't remember. I think it has a two in it. Or a four—I'm not sure."

"That's okay, I know where the gym is now, so it's still a part of the tour."

"But it's not the same," Miles whines. "I wanted you to see the inside."

"I think I can help with that," a male voice comes from behind me, and while it's familiar I don't quite place it until I turn around to find the infamous playboy, Tripp Pierce.

Although I say playboy, Tripp is still a fun guy to hang out with. Really, I don't think I'm much his type considering he usually sticks to the rejections Reagan gives him.

"Yes! Please, please!" Miles yells.

"Calm down, all-star, I got you." Tripp shakes his head with a chuckle before turning to me. "First day, huh?"

"Does news really travel that fast around here?"

"It does now that Callie works here." Tripp turns to type in the code, but when he reaches for the door Miles swats his hand away.

"I got it!"

"Oh, how very gentlemanlike of you," Tripp mocks but sends a cocky smirk my way. "Callie might fight you if you take away her number one fan."

Miles swings the door wide. "No, this is just practice."

Tripp and I walk into the gym and I shake my head. "So that's what instant rejection feels like?"

"Oh, come on, Little Anderson, you'll get used to it. Hell, sometimes it's refreshing."

I snort a laugh. "Ah, now the seeking out rejections from Reagan make sense."

Miles jumps in front of me with a proud grin on his face. I expect Tripp to consider our conversation over and go workout, but I don't think he notices Miles so close. Or he's just so used to saying whatever comes to his mind.

"It's so humbling. She manages to do it in the most brutal fucking—"

I cut him off, unfortunately a little too late. "Geez, can none of you guys watch your language?"

Miles answers before Tripp can even open his mouth. "No, Daddy says it's really annoying. He told me not to repeat words, 'specially from Tripp or Beck."

"What!" Tripp leans back with his hand over his heart for a full dramatic effect.

I snort a small laugh before I can stop it. Miles looks from Tripp to me, and I can see the mischief already there in his eyes.

"Yeah, Dad and Callie sometimes say you don't use your brains to think. I'm not sure what you do use, but clearly it's not smart."

And with that, I full on laugh.

"And that you guys are children sometimes!" Miles adds.

Crap, I gotta pull it together. Bad teacher reaction on this one.

"Excuse me!" Tripp's voice goes up a couple octaves as he grabs Miles to flip him upside down. "Tell me more of what they said."

Miles giggles as Tripp playfully shakes him. "I won't." Giggle. "Tell." Giggle. "You anything."

"Okay, okay. Give him back," I say, reaching out my hands to take Miles back, but Tripp spins him around.

"Sorry, Nanny, gotta fight for him."

"Tripp," I huff out, but don't get to do anything else before a sharper, aggravated voice cuts in.

"Tripp, put him down," Dex snaps, every bit of what I imagine any angry dad sounds like.

One hot...muscular...sweaty...tattoos peeking out from his sleeves dad. I wonder if I can count the abs through his athletic shirt...eek, snap out of it.

Tripp flips Miles back around and sets him on the ground next to me. "Relax, Dex, we were just goofing around. Nanny, here—"

"My nanny is none of your concern," Dex barks.

Oof. Why do I feel like this thick foggy tension in here now? Did I do something wrong? I thought Dex and Tripp got along...

"She's got a name, guys." Beck comes up beside Dex and claps his shoulder. "And I'm sure this was just a stop on their tour, isn't that right, Miles?"

"Yep! Our first stop after seeing Shannon." Miles's face sours as he says her name but then hooks his head over his shoulder to me. "Lucie, don't forget about the schedule problem."

"What problem?" Dex snaps, finally looking my way.

With the tenseness in his gaze, I'm a little torn between wanting to hide and being slightly more attracted to him.

"It's not really a problem. Shannon gave me Callie's schedule instead of yours. When I asked her about it, she said to talk to you, so—"

"I'll talk to her," Dex clips.

Geez, and here I thought our conversation this morning had some hints of normalcy to them. I guess we're back to being sour to Lucie.

Great, a new boss I've irritated in some way.

Is it me? Is this something I need to add to my list to work on?

Swallowing down that thought, I look away from Dex to Miles. "Right, well, this seems like a great start to our tour. What's next, Miles?"

Miles's smile is wide, completely oblivious to the tension around us. "Let's go see if Callie's here."

"That's part of the tour now?" Miles nods his head, and I swear I see hearts in his eyes. "Yeah, Callie's pretty fun, I suppose. Let's go find her."

Miles races to the door while my steps to the door feel heavy. All the guys' eyes are on me, and I can't help but feel like I've done something wrong here. Maybe finding Callie isn't such a bad idea.

I've always watched the Blues play on TV, but it seems the team dynamic is different than I expected. I guess I should have taken into consideration that my brother is usually quite the loner, so his talk about the team is probably just coming from short, passing conversations.

But then again, Will knew Callie was pushing for me to have this job... He would have said something if there was drama that I wouldn't handle well...

Miles waves for me to hurry up. "I think I hear her. Let's go!"

Let's figure out what I've gotten myself into.

Chapter 12
Dex

There's nothing quite like game days. Whether it was my game to pitch or not, I've always loved them. I had hoped that when I took this job that feeling would have stayed...I think I hoped for a lot out of this job that was really a long-fucking-shot.

Tonight's game has been especially hard for many reasons. We have a great line-up of pitchers on the Blues—and even if I'm no longer a part of that, we have a good group. There's just one in particular who I can't fucking stand.

Jordan Clark is our middle reliever and while he's got some solid throws, he's cocky and makes rash game-time decisions that a pitcher like Will, myself, or really any of the other pitchers on this team wouldn't make.

Ignoring signals from our catchers. Being too focused on guys stealing bases to focus on a decent pitch. Mouthing off to umps on calls. No matter what I try, or what the bullpen coach or anyone else says to help rein Jordan in—he doesn't want to listen.

He was our last GM's favorite reliever to call in for some fucking reason. It was probably their matching holier-than-thou asshat personalities. God, I'm so fucking glad he's gone. He started out strong, but if you weren't one of his chosen, you were practically walking on eggshells. Olsson interfered more times than I can count. If he hadn't, I know for damn sure the majority of these players in the dugout would have been traded.

With another clink of a bat, I watch as the ball soars into right field, where, thankfully, it's caught for our third out of the inning. Jordan threw one strike. One.

"God, take him fucking out," I grumble to Olsson. "I already told the guys in the bullpen to get literally anyone else warmed up."

Olsson gives a low chuckle. "Alright, but keep trying with him a little longer. Something's got to get through to him eventually."

As the guys filter into the dugout, I holler at Jordan. "Clark, that's all for today's game."

Jordan spits out a bitter laugh. "I usually pitch two innings."

"Yeah, and most pitchers usually throw more than one strike, so maybe you should go back to the bullpen and work on that."

His nostrils flare. I know I've struck a nerve, but hey, it's not a false statement.

"Yeah, well, since I'm apparently done for this game I think I'll head to the clubhouse."

Figures. I turn back to the field, completely dismissing him because I know I can't stop him.

When he stomps by, Olsson claps my shoulder. "Mr. Personality today, aren't we?"

All I can manage back is a tight nod because, yeah, I know I've been a bit of an ass today. It has everything to do with the sunshiny blonde in the stands.

Without fail, with every change of inning, I do the other thing that has made this game insufferable: look over at Lucie.

Insufferable feels like the wrong word as I watch as she talks to Miles in the stands. My son's hands are making sharp throwing movements, and I can tell from here that he is critiquing the pitches he just saw.

Lucie nods along with that beautiful smile on her face. Her cheeks slightly rosy from the sun that's been beating down on us all game.

I know she has sunscreen because she texted me asking where some was for Miles. Maybe she didn't use it because of her skin? My ex used to have our bathroom full of different lotions and bottles of stuff. I should ask her what kind of sunscreen she wants, or I guess I could get her a hat to keep in my office.

Beck's face blocks my view of Lucie at the best fucking moment because, what the fuck was I just thinking?

"So, care to talk about what happened earlier today?" Beck asks.

"There's nothing to talk about," I grunt out as I turn to look back to the field.

Beck tilts his head back as he raises his eyebrows and plasters that cocky smirk on his face. "Right, because you weren't just looking into the stands for a certain blonde."

"My son's over there, asshole."

Beck folds his arms over the edge of the dugout as we watch our shortstop send a beautiful hit down third base.

"No, of course. I just think Tripp is still feeling the third degree from earlier in the gym."

I clench my jaw at the memory. I could lie to Beck and say it was solely from Tripp messing with Miles, but the guys roughhouse with him all the time. Hell, I think Miles might be a little too aggressive with them half of the time. As a five-year-old, cheap shots are not a thing.

My cut-in was purely spurred by the sound of Lucie's laugh and the fact that it was Tripp who was enjoying it, not me.

"Aren't you up to bat soon? Quit bothering me."

"Nope, I was last batter last inning, so you can cut the bullshit at any time. Will didn't pitch this game, so I know you know he's in the bullpen—"

"Drop it, Beck."

Beck tosses his hands up then waves me off. "Okay, okay. That's fine, it'll be more entertaining when Callie tells Will about what happened, and he'll ask you himself what's going on."

We hear another unmistakable sound of a ball and bat connecting as Adam's hit goes into the back of centerfield. I'll admit, adding Adam and Will to our roster was a very good decision on Olsson's part, but the drawbacks are there too. Unfortunately, they don't have anything to do with how they play baseball.

"Callie wasn't even there." I keep my voice low. Will and Adam may not be around us, but it's not lost on me that we're still in the middle of a fucking game.

Beck hits my shoulder, clearly not caring about being low-key. "Dex, come on, you seriously don't think Callie and Lucie aren't going to talk to each other? Callie has already asked me why you freaked out on Tripp in the gym. So maybe, if you tell me something, I can help you out. I'm your bridge!"

"Fucking hell, lower your voice," I mutter. God, he's just as relentless as Callie. No wonder they're friends. "I may have met Lucie before I knew who she was, okay? I thought she was cute. I halfway, for a second, thought about asking for her number. But then I remembered I'm a single dad with an insane schedule so I didn't. It's just been a little difficult to separate the new connections." That's a major downplay of what happened, but Beck gets what he gets.

"Ahh, now it's starting to make sense. You mean, the first girl you've even thought of attempting to move on with after your divorce ends up being our teammate's sister?"

I don't correct him on the first half, because that's exactly what coffee shop Lucie was, but the second part... "I mean, the much younger sister of a player I coach, who is now my fucking nanny."

Beck huffs a laugh. "Alright, I'll admit the working for you part could complicate things a bit."

"Just that part? I think I named some other important points."

"Not from my point of view. A player's sister? Hello, have you seen who Will takes home every night? Ask Adam if you missed it. And younger? Yes, but Lucie is also an adult. A very mature one, if I can add without it being weird. I've been to the game nights Callie hosts. I don't think the maturity difference between you and Lucie matches the age gap."

I know he's right, hell, I had the same thought earlier today. "Can we possibly drop this, considering we're in the middle of a game?"

Beck chuckles as the umpire calls our final out in the

inning. "Ah, saved by the inning, I suppose." Beck picks up his glove and hits me on the back. "Don't worry, I'll be back."

Fuck, I can already tell this conversation was a mistake. Just like the quick glance I immediately give my sunny nanny in the stands.

We won tonight, barely. Changes over this season have made a huge impact, but it's clear we still have things to work on. The World Series isn't out of the question, but we're struggling to hold on to number three in our division right now. We need to be in the top two to avoid battling it out in wild-card games.

I hold off until after the postgame meeting to go find Miles. Lucie texted that they were hanging out in Callie's office, and I know better than to try to pull him away from that.

Hell, that's just what I'm telling myself to make me feel better about leaving him with them so I can prepare to see Lucie again. Damn it, she's going to move in with us tomorrow—I've got to nip this attraction in the bud.

Walking down our hall, I can hear the unmistakable sound of my son's laugh. Hearing Callie's next, a small pit forms in my stomach when I don't hear Lucie's.

Rounding the corner into Callie's office, I'm not entirely sure what's going on, but I now know the reason I didn't hear Lucie's laugh as I see her standing, juggling three baseballs.

Miles claps his hands as he starts to chant her name, but when Lucie's eyes catch mine, she catches all three balls in her hands and tucks her chin low. I can't exactly tell if the redness on her cheeks is from the sun or if she's blushing.

Miles lets out a groan. "Lucie, keep going!"

Callie shakes Miles's shoulder lightly. "Party's over, kid. Dad's here."

Miles whips his whole body around in his chair and his eyes light up. "Dad, you're here! Finally!"

I take the two steps needed before picking my son up out of the chair. One day, he'll be too big for this type of hug, but until then, I'm going to take full advantage.

Miles's arms squeeze tightly around my neck. "I missed you."

My hold gets a little tighter and the guilt from not getting him sooner hits hard. "I missed you too."

"Oh, don't let him fool you too much, Dex, he was pretty entertained by Lucie's hidden talent," Callie says with a laugh.

Glancing back to Lucie, her cheeks are still red and her eyes avoid mine as she sets the baseballs down on Callie's desk.

"Not a hidden talent, just usually a crowd pleaser amongst children." Lucie's voice is barely above a whisper as she tucks the strands of her hair behind her ears and looks toward Callie.

Miles lets go of his hug and leans back to look me in the eye while talking ninety miles a minute. "It was so cool! I was a little sad when I didn't see you in the hall. I thought about going to the locker room, but then Shannon was walking out, and we've been avoiding her all day. So Lucie and I raced into Callie's office. When I got sad again, Lucie said she knew a way to cheer me up."

I try to ignore the small pang of pain in my chest that

Miles was upset he didn't see me right after the game, but hell, that's hard to hear. Between his mom backing out of their weekend together and me being completely selfish today—

"Miles, why don't you tell your dad about all of the fun we had today?" Lucie's voice cuts through my thoughts.

"Oh yeah, we had so much fun! We went all around the stadium and I got to show Lucie all the big fancy rooms where people watch the games. And we went and got some ice cream, but I did have to eat real food first. Lucie says the same things you do, like eating good food and chewing with my mouth closed."

Callie snorts. "What party poopers."

Miles giggles at Callie while he pushes his hands on my chest for me to put him down. When he sits back down next to Callie, he pulls his legs up on the chair. "Lucie, can you juggle again?"

Lucie hums softly as the corner of her mouth tilts up for a moment. With how sweetly Miles just asked her, I imagine she's considering it. I don't even know how to do it, but hell, I'd figure it out if it meant getting that all-amazed look from my son.

But like Callie said, I'm a bit of a party pooper and I still need to talk to Lucie before we leave.

I kneel next to Miles's chair. "Sorry, bud, maybe another night. We've got to get you to bed, but I do have to talk to Lucie for a minute. Can you stay with Callie until we're done?"

"Oh." Miles frowns for a moment before turning to Callie. "Do you know how to juggle?"

Callie hops up from her chair. "I can surely try!"

Oh, dear Lord.

I give Lucie a small nod to follow me to my office, and before we even make it halfway, we hear squeals and laughs accompanied by a loud thud.

Lucie chuckles. "We have to hurry, or I fear Callie might break a lot of stuff in her office."

I hold the door open and let her walk in first. "Yeah, I'd consider it a safe bet that most of it wouldn't be as accidental as she'd claim."

"No, probably not."

"So, today went okay?" I ask, taking my seat.

"Yeah, I think so. I mean, Miles and I had a good time." Lucie shuffles in her chair and slides the small strands of her blonde hair back again.

This close, I can definitely see the blush but mostly sunburn on her cheeks and her nose.

"Did you not use the sunscreen?"

"Huh?"

"The sunscreen. Your face is red."

The redness on her face intensifies...yeah, I probably could have said that in a less blunt way, but oh well. I'm pushing past my attraction to her right now, and I'm not sure how that's all going to play out. For now, it's bluntness.

Lucie places a hand on her cheek, I'm sure to feel the heat coming from it. "Oh no, I did. I just sunburn really easily. I didn't realize—"

"Maybe bring a hat to keep for the games." *And save me the need to give you one of mine.*

"Right, I can do that." Lucie gives me a slow nod. "So, tomorrow..."

Tomorrow. Fuck, the day she moves in.

Clearing my throat, I look down at the stack of papers on my desk, looking for my schedule that Shannon didn't give

Lucie. Because she needs it, not because I need a break from looking at her. "On the emergency list that Shannon gave you, it has the address and the instructions for the elevator. What time do you think you'll be by to move in?"

"Probably around ten or so. I have an hour drive, but I don't have much stuff, so I think I can get most of it packed tonight, then—"

It takes a minute to process the words Lucie just said, but as I glance at my watch, I see it's already half past nine. "Wait, you have an hour drive?"

"Yeah, I told you that in our non-interview interview in the hall, remember?"

No, I don't. I'm pretty sure I blacked out during half of that conversation.

Looking up from my desk, I study Lucie. "So, you're driving an hour by yourself tonight in the dark after working all day, then turning around and doing it again in the morning? When are you even going to have time to sleep if your plan is to pack?"

"Well, yeah? I'll manage some sleep, and Will's going to meet me to help take some stuff in his SUV because it's bigger. I'll drive my car—"

Nope. Not happening.

"Ride with Will in the morning. I don't want you driving on little sleep. I'll have the car service take you home and get your car to the apartment tomorrow. Just give me your keys."

"Dex, that's not—"

"I said, give me your keys." Okay, yep, teetering blunt and asshole territory. Let's try this again. "The Blues have a car service for many reasons; consider this a perk of the job."

Lucie's lips form a thin line before she sighs and pulls out her keys from her pocket, and drops them in my hand.

Now, is calling the car service this last minute a little bit of an abuse of power? Kind of, but I don't really care.

"Okay, consider it taken care of. I'll have someone out front in fifteen minutes," I say. "We'll see you in the morning."

Lucie tucks her chin down and gives a soft thank you as she stands up. But as she reaches the door, she spins back around. "I...uh, my turtles? No pressure, I just need to get a plan for them."

My final answer is going to be no.

No is what I said in my head when I rehearsed this conversation with her.

But the words that come out of my mouth when I look at Lucie are "I'm not cleaning their tank."

Chapter 13
Lucie

"And we're super sure about this?" Will asks as he holds the turtle tank in the elevator on the way up to the top floor of Dex's apartment complex.

"Yes, we're sure. I need a job," I reply, not even looking back at him as I look for the number of Dex's apartment for the fifteenth time.

"Right, and I don't need to bring up the 'weird vibe' between Dex and Tripp yesterday?"

"Right." The elevator dings and the door slides open.

"Or the fact that Dex got your car moved? *And* got our car service to take you home?"

"Nope," I say, keeping my voice chipper.

Brothers. I walk down the hall and wave him off before he can make another comment.

I knew this whole talk was coming from him. Will's a protector—a "let me take care of you" person—and in a way, I think Dex is too.

His attitude might be a little blunt and prickly at times, but I don't think Dex is being weird about these things. I definitely don't think they mean what Will thinks they could mean.

I scan the numbers on the first door we come to, but then keep going.

"You know it doesn't bother me at all that you took this job, but if you think it's because I'm upset about you getting fired—"

"It's not," I groan out and slide my suitcase further down the hall to the next door. "I really think this could be good for me."

I don't give Will the full reasoning of why I think that, but I know I have to give him a little something. Will's savior complex knows no bounds, especially with me and Reagan. He has every bit of the best intentions, and he'll back off if we tell him, but it's that sibling intuition thing that you have to watch for.

"Alright, if you say so. I know Callie's happy to have another girl around, especially when we travel."

"See, it's a win-win. You can stop worrying now."

I pause at the next door and check the apartment number on my paper for the millionth time. 4878. Yep, this is it.

Will grunts behind me as he tries to readjust his hold. "Alright, alright, but can we hurry it up, please? This thing is really awkward to carry, and I think the duffle bag is about to fall off my shoulder."

"Don't be such a baby, we're here." I snort a laugh as I knock on the door. "You know you wouldn't be whining if Callie came with us."

"Just so you know, I'm flipping you off right now." Will shakes his head with a sigh. "I suppose how you managed to convince Dex to let you keep these things is another question

I'm not allowed to ask?"

"I asked nicely," I sing.

Now if Reagan had said that, Will would have snarled his nose and told her to not be gross, but since it's me, Will just shrugs.

When the door still has not opened, I wonder if I need to knock again, but the moment I raise my hand again, it swings open.

"Lucie's here!" Miles squeals. When he notices Will, he steps out into the hall and looks around. "Did you bring Callie too?"

Will huffs and looks at me. "Think you can work on that for me? Consider it my trade-off for not asking my questions."

"Oh, hush." I wave him off. "Hey, Miles, no Callie today, but look what Will did bring…"

Miles snaps up straight, his eyes growing huge. "The turtles! I thought Daddy was kidding!"

Miles's excitement is so high and as he bounces closer, Will has to take a step back. "Which one's which? Which one is which?"

"Easy, Miles." Dex's voice practically demands my attention.

Turning from Miles to Dex, I see him leaning against the door frame with his arms crossed. A slight corner of his mouth turns up as he watches Miles stumble back a few steps.

Miles snickers. "Sorry."

Will shuffles his grip again. "Can someone please tell me where to put this thing down before Pip and Pop go plop?"

"Hurry, Will, follow me!" Miles shrieks and zips back through the door, nearly knocking into Dex.

"Slow down," Dex huffs, but I don't think it quite registers with Miles. "Will, it's straight back to the living room. Miles cleared the spot he wanted this morning."

"Perfect," Will says as he walks right in.

I, on the other hand, still for just a moment. I meant what I said to Will, I do think this will be good for me, but walking in also feels really weird. I'm going to be living with a guy for the first time ever—minus my brother, he doesn't count.

"You okay?" Dex asks.

I snap out of my trance. "Yeah, I'm good."

Well, here's to figuring myself out, I guess.

Stepping into Dex's apartment, my steps slow as I reach the edge of the living room. Windows make up the entirety of the far wall that looks over an incredible view and a balcony that I fear Dex may never get me off of on nights where we're not traveling.

Even with the elevated aspects of a penthouse, Dex's place feels nice. It feels like a home, despite knowing that he and Miles spend more time in hotel rooms than here. It still gives this well-lived feeling. The living room is full of warm creams and browns, and there are some of Miles's toys on the floor to really hone in on that family feel.

"Is this all you brought?" Dex raises an eyebrow as he reaches for my suitcase. "A duffle bag, a suitcase, and the turtles?"

"Yeah—well, there's still another suitcase in Will's car. I just thought I'd pack for the two weeks' travel, plus have some necessities here, then bring some more stuff later." I shrug.

Does he think it's weird I don't have a ton of stuff?

"My sister is still staying in our apartment for a couple

months, so there's really no rush. You might decide I'm not a good fit after spending two weeks with me," I joke, hoping to lighten the mood, but Dex doesn't laugh or even crack a small smile.

Maybe my leaving in two weeks isn't as much of a joke as I think it could be. Being fired from my second job might really send me into a spiral, but even if Dex doesn't like me, I know I can do this job. I just have to prove it to him.

Dex clears his throat. Yeah, that's a good sign. "Come on, I'll show you your room."

My thin smile is the only response I can muster.

Glancing at Will, he's holding up Miles so he can look up over the tank while he points out each turtle. A more than thin smile tugs at my mouth at that.

Dex continues through the living room and as he starts down a hall, he points to the first door we come to. "Miles's room is this door here, and the next one is his playroom. There's an office space on the other end I'm getting cleaned out. I figured once we get everything situated we can make that into his class-room. Just let me know what you'll need and we'll get it."

"Oh, you don't have to do that. With all the traveling, I'm sure we'll be used to making makeshift classrooms."

Dex doesn't look back and his voice remains just as neutral as can be. "As a teacher, I thought you might like to have a space for that. No one's using it, so why not you?"

I open and close my mouth. This feels like it might be a touchy subject, and you know what, why not me? He wants to give me a classroom, so who am I to argue? "Okay, I'll let you know what we'll need."

"Great," Dex clips as he stops to open the last door on the left. "This is you."

A moment ago I was silent by choice, but now I'm silent due to the view in this freaking room. I knew it looked incredible in the living room but to also have it in my room—I'm completely mesmerized.

Aimlessly walking up to the window that takes up the entire wall, my voice squeaks but I don't care. "Ah, is that Blues Stadium?"

"Yeah, can't see the field, but I imagine any night we do fireworks, the view from here is pretty cool." Dex's tone still sounds completely uninterested, but a more excited child's voice follows.

"And this is Lucie's room!" Miles yells, and as I look at him he's got his arms outstretched as if he were showcasing a grand art piece to my brother.

Will lets out a low whistle. "Nice new view, Luce. I guess this puts your apartment to shame, huh?"

I chuckle. The penthouse in Boston compared to an apartment complex in Rowley...yeah, maybe a bit. "In a way, but yours is still greatly appreciated and loved."

"Yeah, yeah." Will drops my duffle bag onto my new bed that I'm just now really paying attention to. Will seems to notice the bedding too, because he says what I was just thinking. "Hey, yellow's your favorite color."

"It is?" Miles practically radiates excitement at this revelation.

I chuckle. "Sure is, what a happy coincidence."

Miles whips his head to Dex. "You did a good job, Dad!" Miles whips his head back. "He got this at our front door this morning."

"It was the only color with same-day delivery," Dex adds on to Miles's sentence.

Will sends a look my way, but I ignore him. It's bedding, it's really not that deep.

"Well, it's perfect. Thank you."

I send Dex a soft smile first before giving the same one to my nosy brother.

"Alright, well, I'm going to head out. Luce, the suitcase in the car is your travel one, right?"

"Right, can you—"

Will waves me off. "I'll bring it."

"Thank you for helping."

"It's what I do." Will shrugs before turning to head out. I half hold my breath, begging internally that he doesn't say some stupid overprotective brother crap to Dex, but when he walks by he just claps his shoulder then raises his hand in a wave. "I'll see you guys in a couple of hours."

Miles jumps and races to follow Will. "Oh, I'll show you to the front door!"

I chuckle. "Ever the tour guide."

Dex shows the first sign of amusement with what I'd qualify as a humorous huff before going all stoic on me again. "Well, I'll let you get settled."

Clearly, that's all the personality I'm going to be getting out of him today. I give him a small nod as he starts to walk out of my new room.

This is still going to be good for me. I'm sure of it. Miles is my focus, anyway, so what if Dex wants to keep our conversations short? I'm here to do a job, and clearly that's how Dex sees it too.

I pull my suitcase over to the closet space when my phone dings in my pocket.

JENSEN

So, since you're so cool now and getting
to travel with THE Boston Blues, do you
think you could spare a lunch with little ole
me before you leave?

That was really quite dramatic. Also, I'm
not sure… Is asking to leave on your first
day a bad look?

Technically yesterday was your first day,
and today there's no game so from what
I'm assuming it's your day off.

Rather bold assumption, but I suppose I
see your logic.

Just ask, the worst he'll say is "no."

Hmph, yeah a "no" is probably all he'll give me. It would
be nice to see Jensen before I'm gone for nearly two weeks.
And I did tell Dex that on any days off I wanted to have time
for myself. Granted, we haven't clarified a lot of this job…
seems as if that could be a red flag. Maybe that's just how
Dex needs this to be for now. As much of an adjustment as
this is for me, I'm sure it feels life-altering for him.

I can go at his pace, and maybe making myself scarce is
the best way to start—give him space to adjust…but thinking
about asking to leave already has my palms sweating.

Let me feel it out. He had my car
transported here by the team so I'm not
sure if it's here yet either. I'll let you know.

When Jensen thumbs up my message, I slide my phone
back in my pocket.

Okay, just ask. What's the worst that could happen?

Before I let my nerves get too out of hand, I march out the door into the hall and ram right into Dex. Our bodies collide, and the impact starts to send me back onto my butt when Dex's hands reach out quickly to pull me back up.

The only problem—he pulled a little too hard and now I'm completely pressed against him and...oh my gosh, I think I'm touching it. My hand went in a weird position when he grabbed me and now I'm definitely touching something I should not be.

As soon as the realization hits me, I think it hits Dex too, because his hands are now pushing me back.

"Oh my—I—I'm..." I sputter as my brain is still computing what just happened.

Dex's hands steady me for a moment, but then they immediately leave my shoulders once we've both gained our footing. "It's fine," Dex grunts out.

It doesn't feel fine—I, for one, feel mortified. "I-I—I'm sorry. I didn't mean to touch—I mean—run into you like that."

Smooth.

"It's fine." Dex's voice is firm as he takes an extra step back from me. "I was just coming to tell you that your car's in the garage."

"Great!" Unlike Mr. Cool, Calm, and Collected here, my tone is all high and squeaky. "I was going to see if I could meet a friend for lunch before we—"

"Yep, go, that's fine. We leave for the airport at five," Dex barks before he turns around and leaves me to die of embarrassment.

Chapter 14
Lucie

"You did what?!" It doesn't matter that we're sitting outside in downtown Boston, Jensen's voice carries across the whole patio.

I sink lower in my chair. "I think I touched it."

"This is incredible. Please, tell me everything. Leave no inch out."

I can't help but laugh. "Okay, well, I didn't grope it in that much detail. Maybe it was something in his pocket."

"*Ay, dios mío*, Lucie!" Jensen snorts. "It never is."

"Well, shockingly, I've never accidentally touched a man's...equipment before."

Jensen raises an eyebrow. "Equipment? Really?"

"What do you want me to say? I don't cuss and you try thinking of non-cringey words for it." I toss a fry in my mouth as Jensen turns her head up, clearly running all the other options through her head.

"Alright then, just cuss. Ever thought of that?"

I've thought of it many times, every time I try to think of a non-cringey word for a man's penis.

"I'm around kids too much. It just feels weird for me at this point. Unnatural, in a way. I may not know too much about myself, but it'd probably look like Princess Peach cursing. I'd just be forcing it."

Jensen takes a fry and drowns it in the ranch. "I see your logic," she mumbles. "But I've got to disagree on Princess Peach. You know she's dying to cuss Mario out every time she gets kidnapped."

"Well, what princess wouldn't cuss?"

Jensen quirks an eyebrow, then shrugs. "Cinderella? I don't know, we got off track. We were talking about you touching your new boss's dick. Let's get back to that."

"I'd really rather not." I reach for another fry. Am I totally about to ruin the lunch I just ordered by eating way too much of our appetizer? Yep.

"Can you at least tell me if it felt big or not?"

My immediate thought was, of course it freaking felt big, but Dex is *my boss*. A boss who clearly has mixed feelings about hiring me. Talking about this feels wrong. Dex is a private guy. I can respect that.

"Jen, let it go."

"Alright, fine, you prude of a princess. Moving on." Jensen dusts her hands before reaching for her napkin. "How's the whole figuring out yourself going?"

I called Jensen to fill her in on my plan the night Dex officially hired me. She's the only person who knows about it at this point. She is my accountability buddy, making sure I don't lose myself in my siblings again.

"It kind of just started. Taking this job feels more like the start of my who-knows-how-many step plan."

"Don't you have a list?"

"Sort of. I think it's more guidelines really."

Jensen tosses another fry in her mouth. "Run me through them again."

"We've got: venture out more, have a yes day, find a hobby, be more spontaneous, and do something I'm scared of." I tap my finger on each task to make sure I remember all five. I should probably have an official list or something.

"Okay, it seems a little broad. Venture out more? How are you going to venture out? Venturing out to the bar and venturing to the park are two very different levels in my opinion."

"Why can't I venture to both places? The different levels are the whole point. I go to bars with Reagan, and she usually orders my drink without asking me. I go to the park—if we're being honest, I don't remember the last time I've been to a park. But I want to find out. Maybe I'm one of those people who enjoys those park workouts—but I don't know because Reagan hates things that make her sweaty, and Will would rather workout at one of the many top-of-the-line facilities he has access to."

Jensen laughs. "Okay, I'm understanding a little more. So, each item isn't limited to a one-time thing."

"Right, well, except maybe the yes day. Those may be a little more restricted to a once every couple of months deal." I shrug. "Saying yes to myself every single time will result in debt that even Will couldn't pay off."

"Maybe it doesn't have to be yes to monetary things. What about just saying yes more, in general? Like yes to a bubble bath, yes to the whole tub of ice cream in the freezer... Oh, yes to a date! When's the last time you went on a date?"

My mouth forms a thin line as I think. I guess it has been a while since I've been on a date. "I was casually texting one of the teachers that I used to work with, but he ended up ghosting me."

Jensen snorts. "Classy."

I wave my hand off. "As you can see, I'm clearly heart-broken over it. It also solidified my need for these guide-lines. That's the third time I've been ghosted this year alone. I've had some boyfriends over the past but nothing..."

"Toe-curling?"

"Well, yes, but nothing describes it best. Most guys I've texted with seem to end up ghosting, and the two true boyfriends I can recall...well, I just feel like I wasn't really heartbroken over them, ya know? It seems the common denominator is me. Maybe I'm too boring, I don't know."

"Okay, so why not add a spicy side to your list? Venture out more in your dating life. Be Spicy Lucie. Maybe even be a princess who cusses." Her mouth opens in fake shock.

I roll my eyes, tempted to toss a fry at her. "With what time? Remember I'm going to be getting like two days off in the month. It's fine, really. I think I need to figure myself out before I add dating to it."

"Um, figuring out what you like in the bedroom is part of yourself, actually."

She's got me there.

"How about this—hand me a napkin." Jensen digs in her purse when I drop a clean napkin in front of her. After pulling out a Sharpie, she grabs the napkin and starts scrib-bling away.

"Jen—"

She waves her hand, cutting me off. "Shh, I don't want to lose my ideas."

Sitting back in my chair, I let her work.

"Okay, here. As your accountability friend, I insist you add these. Consider it the *Lucie After Dark* side of your list."

Picking up the napkin, I look at the barely legible list— goodness. "Ya know, for a tattoo artist, your penmanship needs work."

"Oh bite me, I was working with a Sharpie and a napkin."

I chuckle and go back to her list. *Try different toys. Find a kink you like. Sexually inspiring outings.*

"Okay, what exactly is a 'sexually inspiring outing'?"

"It could be anything. I tried to be broad, like the rest of your list. You could take a pole dancing class, you could get your nipples pierced, go buy some lingerie, or have a one-night stand. And before you argue, you said you'd have some nights off—women need to not be so judged for them anyway. I had to throw it out there."

"You're right, you're right. Not sure if it's exactly my style, but I can respect the point."

"And hey, none of these things require another person anyway. You can do them all yourself or with someone, but either way, you still get to the core of Lucie."

"Was that supposed to have a double meaning?" I laugh.

"Wasn't intentional, but I'm coining it now for this exact reason."

I fold up the napkin and shove it into my purse. "Anyway, how are things going at the tattoo shop?"

Jensen falls back against her chair with a major eye roll. "I'm so ready to get out of this apprenticeship. Hank is the fucking worst. How Tally stays married to him is beyond me."

"Doesn't he hit on you constantly?"

Jensen throws her hands in the air. "Literally hits on

anyone with a nice rack! I don't know if she doesn't see it, or just doesn't care. I'm honestly scared to bring it up to her but he's been breathing down my fucking neck and getting real touchy."

I hate this for her. Jensen works constantly, and this apprenticeship is the last thing she needs to be officially licensed. "How many hours do you have left?"

Jensen sinks a little lower in her chair. "I'm finally under five hundred. Nearly two years. I've endured his back-handed comments and sleazy pick-up lines this entire time. Now I'm this fucking close, and he starts this shit?"

I can't bring myself to keep the disgust off my face. "Jen, I'm so sorry. Do you think there's any chance you could tell Tally and there not be backlash?"

Jensen lets out a deep, *deep* sigh. "With none whatso-ever? No, I don't think so. I need this apprenticeship, Luce. I push through to get my license, then I'm out of there."

I get it. I'm not happy about it, but I get it. "Swear to me, Jensen, if it escalates, you'll say something."

She holds out her pinky. "Pinky promise, Princess Peach."

Chapter 15
Dex

I have many regrets. So, so many from today. Starting with letting my son see that damn bedspread being delivered. Lucie needed something for the bed and I had nothing on it because I let Kate take whatever the fuck she wanted when she moved out.

Yellow wasn't the only color that was deliverable today, it just reminded me of Lucie. It reminded me of how beautiful she looked in her yellow sundress the first day we met. Finding out it was her favorite color wasn't a total shock, but thanks to my son, I had to come up with a lie on the spot.

Then there was that mishap in the hallway that I'm sure will haunt me for all eternity, but the other main regret of the day was taking the phone back from Miles when he said, "Mommy wants to talk to you."

Again, I should have known that my no-filter son would talk about the new nanny moving in today.

I get that while Kate gave up all rights to decision-making involving Miles, she would still have questions. Despite the short notice, I did get a general background check on Lucie—again, another small abuse of power using the Blues' legal team.

Should I have been the one to tell my ex instead of Miles? Yeah, probably. I definitely got an earful on that one. I'd already had to answer a million and one questions my own mother had about hiring Lucie, but Kate's came with more unnecessary questions. What does Lucie look like? Is she pretty? How old is she?

Answers to those are ones I did not want to give, so it probably made matters worse, but I reminded Kate that none of it really mattered because Lucie's here to stay.

My stress from the phone call must have carried with me throughout the rest of the afternoon, or our run-in in the hall has kept Lucie at a generous arm's length. Which is for the best. In spite of her joke in the living room this morning about being fired after these first two weeks and my attraction to her—I need a nanny and a homeschool teacher for Miles to be able to travel with me.

For the entire plane ride, Lucie gave all her attention to Miles, and while I'd catch her eyes wandering toward me a time or two, her eyes carried more concern for my quiet demeanor than anything else. Not that I should want to see something more in her eyes, that's beside the point.

When our shuttle arrives at our hotel for the week, Miles yawns and holds his arms out for me. "I'm too tired to walk."

I chuckle. "All that sitting for the last couple of hours has worn you out, huh?"

"Travel is exhausting," Miles huffs.

Lucie comes around to my side. Her lips turn up when Miles rests his head on my shoulder. "I second that, bud. I think I'm going to crash as soon as I hit the bed."

Miles giggles and lets out a very fake yawn. "Me too."

Lucie doesn't look exhausted, though. She still shines just as bright with her blonde hair falling loosely over her shoulders and in her damn yellow. It doesn't matter that it's a crewneck, it could be a yellow bag and it would complement her so well.

My hand starts to move to brush some of her hair back behind her shoulder, but then I realize how fucking weird that would be and play it off as if I wanted to scratch Miles's back.

Clearing my throat, I grunt out, "Let's go inside and get checked in then."

I make it about three steps into the lobby before Miles shoots his head up with a squeal. "Lucie, look at the water fountain! They have a water fountain inside! Can we go look at it, Dad? Please, please?"

Miles wiggles in my arms. "I thought you were exhausted?"

"But it's a water fountain!"

"I don't mind taking him, Dex," Lucie says next to me. "Unless you want to? I can try to get us checked in."

This small tug pulls in my chest. It may seem like a small gesture, and while Lucie has given Miles pretty much all of her attention since this whole thing started, she always takes into account my relationship with Miles first.

I set Miles down. "I think I'll have to be the one to check in, but you guys go. I'll meet you over there."

Lucie gives me a small nod, but if she wanted to say anything, it's cut off by Miles grabbing her hand and pulling her away.

"Come on, Lucie, let's go!"

I watch them walk hand in hand for a moment. It's

almost too damn hard to look away. I know I said I need Lucie, but in what capacity, is my next question.

Shit, what have I gotten myself into?

Forcing myself to the reception desk, there's an older lady smiling. "Hi, welcome to the Marriott. What's the last name?"

"Larsen."

After clicking on her keyboard for a moment, she looks back up. "Okay, we have a double queen room ready for you."

"Um, there's supposed to be a conjoined room with that, right? It could be under a different name. Lucie Anderson."

I told Shannon to make sure our rooms going forward were conjoined. I might need her close to help with Miles, but I also need walls between us. I glance at the reception-ist's name tag—Alice. Alice needs to find me some walls.

She continues to type and click on her keyboard, but then frowns. "Nope, I actually don't have that name in my system at all, and unfortunately, there are no conjoining rooms available."

Motherfucker.

"Okay, what other options are there for..." My sentence dies at the conversation behind me.

"Hey, if there's not an extra room, Dex's nanny can bunk with me," Jordan says.

The fuck she can.

"I wonder what that blonde hair would look like wrapped around—"

Spinning away from the lobby desk, I'm ready to jump down his fucking throat, but then Will smacks the back of his head. "That's my sister. Watch it."

"What, like you're one to talk? Don't be a fucking hypocrite, Anderson."

Will takes a step toward Jordan, and, as the coach, I should probably step in, but I'd rather not.

"I'm not," Will says calmly. "I'll say this to anyone on this team, my sister is an adult, she can make her own damn decisions. I don't need to know about them, but you will not disrespect her. Understood?"

Jordan's face is all too smug for my liking, but when Will doesn't step down, he finally nods. "Understood."

The receptionist clears her throat, bringing my attention back to her. "I'm sorry, Mr. Larsen, the only other options are the two king-bed rooms, or we have a suite that has two closed-off rooms and two baths. There is an additional cost—"

"I'll take it." *I just need walls.*

After handing my card over to the receptionist, she returns with our new room keys. "Thank you."

Turning away, I do my best to keep my mouth shut with Jordan.

A small curse is grumbled behind me. I get that I'm his coach. Things should probably be different between us, but I hated playing with the guy, and nothing but my role in the situation has changed.

I make my way over to the fountain but slow to a stop as I watch Lucie dig in her purse while Miles practically dances in anticipation in front of her. The smile on his face is already huge, but when she pulls out what I'm assuming is a coin, Miles's smile grows impossibly bigger.

Taking the coin, Miles walks over to the fountain as Lucie digs in her purse again, but this time she pulls out her phone to take a picture as Miles throws the coin over his shoulder.

In an instant, my phone buzzes in my pocket... God, please don't let it be Kate calling to ruin this moment for me.

Except, it's somehow worse. The text isn't from my ex, it's from Lucie. It's the picture of Miles she just took. Fucking hell.

Walls—I definitely need walls and space between us if I'm going to make this work.

Reaching for my wallet, I go to pull out some more coins to take to Miles when Jordan passes by.

"Hey, Jordan," I call on instinct.

He freezes in his tracks, but that smirk is on his face when he faces me. "Dex."

Stepping in close just as Will did, I keep my voice even and low. "Anderson may not necessarily care if you take a run at his sister, but as for me—keep Lucie's name out of your fucking mouth. I don't want you going near her. Hell, consider her off-fucking-limits to even think about."

"Careful, Dex. You're sounding a little territorial over your nanny."

"I am. So back the fuck off." I walk past him before he can probably even register my response.

Telling him off like that will probably come back to bite me, but right now I can't seem to care. I know Lucie is off-limits for me. It might be selfish, but I want to hold on to her light a little while longer.

Chapter 16
Lucie

Having a job is great, but having a job where I have no clue what I'm supposed to do outside of being the nanny and homeschooling when it's time, is interesting to say the least.

Am I technically on the clock unless told otherwise? Is there something I'm supposed to do when Miles isn't around that's still my job?

I barely know myself and what to do with my own free time. I guess we're just winging everything now.

I practically memorized the Blues' schedule after Shannon gave it to me, so I know today's game isn't a super late one, but me currently up at six in the morning isn't exactly necessary. I'm not sure if it's nerves or the anticipation of being here, but there's no forcing myself back to sleep. I'm wide awake.

Gathering up my shower stuff and some clothes for the day, I tiptoe over to the extra bathroom in our suite, thanks to Shannon's little "slip of her mind". I'm not entirely sure what her angle is. First, leaving out Dex's schedule, and now this?

Avoiding her is a fun game for Miles, but it seems as

though it could be vital for me. Everything has been last minute, so maybe I should give her the benefit of the doubt, but I'm not trusting her as far as I can throw her.

Dex will eventually get used to me, I hope, but I think this whole suite mess has put him a little more off kilter. Here I was wanting to give him space to adjust, but nope.

After hopping out of the shower, I forgo my hair dryer for now since it's still quiet. I guess I could attempt to read or — My stomach growls loudly before I can even finish my thought... Or I could get us some food. Dex did mention wanting Miles to eat more.

If I can't give Dex space, then I might as well do what I can to take the most off his plate.

Pulling my damp hair back into a loose braid and grabbing my shoes, I sneakily head down to the free continental breakfast in the lobby.

Grabbing a plate, I'm not entirely sure what to get. Dex said Miles didn't have any allergies, but does Dex? And I know we're branching Miles out on food, but are there any hard no's?

Well, here's to winging it.

I start by making some waffles as a safe bet on a crowd pleaser, then load up a plate of eggs, bacon, and some potatoes. There are maybe three other people down here at this bright and early 6:30, so I don't feel too bad about making myself at home as I load up our plates.

With three waffles done, I stack them on top of one plate. Hmm, I probably need to bring some extra plates upstairs too. Goodness, I really just jumped on this idea.

"Ah, so she's an early riser," a male's voice says as he comes up beside me. Whipping my head to the side, Olsson has this proud look on his face. "And apparently, she's hungry too."

I chuckle. "True to both, but I was going to take breakfast up for the guys. Granted, I didn't think my plan through fully. I believe it's going to involve multiple trips."

"I think I can help with that a bit." Olsson turns back to a worker passing by at just the right time. "Excuse me, sir, could you possibly bring out a tray and some covers for this young lady to take some food upstairs?"

"Of course," the man replies.

"Thank you, I appreciate it. Oh, also, do you happen to know if Dex is allergic to anything?" Ya know, so I don't accidentally kill my boss. Or imply it since Dex is already leery of me, I'm sure it wouldn't be the best look.

Olsson laughs. "No, he isn't. I like the concern, though. Dex needs a little of that."

Olsson's words hit me hard in my chest. I know I'm just on day three of being Dex's nanny, but his stress isn't lost on me. I may be spurring on some of that stress actually, but it'll get better...I think...I hope.

I shrug off like I'm indifferent. "Oh, well. I'm here to help, right?"

Olsson nods, but before he can say anything, a worker comes up with a tray and two covers. "Here we are. I'll let you take care of the rest, but welcome to the Blues, Lucie. We're happy you're here."

"Me too," I say—and mean it. The best part is that I think Olsson really means it too.

After loading up the plates, I add some muffins, fruit, a juice box, and a couple of water bottles. While the tray does make carrying everything a little easier, I think I walk just as fast as my turtles to get back to our suite.

The workers preparing breakfast will probably hate to see me coming for the rest of the week, but this could be a good way for me to help out in the morning. One step toward getting Dex to relax for a moment.

Getting into our room, I set our food down and immediately start a pot of coffee before unloading our breakfast as quietly as possible.

There's a microwave if we need to heat stuff up, but the moment I get all the waffles laid out, Dex's door swings open, and Miles runs out.

"Good morning, Lucie!" Miles climbs onto the barstool across from our spread. "Wow, you got a lot of food."

I chuckle. "I got all of us a lot of food."

"You did?" Miles's eyes go wide as he takes it all in.

"I did!"

The little cutie's got on pajamas that look just like a baseball player's uniform, and he has those sleep lines on his face where he must have been sleeping hard. He did say travel was exhausting.

"Morning," Dex mumbles low as he walks into the kitchen.

While it looks like Miles just rolled out of bed and ran out the door, Dex, on the other hand, seems like he might have been up for a bit. His hair seems slightly damp from a shower, and whoever designed these T-shirts for the team was doing the Lord's work because they fit in all the right places.

The sleeves end where I can see hints of the ink swirling around on his forearms. Being that Dex has always been a player I enjoy watching on TV, it kind of bugs me that I don't know what his tattoos are...Maybe I should talk Callie into a team calendar.

"Good morning, I got us some breakfast."

Dex walks to the end of the counter as he does the same look around that Miles did.

"I may have gone a little overboard. I wasn't sure what everyone would want."

"I want the fruit cup!" Miles reaches over all of the waffles, eggs, and muffins to snatch the blandest fruit cup I've ever seen. Strawberries and blueberries only.

Dex lets out a breath. "You need something with the fruit, bud."

Miles scrunches his nose and sends a snarled look to his dad. "I don't want anything else."

Alright, here's my opportunity. "You know what I like to eat with my fruit?"

Miles spins back around to me. "What?"

I reach for one plate of waffles and a fruit cup. "I like to put fruit on my waffles."

While the turning up of the nose I get from Miles isn't as dramatic as the one he gave Dex, I still get one. "I don't think I'd like that."

"Have you tried it?"

"No, but—"

I cut him off before he can tell himself he knows he doesn't like it. "Well, I like it. Waffles are better than pancakes, in my opinion. They have these squares that are perfect to keep all the syrup together."

After dumping my fruit and pouring syrup over my waffle, I watch as Miles looks at the plate in front of me. There's no way this kid doesn't want syrup. I get this not-wanting-to-eat attitude is likely stemming from the big changes he's had in his life lately, but now's the time to work through 'em.

Miles and I both—working through it.

"You know what else I like to do?"

Miles sends his little eyebrow up his forehead. "What?"

"I like to dip my bacon in my syrup."

"What!" Miles squeals. "That's crazy!"

My only response is to dip my bacon in my syrup and pop it in my mouth.

Miles giggles as if he can't possibly believe I would actually do such a thing—and Dex, well, he just watches me with his unshakable, stonewall look on his face.

"It's good, I promise," I tell Miles, but when his face scrunches again, I pull out the big guns. "Even Callie thinks so."

Hook. Line. And sinker.

"She does?"

I nod. "Sure does. You don't have to dip—"

"Okay, make me a plate! I mean, make me a plate, please!" Miles turns to Dex, hoping his save came off okay, and finally, the man breaks. Cracks might be a better word for it, but he lets out a small laugh and, dare I say, has a small smile on his handsome face.

"Close. Asking might be a little better with that, please," Dex says.

"Make—"

"Can," Dex corrects.

"Can you make me a plate...please?"

"Yes, I can." Dex reaches for one of the waffles, but then Miles puts his little hand out.

"Actually, can Lucie make my breakfast, and maybe I can watch some shows while I eat?" A beat or two passes, and then Miles adds quickly. "Please!"

An emotion crosses Dex's face that I can't quite read, but then he nods. "Alright, let me help you get a show."

When they walk over to the living room, I get to work on making Miles's breakfast. I drop a few strawberries and blueberries on his waffle before drizzling some syrup over top. I decide to leave some of the berries in the cup just to be safe, then add a piece of bacon on the side.

I drop his food off on the coffee table just as Dex sets down the remote. "Here we are."

"Thanks, Lucie! I can't wait to tell Callie all about my breakfast."

Yep, I'm going to have to tell Callie that waffles are now her favorite, despite my brother's specialty being pancakes. Might be the polar opposite of what he asked me to work on, but, eh.

Walking back to the counter, I grab Miles his juice box, then turn to Dex. "I made us some coffee too."

Dex simply nods. While it might seem like he's slipping back into his stony self, I think I got a little chip in there.

Coming back to my plate, I stay quiet, not wanting to push him any further, but then he appears next to me with two mugs in hand.

Dex slides one to me. "Thank you for that."

"It was nothing, really. I'll try not to always use Callie as my scapegoat, but hey, it worked."

Dex and I both look over to Miles as he shoves a forkful of waffle in his mouth.

"Honestly, I'm a little mad I didn't think of it myself." A small corner of Dex's mouth turns up, but he tries to hide it with a sip of his coffee.

My stomach turns in knots. He hasn't stepped back like he usually does, and his closeness threatens to bring goosebumps to my arms. Maybe I can dig into this stone wall a little deeper.

I keep my voice light and easy. "Eh, you got a lot on your plate, Coach."

Dex makes a small grunt and sets his coffee down on the counter. "Right, well..." He trails off as he walks back over to inspect the stuff by the coffee maker.

Crap, I went too far. So, nicknames are a no-go. I thought it was lighthearted. Dang it.

I know one step forward and two steps back can seem counterproductive, but if you look at the big picture, we still took a step. Maybe I can recover.

Walking to the tray I left on the other side of the counter, I grab the two sugars I brought up.

Deep breaths.

"Dex." When he turns, I hold up the packets. "Two sugars, right?"

I don't get a smile, but a small nod and a moment of those brown eyes meeting mine. "Yeah, that's right."

Chapter 17
Dex

I don't know what I'm doing here. After this morning, I'm not convinced I've ever known what I was doing because I'm a thirty-six-year-old single dad with a job I shouldn't have taken in the first place. And I've, for some reason, hired the first girl I've been attracted to in so damn long who called me "Coach" after getting us breakfast. I'm pretty sure I've had a semi ever since.

And now I've been keeping a healthy distance from her because of it. I keep thinking that space will help, but it's been ten days since I found out Lucie was the girl from the coffee shop, and I'm pretty sure she's surprised me more than Kate ever did in our five-year marriage.

Letting go of this attraction to her feels impossible; each small interaction with her carries with me for hours. Her getting us breakfast and then getting Miles to eat—that's normally a fight every single day. Starting off the day arguing with my son sucks, but that didn't happen this morning.

Lucie packed his backpack to take to the stadium. She helped him brush his teeth so I could work out the hotel issues with Shannon. Lucie asked questions when she felt they were important, like making sure she fixed Miles's hair right, but otherwise, she just helped without me having to tell her to.

Getting to the shuttle was a breeze. We were fifteen minutes early with no meltdowns. Then this thoughtful woman turned to me and handed me some coins to give Miles for the fountain while we waited.

For the first time in months—no, probably years—I haven't had an absolute running wild, stressed to the max pre-game morning. All because of Lucie.

My phone dings in my pocket and I'm really hoping it's Lucie with another picture of Miles.

LUCIE

picture of Miles sitting next to Beck in the dugout

She's sent a couple throughout the day with general updates about what they're doing. It's nice, it's made the low stress of the morning carry throughout the day because I'm not constantly worried about where Miles is or if he's having a good time.

I know Callie was great with Miles, but it's different—I've been able to focus on my actual job today because of Lucie.

Watching the guys warm up in the bullpen, I look over the hitters on the Astros. Will's our starter this game, which is definitely a plus—he's the most consistent while still being able to have a good variety of throws. Between the Astros' lineup and the fact that I know Olsson wants to try Jordan again this game, we're definitely going to need a leg up in the beginning.

"Anderson," I call.

Will makes his way over. "What's up?"

"I know you've played this team many times before, but we've got to start strong." I don't have to explain why to him—as a new trade he hasn't gone numb to Jordan's bullshit like some of the other guys.

"I got ya. What are you thinking? I know some of these guys' weak spots. Hughes hates a low ball and McCormack can't do an outside corner. My issue is Morales—doesn't matter how fast or what angle—fucker hits off me every time."

"Have you tried slowing it down?"

Will gives me a dumbfounded look. "No, can't say that I have."

"Don't be a smartass. I mean, have you tried throwing a circle change on him? If I couldn't strike someone out, I'd try throwing one of those. Morales is a hell of a hitter, so I can't promise he won't adjust to it quickly, but since it's just the grip that changes the speed, it might be enough to trip him up."

Will adjusts his ball cap and shrugs. "Fuck, I'll give it a try. I'll let some of the other guys throw a few, then I'll try it out and see how it feels."

"Alright, I'll tell you if you need to adjust anywhere."

Will nods. "So, how's it going with Lucie?"

His tone doesn't scream any ill-will or double meaning behind the question, but I think my hands just started sweating.

It's torture. Your sister is too young, too nice, and too damn pretty. Oh, and she did the impossible of lowering my blood pressure today, so I'm pretty sure she's some sort of miracle worker.

I clear my throat. "It's going. Miles is definitely enjoying it."

"I'm not surprised, Lucie's always been a natural with kids. Don't repeat this back to Callie because I'm still remaining a neutral party in this whole thing but I'm happy you offered her the job. It really broke her heart to lose her teaching job, and with our other sister moving to Boston, I know it was a lot for her. She seems excited about this, though—said she thought it would be good for her."

"She did?" The response tumbles out of me. While I'm sure she meant the pay and free travel will be good for her, I like hearing it nonetheless.

"Yeah, and for what it's worth, it could be good for you, too. More importantly, it could be good for me because I need Lucie to keep your smooth talker away from my girl."

"If my son is that big of a threat to you, Anderson, I think you might need to step up your game." I wave him off, ignoring the first part that he thinks this could also be good for me. After this morning, it's hard not to see that too.

An even crazier thought enters my brain—if things work out with Lucie, could I actually play again? The way things went today, I can see how much easier it is, and it seems possible. But then again, I'm struggling to see how I can constantly be around Lucie's sunny personality and not get burned.

"Touché." Will tosses a ball my way, pulling me from my thoughts. "Come on, Coach, make sure I'm doing your idea right."

Yeah, this is the only Anderson who needs to call me Coach from here on out.

Starting strong this game, Will manages to throw a damn good first three innings. Specifically, striking out Morales in the bottom of the first. While I figured he would be able to adjust quickly, Will's making him work for each hit now.

Anderson isn't the only one having a good game either. The entire team is playing like a well-oiled machine now. Beck and Tripp had a killer double play this past inning, and Adam hit a home run right out of the gate.

Olsson's got the team morale up with him taking over, and it's a little bittersweet to not be playing when I can see the changes I wished for these past few seasons, but I guess still being a part of it counts in some way.

By the top of the fourth, we're up by two runs and it's looking pretty solid. Will says he's still feeling good to do another couple of innings if possible. I'm not going to argue if that means pushing off bringing in Jordan.

But by the bottom of the inning, the rain starts to fall. It's been overcast all day, but dammit, couldn't it have waited another inning? If this rain doesn't stop in half an hour, then we'll have to reschedule this game.

Everyone works fast to get the tarp pulled out onto the field, and after about twenty minutes of it not letting up, I nudge Olsson. "I'm going to go to the hall and holler at Lucie. Make sure they're somewhere dry."

"Yeah, go for it. I think it's starting to lighten up a bit, so hopefully we can finish this one." Olsson gives me a weird smile. "But take your time, there's no rush here."

"What's that look for?" I groan.

"Just seems like Lucie's working out well. I like her—I think she's just what you needed."

Yeah, that seems to be today's consensus. Unfortunately, so. I think anyone with eyes can see that Lucie is perfect for this job.

Stepping out of the dugout, I pull out my phone as I head toward the guest locker room. Hitting call on Lucie's contact, she picks up on the third ring.

"Hey, Dex." Her voice sounds tense over the phone, and I don't like it.

"Hey, I was checking in to make sure you guys got somewhere dry."

Lucie lets out a small grunt and I can hear a door close. "We're actually headed toward you now. Think you could meet us out in the hall?"

"I'm already out here. Is everything okay?"

But my only answer is the click of the phone. It takes me two seconds to fully register that she just hung up on me, but then I hear her soft voice as she comes around the corner with Miles absolutely clinging to her like a koala bear. "Hey, Dex, sorry. My hands were full. We had a small incident, but we're okay."

"What? What happened?" My brain only seems to register the word incident and the fact that I wasn't there with Miles. I knew today was feeling too good to be true.

When Miles turns his little face to meet mine, he looks so sad. Fuck. Stepping next to Lucie, I pull Miles from her arms. "What happened, bud?"

"I fell down and my knee started bleeding." Miles's little lip quivers as he kicks one leg out.

Looking down to assess the damage, I fully expect to find

the cut for me to take care of but it's already wrapped up with a bandage.

"You were so brave, though." Lucie places her hand on Miles's back. "I took him to the medical tent where we got it all cleaned up. He was a little too excited about dancing in the rain and got tripped up on his feet."

"I fell in a puddle. I don't like the rain anymore. I want to go back to the hotel." Miles's lip hangs so low; his shorts are wet, but his shirt isn't too bad.

Lucie, however, looks soaked. Her light blue Blues T-shirt is a shade darker than it was earlier today, and her straight blonde hair now has a wave to it.

I'm not sure what they were doing or why they stayed out in the rain for so long, but with the sad look on Miles's face, my heart aches.

"Okay, I'll get you and Lucie a ride back to the hotel."

"But why can't you come with us?" Miles cries.

Fuck. I hate this.

"Your dad's got to finish the game, bud," Lucie says with her hand softly rubbing his back. "We can watch him on TV, though."

Miles lays his head on my shoulder as he mumbles, "Okay."

"Think you can make it to the locker room to change? You have extra clothes in your backpack."

Miles lifts his head back up. "Yeah, I think so. I'm just sad now."

"I'll be there in just a second."

When I set him down, he does a pitiful, slow walk to the locker room door. Yep, I'm going to go quit my job now.

"Dex..." Lucie starts off so calm, and I'm sure she's about to say something to try to make me feel better, but when she crosses her arms over her chest, I see the goosebumps on her arms.

"You're soaked, Lucie. What were you guys doing?" My tone comes off harsher than expected, but Lucie doesn't snap back.

Instead, she takes a deep breath. "When the rain started, we were headed to you, thinking we could wait it out in the dugout, but then Miles started dancing while walking. I'm sorry I didn't text you when it happened. Once Miles saw it was bleeding, he started panicking, so I took him straight to the medical tent."

"And you're soaked because..."

Lucie looks down at her shirt as if she didn't even really notice. "Oh, I'm fine. The tent isn't exactly large, and some of the older people thought that would be the perfect place to go for cover in the rain. It was crowded, and where they were treating Miles, my only real option was to stand in the rain."

"You stood in the rain?"

Lucie's eyebrows pull together. "Yes? I told you I'm fine. Miles is the one who hurt himself on my watch. I'm not going to melt. But I am sorry I didn't let you know right away, I just wanted to give him all my attention—he was so upset."

Right, and the thing is, I want to be upset that she didn't tell me right away about it, but I can't. This is not the first scraped knee Miles has had, not by a long shot. The difference is, if it happened on his mom's watch, he was always brought to me at the first sight of blood—it freaked her out, which is probably where Miles's panic stems from. But when it happened with Lucie, she took care of it. She didn't text me because I'm pretty sure I wasn't even a thought to her until Miles was taken care of.

That realization hits me harder than it probably needs to. That's what I need out of Lucie anyway. Her focus and attention on Miles—even if she has mine.

"It's okay, letting me know when you can is all I ask."

Lucie manages a half smile. "I can do that. I still feel bad, though. His sad is making me sad."

Me fucking too. Her being upset isn't helping me either.

I sigh. *Fucking hell.* "I'm going to get his stuff and call you the shuttle to get back to the hotel."

Lucie nods as she runs her hands up and down her arms. Yeah, her being cold also isn't helping.

"Actually, come with me." I don't give her any time to respond as I step to the locker room door and hold it open for her. I don't want to give myself time to change my mind either, so when she walks in, I head straight for my duffle bag and pull out my T-shirt from earlier. It may not be warm, but at least it's dry.

"Here. Bathroom's over there, go put this on."

"Dex, I'm fine, really."

Yeah, "fine" isn't going to work for me right now. I've got a sad kid and chills on my sunny nanny. Tossing it at her probably isn't my smoothest of moves, but she's cold, and I need her to not be.

Miles giggles when Lucie lets out a yelp in surprise. Well, at least I got a laugh out of him.

"Your shirt's on backward," I say to Miles, not wanting to look back to make sure Lucie is actually doing what I told her to do.

He looks down at his shirt and giggles again. "Oops."

Someone's recovery is going well.

After helping him turn his shirt around and calling the shuttle, Lucie makes her way out of the bathroom. My shirt is practically down to her knees, and she's pulled her damp hair back in a braid.

"Better?" I grunt. Fuck, this was a horrible idea. We're getting real close to getting out of the semi territory to full on hard.

"Better, thank you." Lucie's cheeks still have some redness to them from her sunburn, and it intensifies just a little.

"Are we ready to go now?" Miles jumps in between where Lucie and I are standing.

"Yeah, the shuttle said they can take you back." I kneel in front of Miles. "I'll be back as soon as I can, okay?"

Miles launches to wrap his arms around my neck. "Okay, Daddy. I'll miss you."

I chuckle at the surprise attack of a hug, but the ache is still there. "I'll miss you too."

"I'll send proof of life when we get there." Lucie looks down at Miles with a smile, and I already know I'm going to get a picture of Miles in about twenty minutes.

Chapter 18
Dex

"So, is Miles okay?" Beck asks as he falls back into the seat next to me on our shuttle ride back to the hotel.

I check my phone for the fifth time in the past half hour. "I think so. Lucie sent a picture of him wrapped up in some blankets on the couch, but I haven't heard from her since the game ended."

I angle my phone toward Beck to show him some of the best pictures of Miles I've gotten in a long time.

She sent me so many incredible pictures of Miles today that I find it hard to believe she would be ignoring me. Although I will admit the thought to call in a wellness check to our hotel did cross my mind a couple of times.

What's crossed my mind more is the memory of her in my shirt. I know it isn't a good idea, but seeing the chills on her arms was too much for me to handle.

There are a lot of things that seem too much for me to handle with her, and if I'm honest with myself it scares the shit out of me.

Beck puts that stupid smile on his face. "She sends you pictures."

Shit. When he asked me in the locker room where Miles and Lucie were, I should have known he'd come to bug me as soon as the opportunity presented itself.

"She sends me pictures of Miles, you asshole. Don't be weird."

"Well, that's just adorable on her part. You're being weird with your dry-ass responses. Let me see 'em again." Beck tries to grab my phone, but I pull it back. "Would it kill you to show a little bit of personality around Lucie? It could work to your benefit."

"I don't need it to work for my benefit. I need her to be my nanny."

Beck chuckles. "I like how you said that. *My nanny*. It feels very possessive—you should try that with Lucie."

I count to ten in my head before letting out a deep breath. "Go away."

"Don't be so grouchy, Dad."

I'm going to kill him. "Beck."

The fucker just laughs. "I told you I'd be back."

After Lucie and Miles left, the rest of the game felt never-ending. Like some cruel fucking joke, my patience on entertaining Beck's shit is rather low right now.

"Right, and I told you to drop it."

"I'd drop it if I weren't your friend, but, alas, here we are. Don't think Jordan hasn't mentioned your little warning to some of the guys."

"Motherfucker." *Of course he did.*

"I'm just saying—as your friend—you were with Kate for years and never once did you get territorial."

There's no point in arguing with him. He's right. There

have been several things I'd never felt the need to do or say with my ex. Our hookups started out of convenience. We're both very career-driven people, so while the attraction was there, it just never felt like it should be more. That is until a broken condom said otherwise.

Things with Kate felt like settling. That's not a dis on her —she settled with me too. We were simply a situationship, and got married out of obligation, hoping it would work out for the best.

There were never these thoughts of making sure I have an extra hat in my travel bag in case she needed it during the game. I'd never once seen a color and immediately thought of her. There wasn't this pull to be around Kate. From the start, our marriage felt contractual.

Maybe that makes me an asshole, but I think Kate would agree with everything. If anything, Kate treated every part of these last five years as if it were the second job that she didn't want to have.

"I'm asking you—as my friend—to drop it. I can't date her, it's off the table now. Just let me deal with that and quit reminding me of how badly I'm handling it."

"Dex, come on. You deserve—"

"Fuck off, Beck."

Shit, now the confirmation of me being an asshole is coming from the look on Beck's face.

"Fine. Be an unhappy dick for the rest of your life." Beck gets up and walks to the back of the shuttle before I can even say anything.

Fuck, today really went downhill. I've got to pull myself together. I don't know what will make this whole Lucie situation better, but something's got to give.

Finally returning to our hotel, I unlock the door to our

suite. I desperately need sleep, but I can hear the TV. I feel like Lucie would have answered my text if they were still up.

I take roughly three steps deeper into the suite before my heart nearly stops beating in my chest.

Cuddled up on the couch are Lucie and Miles—dead asleep. Miles has his head resting on Lucie's shoulder as her arm drapes around him. They look so peaceful, so at home and natural. My only saving grace is that Lucie's no longer wearing my shirt.

And in that moment, it hits me—this attraction is one-sided. I knew that on some level, but accepting it kind of fucking sucks.

Walking up to them, Miles jostles in his sleep for a moment. I hold my breath, hoping he doesn't wake up. I don't know how long they've been asleep—could be ten minutes or an hour—but I know for damn sure that if he fully wakes up there will be no getting him back down, and I'm too tired to deal with a wired kid.

I take them in one more time, even though I know looking isn't helping me feel better about this whole acceptance thing I'm working through here.

I make my way to our room to get his side of the blankets pulled back and leave the door open so this transfer can go as smoothly as possible.

Back in the living room, I let out a deliberately quiet breath. Neither of them has moved a hair—thank God. Ever so gently, I try to pick Miles up all while doing my best to avoid touching Lucie.

Once Miles is finally secure in my arms, I take a moment to look at his sweet face. There may not have been love in my marriage, but it's always been there with Miles. I never knew such love could exist, really. It took one cry from him when he was born to know there was nothing in this world I could love more than him.

But at the same...if he wakes up, I'm pretty sure I'll lose my damn mind.

I hold my breath again as I slowly lay him down in the bed. I don't exhale until he lets out a sleepy sigh and relaxes when the blankets cover him.

Backing out of the room, I barely make it halfway when I hear "Miles?" coming from Lucie. I can hear the panic in her tone, and while I didn't mean to scare her, I'm not surprised to hear the concern in her voice after realizing Miles wasn't there.

"Miles?" she yells again, this time it's louder. Fuck, I do not want her waking him up.

Swinging the room door open, Lucie practically barrels into me. She lets out a small squeal in surprise as her body hits mine. On instinct, one arm wraps around her waist and carries her out of the room while shutting the door quietly with the other.

"Easy, Luce, it's just me."

Holding her close feels too damn good. I can't quite bring myself to let go either. Her chest is pressed so close against mine, I can practically feel her heart racing...or maybe that's mine.

Fuck.

I set her down, then put as much distance between us as I can manage.

"Dex," Lucie sighs, and her shoulders drop. I can practically see the relief flood her, but it's quickly replaced with anger as she hits my arm. "You scared the crap out of me! Why didn't you wake me up? I was terrified something happened to him."

I can't help the chuckle that escapes me when I see the anger on her face. Here I am wanting to pull her back to me, and she looks like she wants to kill me. Well, kill me in her own way—her sunny demeanor very much still shines through.

"I'm serious, Dex. You took ten years off my life!" She groans as she looks up at the ceiling.

"Will you gain some of those years back when I tell you that he's fast asleep in bed?"

Lucie crosses her arms with a huff. "Probably not."

"Shame," I say, and the smirk comes involuntarily. I try to erase the emotion from my face as quickly as possible, but she sees it, I know she does.

Lucie studies me for a moment. I can tell she's battling her anger, simmering down her panic attack, while simultaneously trying to understand me.

It's the same way she was looking at me on the plane ride here. It never feels like the same way I look at her, more as though I'm a puzzle she's started but can't find the box to know what it's even supposed to look like. Maybe someone should tell her that I have some pieces missing, too.

Hell, what am I even doing here? Why did I even think I could make this work with hiring her?

"Are you hungry?" Lucie asks.

"*Am I hungry?*"

"Yes, Dex, hungry. You know, food...to eat...Have you eaten any actual food since breakfast?"

As my brain processes her words, it becomes painfully obvious that I am now starving. My stomach is seconds away from growling. Shit, I've had so much on my mind—the past twenty minutes especially—but then Lucie walks up with her *let me take care of you* personality, forcing me to actually think about myself.

This is part of the damn problem. I need her to keep all of her focus on Miles. That's how I can make this work.

"Lucie, you know you're not also my nanny, right? I can take care of myself."

That definitely came off a tad dickish, but isn't anger one of the stages of acceptance or something? I don't know what to do here. Maybe she'll yell at me again. Tell me to fuck off or whatever curse replacement she wants to use.

With my ex, that tone would have started an argument instantly, but not with Lucie. Lucie's shoulders roll back before relaxing. She looks me dead in my eyes.

"Okay, Dex, you're right, I'm not *your* nanny. I know it's been a long day for you, and I get this whole thing is an adjustment. Maybe we are both at fault for not setting clear expectations on this job, so allow me to clear things up for you. I'll even explain it with a baseball metaphor. Consider me your teammate—I'll play my position without taking over your job, but it's a team game for a reason. So, I'm sorry if this feels like I'm overstepping, but I'm getting this gut feeling you haven't had a teammate in a long time."

My mouth feels dry all of sudden, so I force a swallow. *Shit, shit, shit.*

She's right, I know I haven't. The thing is, I'm technically retired from the "team" now, and frankly, I don't know if I deserve to join another one.

When I don't respond, Lucie sighs. "You said you didn't need a nanny with one foot out the door—pot, meet kettle. If this isn't going to work, tell me now."

Part of me wants to tell her right here and now that it's

not. I'm one foot in, needing her to help me with Miles and one foot still in that damn coffee shop wanting to ask her out.

I don't know how to make this work. Miles is clearly happy with her being here, and all because I have a fucking crush on his nanny he's going to lose her too?

Fuck. My son deserves better than what I've given him this past year.

I think about what I told her brother about slowing down his pitches. Maybe fighting this is making it worse. Me being a dick and aloof clearly isn't working and damn it, it's selfish for me to fire her.

I can't make it work with Miles's mom, not in the way it was before, but I owe it to Miles to try and make this work.

I swallow all of my fucking pride. "I could eat."

Lucie appeared calm while giving me that fucking speech, but with my response I can visibly see her whole body relax. "Okay, come on, we ordered pizza."

"Did Miles try to only eat the breadsticks?"

One corner of Lucie's mouth turns up. "Didn't order any. I got him to eat two whole slices of pepperoni, actually."

Of course she did. See, this is good for Miles.

"Did you use the Callie card again?"

"Nope." Lucie pops the p with a full smile this time. "They had a make-your-own-pizza option, so I let him 'make' the pizzas. Mine has a lot of veggies on it, so I didn't manage to get him on that one, but—"

"Hey, I'll take it."

I hold back my smile until Lucie turns toward the kitchen. I've hardly gotten Miles to eat without a full-on fight or serious dessert bribery for months, and Lucie's done it twice in one day.

Lucie pulls two boxes out of the fridge and sets them on

the counter. "I also told Miles that since he made the pizza, he had to give them names. So we have Miles's Extreme Pepperoni and Lucie's Veggie Secret. Which one do you want?"

I slide onto the barstool across from her. "Well, I have to try one of Miles's, but is that bacon on the veggie?"

Lucie snorts. "Yeah, that's the secret part. Miles thought it was hilarious."

"Of course he did. I'll take a slice of each then."

"Excellent choice." Lucie takes two slices and plops them on my plate.

When she picks it up to take it to the microwave, I stop her. "Oh no, make your food first."

"Dex, you haven't had real food all day. I can heat mine up after."

"First, it's pizza, I can heat up my own food. Second, it doesn't matter if I haven't eaten all week. I'm pretty sure my mom would appear out of thin air to smack me over the head if I didn't let the woman in my house get her food first."

Rounding the island, I take my plate from her. I watch to make sure my hand doesn't touch hers as I do—I may be letting Lucie in a little bit for the sake of Miles, but let's not push it.

Pulling back, she tucks her blonde hair behind her ears and quickly turns back to the pizza. "Well then, I guess I'll make my plate."

Chapter 19
Lucie

Oh my gosh, I'm getting Dex to talk. *Finally!* I haven't fully broken through his stony demeanor, but the chip from this morning is definitely a crack now. I can see some of the light I know he's hiding behind that *weight of the world* and *stressed dad* armor he's wearing.

I put one slice of my pizza from earlier on a plate and pop it in the microwave. "So, how'd the game turn out? Miles and I didn't make it to the end."

"We won by three runs. I think I'm secure enough to admit that your brother's a damn powerhouse. Between him and the changes Olsson's made, I think we could have a World Series season if we keep it up."

Dex steals a cold pepperoni off one of his slices. I wish he had just made his food first, I'm really not even that hungry, but I don't want to mess up this progress I'm making.

"Hey, I love my brother, but the main thing the Blues needed for a winning season was Olsson. The last GM was a joke."

"Ain't that the fucking truth," Dex agrees right away

then pauses. "You watched our last season? Wasn't Will playing for the Mavericks?"

I nod and turn to watch the time on the microwave. Not sure how it'll come off to Dex that I've always loved watching him play...maybe I'll just stick to the Blues in general.

"I guess I should come clean. I've always been a fan of the Blues. Will may be my favorite player, but—"

Dex gives me a rare chuckle, and I really like it. "Why'd you say it like that?"

"Like what?" I look at him for one second, and just as I do, the microwave beeps. "Ah, fudge," I mumble and whip back around, opening the door to make the noise stop.

"You put a weird emphasis on favorite. Almost as if Will isn't actually your favorite."

Yeah, because technically he's not.

I turn back to the island, tucking a piece of hair behind my ear and avoiding all eye contact. "Microwave's all yours."

"Changing the subject won't work," Dex says.

"What? Will is my favorite." I step around him to sit on the barstool as he puts his food in the microwave next.

"Will is your brother; he's a different kind of favorite. So, him aside—who's your favorite?"

"No, no way. I stand by my answer."

"Oh, come on, you have another favorite. Tell me."

Not happening.

"I changed my mind. Can you go back to ignoring me now?" I joke.

Dex doesn't look my way, and for a minute I'm afraid he actually might. But then I see the corner of his mouth tilt up. It's not a big smile or his laugh, but the crack is still there.

"Alright, I'll find out eventually."

"You know now—it's Will!"

Dex shakes his head and opens the microwave before the beep sounds. He sets his plate on the counter across from me. He doesn't walk around to sit on the extra barstool like he did earlier.

Winning over Dex Larsen seems like it might be a rather slow process, but at least now I think I've actually taken some steps.

He doesn't say anything while we finish our slices. Other than my quiet "thank you" when he takes my plate, it's a peaceful silence instead of the normal tension-filled one.

Dex takes them over to the sink. I prep my small good night spiel because I'm sure he's exhausted, but he turns back around and speaks first. "Hey, I wanted to tell you thank you for the pictures of Miles today. I really appreciated it."

I swallow down my squeal. "You're welcome. I hope it wasn't too annoying."

"No, it was...great. If I can't be with him, it's nice to see what he's doing and know he's having a good time." Dex sighs, avoiding eye contact again.

It's not that I can feel him reverting back to the complete shutdown he would usually give me, but I've pushed enough for tonight.

"Of course. I'm happy to keep sending them."

"I'd like that." Dex's voice stays barely above a whisper. "I've got to ask. Why'd you take this job?"

His question takes me by surprise. I was fully convinced our night was coming to an end. While I can't say I hate that Dex is talking more, I didn't expect this question.

I suppose me being here has been a really vulnerable experience for him. I'm not going to tell him he was actually my favorite player to watch, but I think I owe him a little vulnerability too.

"Well, to be fair, I didn't think you'd offer it to me in the first place. When Callie told me about her plan to annoy you into hiring me, I told her not to waste her breath, but you know how she is."

Dex lets out a huff. Yeah, I'm sure she gave him earfuls.

"I thought taking this job would be good for me. I've recently discovered that I have zero clue who I am as a person—"

Dex snorts a small laugh. "Luce, you just told me off in the calmest and clearest way I've ever experienced maybe fifteen minutes ago. You're going to tell me you don't know who you are?"

My smile is involuntary at him calling me Luce again. I might like it a little too much, but that's beside the point.

"I did not tell you off. I just told you the truth."

Dex shrugs. "Seems like it came from someone pretty confident in herself, if you're asking me."

"Yeah, you're confusing that with the *fake it till you make it* personality. Everything about me feels like it was molded from Will and Reagan. I don't have funny stories from growing up where I was the 'leader' of the group. I'm the side character who went along with things. Scratch that, I'm more of a supporting actress. You know my career and superficial things, but I have no lines and no backstory. Whether I got this job or not wasn't really going to change my plans to figure out who I am, but I am happy you offered it."

Dex looks off to the side as he scratches the back of his neck. "Yeah, me too."

I can't say I entirely believe him, but at least I think I actually have a chance of making him believe it one day.

Chapter 20
Lucie

Tuesday: Boston Blues at Phoenix Astros.

> *picture of Miles eating a hotdog*

> I know he eats hotdogs, but I got him to try it in the bun, now hold your heart…with ketchup.

DEX

Try mustard or chili and then I'll be impressed.

> Hey, baby steps.

Wednesday: Boston Blues at Phoenix Astros.

DEX

Should I ask why I just saw you and Miles hiding around the corner?

> Miles thought he saw Shannon. Avoiding her is a game to him now.

DEX

Don't tell the team that. I think some of the
guys would join you.

Can you blame them?

Thursday: Travel day to Pittsburgh.

Callie has named the group chat: They're just baseball players

CALLIE

So I hear we have a new game.

BECK

Miles told me it was called "Escaping
Grumpiness" but we all know what he
means.

ADAM

Why am I in this chat? We're all on the
fucking airplane together.

TRIPP

Petition to allow Miles a single curse word.
Escaping Bitchiness should be a life motto
really.

CALLIE

Second.

BECK

Third.

WILL

Fourth.

WILL

Callie sent that.

Sorry, petition denied.

BECK

But we have the signatures!

DEX

Luce, how do I leave this chat?

Let me see your phone.

Dex has left the group chat.

Friday: Boston Blues at Pittsburgh Patrons

picture of Miles giving the camera a peace sign next to two Pittsburgh outfielders

Your son just asked them if they were ready to lose today. I swear I nearly died until I realized they were traded from the Blues last season. They said to tell you hi.

DEX

I mean he's not wrong.

Can you do me a favor and bring my hat to the dugout? I think I put it in Miles's bag by accident.

Yeah, headed your way.

DEX

Do you have your hat?

Yes, Coach, I have my hat.

DEX

Good, now put it on.

Saturday: Boston Blues at Pittsburgh Patrons

REAGAN

Okay, this chat has been way too quiet considering two of us are traveling with an MLB team.

JENSEN

Lucie! How's it going with Dex? Has he chilled out any?

CALLIE

Dex showed up today and threw pitches in the bullpen. He was laughing with the guys… I didn't even know what his full laugh sounded like until today.

JENSEN

Damn, Luce. What are you doing to that man? Voodoo? Blowjobs?

No, oh my goodness. I'm just helping with Miles!

REAGAN

Lucie is practically Mary Poppins. Now that she's working for Dex all her thoughts about how hot he is have been shut down.

CALLIE

Just so you know, Luce, Olsson's dating co-workers rule doesn't apply to you. 😊

Listen, I just got Dex on board to like me as his nanny. I think you guys are jumping to conclusions. I've got to start figuring out how homeschooling with Miles is going to work too.

REAGAN

I told you.

JENSEN

Boo, this took a boring turn.

Sunday: Boston Blues at Pittsburgh Patrons

> Hey Coach, consider me your MVP

> *picture of Miles eating a hotdog*

> It has mustard on it.

DEX

Alright, Luce, I'm impressed

Monday: Travel day to Boston.

JENSEN

I know you're off today. I made us a nail
appointment at 10. It's non-negotiable,
babes.

Chapter 21
Dex

We finally land back in Boston bright and early on Monday morning. One thing I can appreciate about travel days is that we always try to book flights either really early or late for us to be able to take in as much time at home as we can. We'll be here for the week, then right back out again.

Miles has apparently been on so many planes that he's slept through landing. With his head lying on Lucie's shoulder, he looks so peaceful.

Lucie looks down at him with a smile. "Part of me is so ready to get off this plane, and the other is perfectly happy sitting here until he wakes up."

Yeah, I know exactly what she means—it was hard enough not to stare at them the entire flight. Lucie worked on her homeschooling plan while Miles rested, perfectly content next to her.

Lucie and I may have found our footing over this week and a half, but it's done jackshit for my attraction to her. Hell, it's only gotten worse.

But instead of focusing on the pure want I have for her, I

think about Miles and how attached to her he already is. I think about how much easier and enjoyable work has been with her around.

When all else fails, I remind myself that she's twelve years younger with goals of figuring out who she is as a person. It's my weakest reasoning of all, but adding that with all the other reasons makes it stack up a little bit more.

I start to nudge Miles's arm from side to side, and his eyes slowly start to blink open. "Are we home now?" he groans.

"Close, we're back in Boston. Just a quick drive in the truck and we'll be home."

Miles groans louder this time as he snuggles closer to Lucie and pulls her arm in front of his face to hide from the light. "But I'm still sleepy."

Lucie chuckles. "Something tells me you're not going to be sleepy for much longer. I know how you work now, kid, sometimes you just need a little encouragement."

Lucie moves to tickle him, and his giggles erupt. "Okay, Lucieeee, I'll get uuuuup."

Lucie stops tickling and helps him with his seatbelt. "Yeah, I thought so."

Making our way off the plane, Miles has now fully woken up and is wired and ready to go. He bounces across the tarmac before spotting Callie.

"Dad! Can I go see Callie for just a little bit, pleeeease?"

"Sure, go ahead."

I watch until he makes it over to Callie and surprises her with a hug. I shake my head as I turn to Lucie and find that she's got the same look on her face that I did.

"I know it's a running joke with the team, but his dedication to winning over Callie is so sweet."

It really is. I halfway feel like I need to be taking notes from him sometimes, but that's a thought I need to counter— *Lucie is here for Miles, not me.*

"He's persistent, that's for sure." I dig into my duffle bag to pull out my keys. "When Casanova's finished, you guys can head to the truck. I can get the bags."

"Are you sure?" Lucie's hand brushes against mine as she takes the keys.

"Yeah, I got it. Plus, that'll make you the bad guy for having to walk away from Callie."

"See, you're doing it wrong. You just need to rope Will in and make *him* the bad guy." Lucie smiles, and I can feel this tightening in my chest. It happens a lot, actually—when she laughs at something I've said or calls me "Coach". When I watch her with Miles. I swear I almost bought heartburn medication at our last hotel.

"Ahh, it all makes sense now. Do you think we should tell Callie and Will that they're our scapegoats?" The need to say "we" and "our" has been an ongoing battle also. Even though Lucie never seems to catch it, I know I've got to stop.

"Oh no, it coincides with their fun aunt and uncle thing they have going." Lucie shrugs. "I'll work on that and meet you at the truck?"

Clearing my throat, I nod. "Yeah, meet you there."

Same as I did with Miles, I watch Lucie walk all the way over to where Callie and Will are standing. Her long blonde hair is pulled up in a ponytail, and while yellow is still my favorite, I think her in any of the Blues merch is second best.

"Hey, I got Miles's suitcase. I think yours and Lucie's are over on the far side." Beck comes up next to me, his words pulling me from my lingering gaze. I know he saw what I was doing, and while we're good after I apologized for being a dick on the shuttle, Beck hasn't brought up the topic of Lucie again.

"Thanks. If you want to leave Miles's here, I'll be—"

"It's luggage, not a big deal, asshole. I'll take this to your truck while you get the rest." Beck doesn't give me any time to argue before he starts to walk off.

I take one more look at Lucie and Miles before grabbing our suitcases from the far side of the plane.

"Oh, hey, Dex, do you have a second?" Shannon stops me.

The need to say "no" is strong. I definitely see why Miles likes to hide from Shannon, but, unfortunately, as a coach, I'm no longer qualified to play the game. "Yeah, what's up?"

"I wanted to offer that if you need someone to help keep Lucie in line, you can ask me."

What the fuck? That's what I really want to say, but professionally, I go with, "Excuse me?"

Shannon flips her black hair behind her shoulder. "You know, make sure her and Miles aren't causing any trouble on game days. I know she's young, but if her being here isn't helping—"

"It is helping," I cut her off. "Last time I talked to Olsson and everyone else on this team, Lucie hasn't caused any issues. Not that their *or your* opinions matter because *I* decide if Lucie's working out or not."

"Dex, she's just young—"

Fucking hell. "You know what will actually help? Calling the hotels for the season. I'm going to need a suite for the rest of our away games. The conjoined rooms in Pittsburgh weren't as functional, and thanks to your oversight in Phoenix, I know that now."

Shannon straightens her spine. I can see her jaw tighten for a second before she grits out, "Fine, I can do that."

I really have tried to give Shannon the benefit of the doubt. I thought her shit attitude came from our last GM, but it seems like she worked so well with him for a reason.

"Great, thank you for the help."

Turning, I head to my truck, grumbling in my head and this time I really do say, "What the fuck?" when I look up.

Jordan is standing by my truck, watching as Lucie gets Miles in. Beck hovers beside Lucie, and I can tell he's saying something to Jordan but I can't make out what.

"...So what you're saying is you have the day off," Jordan says as I walk up behind him.

"Jordan, can I help you?" I clip.

Turning around, Jordan has a smug smirk on his face. "I just came to talk to Lucie for a minute."

"He apparently thought that minute needed to be while she was buckling in Miles," Beck explains. His tone is just as tense as mine. Damn it, I'm going to have to be nicer to him.

Lucie closes Miles's door with a sigh. "Okay, Jordan, what's up?"

"I thought since it was your day off, you might want to have a little fun. A couple of the guys are going out tonight, you should come with."

Say no, say no, say fucking no.

A soft smile comes to Lucie's face, and I swear my heart's in my stomach. "Thank you for thinking of me, but I'm going to pass."

Thank God.

Jordan rocks on his feet for a moment. "Alright, some other time then?"

No.

Lucie glances at me for a moment but I look away. I know I have no say, if she wants to go she has every right to.

"Maybe, I think Dex and I might be able to come one night. It's a team thing, right?"

Holy shit.

Jordan takes a step back at that one. "Right, yeah...maybe some other time."

Lucie's face beams with her bright smile. "Great, just let Dex know. I'm sure I could get my sister to watch Miles, and we could all go together."

"Sure thing," Jordan says as he walks away.

My brain is still trying to process how, rather than just telling him no, Lucie told him she would be bringing me. Fuck, I think that just turned me on.

Beck takes a step forward and turns to look at Lucie.

"What?" She looks back and forth between me and Beck. "What'd I do?"

Beck is silent for another moment, then says, "I think I love you."

"Beck!" I snap. Maybe I won't be nice to him.

Beck holds his hands in the air. "What? I'm kidding! Kind of."

"You do not." Lucie swats her hand at him before turning to me. "Need any help with the bags?"

No, please stay up there because I need you not to see my semi through my sweats.

I clear my throat. "I got it."

"Alright." Lucie shrugs and says bye to Beck before getting in the passenger seat.

Beck waits for her door to shut before turning to me. "I'm not going to say much, but...dude, you're so fucked."

"Well-fucking-aware."

Chapter 22
Lucie

Leaving for my nail appointment felt a little weird. Almost like I didn't want to leave to get my very overgrown nails done. I know I definitely want a nap on a non-hotel mattress, but I also think I just want to spend the day relaxing with Dex and Miles. I feel like that's the one thing we truly haven't gotten to do.

"I need to know everything," Jensen says before her butt even hits the chair next to mine.

My manicurist, Elle, pulls my hand in. Jensen and I always get the same girls—Elle and Kylie—who I believe we'll follow to any salon for the rest of our lives.

"I'm not so sure what you're wanting to know. I'm a nanny to a baseball coach, not a wild celebrity."

Jensen hits me with her free hand. "Oh, come on, let me correct that statement. You're a nanny to a superhot baseball coach. Who, Callie says, is normally all broody, but *you*, Lucie Anderson, make him laugh!"

"Okay, I can agree to that, but you're reading way too much into it. I make him laugh sometimes. He more so has the willingness to laugh with other people now because he has help—it's not directly related to me."

I can admit that I've noticed Dex has relaxed around me a little bit after our little *team* chat over pizza. My crack in his walls is bigger, but every now and then, I notice him trying to add more cement. He'll forget—or pretends to at least—that I'm actually here to help him, so if there's something he needs that I don't think of, he'll try to handle it himself.

I get there are some things that he needs to do as a father, but if I don't jump in where I can, I swear he'd never ask me to do anything.

I try to give him as much space as possible, which helps. Me leaving today is probably something Dex is grateful for, if I'm being honest.

Especially after our little run-in with Jordan. I know Dex can't stand him. I think Dex tries to be civil with Jordan, as a coach, but the animosity from them as players is still there.

I wasn't too sure how volunteering Dex to come with me was going to be received on his end, but there's no way I would ever go out with Jordan. It might seem odd to say, but if Dex doesn't trust him, I don't either.

Jensen purses her lips. "Eh, that could be debated, but I'll let it slide for now. You've spent two weeks with the man, so it's too soon to tell."

"There's nothing to tell. So the man laughs now."

Elle snorts. "There's a lot to tell in a man's laugh."

"Thank you!" Jensen agrees with her entire chest.

Kylie chips in now, too. "Especially if it happens more since you started."

Jensen hums while giving me major side-eye. "Interesting, three to one."

"I think we're very much overanalyzing a laugh."

The girls collectively give each other a look.

Goodness, I can feel my chest turning red. "Okay, full transparency. Do you all seriously think I'm not beyond attracted to him? Have you gotten a look at him? Now imagine what it's like being around him all the time while he's practically the best dad you've ever seen, and you get a front row show of his personality outside of that too... I get to see this man in the mornings when he's still got that adorable sleepy-man look. I can't overthink his laugh, I'm barely holding it together as is."

Another look is exchanged, but this time I feel like I'm being pitied.

"Dex and I have finally seemed to land on good footing with each other. I want to work on myself, and he just wants someone to help with Miles. I'm good. He's good, and Miles is happy. I can't entertain the fantasy."

Jensen tilts her head. "Unless he wanted to entertain?"

I bite back my immediate "yes" and opt to send her a glare as my answer.

Jensen swivels in her chair. "Alright, fine, I get it. I'm a bit of a secret romantic, but believe me, I get why you wouldn't want to get swept up in the idea of it either, knowing that it might not be in the cards. How's working on yourself going anyway? Based on these past two weeks, it seems like you've barely had time."

"Yeah, it's not exactly been the easiest when the guys have a game practically every single day and I'm following a five-year-old around. Miles is great, don't get me wrong, but there's not much time without him either."

"Okay, well, you're off today, right? Get out, get some space, do something for you! Ya know, besides this."

I try to stop the crinkle of my nose at Jensen's idea. I get that I probably should take advantage of this day off, but I don't want to. "I mean, just because I spend a lot of time with them doesn't necessarily mean I need space."

"Lucie! I thought we weren't entertaining the fantasy." Jensen tilts her head again, but now with a blink like she's caught me red-handed.

"I'm not! It's just—I don't know. Can't I just enjoy being around them?"

The collective looks are back.

"Okay, I'm done talking now."

Jensen whips her head back to me. "You know what? As your accountability buddy, I insist you do something on your list today. Even if it includes being with Dex, I added stuff to your list for a reason."

I nearly die in my chair when her eyebrows go up and down with the last part. "Subtle."

Elle snorts a laugh. "I assure you, we've heard way worse. You don't even have to give us the details—I swear, this is tame."

I exhale. "I will figure out something to do, but not from your suggestions, Jen. And this is my official request to no longer talk about Dex the entire appointment."

Jensen mumbles, "Fine," but her smirk tells me everything. The topic of Dex will most definitely be coming up again—I fear it will a lot.

For the rest of the appointment I try to keep the topics going to ensure they don't come back around to me. Jensen lets some of her stress out about Tally's Shop, and Kylie threatens to cut Hank's balls off with her nail scissors. Which is fair.

"So, games every day this week, right?" Jensen asks as we walk out of the nail salon.

"Minus Sunday. We'll be leaving for Detroit that night. Then another week in New York before I'm back."

"Damn, well then, I'll make sure my nail appointments fit your insane schedule, babes. Just text me the date."

"You know you don't have to do that. Your schedule can be just as nuts—don't worry about me if you need to do it on a day I'm not here."

Jensen scoffs. "And miss out on all the Daddy Dex updates? I refuse."

I should have known. I can already feel my cheeks and chest turning red again. "There will be no *Daddy Dex* updates. Please don't say that again."

"We'll see. He might not deserve the title anyway, but with that in mind..." Jensen trails off to dig into her bag. "A-ha."

Jensen pulls out an envelope and hands it over to me. "Since you said I needed to work on my penmanship, this is for you."

Eyeing Jensen while I open the envelope, I'm a little scared about what she could have put in here, but then I pull out this beautiful piece of cardstock. It's got gold embellishments of daisies, small suns, and turtles all around the list.

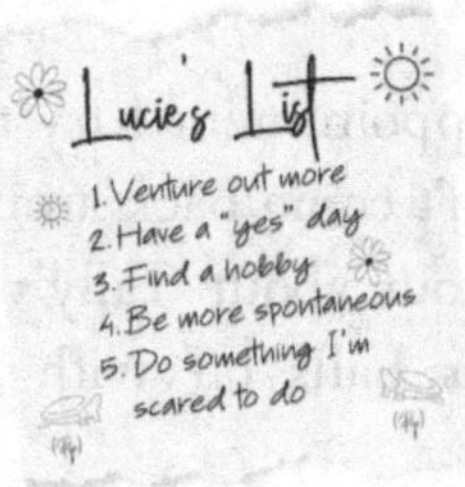

"Flip it over," Jensen says.

And when I do, I'm met with a completely different vibe. Jensen's got *Lucie After Dark* written in a deep red ink. Cherries, snakes, and hearts with flames decorate the spicy additions Jensen made.

"The different vibes felt appropriate. If you're going to stick to this, I thought a visual would help."

"Jen, this is perfect. Thank you."

"So, what are you going to do today? Gotta make it about you in some sort of way, Luce."

"I know, I know. Part of me fears I'll find my new personality in Dex and Miles if I'm not careful."

"You won't, that's what you have me for." Jensen flips her hair behind her shoulder dramatically. "For what it's worth, I think you can still figure out yourself and still want to be around someone all the time. We've already covered that it's not about you not being able to be alone. Finding yourself doesn't exactly have to happen on your own. You just have to have someone who won't dim your light."

"Have I told you how happy I am that we became friends?"

"Yeah, me too. Now, go find Lucie and if she just so happens to like her hot boss, then so be it! Maybe making a move could play into something unexpected." Jensen waggles her eyebrows.

"I was thinking I'd start with something like finding a hobby."

"I hate to break it to you, but I could easily turn every single item on the bright-side list naughty. There are so many hobbies I think you could do with that man."

"Okay, I'm leaving now."

"Good luck on finding your hobby. I hope it brings you a lot of pleasure."

Chapter 23
Dex

Lucie leaving this morning after getting back to the apartment was a damn blessing, but not because I actually wanted her to leave... I just very much needed a cold shower. When that didn't work, I knew talking to my ex-wife would do the trick.

"So, about this weekend, I know it's technically yours, but can I possibly get Miles? I can move some stuff around. I think he'd love to come see me."

"Yeah, I think he also would have loved to see you two weeks ago." The jab comes out before I can stop it. I shouldn't have said it—I know that—but fuck, we're still doing scheduled phone calls because she insisted on it.

"Dex, I told you I had a big case and it needed all of my attention. I'm finally making a name for myself in this firm. I know you disagree with me, but it's where I feel I need to put my focus. Not all of us have a boss who lets their kid run around constantly. And not all of us want to hire a young blonde nanny."

I pinch the bridge of my nose. Fuck, not this again.

Callie took a candid photo of Lucie and Miles for the Blues Instagram story. I think only three hours passed before I got a screenshot and about fifteen texts with it.

I look around to make sure Miles hasn't wandered into the kitchen. I don't want him to overhear any of this pointless bullshit.

"Kate, we've been over this. She's overqualified and can teach our son. I respect that you're Miles's mother, and I'm willing to work with you on the weekend thing. However, let's not forget that you were the one who said you only wanted one weekend a month and granted me full rights on these decisions."

The line goes silent for a moment before she sighs. "Fine. I appreciate the weekend switch. Maybe if it's possible I could get a little more time every now and then? When my work allows it."

I really should have expected this. Kate hasn't asked for any "extra" time in seven months, but now that Miles spent half of their conversations talking about Lucie, suddenly there's time.

As frustrating as it is, Kate will always be Miles's mom and holding petty stuff against her does nothing but make things worse. Despite how she left and the decisions she made, I do know Miles is physically safe with her. If she wants some more time, I won't keep that from either of them. However, I let her set boundaries first, now it's my turn.

"Alright, we'll talk about it. We can do Friday to Sunday this weekend. We can work out some days when we get back from New York."

"Thanks, Dex. I'll look at my schedule and let you know."

"And no more comments about Lucie—you wanted to be

hands off. I didn't hire Lucie to get back at you. I needed help and now I have it."

Kate goes silent again. She's the lawyer so she's strong in an argument, but she also knows when she's lost. I get that being a mother wasn't a part of her plan and I won't judge her for that. At this point I think she's giving what she can, but I'm going to do the same.

"I'll bring Miles over before the game Friday. Is ten okay?"

Kate sighs. "Yeah, that's fine."

"Okay..." I start to say goodbye, but then I hear Miles yell Lucie's name from the living room.

My feet start to move toward them instinctively, completely forgetting that I was on the phone until I hear Kate's voice in my ear again. "One more thing, Dex. Don't be that cliché guy who dates his nanny."

I clench my jaw at her words, but then I see Lucie—I see the smile she has on her face while she greets Miles.

"I have to go. Miles will see you this weekend." I hang up on her before she can respond.

Lucie has grocery bags in her hands, and when I step up to take them from her, the smile she gave Miles doesn't falter. "Hey, I'm back."

Yeah, Kate's parting words don't mean shit to me. There are other reasons to not date Lucie, but being a cliché is not fucking one of them.

Miles doesn't miss a beat as he jumps on the top part of the couch and hangs his arms off the back. "Who will I see this weekend?"

"Your mom. She asked if you could spend the weekend at her house."

"Really?" Miles squeals but then looks at Lucie. "Are you going to come with me?"

Lucie's mouth gapes open for a minute. I get her hesitation, and really I see where Miles would think that since Lucie does go practically everywhere with him while he's with me. Telling a five-year-old "no, because your parents are divorced and I only work for your dad" isn't exactly Lucie's style.

I know it's so far from something Lucie would say, without a shadow of a doubt—if Miles really wanted her to go, she'd do it.

"No, bud, we have to let Lucie have some time off, okay? You and your mom will have lots of fun, though."

Miles's frown isn't exactly what I wanted to see, but as usual, he bounces back pretty fast. "Okay, I guess I'll get to swim! Mom's place has an indoor pool, so make sure to pack my swim stuff."

I chuckle. "Okay, I can do that."

"That sounds like a lot of fun." The relief on her face doesn't go unnoticed by me, but now it hits me that if Miles isn't here...will Lucie leave for the weekend? Will I be alone in this apartment all weekend with just her? I can't think about that. I need a new topic to focus on.

"So, what's all this?" I gesture to the bags I took from her.

"Well, I got some groceries. I thought it could be fun to actually make some homemade pizzas if you guys are up for it? Or I could just make them—"

"No! I want to help!" Miles yells, jumping up from the couch and racing into the kitchen.

Lucie looks to me with that soft smile. I swear I see a damn gleam in her eyes. "What about you, Coach? Want to join us?"

I guess I'm the different side of the same coin because I'll do whatever Lucie asks when she smiles at me like that.

"Yeah, count me in, Luce."

Lucie tucks some of her hair behind her ear and I get a glance at her freshly-painted yellow fingernails. God, I love that color.

Lucie walks around me to the kitchen, but turns back after a few steps. "Heads-up...I cheated a bit. I bought the dough ready to go from the bakery. You have to give it time to rise and—"

"So, we're skipping the boring stuff Miles wouldn't be interested in?"

Lucie chuckles. "Exactly. I thought starting out with rolling and tossing the dough would be the crowd pleaser."

I raise an eyebrow. "Is throwing it really necessary?"

"It is when you're making it with a five-year-old."

Back in the kitchen, I unpack the bags and get everything out on the counter while Lucie helps Miles wash up.

When Miles moves his stool over to the island, he snarls at the spread in front of him. "There's a lot of stuff I don't like, Lucie."

"Miles, manners," I say in a warning.

"But I don't like them." Miles shrugs. "I don't know how to have manners about things I don't like."

Don't laugh. Don't laugh.

Lucie pulls her lips in a thin line, and I can tell she's thinking the same damn thing.

"It's okay to not like things, bud. I know I got some stuff that you don't like, but I do. I also got things that your dad likes. We can each make our own pizzas, and it could be fun to try slices of each."

Miles scrunches his nose while he thinks on Lucie's idea.

"We also need to be appreciative that Lucie bought all of this and wants to do something fun."

Miles finally relents. "Thank you, Lucie. I am excited to make my pizza. But I'm not sure about trying everyone's."

Lucie lets out an amused hum. "Alright, we'll think about it?"

Miles nods. "I'll think about it."

"Good." Lucie looks around the kitchen. "This kind of feels weird to say, but this is the first time I've actually cooked in this kitchen. Where is everything?"

"Whatcha need, Luce?"

"A rolling pin to get the dough ready, a cutting board, and a knife for the veggies."

While I get the things she needs, Miles helps Lucie wipe down the counters. Finding the cutting board and knife is easy; the rolling pin, however, is some weird miracle. I had no fucking clue that I even had one, but there it was in some random drawer full of utensils that I've probably only used a handful of times.

Once the counters are clean, Lucie pulls over the bag of flour and the wrapped-up dough. "Okay, so three pizzas?"

Miles points his finger at himself, then at me and Lucie. "Yep, three."

I chuckle. "I'll let you guys handle that, while I cut up the vegetables. Luce, you like banana peppers, green peppers, and cherry tomatoes?"

Lucie looks at me, her eyes bright as she pulls her hair back in a ponytail. "Yeah, that's right."

Of course it is. I know how she likes her pizza, her coffee, and the concession hotdogs.

Lucie's eyes linger on me for a moment, and it takes a lot not to hold her blue eyes, but I start working on her toppings.

Lucie goes back to Miles with a small nudge. "Alright, Miles, you ready to make a mess?"

"Yes!" Miles cheers.

Lucie splits and rolls out the dough with Miles's help. All while, yes, making a fucking mess with the flour. I don't give a single damn about it either. I don't think this kitchen has heard this much laughter ever.

Miles giggles uncontrollably as Lucie tosses the dough in the air like she's done this forever.

"Please don't get the pizza stuck on my ceiling."

"I think I'm really getting the hang of this." Lucie beams as she catches the dough and then lays it back on the counter.

Miles jumps up and down. "Do the next one! Do mine!"

"Okay, okay." Lucie picks up his next, and Miles's laughter fills the apartment. God, it's the best fucking sound.

I continue to cut the veggies while still watching Miles be completely mesmerized by Lucie. *I'm completely mesmerized by Lucie.*

And that comes at a cost, because as Lucie tosses the dough in the air I completely slice my hand. "Motherfu—"

"Dex?" Lucie cuts me off, keeping her voice even. I'm sure it's not to freak out Miles any more than I just did.

"It's fine, I just cut my finger." It's a cut from a sharp blade, so naturally it's bleeding pretty good.

"It's bleeding, Daddy! Lucie! It's bleeding!" Miles panics.

Shit, I grab a nearby rag to hold on my hand. "It's okay, bud, I promise. I'm okay."

Lucie gives Miles a small smile, then moves to me. She grabs two cherry tomatoes off the board and hands them to

Miles. "I'm going to go help your dad. Why don't you give these to Pip and Pop for me?"

Miles's bottom lip hangs. "But Daddy's bleeding."

"And I'm going to make it stop." Lucie's voice is calm. "I promise. Now, give the turtles their treats and we'll meet you there, okay?"

"Okay." Miles sulks the whole way to the living room.

Lucie turns to me with a small smile. "Let me see, Masterchef."

"Luce, if you weren't just so good with my son, you'd be paying for that comment." The flirt comes out before I can stop it, but Lucie doesn't even blush, or I think even catch it.

She steps in, standing so close to me now—hell, even the way she smells feels bright, like honeysuckle and jasmine.

Lucie looks up to meet my eyes as her hands touch mine. "I'm not afraid of you, Coach."

Fuck, she's killing me. Here I am, thinking my comment will throw her off kilter, but no, it's her throwing me off.

I swallow hard and whisper, "I think I'm afraid of you."

The admission isn't something I want to take back—I am scared of Lucie. Scared of what having her around much more will do to me. Scared of what it could mean if she left, because let's face it, I won't exactly need a nanny and home-school teacher forever.

But to Lucie, I'm pretty sure my whispered confession comes off more as a joke. The corners of her mouth tilt up for a second before she swallows, then looks down at my hand. It's for the fucking best, I guess.

It's finally stopped bleeding, and really, it's fine, but Lucie hums. "I'm going to get a Band-Aid for Miles's sake. Where are they at?"

"Under the sink in the guest bathroom."

Lucie looks back up at me as her hands still rest on mine. Everything about this moment feels charged. One sign—I mean one fucking hint of her wanting more—and I might finally break. One more second of her hands touching me. One hitch of her breath and a part in her lips, and I'm done.

Yeah, I'm fucking afraid of her. I'm afraid I'll never know what she tastes like. What her moans sound like in my ear. What these days could be like if she was more than the fucking nanny. I want her so damn bad that it terrifies me.

Her hand is still touching me. Fuck, what's one lean in?

"Daddy! I got you a Band-Aid!"

Motherfucker.

Lucie and I both jump back from each other as Miles barrels back into the kitchen, waving a Band-Aid in his hand.

When he gets to me, he has the most worried look on his face. "Are you going to be okay?"

I'm not entirely sure if I'm grateful for Miles's intrusion, but it was needed. *Wanted?* That's a different story.

"I'm going to be fine. It's not even bleeding anymore, but I'll still use the Band-Aid."

Miles's face changes instantly, a proud grin pulling at his mouth. "Good, I knew Lucie could fix it, but I wanted to help."

"That was very thoughtful, Miles." Lucie places her hands on Miles's shoulder. "Why don't we finish up our pizzas?"

Miles squeals. "Yay!"

Lucie is here for Miles. Not for me. Lucie is here for Miles. Not for me.

I watch her as she picks up Miles's pizza dough, repeating that in my head. Her eyes connect with mine.

Damn it. I want her for us.

Chapter 24
Lucie

I slept horribly last night. It felt like my skin was on fire. The sheets felt like sandpaper, and my pajama set was the most uncomfortable thing I have ever put on my body.

All I could think about was Dex. The way he looked at me in the kitchen...his words...*I think I'm afraid of you.* It's like they vibrated through me.

All night, I wanted to knock on his door and ask what exactly he's afraid of. The only thing that managed to keep me in my uncomfortable bed was the fantasy of him pulling me to him and kissing me as his answer. Not because I didn't want that to be his answer, but I didn't want to find out if it wasn't. That, and the fact that I'd have to pass Miles asleep in his bedroom first.

I'm not going to deny that there could be something between me and Dex. I didn't dream up that moment yesterday. But he hired me for a reason, and if—that's a big if—there's something that could happen between me and Dex, he's going to have to make the first move. I meant what I told

Jensen. I can't entertain the fantasy of Dex—I will only entertain the reality of him.

I felt the pull to Dex yesterday in the kitchen. I felt that tension in his gaze. I didn't get any clear action.

I pull out my phone to text Jensen. Last night, while I wanted to use all of us cooking together as something spontaneous from my list, I'm going to need a Lucie After Dark one very soon.

> Alright, where do I need to go to get a new vibrator?

JENSEN

> Hi, good morning, I love the bluntness, Princess Peach. New hobby not pleasurable enough for you?

> Jensennnn, help me. It's on the list, I don't need to elaborate more than that.

> Fair. Why don't you come tomorrow morning on my run around town for a venturing out on the Nice Lucie List, then we'll go to a store together after.

> Obviously going to leave out the sex store part, but I'll make sure it's okay with Dex since I'll have to be back to help with Miles by two.

> That works. I work at Tally's shop at three. The run helps me get out my aggression, so I don't hit Hank while he makes derogatory remarks as he tattoos.

> Hitting is low on the list of things that man deserves.

> Tell me the fuck about it.

Sliding out of my bed, I take a shower and get ready for the day. Normally I would wear some Blues merch on game days, but I've been wearing it so much I want something different.

I want something I feel good in, something I don't want to even daydream about my hot boss ripping off because I love it that much.

Flipping through the few things hanging up in my closet, I decide on my yellow athletic dress. Yep, this will do.

Making my way to the kitchen, I pass Miles sitting on the couch with a bowl of cereal, watching some cartoon. "Good morning, Lucie. You look really pretty."

My heart. "Thank you, that's so sweet. I like that you're eating cereal with milk."

Miles gives me a toothy grin. "It's good sometimes. Daddy made it, but not as good as you do."

I chuckle. "I won't tell him. I'm gonna go get myself some breakfast now too."

"Okay," Miles mumbles with his mouth full, but then swallows. "Sorry."

"That's okay." I squeeze his shoulder before I turn the corner into the kitchen to find Dex.

When he notices me, I swear his eyes scan me from head to toe. I can't really tell if he's thinking I look pretty like Miles said, but that's Dex. I've been making cracks in his stony demeanor, but they're just that—cracks. No wall tumbling down. No clear actions.

"Morning," he huffs before taking a sip of his coffee.

"Morning," I reply with only slightly more enthusiasm. I need caffeine before anyone gets extra happy Lucie today.

I make it two steps to the coffee pot before Dex sets a full mug in front of me. "I just poured and added milk to it."

"Thank you."

Of course he knows how I like my coffee. I know how he likes his and it's not necessarily a sweet gesture. We just know these things because of our situation. Let's face it, Dex didn't even like me a week and a half ago. Maybe yesterday was a fluke.

I'm just feeling...pentup from no sleep. It'll pass.

Dex takes another sip of his coffee and I note the trails of his tattoos peeking out of the sleeves of his shirt again.

No, pent up is the wrong wording. I need an orgasm—tomorrow's plans to go to a sex store are non-negotiable.

"So, tomorrow, could I possibly meet up with Jensen? She runs in the mornings and wants me to join her. I know I'm not technically off, but I'll be back before two to help with Miles still."

Dex raises an eyebrow. "You like to run?"

Umm, I didn't think that part through. I'm sure Jensen will go easy on me; she did say it's a venturing-out activity. "I might."

Dex hums as a small tug pulls on the corner of his mouth. "That's fine, Luce."

"Thank you," I mutter as I try to fight off a yawn.

"Didn't sleep well?" Dex asks.

"Hmm?" I hum, his tone was so nonchalant, and honestly, my brain feels foggy. "Oh, no, I didn't."

Dex picks up his coffee and rounds the counter as he heads for the living room. His body lingers behind me for a moment, then he mumbles, "Yeah, I didn't either."

You know what really doesn't help when you're feeling like you want to climb your boss like a tree? Baseball pants. Dex should not be allowed to wear his baseball pants today.

Some days he wears just athletic shorts and a T-shirt in the bullpen, but today he put on his baseball pants. And naturally, Miles chooses today to follow his dad around every place he can.

Miles and I sit over to the side in the shade. He watches each ball being thrown with this bright gleam in his eyes. I really need to switch up my focus here. Miles is in heaven right now—even if I'm in a weird heaven and hell situation.

"So, do you still want to be a pitcher?"

"Yes!" He doesn't miss a beat. "We've talked about this, Lucieeee. It's the best position, it's what Daddy was."

I snort a laugh at his dramatic response—like this kid didn't change his mind about ten different things this morning alone.

I look over to Dex again as he talks to one of the closing pitchers. I've been meaning to talk to Dex about his retirement. I don't want to pry or overstep—we've been making good progress on our daily work routine, minus this attraction sparking up fast—but I really think we could make it work so Dex could actually play again.

"That he was. Did you know that your dad was my favorite player to watch?"

Ope, that was a mistake.

Miles's eyes go wide. "He was?"

Oh no, that's definitely going to come back up with horrible timing, I'm sure of it. I open my mouth, unsure of how to dial this admission down, but then my eye catches on Will walking our way.

"Yeah, he was, but let's keep that between us because I don't want to hurt my brother's feelings." Not a big fan of suggesting secrets between me and Miles, but desperate times call for desperate measures, and I'm not afraid to use Will as my out.

When Will reaches us, he slides in on the bench next to Miles. "Hey, what are you two doing?"

"Watching." Miles giggles an evil laugh.

Will gives me a small look, but I only shrug. Yep, Miles won't be able to keep this quiet for long.

"Well, I'm done warming up, and I happen to know that Beck brought his PlayStation if you want to come play some games with us?"

Miles's eyes go wide. "Really? Can I go, Lucie?"

"What kind of games?" I can see it now, Dex going into the locker room to find Miles playing a game he's not supposed to, and there goes all my good progress.

"Normal games," Will snarks back. "I already talked to Dex about it."

"Please, Lucieeeee?" Miles begs.

"Okay, but—"

Miles jumps off the bench, cutting me off. "Yay! Let's go, let's go!"

"So, all I need to do is bring video games for you to like me?" Will laughs as Miles tugs on his arms to pull him up. "Head to the Clubhouse, I'll be right behind you."

Miles races back into the stadium without even a goodbye.

I chuckle. "Text me when you need me to take back over."

"I will. Now go take a break. You look tired."

"Hey, Miles said I looked pretty today."

"You do, but I'm your brother—I see the tired."

That's the sibling radar for ya. I guess I shouldn't mention that I'm tired from being up and thinking about his coach all night.

"Thank you," I mutter as Will squeezes my shoulder on his way to chase Miles to the Clubhouse.

I'm not exactly sure what to do now. I guess I could go find Callie, but she's usually running around just as much as I do with Miles. Looking over the bullpen, I find Dex thoroughly occupied talking to Jordan.

The tense face he's making gives me all the context I need. I nearly laugh when I see the deep breath he takes before speaking again all the way from here.

It seems like he might be here for a bit, maybe I can hide out in his office. Can't say I wouldn't mind some peace and quiet before the game starts.

Walking through the hall, some of the players say hi as I pass them by. You'd think that having my brother play in the MLB for years, I would be completely immune to this, and in a way, I guess I am. But considering the Blues are secretly my favorite team, I still feel a bit like pinching myself as I walk through the halls.

Turning on the lights in Dex's office, I look over his setup. It wouldn't surprise me if this office didn't change at all from the person who had it before. It's basic, with a picture of Miles on the desk as the only form of decor. Well, that and a plant that looks like it's seen better days. I bet it's missing its previous owner.

Grabbing a water bottle out of the mini fridge, I pour a little into the small wilting thing. I'm not a wiz with plants like my sister, but I can't imagine a little water will hurt. Really, I can't even say if it can be saved.

Pulling out my phone, I take a picture of the plant and send it to Reagan.

So is there any hope for this baby?

It's been a few days since I've heard from Rea, which feels weird…I'm not exactly sure what to make of it. Reagan's personality has a tendency to steamroll me in a different way than Will's does. I mean, she was standing me up before I got this job to begin with because of all the stuff her and Julie were doing.

Doesn't exactly help my indifference about her silence, but maybe she'll text back soon with some smart-aleck remark.

Setting my phone down on Dex's desk, I look back and forth between all of the chairs he has in here. Not a single one seems truly comfy. My yawn comes hard. Hmm, how weird would it be to sit in his office chair?

It definitely seems like the best option since it has more cushioning than the two across from his desk. I kind of feel like I could use just a small power nap. Ten minutes, tops. I mean it's not like Dex would care…I think.

Sitting back in the chair, I sigh, closing my eyes. Yep, twenty minutes max.

"What are you doing?" Shannon's voice snaps.

Jumping in Dex's chair, my eyes fly open. "Goodness, you scared me."

So, that's what immediate consequences feel like.

Shannon's *hmph* is full of disdain. I hadn't actually realized how much annoyance could be carried in such a small sound, but there it was.

"Will has Miles, so I was taking a little break."

"In Dex's chair? Napping?"

My heart still feels like it's beating out of my chest. How was she that quiet? I can normally hear her heels halfway down the hall. "Not napping, just resting…"

"Right, and in Dex's chair, because…" Shannon waves her hand for me to fill in the rest of her sentence.

I don't know how to answer her. I don't think "because it looked the coziest" is an answer that will go over well with her. Although it's not like she caught me rifling through his desk or trying to break into his computer. What does it matter that I was sitting with my eyes closed?

"Because she can," Dex says as he walks around her into his office and sits in one of the chairs across from me. "Anything else?"

Shannon's spine straightens. "Don't forget you have a pre-game coaches' meeting in an hour."

Dex doesn't even look at her when he replies, "We have one every game, I'm pretty sure muscle memory won't let me forget at this point."

When the laugh bubbles out of me, I quickly force my lips into a thin line.

Shannon mumbles something under her breath, but it's drowned out by the clicks of her heels as she turns. Ah, there they are.

As the sound gets further away, I let my laugh out. "Do you want your seat back?"

Dex shakes his head. "No, it's fine, Luce."

"Are you sure? If you need to get some work done, I can go—"

"No," Dex cuts me off. "Stay here. Miles is having fun with the guys, and as Shannon just reminded me, I've got an hour to waste."

The smirk tugging on his lips makes butterflies erupt in my stomach. "Okay. What do you want to do, Coach?"

Chapter 25
Dex

"We're going to people watch?" Lucie laughs as I bring one of the chairs around behind my desk to the window to watch Baltimore's team warm up.

"You got any better ideas?"

Lucie shrugs and rolls my office chair next to me. "I guess not."

She's wearing that damn yellow dress she wore in the coffee shop the first time we met. Seeing her in yellow has been torture enough, but I've been simultaneously dreading and praying to see this dress on her again.

Lucie seems to notice my stare because when her eyes meet mine, there's a small blush to her cheeks.

Clearing my throat, I turn to look back over the field as one of the hitters sends a ball out to right field.

"I feel like there's some sort of betting game in here somewhere," Lucie says softly.

I watch as the same hitter sends his next hit to right field again. "Okay, how about this— we bet questions. So if I bet the next hit lands in left field and it does, I get to ask you a question, but if it doesn't, you get to ask."

Lucie's smile is soft, but I can see the excitement in her eyes. "Okay, let's do it."

We both turn back to the field as the ball gets hit into left field. "I win. Tell me more about figuring yourself out."

Lucie hums. "That's not a question."

"Alright, fair. How are you figuring yourself out?" I'm still having a hard time understanding how Lucie thinks she's not exactly who she needs to be.

Lucie shuffles in my office chair, angling slightly away from me. "Well, I have this list, or guidelines might be the better word. I guess it's not necessarily that I don't know anything about myself, it's more that I feel like a lot of stuff stems from my siblings."

"Is that why you're going to try to go running tomorrow?"

Lucie's face turns bright red. "Yeah, you could say that."

"Wh—"

"It's my turn," Lucie cuts me off as the next batter comes up. "I bet that he hits it to center field."

The pitch comes and it's hit to...left field.

"What are the guidelines?"

Lucie swallows. 'Um, there's venture out more—"

"Running," I offer, and Lucie shakes her head before continuing.

"Find a hobby, have a yes day, do something that scares me, and be more spontaneous. There's not really a limit on them either, just to keep me on the path."

"Does that path have an ending?"

"What do you mean?"

"You know, a goal or some life milestone?"

Lucie shrugs. "Do they have to have an ending?"

"I don't know. I guess they don't. I mean, you're young—"

Lucie snorts a laugh. "Oh no, not the 'you've got your whole life ahead of you' speech."

The smirk tugs at my mouth. "God, I hated it the moment it came out of my mouth. How patronizing did that sound?"

"Eh, I think I cut you off in time." Lucie laughs again. "Even though I believe I'm way past the bet requirements, there's not necessarily this big end goal. It's not that I'm doing any of this to be ready for a relationship or a big career move. It's just for me."

Shit. I don't know if I like or hate that answer. I like that this is for her—hearing she wants to better herself for a guy would have pissed me the fuck off. But, then again, I kind of want to be that guy. That's part of the damn problem.

My feelings for Lucie are getting too hard to ignore. We already had one close call, and I don't see myself recovering from too many more moments like that with her.

Lucie continues on, not helping my internal downfall.

"It's not to keep me from finding someone either, just making sure they don't try to make their light my own or more likely, that I make their personality mine like I did with my siblings...I probably sound nuts."

"No, you don't." I don't see how anyone could ever outshine Lucie. Hell, I hardly understand how she doesn't see it herself. She's a nurturer, but she's also resilient in the best way. No matter how many times I tried to push her away, she's stayed put. She's calm and even-tempered, but full of passion when it comes to the people she cares about.

She can claim she's the side character—or extra...whatever the fuck she said—all she wants. I think she's a main character who just hasn't found her story yet.

Lucie gives me a half smile. "Okay, it's my turn. I bet two questions—"

"Whoa, I never said you could wager multiple questions."

"You never said I couldn't. Plus, I just overpaid on that one."

See, that's light.

I hold out my hand for her to continue.

"I bet two questions that the next one lands in left field."

The pitch comes and with the swing, the ball flies into left field where one of the players shagging balls makes a diving catch. Lucie mumbles a small celebratory "yes" and angles her chair back to me.

"First question. Why'd you retire?"

I lift an eyebrow and laugh. "Is that not obvious? I think having to hire you is part of the answer."

Lucie nudges my arm. "Part of the answer, Dex. Come on, tell me the full answer."

I fight the urge to push back on this question more if it means she'll touch my arm again, but I know she was vulnerable with me just now. I can do the same, but only because it's *her*.

"Alright. Not having someone to take care of Miles was a big part of it. The travel and schedule were hard enough as is —I missed him like crazy when my mom or Kate couldn't travel with me to the away games.

"The other part is guilt. Kate and I were never going to work. There was no real love lost there, just two people who made decisions and are now dealing with the outcomes. Kate never really wanted to be a mother, and I knew that. When we found out she was pregnant, I told her I would support whatever decision she made moving forward with the pregnancy. It was her choice completely, and I respected it. It wasn't until she decided to have Miles that I started fucking up.

"We should never have gotten married. I'm man enough to own that I played a bigger role in that than she did. The idea of having that family dynamic was something I wanted. The pressure from my own parents didn't help—their hearts weren't necessarily in the wrong place, more that generational bullshit of getting married when you have a baby and all that."

I sigh, running my hands over my face. Fuck, the shit I'm putting Miles through kills me. I can't say I'm putting him through it alone, but I'm the one who caused it. Who knows if Kate and I could have just made co-parenting work better had we not gotten married. Maybe I could have even taken on this full-time role sooner...

"I may not completely understand or even agree with how Kate's handled the divorce when it comes to Miles, but I can't blame her for it."

"You blame yourself," Lucie says the words that I couldn't.

"Yeah, I blame myself. I just want him to have a happy life—the best life I can give him. Retiring felt like the only way to do that. Then Olsson made me this offer, and I selfishly took it."

Lucie stays silent for a moment, but then shuffles in her chair to angle more toward me. "You know, my dad left when I was six. He was a horrible alcoholic—it's why Will doesn't drink at all, actually. With me being the youngest, I don't have a lot of memories of him, and while I've seen pictures that my mom still has hidden in a box under her bed, I haven't seen him since the day he left.

"If you asked my siblings if they thought him choosing to leave was selfish, you might get a different answer, but for me, I think it was the right one. It's not really my story to tell, but with what happened to Will—him staying would have put all of us at risk." Lucie's hand lands on top of mine. "So while I don't completely understand or even agree with him, I won't blame him for what I believe was the right decision at the core of it."

"Luce." My voice is low, with what I can't decide is a warning or plea, because her hand is still holding mine.

"I have one more question left," Lucie whispers. "Why are you afraid of me?"

So many reasons, but the one that sums it up the most is that I don't want to lose her if I ever were to get the pleasure of being hers.

I swallow hard. "I don't want to ever blame myself over you."

Chapter 26
Lucie

"I'm dying, Jensen," I pant out while bending over with my hands on my knees. We've run maybe a mile, and I'm regretting my life choices.

"That's funny, you said the same thing about Dex before we got started."

"Because it's true. He's killing me—you're killing me. All this run has done is made my legs feel like Jell-O...my lungs feel like they are going to collapse....and I'm still thinking about Dex. At this point, I don't even think a vibrator will help."

After our emotional confessions, we continued playing our betting question game, but the topics got much lighter... like how Dex got drafted, how I got my turtles, and why I don't cuss. But the thing was, Dex never let go of my hand, and I didn't pull it away.

We sat there talking, holding hands, and watching baseball warm-ups. I don't think I ever felt more content in my life. I can't say when it changed between us, but I never wanted that moment to end.

Jensen's border collie, Dottie, comes up and licks the side of my face. "She's telling you to pull yourself together because we're only halfway through our normal route. You told me to help you get Dex off your mind."

Standing up straight, a cool breeze comes off the waterfront. I huff. Goodness, I think my ears are ringing.

"I would rather go back to Dex's apartment right now and tell him I need him to help me do my Lucie After Dark list than finish this run."

Jensen hums; she doesn't even look like she's broken a sweat yet. "Oh, please let me call your bluff."

Part of me wishes she could. "You know you can't."

Just as much as I know I can't force Dex's hand. I didn't give Jensen all of the details about our conversation yesterday, but I gave her the CliffNotes because I think I'm falling for my boss when it's just as unfair for me as it is to him.

Hearing him say all of those things yesterday meant so much to me. It was as if I'd managed to get a big enough hole in his thick wall that I could step all the way through, but I'm not entirely sure Dex wants me to stay there. Or well, I think he might, but doesn't know if he has the capability to.

He's made his interest in me clear, I can see it now. But it's not just about me and him—Miles plays a huge role. Dex blames himself for the things that have changed in his son's life, and now I'm a part of that. Whatever this is between us, it directly affects Miles, no matter how we look at it.

I don't know what angle Dex is looking at it from, but I selfishly want it to be the one that eventually wants to give us a try.

"Luce, you both can't just live together and not ever address this. I get self-sacrificing to a degree, but you're not even trying."

I huff another deep breath, finally feeling like my heart rate is coming down. "That's not true. Dex needs me as Miles's nanny and teacher. Me being more has to come from him when he's ready."

Even if I'm afraid he never will be, I know I can't tell him I think he deserves his happiness too when I know that he already carries so much guilt.

"If that's what you want. Either way, you're not getting out of the rest of this run."

"Just so we're clear, venturing out with running is a no. Lucie Anderson is not a running girlie."

Dottie lets out a small bark, and Jensen laughs. "She just called you a pussy."

"She did? Or you did?"

"Both. Hers is for stalling her run, and mine is for not making a move on Dex."

"I want to! But I can't. I can't be the one that makes the first move in good conscience, and I definitely can't finish this run."

"Yes, you can—" Jensen stops and her spine snaps straight up. "You have got to be kidding me."

I follow her gaze and find Beck slowing down his run and walking up to us.

"Well, if this isn't the best way to start my day, then I don't know what is." Beck's cocky smirk flashes to Jensen. "Hey, Jenni-cakes, I missed our runs while I was gone."

I tilt my head to Jensen. Suddenly, I'm feeling much better. "Your runs?"

Jensen clenches her jaw as she crosses her arms over her chest. "He means how I run away from him because he's a stalker."

Beck laughs, completely unfazed, and kneels down to pet

Dottie. "I'm not a stalker, right, Dottie? You like when I run with you guys?"

Dottie rolls over, practically putty as Beck pets her. My smile grows bigger, and Jensen just seems more pissed.

"She likes that it makes us run faster—my goal is to lose you as quickly as possible."

Beck stands back up, and Dottie practically whimpers at his feet. "You know, I like that I drive you, J. You should always be with someone who makes you want to keep improving."

My whole day has officially turned around.

"Wait, Beck, do you have a thigh tattoo?" I don't know how I've never noticed it before, but I can see tips of ink at the end of his shorts, similar to how Dex's do with his shirts.

Ah, yeah, that's why I haven't noticed—Dex.

"Oh yeah, I just got this started over the offseason." Beck pulls the hem of his athletic shorts up to show us more of the lightning tattooed on his thigh. He looks up to Jensen with the same smirk. "I'll be waiting to get the rest of my idea until this new artist starts. I think I'll like her style more."

I swear Jensen's jaw clenches even harder. How she hasn't cracked a tooth is impressive. "In your dreams, Beckham."

"Oh, it does happen in my dreams—a lot. Don't worry, your personality doesn't change there either."

Jensen's nostrils flare as she takes a deep breath. "Well, we're actually about to get back to our run, so—"

This might be a bit of a bad friend move—or good friend, considering I think Jensen is actually sweating now. A mile into this run and she was glowing. Two minutes of this conversation and her chest and the tips of her ears are red.

"Actually, I think I might be holding you back. Maybe you should finish with Beck."

Jensen looks at me like she wants to absolutely murder me. "No, we have plans after this. Remember?"

"We can do that another day." I can sacrifice my store trip for this.

"We're a mile away from your car, Luce," Jensen huffs. "What are you going to do, walk back with no one with you?"

"Yep," I state.

Do I need to be pushed with Dex? Maybe, but it seems like I'm not the only one in need of a shove.

Beck eyes me for a minute, I know he's thinking through what I've suggested. I've noticed this big brother personality with Beck over the past two weeks. It comes out a lot with Callie, but I've noticed it's extended to me a little bit more.

"I'll be just fine." I pull my phone from the pocket in my leggings. "I'll text you when I get back."

Beck turns to Jensen. "What do you say, Jennie-cakes? Up for a little driving?"

As if Dottie can understand, she barks.

"Damn traitors," Jensen grumbles.

"Good luck, Jen, I'll text you," I say over my shoulder, already turning to start my walk back.

"Yes, you will!" Jensen's tone gives me enough indication that she will most definitely be getting me back for this, but it's so worth it.

Walking along the waterfront, another breeze hits me. I'm definitely not a running girl, but I think I'd be down for some walks. This could be a good form of venturing out.

Talking to Dex about the idea of what these guidelines

are felt different from when I spoke to Jensen about it. Yes, I feel like I'm this extra in my own story, but I can't really pinpoint why I feel that way.

The list, ideas, or whatever I'm doing will help with that, I hope. Maybe that's why it's better for me to leave the ball in Dex's court. While he may have this new attraction to me, once I figure my own self out, he might change his mind.

Okay, I don't like that mindset. Maybe walking is a no-go too. It's too quiet—too many opportunities for my brain to wander. I could look into some low-impact stuff later today. A class might be more my style.

My phone dings in my pocket. I'm hoping it's Reagan finally texting me back. Her ignoring my text about the wilting plant has me feeling a little more unnerved. Will said he checked in with her Sunday when we got back, and said she seemed busy—but that's her normal.

But when I look at my phone, my stomach does a small flip.

DEX

Want to tell me why Beck just messaged me that you're walking a mile back to your car all by yourself?

Of course Beck messaged him.

Turns out running isn't my thing. Mark that down about things we now know about Lucie.

Let me pretend to be shocked for a second.

Dex! I could have liked it.

> No, you liked the idea of doing something
> with Jensen that she wanted to do.

I stop walking as I read his message. Dang, how did he see that? I know that wasn't my intention. And granted, he doesn't know about the plans to get a sex toy after, but still. I wanted to get out and try new things. I guess running wouldn't have been my initial first choice in a workout, per se. Then again, I hadn't ever *tried* running before.

> I liked that it was with Jensen, but that was
> still for me. What if I did like it?

> I never said it wasn't for you in some way. I
> said I'm not surprised you didn't like it.

> And what would I like, Coach?

I watch as the bubbles dance, waiting for Dex's reply. When they disappear, I think I might have actually stumped him, but then a link comes through for a yoga studio.

Clicking on the link pulls up the website for Sunbeam Yoga. My mouth goes dry as I scroll through the website. It's perfect—exactly what I would have picked out for myself if I actually looked for it. There are classes every day, but every Sunday has a different class with a fun activity. Wine and yoga. Goats with yoga. Parents and kid sessions. Couples classes.

> I got you a membership already. There's a
> class in half an hour. Text me when you get
> to your car safely, then go try it out.

> Dex, this is perfect, but you didn't have to
> do this.

Today may not have started completely as planned, but it got so much better. I loved the yoga class. It was absolutely incredible. The people there were so nice, and the whole place had this sunrise-sunset vibe. I loved everything about it.

After it ended, I felt so empowered that I even decided to go buy a vibrator all by myself. That was the whole purpose of this list to start—doing things on my own.

Walking down the hall to Dex's place, I stuff the new bullet vibrator to the very bottom of my bag. The store was an experience for sure, but with all the traveling, I thought small and discreet might be best.

Unlocking the door, I make it a step into the living room before Miles pops up in front of me. "Lucie's back!"

"I am." I chuckle, but then I notice something's different. "Miles, did you get a haircut?"

"I did! Daddy took me to the barbershop. Doesn't it look really good?"

"It does. I love it, bud."

"Good, that means Callie will too." Miles beams, but within a second, his mood shifts. He puts his hands together and gives me the sweet puppy dog eyes. "Can we please bring one of the turtles to the stadium today?"

I open my mouth to tell him that they need to stay in their home, but then I hear Dex's voice behind me. "We already talked about this, Miles. Don't ask Lucie when I've already said no."

Miles groans with a major pout with his bottom lip.

I fold my lips together to hold in a laugh. Poor kid. I swear, one day Miles is going to kidnap them and sneak them into a game, or worse, an away game.

"Why don't you grab them two strawberries from the fridge for their treat?"

Miles's lip comes straight up and now we're back to a smile. "Okay!"

I watch Miles race around me to the kitchen, but then my eyes find Dex, and I have to do a double-take. "Ah, Dex, you got a haircut too!"

Dex tilts his head with a laugh. "Shit, Luce, what are you trying to say? Was it that bad before or that bad now?"

The smile on my face has got to be huge. "No, no, it was great before too, but this is how you would wear it during the season when you played..." My words die off, because Lord help me, he looks so hot right now. Good thing I still went to get that vibrator.

The corner of Dex's mouth turns up, and he takes a small step closer to me. "You remember what it looked like when I played?"

Ope, I need to throw together some sort of answer, but then my mistake from yesterday catches up to me.

"Because you were Lucie's favorite baseball player, Daddy," Miles says as he munches on a strawberry with two extra ones in his other hand.

Yep, I knew that secret wasn't going to last long.

Dex's smile grows as he processes Miles's words. "Really?"

You know what? I'm not embarrassed. Looking at this man—yeah, he was my favorite.

I dare a small step toward him, for what reason I don't know, other than I just want to be closer to him. Dex seems to feel the same as he steps another inch in.

I look up at him with a smile. "You did say you would find out eventually."

Dex's eyes soften. "Yeah, I did."

"Can I give the turtles their strawberries now?" Miles asks, completely oblivious to the moment around him.

Taking a step back, I turn to Miles. "Sure can, but then I need to get some water and a shower before we head to the game, okay?"

"Okay!" Miles skips over to the tank, and I help him get them set in place. I try not to think too much about Dex behind me, but when I turn back, he's no longer in the living room.

I didn't think him finding out he was my favorite player freaked him out, but maybe he's having a delayed freak-out.

Okay, deep breaths, we're keeping the ball in his court for a reason.

Miles hops off his stool with a thud. "I'm going to go play until we have to leave, okay?"

I barely get "okay" out before he races down the hall to his room.

Goodness, his energy—I wish I had it. Between my unenjoyable run and super uplifting yoga class, I'm feeling beat already and the day's barely even started.

Making my way to the kitchen to grab some water, I stall when Dex meets me halfway with a glass. "So, how'd you like the class?"

Okay, maybe no freak out, but still proceed with caution.

"You were right, it was perfect." I take the glass of water

from him while making sure to keep my hand from brushing against his. "Thank you for finding it for me."

I take a heavy sip, not realizing how much I needed it until now.

"I thought you would." A smirk tugs at Dex's lips.

Setting my glass down on the side table, I know we need to talk about the payment of it all because I definitely want to go back.

"I know you said you paid for the first membership, so if you want to take that out of my pay—"

Dex holds up his hand. "Gonna stop you there, Luce. It's paid for, don't worry about it."

"Dex, no. It's my thing, let me pay for it."

"Not happening." He shrugs.

"Yes, yes happening. Dex, part of why all of this got started is because I rely so much on my siblings. Will has always paid for the majority of my stuff. I don't want to keep being this spoiled—"

Dex takes a step in, his cool peppermint scent demanding even more of my attention to his closeness. For weeks, he's taken steps back, and now he's inching closer. There's maybe two inches between us now, and yet, it still doesn't feel like it's close enough.

He tucks a loose strand behind my ear, and his voice comes out calm and even. "I can see I've hit a nerve. Lucie, you're not spoiled. I think you are the furthest from spoiled, actually. For two weeks, you've traveled with me and Miles. You've eaten nothing but shitty hotel food and bad concession hotdogs. You haven't gotten to visit a single place we've been to because you take care of Miles nearly twenty-four fucking seven just like me, without a single complaint."

"I like the concession hotdogs," I grumble. "They're underrated. And I still want to pay for the classes."

"Too fucking bad, Luce." Dex chuckles. "You can stop taking your brother's money all you want, but if *I* want to spoil you, then I'm going to."

An argument doesn't even start in my head. "Okay, Coach."

Chapter 27
Dex

"Miles, slow down. You have to chew your food, not inhale it." Lucie laughs from where she's sitting on the barstool next to Miles.

They've had breakfast together here for the past three days, and each morning the dam is closer to breaking. I like Lucie, there's no denying it to myself—or even to her. And I think she might feel this attraction to me too.

I know it doesn't mean we should date. Every morning as I watch them together over breakfast, I tell myself, "I can't break today for my son." I can't put Miles through another loss, and losing Lucie would devastate him. Hell, the thought even devastates me.

Although it might be unfair to both of us, I can't seem to stop seeking her out. I don't want to stop. I like watching her with Miles. I like talking to her and finding out all of her hidden talents. Hell, I feel like I'm in fucking high school again. I like her a lot.

I'm not entirely sure how this weekend alone with her is going to go.

"All done." Miles slides his empty bowl of cereal forward.

I especially like how, since Lucie started, Miles is eating normally again.

I grab his bowl to take it to the sink. "Okay, Miles, why don't you go grab some of the stuff you want to take to your mom's."

Miles's eyebrows raise, and this mischievous smile appears on his face. "Can I bring Pip and Pop?"

Lucie gives me a thin-lipped smile. Miles has asked me every single day to take these damn turtles somewhere.

"Do you like having the turtles?"

"Yes." Miles's smile hasn't completely depleted yet.

"Then they stay here."

Miles's shoulders sink. "But I'll be gone for two whole sleeps, and then we get on a plane again. They're going to miss me like I miss them."

Lucie looks at me again with a sweet pout—that was cute, I get it, but I'm not strong enough to tell them both no if they push me on this.

"No," I point at her, "not you too."

Lucie's jaw drops with a scoff. "I didn't say anything."

"You're both pouting over turtles staying in the place that keeps them alive. Mind you, I didn't want them to begin with."

"What!?" Miles's voice goes up at least five octaves.

Lucie laughs and ruffles Miles's head. "Don't listen to him, he was so excited about the idea of Pip and Pop. But he is right, they do need to stay where they are. While I totally understand them missing you, they are happiest here."

"Okay, I guess so," Miles grumbles as he hops off the

barstool. "Lucie, can I take one of the new coloring books you got me?"

"Go for it. They're in the bags in our soon-to-be classroom. I'll be there in just a minute to help."

Miles shoots off like a rocket. "I can find it first."

I shake my head with a sigh. "You know he's going to take those damn things somewhere one day."

Lucie rests her chin on her hand with a sweet smile. "I know. I'm just waiting to find them in his backpack midflight."

"Remind me to check on them Sunday before we leave," I say, finally dropping Miles's bowl in the sink. "So what're your plans for this weekend?"

I want her to say that nothing changes and she'll still be the brightness in my day. I need her to say that she's going to go visit her brother or sister, mom, anyone that keeps me from breaking.

"No plans in particular." Lucie slides off her stool and meets me at the sink with her breakfast. "I think I'll go to one of the yoga classes today. Maybe go around to some stores, then come to the game later."

"You still want to come to the game even though you don't have to be there? I mean, your favorite player isn't even on the team anymore."

Lucie bites back a smirk. "I regret telling Miles that, ya know?"

Hmph, I sure as hell don't.

Taking some steps back from her, I lean against the island. "Don't worry, I'm just going to hold it over your head for the foreseeable future."

Our future.

Lucie hums with a smile. "Well, we obviously don't have

to talk about this right now, but just floating the idea by you. What if you did want to be a player again?"

Lucie's eyes dart to mine cautiously. I don't know how to respond to her honestly. The idea has crossed my mind, but I only let it cross it—I don't think about it more than that because it's the decision I made, even if I wish I could play again.

"I've just been thinking we seem to have a pretty good routine here. Like Miles said, you were my favorite, and I know you retired for him, but it seemed like a choice you maybe regret..."

And this is coming from the girl who can't even see what makes her so damn special. How she doesn't see that blows my fucking mind.

"Luce, I appreciate the offer, but I don't know if that's—"

"Lucie!" Miles yells from down the hall.

Lucie chuckles, then steps toward me.

I swear we're just two magnets constantly feeling this pull, because I was just about to meet her in the middle.

"Just think about it..." Lucie whispers. "For me?"

I swallow hard and nod, because I'm pretty sure I'm unable to give a verbal response.

Is she right? Could I play again? I would really like to do that, but, hell, it almost feels as uncertain as acting on my feelings with Lucie.

I dwell on each variable—each possible outcome of playing again as we get ready to go. When Miles launches himself into Lucie's arms with a goodbye hug, I can only think of the variables and outcomes that involve me getting to have more of Lucie.

Fuck, I know hiring Lucie was supposed to lighten the weight on my shoulders—not fucking add new ones. Stay coaching—play again? Tell Lucie how I fucking feel and maybe end up with the girl I was supposed to have all along, or fuck everything up for the second time and hurt my son, yet again, in the process.

My mood has completely tanked. God, I just want to get one thing right.

On our way, Miles kicks his feet happily on the back of my seat. "Hey, bud, think we can maybe stop kicking my seat?"

"Sorry," Miles snorts. "Hey, Daddy, do you think you can read this paper? I think Lucie drew it, and it's really pretty."

I look in the rearview mirror, angling it so I can see Miles. He's flipping around what looks like an invitation. "I'm kind of driving, so not really, but are you sure that's one of the things for you? Where did you get that?"

"I got it from Lucie's bag. She said there was coloring stuff in the bags, and I found this in one of them. I think Lucie drew it, and I'm supposed to color it in."

I'm not sure about that. It's hard to tell while driving, but from quick glances, it seems more likely that Miles grabbed something he wasn't supposed to.

"Can I see it?" I reach my hand back just as we come to a red light.

Miles slaps it in my palm. "Here you go."

I glance ahead to make sure the light is still red, then look at the front of the paper. It's framed with gold and yellow drawings, and Lucie's name is written all fancy up top. Then in the middle are the guidelines she told me about that she has been keeping to.

Yeah, this definitely isn't something Miles is supposed to

have. I look back at the light again to make sure it's still red, then flip it over—holy fuck.

A car behind me honks loudly. "Fuck." I drop the paper on my dash and start moving again. Holy shit. Lucie didn't mention anything about *those* guidelines.

"Daddy?" Miles's voice cracks in the back. "Is everything okay? You said a bad word."

I did, didn't I? It's like my brain short-circuited, and the honking pulled me out of it. "Everything's fine. I'm sorry, I didn't mean to scare you. The honk was just to tell me it's time to move again."

"Okay, can I have the paper back now?"

Absolutely not.

"I think this paper is for Lucie, Miles. This wasn't actually meant for you."

I don't think it was meant to be seen by anyone—I don't know how I can unsee it. *Get a toy. Find a kink. Sexually inspiring outings.* It's seared in my brain.

Okay, deep breath. You're about to take your son to your ex-wife, and showing up with a hard-on is not what's about to happen.

Christ, this day has sent me on loop after fucking loop. Is she doing these things with other people? She said they were just for her, but the thought of her doing any of these with anyone but me fills me with this out-of-body rage.

No one deserves to do these things with her unless they see what I see. Granted, I'm not entirely sure I deserve to do them with her considering I've done nothing but fight this attraction to her.

How did running into a girl at a coffee shop get so damn complicated?

Standing outside Kate's apartment, Miles knocks wildly.

"Mommy!" Miles jumps to Kate the second she opens the door.

"Hey, sweetie, I'm happy you're here."

"Me too! Daddy said I couldn't bring Pip and Pop." Miles's face drops for a minute but then bounces back. "But Lucie packed all my swim stuff."

"Did she now?" Kate shoots me a small look I'm not really in the mood to entertain. "We'll see if we have time for that."

Don't say anything. Don't say anything.

I kneel down to meet Miles's height. "I'll see you in two sleeps, okay? You can call me anytime too."

"Okay, Daddy. Love you!" Miles gives me a quick hug but the excitement of being at a new place has taken over. Once his hands let me go, he's bolting through the door.

"Love you too," I say, but can't be sure if he heard me. "Call me if he needs anything, Kate."

"Call you or your nanny?"

"I'm not entertaining that question right now. Have a good weekend with him. I'll pick him up whenever you're ready on Sunday."

"Alright. Oh, and I have a work trip to New York next weekend. Same time you'll be playing the Crimsons. I thought it would be good if we all got to spend some time together."

Shit. I know this isn't about me. The mention of Lucie right off the bat by Miles has gone straight to her head.

"You know we're going to be pretty busy at the games. I'm not saying you can't come to a game, but Lucie's going to be in charge of Miles on those days."

"Dex, is that really necessary?"

"Necessary isn't the word to use here. I'm flexible, but

we have to have boundaries. It's her job, and she knows the routine on game days."

Kate rolls her shoulders back. "We'll talk about it later."

You know what, it's not worth the argument right now. "Fine. You guys have fun. Let me know the time for Sunday."

I don't wait around for her answer; I know she'll decide on the time based on Miles's energy level over the next two days.

Back in my car, my eyes catch on Lucie's paper. There isn't a single rational thing that goes through my mind when I look at that list written in red...

My resolve is fucking breaking.

LUCIE

I'm done with the yoga class, I'm going to go around to some stores. I might have an idea to help with our turtle situation but we'll see.

I'm back. I'll head over to the stadium around the start of first pitch. Let me know if you need anything.

Okay, leaving now. See you soon, Coach.

I think I've typed and erased at least fifty messages to Lucie today. As a saving grace, she wasn't home when I got back from dropping off Miles, and I didn't wait around to see when she'd come back.

I immediately got ready and did a two-hour workout in the gym. It helped me in no way—all I've been able to think about is her. How badly I want her but can't fucking have her.

"So, are you ever going to answer her, or are you just going to keep looking at your phone all day?" Beck's voice pulls me out of my trance.

I shove my phone in my back pocket and keep my eyes on the field, watching all the cameras as the people start the ceremonial first pitch. I'm not sure who's doing it today, some comedian or something, I think. "What's up, Beck?"

"Just wondering what's climbed up your ass today. I think I'm the only player not afraid of talking to you right now."

"That seems a tad dramatic. Will and Callie talked to me earlier with no complaints."

Beck gives me this annoying hum. "I really want to make a very important distinction about what you just said, but I think it's best I don't."

Yeah, he's probably right.

"Want to tell me why you're ignoring her?"

"Nope."

"Do you think ignoring her is actually going to help you?"

"Go away, Beck." I dismiss him and look into the stands for Lucie. I don't know how well I'll actually talk to Lucie right now without taking her back to my office.

The moment my eyes land on her I know I'm fucked. Her in damn yellow.

With each step closer to me, that magnet pull feels so strong.

She's my son's nanny, whom he loves. And he's finally starting to heal at home since the divorce. She's my player's little sister. Twelve years younger than me, even if it doesn't feel like it.

She's...She's...damn it, I just want her to be mine.

Walking away from Beck without another thought, I meet Lucie at the stands.

"Hey, Coach." She smiles and everything else seems to fade away.

Thank God for this netting between us.

"Hey," I grunt out. Hell, I'm going to fuck this up.

"I didn't want to interrupt, but I just wanted to let you know I was here."

"I knew you were, Luce. I think I spotted you the moment you hit the stairs."

She looks so beautiful in this dress; I don't think I've ever seen this one on her. I can't help but let my eyes travel up from her white Converse to the dress that makes me want to fill my entire life with yellow, to Lucie's lips that I need to taste, and the pink on her cheeks.

Wait. I know right now she's blushing, but... "Where's your hat?"

Lucie shrugs. "It's back at the apartment. It totally slipped my mind to grab it, but it's no big deal."

"Yes, it is a big deal. You said you get sunburned easily, so—" I let out an exasperated breath. "Come over here."

"Dex—" Lucie starts to argue, but it's not up for negotiation.

Lucie follows a few steps behind until we meet where there's a small gap in the netting. I take my hat off and hold it out to her. "Put it on."

Lucie shakes her head with a stressed laugh. "I can't take your—"

"Put. It. On. Lucie."

I'm already going to be thinking about her the whole damn game, and I'd rather not constantly be thinking about her getting burned in the sun on top of that.

Lucie gives me a tight-lipped smile as she takes my hat and puts it on her head. "There, better?"

"Nope," I clip out, because now I really want to take her back to my office. God, she can wear no other hat but my own from here on out. "I have to get back to the dugout. Keep that on or I'll come out in the stadium to put it back, got it?"

"Got it." Lucie's voice is tighter than it normally is—not that I'm surprised. To her, I'm probably coming off like a total dick, but that's essentially the only dynamic I can manage right now to keep me from walking away from this game entirely.

Making my way over to the dugout, I take some deep breaths. I just need a solid ten seconds of silence.

But do I get it? No. Instead, I get Will coming up beside me. Motherfucker.

"Ya know, watching you with my sister kind of makes me feel bad for Adam. That's really the only unforgivable part here."

Shit. "I don't know what you're talking about."

Will laughs. "Said that before myself. I'll tell you what, though. I have an extra hat to give Lucie if the sun really bothers her that much."

I clench my jaw to physically stop myself from telling him to not even fucking try it. But that's all Will needs to see to know exactly what I was thinking.

"Yeah, Callie only wears my stuff too."

My eyes wander over to where Lucie is sitting, my hat

still on her head, exactly where it should be. "You know we're talking about *your* sister right now?"

"Hey, I don't need details. I want my sister to be happy. I don't know what's fully going on here—and again I can't stress this enough, I don't need details—but if you're worried about me, don't be. I'm not about to spend my time being upset about someone treating my sister with respect and making her happy."

I let his words register in my brain. Part of me knew he wouldn't be upset, that's just not Will. But using it as an excuse to not move forward with Lucie was one thread I had holding me back. It was a weak one, but it's snapped completely now.

"I didn't ask for your blessing, Anderson."

"Yeah, the thing is, you don't need it." Will claps my shoulder. "Now I'm going to go kiss my teammate's sister before the game starts, and her brother isn't going to care because he knows I love her."

Fuck.

Chapter 28
Lucie

I'm not sure what happened to Dex today, but clearly something's gone wrong. Him giving me a hat should have been a sweet gesture, but the tone he did it in felt harsh.

I'm not sure if it was me suggesting that he could play again, or maybe it's just not having Miles here. This is the first weekend I've been around when Miles goes to his mom's house.

And add in the fact that he ignored my texts all day...I guess he doesn't care to respond since I don't have Miles? That seems so out of character for him, especially with the moments we've had lately.

I thought of waiting for him after the game, but that felt a little pathetic. If this is how he is when Miles is gone, then maybe I should stay out of his way. I knew doing this with him would be a slow process. I'm learning that although I'm patient, I'm not a pushover. If he wanted me to wait, then he would have made that clear.

Besides, I have a fun project waiting for me back at Dex's house anyway. After my yoga class, I went around to some craft stores in search of animal crochet kits—specifically, two turtle ones.

It might not be as fun and exciting as bringing the actual Pip and Pop to away games, but at least it'll help keep the real ones safe in their tank.

I probably should have bought backup stuffed animal ones, because based on the progress I made earlier…it's not exactly going to be the hobby for me. But it's the thought that counts, I suppose.

Back at Dex's, I grab a blanket, my crochet kit, and head straight for the balcony to get settled in. I honestly can't say that Miles will even be able to tell that these are turtles, but, eh, maybe it's just because I'm not finished.

I lay everything out again as the instructions say and pick up where I left off.

Wrapping the yarn around with the needle seems like it should be so simple, but it takes me a few minutes to really get back into the groove of it.

Although the further along I get, the more I can actually see the turtle now. It's not necessarily as pretty as the pictures on the instructions, but it's coming along.

I'm not sure how long I work, but eventually I tune everything else out as I add the stuffing to close up the body. I pull the needle through the middle to tie it off when I hear the sliding door open, then close.

My heart starts to beat out of my chest. I look up as Dex walks toward me. He's out of the uniform and back in athletic shorts and those T-shirts I love. It's a blessing and a curse that I haven't happened upon Dex with his shirt off yet.

I want to know what those tattoos look like, but with his mood at the baseball field, I'm not too sure I'll ever see them.

"Hey, you're back," I say, barely above a whisper, and give him a cautious smile.

"I am." Well, I see Dex's stoic demeanor still stands, but he takes the seat in the chair next to me anyway. "What are you doing out here?"

"I'm attempting to crochet." I shrug.

Maybe he just needs some normalcy. I'm not sure what happened to make him act so out of it earlier; maybe he needs a little light.

"I never claimed I was going to be the *cool* main character in the movie. I'm trying it out as a new hobby. What do you think it is?"

I hold up the little ball of green. I know there's no way to tell without adding in the extra details, but the small scrunch of his nose makes it worth it.

"I...don't think I like this game, Luce."

"Yeah, I'm not sure if I'm going to be the best at it, but it's supposed to be a turtle. Miles said he misses Pip and Pop, and I know we're another two-week away game rotation before he tries to sneak them out somewhere. I thought I could make him some travel ones to see if that helps."

"Wait, these are for Miles? I thought the list was supposed to be for things that are just for you?"

"Eh, it's still for me." I gather up all of the stuff in my lap to set it in the bag next to me. "I probably should just get him already-made stuffies, but the idea to try out a new hobby while making him something seemed more fun."

Dex sighs and shuffles in his seat. "I'm sorry for being a dick today."

"That's okay. Want to tell me why?"

Dex stares deep into my eyes. "Yes and no."

"Okay." I slide my legs off the lounger so I'm facing him.

I lean my elbow on my knee, resting my chin on my hand. "Was it something I did?"

"Fuck." Dex scoffs a laugh as he shoots up from where he was sitting. He puts a healthy distance between us before he speaks again. "I'm at my wits fucking end here. I want you, Luce. I have since I met you at the coffee shop."

I'm frozen in my seat. Since the first time we met?

My brain is still trying to process this information when Dex drops the cardstock of my list on the lounger between us.

That definitely gets my body back in motion. Standing up, I pick up the paper and stalk toward him. "Where did you get this?"

Dex goes still. "Miles took this out of your purse today. I'm sorry he did, and I'm sorry I looked at it...but every time I think of you doing any of these things with someone else, I want to lose my damn mind."

Dex grabs my hips and turns us to the side and backs me up against the window. "But then I think about all the ways I could do these things with you. All the ways I could make you scream my name. All the ways I want to worship that damn light of yours that you somehow can't see. I fucking live to see your light, Lucie. It's taking over every fiber of my being.

"I know you said you don't want to be with someone who tries to dim your light, or turn it into their own... but that's not what's happening here. Baby, I want yours. I want it so fucking badly, but I know I shouldn't."

All of the breath is knocked out of me as his eyes peer into mine. I can physically see him struggling to hold back.

Not leaning in to make the first move has to be one of the

hardest things I've ever done. I have to let him lead this if it's ever going to work.

I don't want to be Dex's regret or something he blames himself over, but he has to want this—he has to want us enough.

I suck in a small breath as Dex tucks a strand of my hair behind my ear then trails his hand back down my jaw.

"Dex..." I breathe out.

"Tell me we shouldn't do this, Luce. Tell me to stop."

That I won't do. My heart continues to beat out of my chest, but I try to keep my voice as calm as possible. "Dex, I have all the patience in the world, but I'm not going to lie to you. If you want to kiss me, do it when you're ready because I want you just as badly."

"I don't know if I'll be able to stop," Dex whispers as his hands cup my face.

I stare deep into those eyes—the longing is practically written all over his face. He needs something to push him over the edge. I won't make the first move, but if he wants reassurance that I'm just as much in this as he is, I can give him that.

"Then maybe you don't. I trust you, Dex. I like being on your team."

Dex's hands tense against my cheeks, but then he pulls me in close. "Fuck it."

Chapter 29
Dex

Kissing Lucie is my point of no return. There's no denying that every single thread has effectively broken.

Our lips move in tandem with each other. Each pass of my tongue pulls a small whimper out of her. Fuck, is there a way I can bottle up this sound?

One of my hands moves down to the small of her back while the other threads behind her head so I can pin her up against the window and deepen this incredible kiss.

Lucie lifts one leg and hooks it around my hip. I reach for the other leg and lift her the rest of the way up so they both can wrap around my waist.

Her dress bunches up, and I can't help but travel my hands across her smooth skin to grip her ass. "You in fucking yellow, baby. It's quickly becoming my favorite color."

"I'll wear it whenever you want," Lucie pants out as she pulls me back in for a demanding kiss.

"Just know that whenever you do, it's going to end up on the floor of my bedroom." I've got her pinned at just the right angle, and when I press into her deeper, she lets out a muffled moan.

I kiss down Lucie's neck as she tightens her legs around me and starts to rotate her hips. "Please, Dex, give me more."

"I want to give you everything, baby." I kiss back up to her jaw and pepper the kisses slowly. "It's been fucking terrifying."

Lucie's hands find my face, and she brings my eyes to meet hers. "I'm still not afraid of you, Coach. Give it to me. I can take it."

"Fuck, Luce." I give her one more slow kiss before I pull her away from the window, and I carry her back inside to my room. I'm tempted to take her to the couch, but I meant what I said. I want this dress on my bedroom floor.

I want every stitch of clothing off her body and not to be put back on for the rest of the night. I want her sweet jasmine scent to take over my pillows. I want her lying back on my bed completely bare for me, and I want to get every orgasm I can out of her.

I damn near kick my door open at the thought.

When I reach the edge of the mattress, I hold her there for just a moment. "Tell me again that you want this."

Lucie places her delicate hands on either side of my face. "Dex, I want this. And not just for that list either. I told you those things are for me. I want this for us."

For us.

I didn't know how much I needed that to be her answer. I can't say that Lucie feels as strongly about me as I do her, but she doesn't need to. She feels enough for there to be an us to figure out.

I kiss her slow and deep. The manic need I've felt all

these weeks has shifted at the simple word—us. I don't want to rush us.

Lucie's body melts against mine, bringing even more passion to this kiss. Time and reality all seem to slip away in this moment here with her. All the regret I've held disappears because it's brought me to her—I can see that now. I can see with Lucie's light.

I lay her down on the bed, and kiss slowly down her jaw to her neck, down her collarbone and her chest until I'm stopped by the fabric of her dress. Lucie shivers underneath me as her hands go to the back of my head.

"Dex." She lets out a breathy moan.

Fuck, when she says my name like that I want to speed things back up again, but we have plenty of time for that later.

Sliding off the mattress, I pull my shirt off my head, then reach for her dress, but she holds up her hand.

"Wait. I've been dying to see your tattoos." Lucie gets up on her knees and meets me at the edge of the bed. Her fingers lightly trace the lines of the ink on my skin. She starts on my left bicep. Her fingers swirl around the clouds, then around the clock. She looks to me with a silent question about the meaning.

"It has Miles's birth time on it." I reach up to tuck a strand of hair behind her ear and let her continue exploring.

She continues to trace the ink through my chest. "Why the storm?"

"There was a horrible one the night Miles was born."

Her smile grows as she finally lands on the end of the other arm that has the sun peeking out over the edge of the clouds and sunbeams shining down. "This side especially, every time you wear your Blues T-shirts, I can see the ends. And every time I'd wonder what they looked like in a situation just like this one."

I let out an amused huff and my hands graze her thighs. "Now you know how I felt every fucking morning when I'd see you."

"I thought it was when I wore yellow?"

"No, you wearing yellow tested my fucking resolve the most." I grip the hem of her dress and pull it up over her head. "But every single morning—every single interaction I had with you—I thought of how badly I wanted this."

I toss her dress on my floor, then look back at her. Seeing her in this light pink lace bra and thong nearly brings me to my knees. "Fuck, I might have a new favorite color."

Lucie lets out this light, adorable laugh. I've always enjoyed hearing her laugh, but this one, this one nearly makes me come in my shorts.

I pull her face to me and bottle up that laugh with a kiss. Hearing it again will make taking it slow end very quickly.

"Dex," Lucie moans my name again.

I trail one hand down her body to the edge of her underwear. My fingers slide lightly across the hem.

I hadn't meant for it to come off as hesitation, but Lucie being Lucie, she breathes out. "I want this, Dex."

"Fuck, Luce." My hand goes down to her wet slit and I tease at her entrance. "This all for me, baby?"

Lucie's head tilts back for a second, but then she comes back to meet my eyes with a slow nod. "I want you."

The groan I let out is damn near animalistic as I slide one finger in her slowly then curve it in slightly to rub my finger against her wall. Only pulling back a little before doing it again.

"Oh, God," Lucie moans.

Repeating the motion over and over, I can feel her squeeze around my finger.

"No, Luce. You say my name when you come because I'm going to be the one worshiping you."

Chapter 30
Lucie

Dex guides me back on his bed while his lips kiss me with what feels like a perfect tempo to mirror the movements of his finger inside me.

I don't know how to explain it, but when his finger glides slowly down ever so slightly, his lips move slower, and his tongue teases mine playfully. When he slides back in and taps against my G-spot, our kiss feels charged, and he bites at my lip.

After a few times, I feel him add another finger. A small whimper is all I can manage while holding on for dear life with all the sensation Dex is giving me.

I knew he would be great in bed— there wasn't a single doubt in my mind— but this? He's put in two fingers, but I was so close to exploding already by his lips on mine alone.

I moan his name in a plea as I writhe beneath him. "More, please."

Dex leans back on his knees, watching as he works his fingers inside of me. "Fuck, baby. You are extraordinary." Dex reaches for the pillow next to me and gives my G-spot another slow rub until my back arches, so close to the edge when he pulls his fingers out. "Lift your hips for me, Lucie."

My whole body vibrates at the tone and words coming from his mouth. He slides the pillow underneath my hips. I start to lower back down, but his finger circles my clit through my underwear. "Not yet, keep 'em up."

Dex slows his circles as he leans down to place a kiss on one side of my hip and the other.

Oh my gosh, I think I'm on fire. My fingers thread through his curls, and I bring my hips up even higher as my back arches again. "Dex."

I feel the breath of Dex's small chuckle against my skin then his finger drags slowly down over my panties all the way around to squeeze my ass before I feel his fingers grip the hem. "I'm just as desperate for you, baby, but I need to taste this perfect cunt of yours first. What do you say, can I taste you?"

Oh, good God, please.

I nod my head and somehow manage a "yes."

Dex doesn't slide my thong down—no, he rips it. Snaps the fabric like it's nothing. I gasp at the surprise and drop my hips down to the pillow. Before I can even recover from how hot that was, Dex's mouth is on me.

The moan I let out isn't quiet, and Dex hears. "Be loud for me, Luce." His breath against my clit sends shivers up my spine. "Moan louder."

As his tongue flicks over my clit this time, I feel like a bottle rocket just waiting to shoot off. My grip on his hair tightens. "Earn it, Coach."

Dex looks up at me with a wicked glint in his eyes. "Gladly. Now spread your legs wider and let me worship."

I let my knees fall to the side as far as they can as Dex

sucks my clit in between his teeth, not full on biting but enough to send shockwaves radiating through me.

The scream of his name comes fast. Yep—he earned that one.

Dex rolls his tongue lightly now, somehow bringing the same feeling back.

My legs start to shake and my grip on his hair tightens. "Yes, Dex. Yes!"

Dex's groan vibrates against me. "That's my girl."

"Dex, please. More, please, give—" I can't even finish my request before Dex slides his two fingers in my center, curving them slightly like earlier.

He follows the rhythm of his fingers like he did with the kiss. Dex gives slow rolls of his tongue as his fingers slide up and down slightly, but when he taps on my G-spot he sucks my clit with his teeth.

The mirroring of the two sensations is overwhelming. I feel my core tightening and my toes curling. The chant of his name starts loud, but with each rotation, it dies down until I break.

No, break is too simple a word. I shatter. I evaporate into nothing.

Dex lets out a moan of his own as one hand grips my ass to hold me in place as he coaxes me through it.

"Dex..." I breathe out when my high finally plateaus.

"I know, baby." Dex rocks back off the bed and takes off his shorts.

I rise up to my elbows as he pulls down his boxer briefs. "God," I mutter. I knew it felt big after our little run in the hall, but wow, it's perfect.

I move to sit up, but Dex gets back on the bed to lower me back down. "I can see what you're thinking in your eyes,

Luce. Believe me, I want your mouth on my cock too, but fuck—right now..."

Dex trails his lips up my stomach, peppering a few kisses over my breasts before meeting my eyes as he hovers over me.

I understand why missionary can be so great now. I've definitely gotten off to the thought of him, but with him peering down like he wants everything from me? Yeah, I'm done for.

He leans down with a kiss that has me tasting myself. It's slow and purposeful. It might not seem like a desperate kiss, but it's carried out like a promise.

"I'm so fucking desperate to be inside you."

He lines up at my center but doesn't push in. I can practically feel the thought process in his mind.

If we really think about it, and that's exactly what Dex is doing right now—thinking—the start of all of this truthfully came from a defective condom.

"Dex, I'm patient. Nothing will make me change my mind about us tonight." Cupping his face, I give him a soft smile. "I'm also on birth control."

Dex's laugh fills the air between us. God, I love that sound.

"How'd you know exactly what I was thinking, Luce?"

"Well, I mean, you were my favorite baseball player." I laugh next. It should probably feel weird to have these giggles in our current situation, but it doesn't. It just feels natural with him.

Dex leans back in to kiss me until my laugh dies, and I place my hand gently on his shoulder to push him back an inch.

"Like you said, I can see it in your eyes. You've slowly let me in, Dex, I couldn't help but pay attention."

Dex cradles my face in his hands. "Baby, you demanded my attention from the start."

When he leans in for another kiss, he slowly slides in. My breath hitches and my fingers dig into his back.

Okay, so it also feels bigger than it looks. I take a deep breath and adjust my hips.

"That's it, baby, breathe for me. Let me know when you're ready for more."

I hold his eyes as I take another slow breath. "I can take it."

"Yeah, you can, Luce." Dex lets out a low growl and pushes the rest of the way in. "Fuck, you feel so good."

Dex rests at the hilt, not moving yet. As much as I want him to, I also want to live in this feeling with him. It may be too soon to say with certainty where Dex sees this—us—going, but I knew the moment he kissed me on the balcony that I would be the one not able to stop.

Dex cups my face and brings me in for another sensual kiss. His hips match the pacing as he rocks in me with slow yet powerful strokes.

"God, Luce," Dex breathes out. "Tell me how to get you there, I want to come with you."

"Just give me you, Dex. No more holding back."

Dex buries his head in the crook of my neck and lets out a deep groan. "Fuck."

In an instant, he flips us over. He holds me tight to his chest as his thrusts turn from slow and meticulous to thrusts so intense my eyes roll back.

I'm on top, but I'm completely at Dex's mercy. The chants of his name come with many moans and pleas as my orgasm grows.

The buildup almost feels like too much. I swore the first

one was powerful, but I'm not sure if I even have words for how this one feels.

Dex whispers in my ear, "That's it, Luce, come with me."

With a few more strokes, I have to bite down on Dex's shoulder.

"Fuck," Dex huffs and smacks my backside.

Dex holds my body tight against his, grounding me as my orgasm takes off in full force. His thrusts suddenly turn manic, which somehow only spurs my climax on, and with my name on his lips, Dex comes inside me.

When the sensation slows for both of us, I rest my head on his shoulder. Dex runs his fingers over my back lightly as we catch our breath.

"That was incredible," I whisper, trying to even my heart rate.

Dex places a small kiss on the side of my head. "It was."

Finally managing a little bit of muscle strength, I lift my head up to meet Dex's eyes. The smile that comes to my lips is effortless.

Then it really hits me. I just had sex with *Dex Larsen*.

The girly giggle bubbles out of me. "Oh my gosh, we just had sex and it was really, *really* good."

Dex smiles and tucks my hair behind my ear, then brushes behind my shoulder. "Did you ever think you'd fuck your favorite player, Luce?"

My laugh comes again, and Dex rolls me to my back and hovers with a slanted smile.

"You better watch that laugh, baby. It's making my dick hard again."

Chapter 31
Dex

Holy fuck. I mean, really. Holy fuck. That was incredible.

As I hover over Lucie, she looks up at me with this satisfied gleam in her eyes. Her hair is a bit of a mess in the best way possible. She looks thoroughly fucked.

Thoroughly fucked by me.

Her adorable laughter isn't a turn-off in the slightest. I love it. It feels good, actually. There's this level of trust that comes with her laugh, a level of comfort. This might have been our first time, but it also felt like we'd been doing this for years.

It's definitely the start of doing it for years, that's for sure.

Lucie's hands start to slowly scratch my back. "So, did you eat anything today?"

I know she doesn't mean any sort of innuendo, but she really walked right into this one. "I just did, Luce."

"Dex!" Lucie pushes against my chest, but I don't budge. "You know what I mean. Actual food."

"I mean, really—"

"Dex!"

I chuckle. "Yes, they had sandwiches for us after the game."

Lucie gives a small pout. "Oh, good."

"Luce, baby, are you hungry?"

"A little bit, but it's okay—"

I roll off the mattress and pick up my shirt. "Come here."

Lucie sits up, but doesn't move closer. "Dex, really, it's fine. We can just stay here."

I lean down to meet her eyes. "Me and you both know we'll be back here for the rest of the night—but not until you eat."

While Lucie bites at her lip—I'm sure trying to decide if she wants to argue with me—I slide my shirt over her head, then throw on my shorts while she slides her arms through the sleeves.

Finally, she speaks. "We could just—"

I scoop her up from my bed. "Quick snack, Luce, okay?"

Lucie tightens her legs around my waist with a smirk. "If you insist."

Making our way into the kitchen, I sit Lucie down on the island. "Whatcha thinking?"

Her eyes light up. "Popcorn?"

"Popcorn? You really have a thing for stadium food, don't you?"

Lucie scoffs. "Listen, I blame you for this."

"Me?" I go to the cabinet and pull out a bag to pop in the microwave.

"Yes, you. I finally moved on from concession food when Will moved across the country—but then *you* hired me, and now my addiction is back."

I laugh as I toss the pack on the tray, then hit the button

on the microwave. "Guilty pleasure meal is stadium food, got it."

"Another thanks to my siblings." Lucie shifts on the counter, then runs her hands up and down her thighs. "I actually haven't heard from Reagan all week. It's been a little weird."

I walk over to her and let my hands take over. "Have you reached out to her?"

"Kind of. I sent her a picture of that dying plant in your office to see if it was savable, but she never responded. I'm pretty sure the plant has given up hope now."

I look at her sideways. "I have a plant in my office?"

Lucie's mouth gapes with a hint of a smile tugging at the corners. "That poor thing never stood a chance."

"No, it very much did not."

"Well, maybe I'll try to text Rea tomorrow and see if she wants to get it before we leave." Lucie shrugs. "I know I wanted to branch out solo on my own, but I don't know...it's weird not hearing from her. Will said he's talked to her, but he's the caretaker of the group, so he probably forced her to talk to him."

"He's the caretaker?" I ask with a raised brow as the microwave beeps.

While I grab the bag, Lucie hops off the counter to grab a bowl. "Yeah, after our dad left, Will sort of adopted this brotherly-fatherly role. Like, when I was in the eighth grade, I was in the top ten for education. Our school was doing some midday assembly that family members could come to. I knew our mom wouldn't be able to come because she worked so much as an ER nurse, so I didn't even bring it up to her. I was perfectly fine having no one come, it honestly felt like a silly thing to acknowledge in the first place, but after Reagan found out about it, she had to tell Will."

Lucie laughs. "He told his second-period teacher he needed to get something out of the baseball players' locker room, then snuck out the bathroom window, so he could come watch me get a piece of paper that I couldn't even begin to tell you where it is now."

Lucie hops back on the counter with another shrug. "He tries to stick to brother duties for the most part, but Reagan and I always say he's both."

I break open the bag with a little more understanding now. I think all the Andersons may be caretakers in their own way, based on how they grew up. Maybe that's why Lucie has a hard time seeing it.

"Okay, if you tell him this, I'll deny it—but I like your brother."

Lucie's eyes go wide as she gives me a thin-lipped smile.

"I mean it, Luce, I'll deny it."

She finally lets her lips go and scrunches her nose. "Me knowing is enough."

I shake my head as I pour the popcorn into the bowl. "Will's version of caretaking is completely different from yours—I know the least about Reagan, but I can already tell that hers is different. Just because they're also caretakers doesn't mean that you got your personality from them."

Lucie scrunches her nose and picks a couple pieces of popcorn. "I feel like I did."

"You're different, and I have examples to prove it." I step to her, running my hands up and down her thighs again. "Will takes care of monetary things because he has the means to do it. Outside of that, he makes sure things get done and shows up when he's needed. He also has a bit of a hot head at times. It's mellowed over the years, but it's still there when he feels protective."

Lucie smiles and takes a bite of the popcorn. "Okay, and?"

"Reagan, from what I've gathered, is more of a quiet caretaker. She told Will about something that was important to you, because even though you said you would be fine, she knows you deserve more. She didn't sneak out with Will to come to your school thing, but she looks for indirect ways to care for people."

"When did you become so philosophical? Is that what happens in old age?"

My laugh takes me by surprise. *She's got jokes, alright.* "Luce, do you know how many times I told myself I shouldn't date you because of our age difference?"

Lucie scrunches her nose. "Not enough, thank goodness."

I shake my head with another chuckle, and Lucie nudges me as she reaches for some more popcorn.

"We're adults, Dex. Now, go on. You were about to tell me how I'm different from my siblings."

"I don't know if I should tell you. Isn't your whole thing supposed to be about figuring it out yourself?"

"Yeah, but—"

I caress her cheek. "Luce, baby, I see you. I see you so fucking clearly, and I want you to see it for yourself too. If these rules or list, whatever it is, is what you feel like you need right now, then do it." Lucie's eyes dip down for a second, but I tilt her face back up. "I like you, Lucie. I'll gladly take on your light."

Lucie gives me a soft smile. "Thank you."

I let go of her face so she can eat some more of the

popcorn. "So, tell me about the other side of things that you didn't mention in my office."

Lucie chuckles, tossing a piece in her mouth. "What, like you actually expected me to tell you those? Are you kidding? 'Yeah, Dex, I have these safe-for-work ones, then I have these not-safe-for-work ones because Jensen insisted I have spicy ones to do myself. But don't worry, you could do them with me if you want.'"

"I know you're mocking me, but to be fair, I wouldn't have said no." Even if I think we're more than that list.

Lucie's cheeks blush, and I can't help my next question. "So...can I?"

Lucie bites her lip and wraps her arms around my shoulders. "I'm not entirely sure we need that list."

"Oh, no, those are for you, remember? I think we actually just covered that."

Lucie's laugh goes straight to my dick. Fuck, that's going to be a real problem now. "What did I tell you about your laugh?"

"Goodness, can't laugh, can't wear yell—"

Again, she's mocking me, but I grab her chin, cutting off her words. "Never stop. I'm begging you, actually."

Lucie's eyes soften. "Since you're begging, I suppose."

"I am." I lean in for what I intend to be a small kiss, but then my tongue's in her mouth and I don't want to pull away.

Lucie hums happily, and I pull her to the edge of the counter by her knees. "Are you still hungry?"

"Starved." Her arms snake around my shoulders and pull me closer to her.

I kiss down her neck. "So, have you done anything off the list?"

Lucie gives me a soft moan when I kiss the crook of her neck and down her collarbone. "Only one."

"Oh yeah? Which one?"

"I bought a vibrator."

"Have you used it?"

Lucie's breath hitches when I slide my hand up her shirt and palm her tits. "Y-yes."

I roll her hard nipple between my fingers. "And?"

Lucie moans as her body melts from my touch. "It wasn't exactly what I was wanting...but the thought of you helped."

Fucking hell.

I pick her up from the counter and start to walk to her room. I'm praying that Miles hasn't left some random ass toy in the hall because I can't stop kissing her to see where I'm going. The last thing I need right now is to trip over a fucking kid's toy when I'm trying to use an adult one on Lucie.

Thankfully, we make it to her room, and I lay her down on the yellow bedspread. "Fuck, I should have come in here to begin with. Remind me to make an order for new bedding tomorrow."

Lucie's laugh bubbles out of her again, and I swallow it up with my mouth on hers.

"Where's it at?" I ask in between breaths.

"Nightstand, top drawer," Lucie whispers.

Finding the willpower to break away from her comes from the fact that I actually need the toy to use it on her, but damn, kissing her is addicting.

Rifling through the drawer like a madman, I finally pull out a little blue bullet vibrator. "This is all you got, Luce?"

"Hey, I wanted discreet and travel-sized." Lucie snatches it from my hand with a scoff. "Like you said Dex, this is for me."

Lucie slides off the bed with a wicked smile. "Who said you get to use it?"

"Please, baby." My hand covers Lucie's, waiting for her to hand it over, but she doesn't.

Instead, she pushes me a step back, then sinks down to her knees. "It's my thing, remember. You said you'd gladly watch. Maybe that could even be my kink—you watching me. Or maybe it's more dirty talk..."

Lucie hooks her thumbs under my shorts and pulls them down. "You know what, Coach?" Lucie's hand wraps around my cock as she peers up at me. "Why don't you coach me through using my vibrator while I suck you?"

"Fuck, Luce." I reach down and pull my shirt over Lucie's head, then gather her hair back behind her head, pulling it back so she's looking up at me. "Be a good girl and give me that toy."

Lucie's eyes narrow, and I see her grip tighten on the vibrator.

I almost want to tell her that the brat submissive kink isn't for her, but I know that's not what this is about.

"Trust me, Luce. I'll give it back. First, I want you to slide your fingers in that tight pussy of yours and do the same thing I did to you earlier."

The excitement sparks in Lucie's eyes first, then she hands me her vibrator.

"Good girl. Now"—I take the hand she has wrapped around my dick and spit on it before putting it back—"use your hands, Luce."

Lucie's hand slowly starts to work me over as her other slides down to that perfect cunt of hers. Her eyes peer up at me. "Yes, Coach."

I'm so fucked. I'm absolutely fucked.

Lucie's moans start soft. I can tell when she starts to tap on her G-spot because her hand on my shaft nearly stops from her pleasure.

"Yeah, just like that. God, you look so fucking sexy like this."

Lucie opens her mouth, and while my dick hates me for it, I stop her. "I didn't say you could suck me yet. I want to hear how wet you are before I hear you choking on my cock."

Lucie's pout has me on the verge of caving. God, I want her mouth on me so bad, it's killing me, but that's not what this is about.

"Now, slide your fingers out to circle your clit twice then fill yourself again."

Lucie follows my instructions so beautifully. "That's my girl. Again."

"Dex," Lucie pants as her fingers circle her clit.

"Don't come yet, baby." I reach down to play with one of her hard, little pink nipples. Pink really is starting to rival yellow with her.

I click on her little bullet vibrator, and the low hum has that light brightening in her eyes again. "Take your fingers out, Lucie."

She does so slowly, then reaches up for the toy, and she'll get it—but first, I lean down and suck the taste of her off her fingers.

She tastes just as sweet as everything else about her. That bright floral light she just exudes. Hell, she really is addictive.

Lucie's breath catches as I swirl my tongue around the tip of her finger, just like I would if my face were between her legs.

"Dex." Lucie's hand flexes around my cock.

"You taste so good, baby. I couldn't resist." I hand her the buzzing toy, then pull her hair back again. "Do you want to taste me?"

Lucie nods. "Please."

My grip on her hair tightens. "Good, now put that on your clit and open your mouth."

I hold her head back by her hair until I see the toy settle in between her legs, then as she lets out a moan, I slide my dick in her mouth.

"Fuck, Lucie." I knew her mouth would feel incredible, but shit.

Lucie peers up at me with her blue eyes as her head bobs back and forth. "Yes, baby, suck my cock. You're so good at it."

Lucie's moan threatens my willpower. It vibrates around me—like that damn toy she's using.

I gather up her hair in one hand then lean down to play with her tit again. Lucie's other hand still works at my base, and while this is already the best blowjob I've ever had, I kind of want to push her a bit.

"I think you can take more, though, baby. You told me you could take it, didn't you?"

Lucie nods the best she can while my dick's in her mouth. God, she's perfect.

My thrusts stay slow. "If you need a break, take it, Luce. Do you understand?"

I wait for a small nod or muffled yes, but instead, Lucie moves the hand that was at the base of my shaft to play with my balls.

"I'll take that as a yes." My thrusts pick up, and she gags for just a moment, but then she adjusts. "That's my girl. Let me fuck your face."

Lucie peers up at me for a moment, then takes me as deep as she can, before she pauses.

"Fuck, Lucie." I was not expecting that, nor am I ready when her tongue starts to flick mid-shaft before sliding it all the way back up to the tip.

I struggle to stay upright. "Hell, baby, you better be on the verge of coming yourself when you do that again—*shit*—I'll come down your throat next time."

I swear I can see the wicked smile in her eyes. She's killing me—I'm so fucking gone for her already.

"How does it feel to know you have that power over me, Luce?" I let go of her hair just to brush it back again. "How does it feel to know you make me feel more alive than any game I've ever played over my career? That you've had me fucking my hand at the thought of this very moment and now I know I'll never be able to go back?"

Lucie's whimpers grow faster, and her knees slide out slightly on the carpet, her hips moving slightly. She's close too. I can feel it.

"Yes, baby. I can't wait for you to sit on my face, moving your hips ever so slowly just like that. Picture that right now, Luce."

Right as I think Lucie's about to break, she takes me all the way back again and then she fucking comes.

"Fuck," I bark and then I'm done too. I come right down her throat, and she swallows every single drop.

She holds me in her mouth until her climax ebbs. The moment she's off, I scoop her up and fall back onto her bed with her straddled on top of me. She giggles for a moment, and then I lift her up over my head.

"Sit, Luce. Let me clean you up."

"Dex...you don't have to do this again." Her chest rises and falls rapidly, but I still see that excitement in her eyes.

Raising my head, I lick from her pussy to her clit and her legs shake around my shoulders as she fucking sits.

Her hands grip onto the headboard as her head falls back. "Dex, it's too—"

"Don't you dare say it's too much." I slowly circle her clit before backing off again. "We both know you can handle it just fine."

Lucie's hums turn into a low moan as I continue to lick her sweet pussy.

"I guess you did warn me that you might not be able to stop." Lucie's hips start to move just like they did moments ago. "I don't think I want you to ever stop."

My hands grip on to her ass—there is no *think* that fits this feeling with her. There's no stopping. Not this and not us.

Chapter 32
Dex

This might be the first time I've woken up with a damn smile on my face. A naked Lucie, all wrapped up in her yellow sheets, lies next to me, still fast asleep. I check my phone on her nightstand for the time—shit, this is also the first time since Miles was born that I've slept until nine.

I gently slide over to her and wrap her up in my arms. She makes a little satisfied noise as her body molds to mine.

"Good morning." She sighs.

I place a small kiss at the crook of her neck. "Good morning, baby."

Lucie rolls over with a sleepy smile on her face. "Last night was..."

When she trails off, a small pit forms in my stomach that she might finish it with a "one night" situation, but that's not what this is. I want to establish that now.

I cup her face. "Was really great and will continue to be really great."

Lucie's smile grows before snuggling on my chest with a yawn. "Sounds good to me, Coach."

I trace small, inconsistent circles up and down Lucie's side as she tangles her legs around mine.

"What time do we have to get out of this bed?"

Before I can even answer, my phone vibrates on the dresser. I hold one arm around Luce so she doesn't even think to try to pull away while I grab it, but when I see who's calling, I sit straight up. Lucie lets out a little yelp at my full change in position.

"Shit. Kate's FaceTiming me to talk to Miles."

Lucie laughs. "Okay. Your clothes are on the floor. Go talk to Miles. I'm going to freshen up, then start some breakfast."

I let out a small exhale as Lucie rolls out of the bed, seemingly unbothered by my panicked tone. It's not that I'm worried about what anyone else thinks, but I can't exactly answer the phone like this to talk to my five-year-old.

Throwing on my shorts and shirt, I answer the moment I step out into the hall, then walk as quickly as possible away from Lucie's door while it's connecting. If Kate is with Miles, I know she'll be looking around for any signs of what happened between Lucie and me last night.

Not that I care about her thoughts, but Miles is the priority. I have zero clue how to explain to him that I think I could be in love with his nanny when he still gets confused about why his mom doesn't live with us anymore.

"Hi, Daddy," Miles says the moment his face pops up on the screen.

"Hey, bud, good morning." I let out a sigh when I don't see Kate, but then she slides into frame.

"Hey, Dex, took you a while to answer. Surely you weren't still sleeping." Her head tilts to the side, and I can tell her eyes are scanning her screen.

When she realizes I'm in the living room, she leans slightly out of view. The thing with Kate is that this jealousy isn't exactly about me; it's more that she thinks Lucie is excelling in something she didn't.

But based on the way Lucie laughed and smiled—even though I was trying to get out of her room like a bat out of hell—I don't think Lucie sees this as a competition. It'll take some time, but I think Kate will be able to see it too.

I fall back on the couch, and instead of giving Kate's little comment a direct response, I remind her that I am indeed kid-free right now. "How was your night, Miles? Wake up bright and early like usual?"

"Yep," Miles and Kate respond at the same time.

Miles picks up the phone and brings it really close to his face. "I had the craziest dream last night, Daddy. It was wild! So, I dreamed that Pip and Pop grew huge! Like monster truck big, and..."

I nod along as Miles begins to tell me the longest dream I've ever heard. At some point, it definitely felt like he was more wanting to hear himself talk than actually telling me about the dream he had.

"And then Lucie showed up, and she was dressed up like a princess." Miles tilts his head to the side. "Where is Lucie, Daddy?"

I open my mouth to tell him she's in her room, but before I can, Lucie walks into the living room. I can't stop the smile that comes to my face.

Her long blonde hair falls over her shoulders in soft waves—all signs of it being mussed from hands running through it last night are gone. Unfortunately, no longer wearing my clothes, but instead some black leggings and one of her Blues crewnecks.

"She just walked into the living room. Do you want to say hi?"

"Yes, please!" Miles beams.

Lucie chuckles and walks around to lean over into the frame from behind the couch. "Hey, Miles."

"Hi Lucie, do you want to hear about my dream?"

Oh great, we'll be on this phone for hours.

"You know, I would love to Miles, but what about you save it for our plane ride tomorrow? I always get so bored, and I bet your dream is very entertaining."

"Oh, good idea. Maybe Callie will want to listen too. It'll be like story time!"

Lucie laughs. "That sounds perfect. I'm going to make breakfast, so you can finish talking to your dad, okay?"

"Okie, can you give Pip and Pop some strawberries? Tell them it's from me!"

"You know I will. Enjoy your time with your mom."

Miles yells bye to Lucie, Kate pulls the phone back from Miles, and sets it back to where she's in the frame. "She stayed the night?"

Her catty tone thankfully isn't one I think Miles completely understands yet.

"She lives here," I respond, keeping my tone free of any emotion.

"She does, Mommy. Lucie has her own room and everything. Her room is close to mine because she helps take care of me when Daddy's working. What is it that Lucie is again?"

"A nanny," I mutter.

Fuck.

Miles continues on with each word, making my guilt weigh about ten tons.

"Right! Lucie's my nanny. She's also supposed to be my teacher when school starts. She said we'll have lessons and fun experiments. We already have a lot of fun together, but —" Miles's head whips to his mom. "Do you think Lucie can come here with me since you work too? Or you could come to Daddy, and then Lucie can help while you and Daddy work."

Shit. Shit. Shit.

Kate's mouth opens, but she doesn't say anything. She simply looks to me like a deer caught in headlights.

Fuck! I don't know how to respond either, but I know I can't explain again why his mom and dad don't live together anymore over the phone.

"Miles, we'll talk about that more tomorrow, okay?"

"Okay." Miles shrugs.

If we can move on from this topic for now, I can think of ways to explain it better and have a more productive conversation when I'm with him.

But then Kate finally speaks. "Lucie also only works for your dad, Miles. She's his *employee*."

Motherfucker. She said that more for me than anyone.

Miles tilts his head. "What's an employee?"

Kate doesn't miss a beat this time. "That means it's someone your dad pays. He is her boss, and being your nanny is her job as the employee."

Yep, that's fucking helpful. "Okay, well, I need to get ready to head to the stadium. Miles, you can call me before the game, and I'll see you tomorrow, okay?"

"Okay, Daddy." Miles beams. "Have a good game, I love you."

"I love you too, bud." I don't want to give Kate any room to say anything else, so I remind Miles of how much he loves to press that red button. "Why don't you hang up—"

The FaceTime ends abruptly—yep, that's a five-year-old for ya.

I toss my phone to the other side of the couch. Leaning back, I run my hands over my face.

Fuck, how do I approach this? I don't want to fuck this up with her, nor do I want to fuck up my kid any more than I already have.

Walking into the kitchen, Lucie gives me a soft smile as she cuts up some strawberries. "I was thinking of making a yogurt bowl. Do you want one?"

I clear my throat. "Yeah, that's fine."

Lucie walks around the island, and just when I think she's headed for the fridge, she's in front of me and her hands land softly on my face. "Dex, I'm patient. It's one of the few things I'm very sure of about myself."

I let out a small sigh of relief. Of course she knew what I needed to hear. "I like you, Lucie, I need you to know that. I also need you to know that it's not the divorce that gives me pause, it's—"

"It's Miles, and how Miles handled and will continue to handle the divorce. Dex, I'll repeat myself—I'm patient. You telling me how you feel about me...and with last night...it's enough for now. I don't mind finding these moments with you while you navigate this."

God, I'm falling so fucking hard for the nanny.

"Luce?"

She looks up to me with a blush tinting her cheeks. "Yeah?"

"Thank you for telling me to get over myself that night. I like having you on my team." I place a kiss on her forehead.

Lucie's breath catches for a moment. "I like being on your team. Thank you for trusting me to join."

"So someone's in a better mood today." Beck appears next to me on the field with a stupid cocky grin on his face.

I've been in the bullpen helping the guys warm up for the past couple hours, but the moment I stepped on to this field, I should have known the nosy asshole would find me.

Yeah, my mood is definitely better. After our talk in the kitchen and breakfast together on the balcony, I pulled Lucie into the shower with me...then we may have also had a quickie on the couch before I left for the stadium.

If we're working on moments we have together right now, then I'm going to take advantage of them. Lucie may be patient, but that doesn't mean I should let her think there isn't something to be patient for.

"Go away, Beck." I'm trying to come off short, but I fail.

"You know...you really should be nicer to me. Here I am, concerned about your well-being. I walked by the bullpen and saw you actually talking to Jordan, while not looking like you wanted to kill him or yourself. Want to tell me what that's about? Are you sick?"

"That's not the question you want to ask." I laugh.

"Holy shit, you're laughing? I guess I got my answer. Damn it, Tripp and I owe Adam fifty bucks."

I snap my head to him. "What the hell are you talking about?"

Beck gives me that cocky grin. "We might have had a

little pool going on when you would finally get over yourself and be with Lucie."

Adam comes up next with two bats in his hand, then tosses one to Beck. "You got my money?"

You've got to be fucking kidding me.

"You all seriously bet on this?"

"Obviously. I needed one more month of you holding out. Actually, I thought you'd need more time to win over Lucie...she's all happy. You're kind of an asshole sometimes." Beck tosses his bat around mindlessly. "Even though I feel like it's unfair now. I knew Anderson would be fine with it, but I didn't expect him to give his fucking stamp of approval."

Adam gives an arrogant *hmph*. "I may have casually reminded him of how obvious he was in the beginning. Worked like a damn charm. I expect cash from you and Tripp."

Beck scoffs. "Dude, you fucking cheater."

"What the fuck, you guys?" I mutter, pinching the bridge of my nose. "Does Will know you all bet on his sister? He may not care about me, but—"

Adam laughs again. "I'll tell you what. I'll give you the money if you go tell Will that we made a bet about you hooking up with his sister, and it's over now."

Yeah, no, not doing that.

"Yeah, that's what I thought. I'm okay with Callie and Will, but I don't ask fucking questions." Adam puts his helmet on his head. "I'm gonna go hit a few. Daines—cash only."

Beck waves him off, then claps my shoulder. "The one and only time I'm happy I've lost a bet. Don't fuck it up."

"I don't plan to." I can't. I *won't*.

My phone vibrates in my pocket.

LUCIE

It felt too weird not being at the stadium.
I'm going to finish up these turtles for
Miles in your office.

Are you in my office now?

Yeah, is that okay? I can go to Callie's if
you need me to.

Don't you dare.

I start to walk to the dugout so I can go meet her, but then Beck calls for me.

"Hey, Dex, the pitching machine keeps getting jammed. Why don't you come out of retirement for a minute and throw some?"

My knee-jerk reaction is no, but then I think about Lucie watching me from my office. I was her favorite player, right?

"Alright, hold on," I holler back to Beck.

Fucker probably thought I'd say no, but I pull my phone back out.

Bring my chair over by the window if you
want to see your favorite player throw
some pitches.

Chapter 33
Lucie

Well, today just keeps getting better and better. I knew coming to the stadium early was a good idea.

My smile at Dex's text about him throwing some balls was downright cheesy. If he wants to keep playing, I want him to be able to pursue that. Even if it's selfish on my end because I really like watching this man throw some baseballs.

Even if it's just hitting practice, and I can tell he's not actively trying to strike people out—well, except for Beck, Adam, and Tripp. I'm not exactly sure what happened there, but Dex throws hard every time they step up to the plate. It's been quite comical.

By the time I'm finishing the final touches on the first crochet turtle, Dex starts rolling his left shoulder. I reach for the second kit and start on it as he continues throwing.

I could actually be getting the hang of this. Will it be a hobby I continue? Probably not, but I think Miles will love it —and that's all that matters.

I make some good progress by the time Dex starts to full on stretch his arm. Someone might be a little out of practice.

I watch as he tosses a ball off to my brother to take over, but before he walks off the mound, he looks up toward me and winks. I'm not entirely sure if he can see me up here or if these are tinted windows, but I wave anyway.

When I see him disappear into the dugout, my heart rate kicks up. I really hope he's coming up here. I didn't necessarily want to be a distraction for him today, but I also couldn't sit in that penthouse without him there for a minute longer.

I make a few more passes on the turtle before I hear the office door open. I spin around in his chair to find Dex absolutely beaming.

This man. I swear, if I can't talk him into playing again, I might just ask Olsson to draw up a contract and I'll forge his signature myself.

I put on my best fan girl voice. "Oh my gosh, it's *the* Dex Larsen. Pitcher for—"

Dex cuts me off the moment he reaches me, his hands threading through my hair, and gives me a lustful kiss that sends shockwaves through my body.

When he pulls back, he rests his forehead on mine.

"Looks like you still have some of it left in ya, Coach."

Dex chuckles softly, then scoops me up from the chair and promptly sits back down with me in his lap.

"I think that was another crack at our age difference."

"What? *Me?* No. What age difference?"

Dex shakes his head as a smirk tugs at the corners of his mouth. "You still working on these for Miles?"

"Yep." I reach over to my canvas bag of stuff and Dex's grip tightens instinctively so I don't roll out of his lap as I grab the one I finished. "Ta-da!"

"Hey, it actually looks like something now." Dex takes it from my hand to look closer at it. "So, is this Pip or Pop?"

"Considering I bought two of the exact same turtles, I figured they'll get mixed up anyway."

Dex kisses my head. "He's going to love them. Thank you for thinking of him."

"He's too cute not to think of," I say, taking the turtle back and setting it back in the bag. "Who knows, maybe this will keep my actual turtles alive in their tank and not thousands of feet in the air on a plane full of baseball players."

Dex shakes his head. "You and those fucking turtles. I can't believe I caved on those things."

I snort. "I asked nicely. It works every time."

"No, baby, you could have demanded to bring those things and I would have said okay. You could have said you're bringing a circus, and I would have said there's room. I would only be saying no in my head." Dex leans in to whisper in my ear. "But what would come out would be 'anything you want.'"

I giggle at the feel of his words so close, but the moment Dex hears my laugh, he cups my face and kisses right where he just whispered. "Fuck, that laugh."

A blush comes to my cheeks as he lets my face go. "And here I was, thinking you were this prickly man who didn't want to hire me."

"Oh, I didn't, but not for the reason you're thinking." Dex tucks a strand of hair behind my ear. "Hey, I actually have something to run by you."

At the change in Dex's tone, I clip my last loop and set down the unfinished turtle to give him my full attention. "What's up?"

"So, when I dropped off Miles, Kate mentioned that she

would be in New York this weekend and wants to come to one of the games to spend more time with Miles. The thing is, she wants to come for the whole day. I told her you're the person in charge of him, you know how it is on game days and the schedule of everything."

"Oh, Dex..." I bet that went over well.

"I know, I told her we'd talk about it because I don't want to keep Miles from his mom, but I have to set boundaries somewhere. That was her whole thing to begin with. She still has Miles call at the scheduled times, but I'm supposed to bend whenever she wants me to?"

I place my hand lightly on his chest and feel his heart beating fast. "Dex, it's okay. You're doing what you think is right. I'm assuming, since you're bringing this up, that she does actually want to come to one of the games?"

"Yeah, on my way up here, she sent a text saying she wants me to pick Miles up after breakfast tomorrow and that she wants one game with him this weekend." Dex exhales. "I want to be flexible when it benefits Miles, but I also don't want to allow a break in the boundary I set with you being in charge when it's not legally one of her times to begin with."

Dex runs his hand lightly on my thigh. "I'm sorry, I didn't mean to put you in this situation, Lucie. If you're uncomfortable with it, please tell me. I'll take care of it."

"This might sound really weird to hear, but in a way, I kind of need to be a teammate to Kate too. Us aside—"

"No, not us aside," Dex interrupts, and while it's a sweet gesture, there's more to it than us—there's no other way for me to look at it.

"Not entirely what I meant. Look, Dex, Kate's a part of your team whether either of you likes it or not. Actually, scratch that—we're all on Miles's team. I can spend the day with Kate and try to find the balance of not overstepping her role on this team and still keeping your boundaries. Will it be awkward? Probably, but you also walked in on me juggling on my first day. I don't think I've ever felt more awkward in my life than at that moment."

Dex shakes his head with a small laugh. I know this is hard for him, and just as he thinks he's figuring out a good routine with Miles, it shifts.

"Miles is the priority here, Dex. You know that, I know that. I believe that Kate knows it too."

Dex cups my face. "You're incredible."

I shrug. "What was incredible was watching you pitch again."

Dex rolls his eyes playfully. I knew he enjoyed it. He just needs a few nudges, and I think I could talk him into it.

"Any reason you threw harder for Beck, Tripp, and Adam? I didn't think the purpose of batting practice was to strike them out necessarily."

"Eh, they made a stupid bet. They all owe me fifty bucks now."

"Aren't you all, oh, what's that word again? Rich? Millionaires?"

"Yep." Dex places a kiss on my forehead. "They started it."

I shake my head. "Boys."

Dex and I spend the next hour watching as warm-ups change from the Blues to Baltimore's team. I work on Miles's last turtle and I swear I'm never doing this again. Dex gets a good laugh every time I miscount my stitches and nearly scream in frustration.

By the time I finish the body, Dex has to head out for his meeting with Olsson.

"You going to stay here for a little bit longer?" Dex asks as he stands us both up.

I set all of my stuff back in my canvas bag. "I think I'll go find Callie, maybe walk around with her for a bit."

"Okay, Luce, after you." Dex motions for me to head out first, but then his hand catches my arm. "Shit, hold on."

"What's up, Coach?" I chuckle at his abrupt change, but Dex doesn't say anything, he simply reaches for his duffle bag on the floor and pulls out his hat from last season—*his* last season.

Yesterday, when he gave me his hat to wear, it felt tense. Even though I know now why it was tense. This time, he's looking at me like it means something to him. Which is good because this means a lot to me.

Dex places his hat on my head gently, then softly brushes my hair to my back and slides his hands slowly down, causing chills to pop up on my arms.

He lets out a small exhale. "That's better."

My heart nearly explodes, considering I snarkily asked him yesterday if he was better after I put on his hat, and he told me no.

I can feel the blush coming to my cheeks. "Yeah, it is."

I agreed to moments with Dex because I think he'll be worth the wait. I don't need him to make all these big declarations, and, yeah, I love the grand gestures, but these small ones seem to pack a pretty good punch too.

Dex's eyes slowly trail down to my lips.

I'm not entirely sure what it is, but I need him to kiss me. I should probably be tapped out on make outs and orgasms with him for at least a little bit...but I'm not. I want more.

Dex must clearly feel the same as he snakes one arm through to the small of my back, pulling me to him while his other hand threads through my hair, knocking the hat he just placed on my head to the floor before claiming my lips with his.

I wrap my arms around his shoulders with a pleased hum as I lean my body deeper into his. Dex's hands find the back of my thighs, picking me up and setting me down right on top of his desk.

This kiss is more manic than it has been. Something about it feels so demanding, yet desperate at the same time. I don't even think I need more than this—I just need this kiss to keep going.

Dex pulls my hips to the edge of the desk, then grinds his hard length against me. Yep, our clothes can stay on if they have to. I have no doubt in my mind that Dex can make me come from a serious dry hump and make out sesh.

My hands slide under his shirt, feeling every muscle from his incredible abs to his chest. My fingers glide over his nipples, and I can feel the shiver radiate through him. Dex moans deep against my mouth. "You're going to be the death of me, baby."

He yanks my body impossibly closer, grinding against me harder. Our kiss loses the small shred of rhythm we had. It's messy, yet so hot. I start to roll my hips with Dex's thrusts. It doesn't matter that our pants separate us. I'm seconds away, and I know Dex is too.

My hands slide around to his chest again as Dex grabs a fistful of my hair.

"Oh, shit," a woman's voice cuts through the moment, and our bodies go rigid.

Wait, I know that voice.

Chapter 34
Lucie

Dex pulls back from our kiss to turn his head, but doesn't step away. "We're a little busy—"

I lean around him and, much to my horror, see my sister standing at his door. "Reagan? What are you doing here?"

Dex whips his head to me as he processes that he just tried to tell my sister to leave because he wanted to finish our dry hump session. "Reagan...like?"

"Like, her sister," Reagan finishes for him.

Dex gives me a small look as he lifts me off his desk to stand me back up. "Not the first impression I wanted to make," he whispers in my ear.

When I let out a small giggle, Dex kisses my temple as if he just can't help himself any time I laugh. It's really sweet actually.

Reagan cuts through our moment again. "Well, I just thought I'd come grab that plant you sent me a picture of earlier this week. I want to get out of here before traffic gets bad."

She's here for the plant...*She's here for the plant?!*

She hasn't talked to me all week, and yet she somehow manages to find me mid-makeout with Dex—because she wants his dying plant?

My spine snaps up—I'm finding my backbone today apparently. "Well, maybe answering my text would have been a better way to go about that, Rea. What were you going to do? Just take it out of his office without saying anything?"

"Maybe." Reagan shrugs. "It would have been nice if you brought it to me instead."

She has got to be joking right now. "You never even responded to my text about it! Why would I bring it to you?"

Reagan flinches back at my tone. "What's your problem? You're the one who's made time to see Jensen this week and not me."

"Yeah, Jensen actually answers my texts."

The room goes deadly silent, and the sister tension is so very thick.

Dex clears his throat as he places his hand on the small of my back. "Why don't I give you two a minute?"

I give him a small nod and whisper, "Thank you."

"I'll be in my meeting, but text me if you need me." He kisses my temple again, then gives Reagan a curt nod as he walks past.

With the click of his office door, Reagan crosses her arms over her chest. "Well, I can say I definitely didn't expect to walk in on that little pregame."

I sigh. "What's that supposed to mean, Rea?"

"I'm just saying, as your older sister, I'm surprised that you are now dating your boss. Plus, didn't you say he was super standoffish at the beginning of all this? I mean, good for you if the sex is good, but keep your expectations low, Luce. This could just be a convenience thing for him."

She's not serious, she can't be.

"You came here, not to see me, but to steal a plant, act like it's completely my fault for also not seeing you, then you throw a backhanded comment like that?"

Reagan waves her hand. "That's not what I meant to do, but come on, Luce—have you really thought this through? He was divorced, what, seven months ago? Seven months to his nearly five-year marriage. Not to mention the marriage that includes their child...who you nanny and are supposed to start homeschooling."

Okay, I get how Dex's divorce seems like it could be an issue from her perspective, but with what Dex has told me actually happened between him and Kate, I don't feel like I'm this rebound or means to make her jealous. Granted, I can't tell her any of that. Dex told me that in confidence, and I won't betray that.

"Rea, don't you think that if Dex wasn't a good fit for me, that Will would have said something?"

Reagan snorts a sarcastic laugh. "Will's got rose-colored glasses now that he's with Callie. He's still in that *blinded-by-love* phase. Does he even know about you two?"

Shoot, I can't say with confidence that he does. I mean, everything is so new between us, but I still think Will would have said something. He's bound to at least be suspicious.

Will's never even mentioned anything bad about Dex ever actually. Boss or potential boyfriend, Will would have said something to me if he thought I was getting into something messy.

"That's not the point—"

"It is the point, actually," Reagan huffs. "Listen, I'm

saying this as your older sister, as the person who has always looked out for you. Sweet angel sister Lucie sometimes doesn't see the full picture, so it's my job to do that for you. If Dex is actually serious about you, then great, I'd love that for you. But maybe you should also consider that you could be just a fling. Don't get me wrong, there's nothing wrong with being a fling when feelings aren't involved, but you and I know that's already off the table for you."

Rage rolls through and out of my body. I could argue until I'm blue in the face, but it won't change the words she's already said.

"Just take the plant, okay? I don't really want to talk about this with you if you're not even going to listen to me."

Reagan shrugs, then walks around to look out Dex's window. "This view is awesome."

"Reagan, seriously!" Okay, rage coming back.

Reagan doesn't flinch or even change her casual tone. She looks completely uninterested in hearing anything I have to say, and that's what's hurting me the most.

"Look, I really don't mean to be harsh, but I'm just looking out for you, Luce. We aren't glued to each other's hips anymore, but I'm still your older sister. If I can't tell you the things you don't want to hear, then who can?"

I scoff a breath. "Yeah, well, you're wrong."

Reagan finally steps back to me and rests her hands on my shoulders. "Maybe I am, but I also can't help but think that this is why you've been avoiding me. You knew I'd see your feelings even though you know it could end badly and that I would point them out."

I step back from her touch. "We just started this thing between us *last night*. Maybe you're just being pessimistic."

Reagan snorts. "Considering you just called it a 'thing'

instead of clear terminology tells me enough already. You also didn't develop these feelings overnight. I can't tell you to be cautious if I don't see it for myself."

"Let's not forget that you were the one who ditched me all week before I took this job, and it was you who didn't return my text."

Reagan folds her lips together. "I've been busy. You know that."

You know what, egging this on will get me nowhere. "Just take the plant, Reagan."

Reagan sighs. "I'm just looking out for you, Lucie. You know I love you, and I don't want to see you lose the job you were excited for and get your heart broken at the same time."

Her words cut through my chest. I see that point. I really do appreciate her wanting to look out for me, but her execution could have been so much better. "Thanks, I love you too, but in all fairness, just take the plant and go. Please."

Reagan nods and turns to grab the pathetic little plant that looks about how I feel right now, then leaves without another word.

When the door clicks, my sanity snaps. I want to be angry at her and tell her she's wrong about everything she said. I want to cry a little because I hate that, while I don't like her words, could there possibly be any merit to them?

No, she's wrong. I'm not a rebound or a fling. Granted, I don't know entirely what I am. Part of me wants to walk right up to Dex and ask him straight up, "What are we, exactly?"

But we literally started this last night. I told him I could be patient. This has been my whole thing to begin with, letting Dex lead. Letting Reagan's words affect me this much isn't fair when I have no real reasons to believe her words either.

I'm patient, but not a pushover. Just because I don't feel like I need to get an answer out of Dex right now, doesn't mean I won't ever ask him.

I take deep breaths before walking back over to Dex's office chair. There's no way I can walk around now, I'm too worked up to talk to anyone.

I reach for my canvas bag. Maybe finishing this turtle for Miles will help. It forces me to focus on something instead of Reagan's words bouncing through my mind. Not to mention, it reminds me of the sole reason Dex and I are taking this one step at a time to begin with. *Miles.*

Growing up, our mom always said she never introduced us to any dates she went on because they were never serious. She never wanted to bring someone into our lives who wasn't even thinking about staying.

I knew this would be complicated. I'm already so entangled in Miles's life. I need to take it one step at a time. I can't say how Miles would feel about me dating his dad. I have to trust that Dex knows the best way to handle this, because I am serious. I'm serious about both of them.

I get my stuff set back up and start my first loop when there's a knock at the door. I swear, I won't be able to handle another round with Reagan, and honestly, I'd prefer it not to be Dex either, with my brain feeling all twisted.

"Hey, Luce, can I come in?" Will's voice comes from behind me.

I spin around in the chair to find him standing in the doorway. I have to blink my eyes a lot because my immediate reaction is to cry. I don't know why—it's the dad-effect, I guess. That safe feeling of knowing I can cry and he won't judge me.

But *I'm* judging me. It takes quite a lot of willpower, but I swallow down enough emotion to speak. "You can come in, but don't you dare hug me. I don't want to cry."

Will chuckles before stepping in and closing the door behind him. "You know, when Dex texted me asking to come check on you, I wasn't entirely sure what to expect. But I did not think I'd find a grandma. Are you knitting?"

"I'm crocheting for Miles. I will never do this again." I can't form a full laugh yet, but a smile threatens my lips for a moment. "Dex texted you?"

"Yep, he said Reagan showed up, and I might want to come check on you." Will picks up one of the small chairs and brings it around to the window. "Want to talk about it?"

"Reagan..." I exhale. I don't know what to even say to him about what happened. Frankly, I'm a little worried that Will might have the same opinions as her—two sibling lectures back to back, I can't handle. "It was fine. I just haven't seen her all week, that's all."

"Phew, lying to me...that bad, huh?" When I can't bring myself to answer, let alone look at him, he curses. "Don't get mad, but I told Rea to give you some space."

My needle falls. I don't even care how it will mess me up later. "What? Why?"

Will gives me a pointed look. "I think the answer comes from you actually telling me why you're upset at her. I know it's not about her not texting you back. That might be part of it, but she had opinions about you and Dex, didn't she?"

"H-how do you know about me and Dex?" I figured he did, but to go as far as telling Reagan not to message me... what is going on?

"How did you and Reagan know I liked Callie?"

Oh, dang, was I really *that* obvious?

Will leans back in the chair. "I could tell he liked you the day you moved in, but I told you I wasn't asking questions, so I just watched."

"He wasn't even that nice to me in the first week of hiring."

Will shrugs. "And I avoided Callie for a whole month. Sorry, sis, but the tables have turned. You were less obvious than Dex was, I'll give you that."

I attempt an amused *hmph*. "You're being a lot nicer than Reagan was about me potentially dating *your* coach."

Will laughs. "And now you know why I asked her to give you some space."

"Not really. Part of me sees the logic, but I don't understand. She knew I had always enjoyed watching him play and...stuff." Hmm, maybe I don't tell my brother that I've always been attracted to Dex.

Will shakes his head. "Do you remember your sophomore year when Miller Richardson asked you to the homecoming dance?"

I look at him sideways. "Yeah? He also stood me up at the last minute, and you raced me across town so I could meet up with my friends."

"Yeah, well, Reagan told him he wasn't taking you because she knew he was actually still seeing a girl in the next town over."

Oh, *that* I didn't know. I blink as I try to wrap my head around this. "Why tell him not to take me instead of telling me that? We could have actually made a plan instead of—" I stop with a deep exhale. I'm getting too worked up over a high school dance.

"Yeah, take another deep breath. You'll need it." Will shakes my leg. "That was the first of many guys Reagan ran off."

"What? You mean she's done this to me multiple times? Talking to the guys instead of just telling me about it?"

"The latest was that teacher you were talking to. Yeah, he came to Reagan's shop to buy his wife some flowers." Will gives me a slanted smile. "She had good reasons, Luce. I get that it's frustrating, but her heart is always in the right place."

Oh my gosh. Every random ghosting or numbers I've had disappear from my phone makes sense. "I can't believe this. She's been doing this for years?"

Will winces. "You could just look at it as dodged bullets."

My heart sinks a bit. In a way, I could see her doing this on a couple of occasions, but this feels like crossing a line. "Just because it was a bullet dodged doesn't mean it shouldn't have been a lesson learned, Will."

"I agree." Will holds up his hands. "I told her many times to stop, but she just wants to protect you, Luce. I know it's hard to see, and her methods aren't always the softest. When I asked her to keep her distance, I told her that there was nothing to run off this time."

"I don't think she completely agrees with you," I huff out. "She definitely let me know she has doubts."

Will squeezes my knee. "Not exactly. This is the first time she's actually said something to you about it. She usually intimidates the guys or threatens their livelihoods to get them to back off."

I look at Will with a face that I can't decide is horrified or amused at the thought of her threatening who knows how many guys. "Make it stop, this is too much for me to take in."

Will laughs. "This time, she told *you* because I think she knows there's no scaring Dex. She knows I wouldn't come to her and say 'let them figure it out' without any reasoning behind it. She can't help herself—she wants you to be happy, Luce. She just has a little bit of an overbearing way of showing it. I don't know what warnings she gave you exactly, but it was her best attempt at letting you do this relationship on your own while trying to prepare you for any downfalls."

I take another deep breath and let some of the weight Reagan's words placed on my shoulders roll off. "I know Dex and I are still figuring things out. There's no guarantee we will work out, given the stakes of the situation. I want Dex to keep Miles at the forefront here, but I deserve to be able to figure this out on my own. If I get hurt, then so be it."

"I agree." Will pushes back to his feet. "Give it some time to cool off. You deserve a chance to figure this out on your own, Luce. But if you need me or Rea, we're always here."

"Thanks, Will." Dang it. Tears threaten again, but I force them down. "Still don't hug me, I want to be strong."

"Okay." Will pats my head with a laugh. "I have to finish getting ready for the game. Take it one day at a time. It'll work out how it needs to."

I look up to my older brother, the dad of our family, whether he wants to be or not. "I know I don't need your blessing, but—"

"That's right, you don't," Will cuts me off. "Lucie, do you like Dex?"

"Yes," I answer him immediately.

"Are you happy?"

"Yes."

Will smiles. "Okay, that's all that matters."

With a squeeze to my shoulder, Will heads out to get ready for the game. I exhale in this new silence, letting everything Will said process in my brain. I can't entirely decide how I feel about Reagan right now, but Will's right, I don't need anyone's blessing here.

With this newfound clarity, I get back to work on the last turtle and nearly finish it when I realize the game's starting. I know Dex wouldn't mind if I watched the game from his office, and part of me is tempted to, but I like being in the stands for the games. Plus, I get a better view of Dex. Even if he's not playing, the baseball pants work—no matter the context.

Tying off the last piece of the head, I put everything back in my canvas bag and head down to Dex's reserved seats.

The moment my butt hits the hot plastic I feel Dex's eyes on me. I'm sure Will told him I was fine after our little talk, but I give him a reassuring smile to affirm I'm okay. He sends a smirk my way before disappearing back into the dugout.

I let that smile of his put everything Reagan said in a box and shove it to the back of my brain. Will's right, everything will work out how it needs to. I can hear her warnings, but I don't have to listen to them.

As the game starts, I do my best to pay attention, but my eyes tend to wander over to the dugout for a specific coach to step back into view.

With another glance back, I notice Callie pointing her camera my way. I send her a confused look. I reach for my phone to text her, but then a shadow falls over me.

"I think you forgot something, baby." Dex stands over me with that same smirk he gave me earlier.

The crowd starts to whistle and yell louder as the jumbotron shows Dex standing over me in the crowd.

"Dex? What are you doing?" My nervous laughter comes out soft, and I swear my hands start to shake. There's now a whole lot of attention on us, not to mention, this is a televised game.

"You wear my hat to games, Luce." Dex kneels beside me as he places his hat on my head. "My girl wears my hat, got it?"

I have to be blushing so hard right now. "Got it, Coach."

Chapter 35
Dex

Monday: Boston Blues at Detroit Cubs

> I think our real turtles are safe now.

LUCE

> I know I said I would never crochet again,
> but Miles loving them makes me want to
> keep going.

> How about I buy already made ones and
> we tell him you did it?

LUCE

> Noo, that ruins the love part of it, Dex.

> I think you hating it takes the love part out
> of it, baby.

LUCE

> Some sacrifices must be made for Miles.

> Believe me, I know.

Tuesday: Boston Blues at Detroit Cubs

They're just baseball players

CALLIE

Can we still play the escaping bitchiness game? Shannon's in fine form.

LUCE

That's not the legal name of the game, Cals.

BECK

Count me in, Callie Bear. Come to the locker room and we'll hide out.

WILL

My arm is feeling out of sorts. Should a ball go a little sideways toward Shannon or Beck at warm-ups… it was an accident.

BECK

Me?! What did I do?

CALLIE

You know he doesn't like your nicknames.

WILL

Or how about you telling MY girlfriend to come to the locker room with you.

ADAM

Why is there a stuffed turtle in my catcher's bag?

LUCE

OMG, I've been trying to get Miles to remember where he put it down for hours.

Didn't I leave this group chat?

Wednesday: Boston Blues at Detroit Cubs

I think you packed this yellow dress just to torture me.

LUCE

Who? Me? I would never do such a thing.

Is it working?

Send Miles with Callie for a bit. I want to see that dress on the floor of the first room I can find with a lock.

LUCE

Yes, Coach.

Thursday: Boston Blues at Detroit Cubs

KATE

I've cleared my schedule for Saturday's game. What time can I meet you at the stadium?

You can meet Lucie and Miles at the gate at noon. The game doesn't start until two though. Up to you.

KATE

Just so I can mentally prepare myself, will you be making your way into the crowd at this game too? Or will you put your hat on Lucie earlier?

Not entertaining this.

KATE

I didn't think you'd be the cliché.

Guilty.

Friday: Boston Blues at New York Crimsons

They're just baseball players

TRIPP

So… fighting this game?

CALLIE

Ugh, trauma warning would have been nice.

BECK

We fight for honor, Callie Bear.

WILL

Dex, how much trouble will I get in if I hit Beck?

No broken bones, no consequences.

BECK

This isn't fair. Of course he's going to let you do whatever, he's dating your sister!

TRIPP

Does anyone else have any other sisters?

ADAM

No, we're actually all grateful that none of our sisters picked you.

TRIPP

Ouch. What about that Jensen girl? What about her?

BECK

In your fucking dreams.

LUCE

Someone replied awfully fast. Care to elaborate on that, Beck?

BECK

In your fucking dreams, Luce.

Don't call her Luce. Don't cuss at her either.

ADAM

Lucie, the turtle is back in my catcher's bag.

LUCE

Alright, you're my first text now when one goes missing. I've been looking for hours!

Chapter 36
Lucie

"Lucie, I can't wait for you to meet Mommy. We're going to have such a fun day!" Miles bounces in front of me with nothing but pure joy on his face.

I, however, am trying not to panic. I know I told Dex I could handle this—and I can—but as I'm standing here waiting on Dex's ex-wife, my anxiety is really kicking in.

Dex mentioned that she knows about us. Apparently, Dex putting his hat on my head during the game was a little more newsworthy than either of us really anticipated. It got back around to Kate, thankfully after Miles left.

He's still blissfully unaware about me and Dex. It helps in a way. I don't feel like a secret fling at all when Dex is perfectly fine letting everyone else know we're together. It's simply navigating Miles. I love this kid so much it hurts. If I have to wait to tell him that I'm falling in love with his dad for his benefit, then that's perfectly fine with me.

I look at my phone to check the time and find a text from Dex.

FAV PLAYER

> Please come get me if you need me, Luce.

> Doubting me already?

> Never, baby.

Dex gave me another chance to back out of this, and for a moment, I considered it. I'm not sure what Kate will throw my way today, but if Dex and I are ever going to work, I know I have to make it work with Kate too. I can't say she'll like me— she doesn't have to— we just need common ground.

I'm more than capable of swallowing some pride. I did it plenty as a teacher with overbearing parents, I can do it here.

My game plan is simple: be the nanny. I've been "in charge" of Miles while Dex is around. I'll keep Kate in consideration as the parent, but really, Miles and I have these days down pat. I can handle the little things, but if something major comes up, I can give Kate the opportunity to handle it.

Miles squeals. "Mommy!"

Now I prepped myself all week for how beautiful I knew Kate had to be—I was very much right. She has flawless olive skin, long brown hair, and even without the heels she's wearing, I'm sure she's at least a couple of inches taller than me.

Miles races to wrap his little arms around her waist, and she chuckles, leaning over to hug him back. "Hey, baby. I'm so happy to see you."

Okay, deep breaths. I've got this. "Hi, I'm Lucie."

I hold out my hand for a shake. For a moment, Kate just looks at it, but with a quick glance down at Miles, she caves. "Kate."

"We're going to have the best day ever!" Miles giggles. "I was thinking we could play 'Escaping Grumpiness' and get hotdogs. Oh! Can I get mustard on my hotdog?"

Not every food venture has stuck with Miles, but I consider the condiments he now likes on hotdogs as my biggest accomplishment.

"Yeah, I think we can get some mustard for you, bud."

Kate huffs a small laugh. "And what's 'Escaping Grumpiness?' Is that what you call hiding from your father?"

Don't answer, Luce, it's a trap.

Miles shakes his head. "No, silly Mommy. It's hiding from Shannon. She's always grumpy."

Kate raises her eyebrows as she looks at me and says with a whisper, "So, grumpy is code for bitchy, yes?"

Okay, common ground topic. "You guessed it."

Miles grabs hold of each of our hands and pulls. "Come on, let's get going."

I laugh. "And what exactly are you wanting to do first?"

Miles drops our hands and looks up to the ceiling as he thinks. "Is it time for warm-ups?"

I check the time again. "Batting practice should be starting. Do you want to shag some balls?"

"Yes!" Miles's eyes go wide. "And maybe Mommy can meet Callie!"

"Oh, I must meet the girl you claim you're going to marry." Kate's excitement holds what sounds a bit like condescension, but we're swallowing it all down.

"Alright, Miles, do you remember how to get to the door that leads to the field?"

"Yes!" He nods, then scrunches his nose. "Will you tell me if I go the wrong way?"

I laugh. "Yes, I'll tell you if we start going the wrong way."

Kate and I walk in silence. Our eyes focused on Miles as he skips down the hall. Kate's heels click just like Shannon's, but they sound different in a way. Maybe just because I know Shannon, they come off annoying, but with Kate, I swear they sound different. Her heels sound like power. I know that might sound crazy, but it's the first thing I think of.

Dex mentioned that she's a lawyer, and from what I've stalked, a pretty good one too. Her appearance is intimidating, while still gorgeous. I'd hire her, that's for sure.

"I'm sure you won't be surprised when I tell you that this wasn't how I wanted today to go." Kate keeps her voice low. "Did Dex tell you I wanted time with just Miles or both of them?"

My mouth goes bone dry. "Um, Miles."

Kate gives me a slow nod. "I thought he might've."

Does that mean she wanted to see Dex today too? I'm assuming he told her no, considering I'm the one walking around with her today. I'm not entirely sure how I feel about that...I mean, he didn't tell me that she mentioned adding him into this mix, but okay, let's not overthink this.

"Look, I'm just the nanny for today. As weird as it sounds, just think of me that way."

Kate huffs an amused breath. "Does that mean I can fire you?"

I press my lips in a thin line. "Well—"

"Yeah, I know." Kate gives what barely qualifies as a half-smile. "You're also not just the nanny, though. Seems like you're also a teacher and something more from what I can tell."

"Uhh, yeah..." I trail off as Miles skips right past the stairs. "Hey, Miles, down this way."

He skids to a stop. "Oh, oopsies."

Miles races back to us and down the stairs. "Handrail, please," I say on instinct, then snap my mouth shut. Maybe I should have let Kate take that one. I don't know, she's hard to read—just like Dex.

Oh my goodness, did they not work out because they are kind of the same person? Tough, hard-working, attention-demanding presence, and getting emotions out of them is like pulling teeth. This is probably a revelation I should keep to myself.

I let him get a few good stairs in between us before I speak again. Keeping the focus on Miles was my tactic with Dex, maybe it will work here too.

"So, for school, we've started the process of getting it approved with the school district. I'll submit a home-schooling plan to them over the next couple of weeks. As long as that gets approved, we should be good to start after that."

Kate raises an eyebrow. "Can I see the plan?"

My mouth opens with what I think I'm going to say is "yes", but then snaps shut. Is this something I need to ask Dex about first? Then again, we're all Team Miles, right?

"I'm sure we can work something out."

Kate hums. I'm sure it's a *yeah, right* kind of hum, but there's nothing I can do about it at this moment other than what I've just offered.

The rest of our walk down to the field is in silence. Thick, awkward, painful silence.

My anxiety only gets greater the closer we get to the field. If Dex is out here, I'm not entirely sure how things will play out. I'm not here to stand in between them being parents, but this gray area of what Dex and I are feels like it makes things...complicated.

Kate's words replay in my mind. She wanted time with Dex today too? Or was that just a way to get a rise out of me? If I were Reagan in this situation, I'm sure a comment like that would have definitely started some sort of competition of undermining each other.

The thought of Reagan threatens to pull that locked box out of the back of my head. Maybe that's why I even thought of her to begin with. Dang subconscious is spiraling right now because I've never really dealt with this type of cattiness to begin with. Reagan dealt with those passive aggressive, mean girls growing up—and apparently the douche bags too. I just didn't know about that.

The thing is, it's not in me to compete with Kate; there's no point. She's Miles's mom, Dex's ex-wife. Those are facts I can't change.

I'm not sure what the true reason is for Kate wanting to come today—whether it's actually for Miles or some sort of excuse to be around Dex, but a heads-up would have been nice. Maybe agreeing to this wasn't my smartest decision. I can swallow my pride, but I don't think I'm cut out for head games if that's the tactic she's using.

Walking out to the field, Miles jumps on the first person he sees. "Beck! Can I come catch balls with you?"

Beck holds out his hand for a high five that's raised slightly too tall for Miles to reach without jumping. "Hell yeah."

"Beck." My correction comes out on instinct again. Crap, maybe she does think I'm competing with her. Ugh, I'm definitely overthinking all of this now.

Beck scoops Miles up and places him on his shoulders. "Hey, Luce," he says, giving me a warm smile, then a curt nod to Kate. "Kate."

"Beck." She matches his tone.

Well, at least I'm not the only person living in this awkward moment now.

Like the teacher I am, I clap my hands together. "Okay, so, outfield?"

Cool, Luce, way to be cool.

Beck adjusts Miles on his shoulders. "Yeah. Kate, you can come with us. There's a place you can stand to watch off to the side. Lucie, I need you to do me a *huge* favor. Can you go grab my bat? I left it in the locker room."

And leave Miles... "Beck, I don't—"

"Please, Luce. I'll owe you so much!" Beck gives me this pleading look.

I look around the field. Okay, I trust Beck. Adam's here, and Miles loves Adam. Plus, Dex said that Miles isn't unsafe with Kate, but then again, this was his boundary, right?

"It's fine, Lucie. I think we can be alone for five minutes," Kate says in a very condescending tone this time.

Great, now if I don't go, it will definitely look like I'm undermining her.

Beck sends her a snarky smile. "I'll be here too."

I'll be gone, what? Just a few minutes? But then, what if Dex sees me not with Miles like we talked about? Okay, my brain is about to explode.

Kate gives me a glare. I know my answer is definitely about to play into the rest of our day together.

I exhale, trying to actually think out all my options when Callie comes up by Beck.

"Ahh, Miles, are you about to help shag some balls? I'd love to take your picture!"

Thank goodness. Okay, Callie I can trust without question. A person Dex also trusts.

"You guys get started, I'll be right back."

I give Beck and Callie one quick look in warning to please not let anything happen to Miles.

"Thanks, Luce!" Beck calls as I head over to the dugout and back into the hall.

Okay, get a bat and get out. What could happen, really? I let out a breath full of my stress, then look up to find Dex.

He smirks as he leans against the wall. "I have to know, who got you to finally come in here, Beck or Callie?"

"I—uh." *Wait, what did he just say?* I walk to him as I process his words. "Dex, did you plan this? I was having an anxiety attack trying to decide if I should leave Miles." I smack at his crossed arms, but he grabs my wrist and pulls me into the supply closet.

With the switch of the lights, he pulls me to him with a wicked grin.

"I think you're the one who told me to start using my teammates, baby. Beck and Callie are more than capable of taking care of Miles. Even if they might teach him a bad word or two." Dex's hands find my face, and his eyes soften. "I wanted to check on you."

Strings pull at my heart. That's why I agreed to this, because even though getting through Dex's walls was tough, I like that I'm starting to get more emotions out of him.

"I'm good," I lie, and Dex knows it.

"Luce, let me fix this. I never should have let you be put in this situation."

I bite at my lip. Does it make me a terrible person that I

really don't want to take him up on his offer because I'm afraid the only solution is him spending the day with them, and that thought kind of makes my chest burn?

"Dex, why didn't you tell me that Kate actually wanted to spend the day with you and Miles?"

Dex doesn't flinch or step back—he doesn't look surprised by my question at all, actually. "I should have known she'd bring up the one thing I told her was off the table. That wasn't ever an option, baby. Kate and I will spend time together as Miles's parents many times throughout his life, but today isn't one of them. You not spending the rest of the day with them doesn't mean that I'm going to either."

Dex walks me back against the wall, his arms now caging me in as he places a light kiss on my lips. "I have to admit, I like seeing you jealous, Luce. But you don't have to be. Kate called my bluff, and I'm sorry I used you in my bet; it'll never happen again. If you want to spend the game by yourself, do it. If you're worried that I have any feelings for Kate, you're wrong. I'll text Kate without hesitation and tell her she'll be on her own with Miles for the rest of the day if you're uncomfortable."

I sigh. "I'm fine, really. Miles was excited for today, and I don't want to ruin it. I just got in my head for a second."

"Then allow me to pull you out of it." Dex's hand traces along my jaw and threads through my hair.

When the smile barely touches my lips, Dex leans in to devour it. The kiss is...it's just Dex. It makes my stomach flip and my heart beats out of my chest, but I've also never felt safer and so completely adored in my life.

"You, Lucie Anderson," Dex whispers against my skin as he kisses down my neck, "are the woman I want"—he kisses back up and across my jaw—"the woman I need." He gives one more deep, sensual kiss to my lips, then pulls back to meet my eyes.

He lets out a low sigh. "I want to tell Miles about us, Luce. I know you said you were patient, but I don't know if I am."

"Dex...if this is about what Kate—"

"It's not. Not even in the slightest. It's about the fact that Miles knows you as his nanny but you're so much fucking more."

"Yeah, I'm also the teacher, right?" I try to joke, but my laugh comes out shaky.

I want to be more. I want to be the one for Dex. I also just want to be the right one for Miles too. I don't want to replace his mom, but this is such a tricky situation. I can be in love with Dex and still not be the right person when he takes Miles into account.

My love for Miles isn't tied to Dex either. It could be a fair argument that it's the other way around, actually.

"You are more, Lucie. I knew you could've been more the moment you slid your coffee cup in front of me. I didn't quite realize how much more, but..." Dex's eyes track over my face before tucking a strand of hair behind my ear. "I think you could be everything that Miles and I are missing."

My breath hitches as Dex captures my lips again. I melt at this man's touch. His words. His kiss.

God, I want to stay in here for hours longer with this kiss, but Dex pulls back. "I mean it, Luce. No matter what back-handed, undermining comment Kate says, she's the one who didn't want this extra time to begin with. I know today is putting you in a real shitty spot. I know you want to find that balance to make this work, but cut yourself a little slack. It took two people to get you in here."

I crinkle my nose at the reminder of my near panic attack of coming down here. "I didn't want to let you down by leaving Miles, but then the comment about Kate wanting to spend time with you...it was just a lot in a really short amount of time."

Dex chuckles. "I know. I'm sorry I roped you into this today. Just think of Kate as Beck."

I raise my eyebrow. "Oh, I'm so telling him you said that."

"Hear me out, she's a bitchier Beck, but I know he wouldn't do anything on purpose to put Miles in danger and his opinion about you would never have any impact on the way I feel about *you*."

I exhale some of the weight off my shoulders. A grumpy Beck, I can do that.

"I should probably get back out there."

A smirk plays at Dex's mouth. "A few more minutes won't hurt."

He leans back in for another one of those body-melting kisses. I push him back. "Dex," I draw his name out with a giggle. "Miles might start to wonder where I am."

Dex lets out a curse. "Not fair, Luce. Now I'm jealous of my own son."

I playfully run my hands down his chest. "Sorry, right now I am his nanny."

Dex lets out a low growl. "Tonight I'm going to fuck the word 'nanny' right out of you."

"I'll hold you to it, Coach." I lean into him slightly, and just as he goes in for a kiss, I slide around him with a smirk. "So, does Beck actually need his bat? Or is your ploy to get me down here supposed to be obvious when I go back out there empty-handed?"

Dex shakes his head with an amused grin tugging at the corners of his mouth. He grabs the bat I hadn't even realized was next to the door the entire time. "I thought ahead, baby."

I take the bat from him with a sweet smile. "Wish me luck."

After making my way back out to the field with the mentality of looking at Kate like Beck, things get a lot simpler. I didn't have a panic attack when Miles wanted his mom to walk him to the locker room to get his glove so he could play catch with Adam. Any subtle remarks she made didn't hit as hard with Dex's words fresh in my mind.

With warm-ups coming to an end and the official game-day field events starting, Miles wants us to hide out in the dugout for most of it.

When I notice Dex not filtering in with some of the players, I shoot him a text.

> What, are you avoiding the dugout now?

FAV PLAYER
> I'm in the bullpen helping your brother with something actually.

> What a coincidence.

Miles taps on my shoulder. "Lucie, can we get our hotdogs now?"

I slide my phone in my back pocket. "Of course. You know they're my favorite." I stand up, reaching for his hand. "We can go to our seats after."

"Okie," Miles cheers, then reaches for his mom's hand. "Come on, let's go."

Kate holds Miles's hand while he pulls her, but eventually she lets go. I force my lips shut when I notice, but Miles swings our joined hands happily as we walk back up to the concessions.

Honestly, I'm grateful he doesn't let go because the crowd today is insane. We've had sold-out games at home, but this place feels absolutely packed. It could be the Crimson fan base, everyone is cutting in front of us as we walk, and we even get some already drunken fans yelling Crimson chants when they notice our Blues game-day attire.

I hold Miles's hand tightly as we wait in line at the concessions. "You want the usual, bud?"

Miles looks up at me with a toothy grin. "Hotdog with mustard. Oh, and a Sprite."

"Coming right up." I look toward Kate. "Do you want anything?"

She snarls her nose as she looks at the menu. "I'll get something later."

"Okay," I say with a smile.

After ordering our food, I swallow down a little pride and put on my best teacher voice to ask Miles to hold his mom's hand so I can carry the food.

"Got it." Miles grabs Kate's hand again and swings it up to show me.

"Perfect, I think we can get to our seats this—" My sentence ends as a random person runs into my back, sending all of my food to the ground.

"Oh, I'm so sorry! This other guy ran into me..." the man starts as he picks up our sodas, but unfortunately, the dogs can't be salvaged. "Let me give you some cash for more," he blurts out.

"It's okay, it was—" I stop short as I look at the man in front of me. I blink several times. This can't be right. No, I think I'm going insane.

"Lucie?" My name comes out as a question, and my heart rate skyrockets.

I look back at this man, who definitely looks older than I would have thought, but there is a resemblance to Will and Reagan. "Dad?"

The word feels so weird coming out of my mouth. I guess I show how I feel on my face because the man in front of me pales.

Miles tugs on my shirt, looking up at me so pitifully. "Lucie, our hotdogs...they're your favorite."

"It's okay bud, I...um..." I look from Miles to *my dad*, then to Kate, who's looking at me like I've gone insane. Maybe I have, that could actually be what's happening here.

Kate puts her hands on Miles's shoulder. "We will wait for you just right over there."

I contemplate her words for a minute before giving her a small nod. "I won't be long."

When they get far enough away, I slowly look to the man in front of me. Ian Anderson feels like a ghost to me, and yet here he stands.

His hair is dark brown, just like my siblings, the wrinkles are deeper, but I'm sure years of drinking did that. Although he's standing in front of me, Diet Coke in hand, and besides us running into each other, he doesn't seem out of sorts. He doesn't smell like alcohol. He's not stumbling or slurring his words.

He looks at me for just a moment and curses under his breath. "I'm sorry, I know this might be hard to believe, but I didn't mean to run into you like that. I try to stay out of sight when I come and watch Will. I didn't realize it was you until..." His face softens with a small sigh. "You look so much like your mother, Lucie."

Wait, what? He came to watch Will? Actually, it sounded like he does it often. And I know I look like my mom, but hearing it from a man I haven't seen in over a decade...

"I think I need to sit down."

He nods and holds his hand out to the nearby bench. When his hand touches the back of my arm, I jump. "I got it."

"Right, sorry." He tucks his lips in a thin line. "I can walk away if you need me to, Lucie. I promise I'm not here to cause trouble. I just came to watch Will pitch."

Sitting down, I rest my elbows on my knees and rub my temples. "You're here to watch Will? You've watched him before?"

He sighs. "Every game I can make it to for the past few years."

"Well, he has no idea you do, I can assure you of that." Oh my gosh, Will. He's...he—I don't know what he would do if he found out. I don't know what I'm doing. I shoot back up to pace in front of the bench.

"I'm sorry. This is just a lot to process. I should really get back to Miles." My nervous laughter comes out involuntarily. "I just—you watch Will play?"

"I know this is a lot. I'm sorry. I don't expect anything from you guys, especially from Will, but I've been sober for nearly five years. I just want to watch him play—that's it."

I pause in front of him. "You're sober?"

"I swear." His response is immediate.

My heart swells a bit because I can see that he means it.

"Lucie, I get that I walked out. I'm not expecting anything from any of you. I promise. I'll go to my seat now and not get up for the rest of the night."

My shoulders finally fall down from being pinned up to my ears with tension. "I—"

But I don't get to finish my sentence because Kate's running up to me. "Lucie, I can't find Miles."

"Wh-what?" My heart falls into my stomach. "What do you mean you can't find Miles?"

"He was there one second, then he was gone." Kate scratches at her face as she squeezes her eyes shut before shooting them back open with a muffled shriek. "Lucie, what do we do?"

Chapter 37
Miles

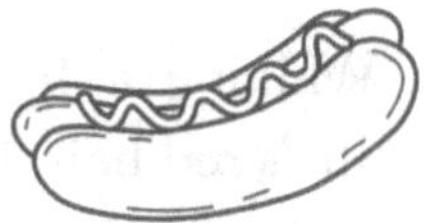

I don't know who that man is talking to Lucie, but he knocked over our hotdogs. That really wasn't very nice.

Mommy's phone starts to ring loudly. It does that a lot. When she pulls it out, she makes this really excited face. "Miles, sweetie, this is a really important phone call. Can you let me have a minute?"

"Okay, Mommy." I nod.

Looking back at Lucie, she's sitting on a bench now. I hope she's feeling okay. Maybe I should go check on her? Oh, I think I need to go pee first.

Jumping, I turn around and tap on Mommy's hip. "Mommy, Mommy."

Her hand swats around in the air, then she holds up one of her fingers.

"Mommy, Mommy." I tug again.

This time, she turns to me, but she puts her finger on her mouth, then turns back around.

But I really have to go. Maybe Lucie can take me? But if she's sick maybe she can't either. Spinning around, I look for

Lucie again, but then I hear the sound of a flush coming from the open door next to me.

Hey, it's just right here. Looking back at Mommy, she's still talking on her phone. She usually talks a long time. I can be super fast. She'll be really impressed.

And I am. In and out like a flash, but I don't see Mommy anymore.

"Mommy," I call. Walking a little further, I start to worry, but then I see Callie's red hair. I bet she knows where my mommy is!

Skipping after her, I follow her back out into the stadium, down some stairs, and over to this far side. I keep calling her name, but she doesn't turn around. It's weird, can she not hear me with all the people?

When she stops and takes a seat, I see it's not actually Callie.

Oh no.

Spinning around, I race back. Maybe Lucie's still sitting down. But wait, how many stairs did I do? One. I think it was one. Or was it two?

People move so fast around me. I don't know which way to go. I feel the tears start to trickle, but I'm a big boy. I don't want to show that I'm crying. Maybe if I just run really fast, I'll find Lucie again.

Finally, I get back in the hall, but I don't see the concession.

Looking around again, I find Shannon. I know I'm usually supposed to hide from her, but I really want Lucie.

"Shannon! Shannon!" I call, and she actually seems to hear me.

She turns around, holding her phone up to her ear. "Miles, what are you doing?"

"I can't find Lucie. Do you know where she is?"

"Hold on." Shannon holds her phone out weird, then leans down. "Nope. Go find your nanny, kid. I don't have time for this."

"B-but...but I don't know where she is," I tell her, but she's already walking away.

Chapter 38
Dex

My message sits unread. Things feel weird. I can't explain it, call it a dad's intuition if you want, but something feels off. Especially with Lucie not answering my text. Then, add in the fact that I can see the seats I know they are supposed to be in, but there's no one there.

I know it was unfair for me to stick Lucie with this today, but I meant every word in that closet. I want to tell Miles about us. I want him to know what she means to me. What she could mean for both of us, really.

Kate is Miles's mother, no one can take that from her, even if I know she doesn't really want it. But Lucie...I think it's very possible that she loves Miles more than she could ever love me and something about that thought makes me so fucking happy.

I want that for my son. I know Miles deserves Lucie's love more than I do, and maybe a good father would have let her stay the nanny, but I think I'm so fucking in love with her that I can't stay away.

The first inning sails by with neither team scoring any runs. When Beck steps up to the plate for the start of the second, my eyes drift back over to the seats. Fucking empty.

They're probably getting food or something, and there's an insane line. But something deep in my gut isn't sitting right. I should just step out and call Lucie to alleviate all this worrying.

I step back to make my way out of the dugout, but then Olsson calls, "Hey, Larsen, come here for a second."

I pinch my eyebrows and weave through the players. I recognize the security guard who's posted outside our entry to the dugout with Kate right next to him.

I can feel my blood pressure rising. *Fuck.* I knew something didn't feel right, but then again, it's just Kate here...no Miles or Lucie.

The security guard clears his throat as I reach them. "I'm sorry to interrupt, but this woman is stating she needed to speak with you—"

"I'm the mother of his child, I think I—"

For fuck's sake. "Kate, what's going on?"

Her face pales. "It wasn't my fault, Dex, really."

Bile immediately climbs up my throat. What wasn't her fault?

"Where are Miles and Lucie?" I grit out, my volume rising like my oncoming anger.

Will appears next to me, as I'm sure he heard his sister's name. "What's going on?"

Kate starts waving her hands as she speaks, and I know I'm about to get nothing but excuses. "It happened so fast, I don't know. Lucie ran into this guy...her dad or something..."

"Her dad?" Will echoes. I can hear the struggle in his voice. While I want to comfort Lucie at the moment, I need to know where my son is.

"Miles, Kate. Where is Miles?"

Kate practically shrinks in front of me. "He's...missing."

It's a weird thing, feeling panic and fear. In this moment, I feel them both so immensely that it's physically painful. Almost as if I'm being choked or strangled. Missing. My son is missing.

"Explain. Now."

"I'm trying to!" Kate whines and throws her hands up in the air.

"No, stop that. Do not play the victim. Do not tell me anything other than what happened. I don't care about the outside circumstances around it right now. I want the truth and I want it now."

Kate swallows hard. "We were walking to our seats from the concession stands when Lucie ran into this guy. She called him Dad, but she looked terrified—"

"Fuck," Will mutters next to me. I want to acknowledge it, I do, but my son holds priority right now.

"Well, I told her I would take Miles over to the side so she could have a moment alone...but then I got this call from Cedar and Park that I've been waiting weeks for..." My glare says every bit of I don't fucking care, and Kate sighs. "I don't know, Dex, he was just gone."

My body goes rigid with terror.

"Fuck!" I yell and storm past Kate and the security guard. I don't care if I'm on the job. I don't care that it's the start of the game, and Olsson knows that.

Storming through the hall, I don't know where to start but, fuck, I'll tear this place apart if it means finding Miles.

In my rage, I don't hear the cleats running up behind me until Will's right next to me.

"What are you doing?" I snap. I can storm out and most likely get away with it, but Will's supposed to be pitching tonight.

Will doesn't stop, he doesn't tell me to slow down or take a deep breath. He simply matches my pace. "After hearing that two people—who are very important to me—need help, someone else can fucking pitch. We'll find him, Dex...more likely Lucie will, but you're getting my help either way."

All I can manage is to nod back to him. After we find Miles, I'll tell him how fucking much this means to me, but for now I have to find my son.

"Wait for me!" Kate calls. "He's my son too, you know. I'm just as upset as you."

I don't stop. I physically can't, so I just holler over my shoulder, not caring if I sound like an ass. "I'm well aware, but this is not the fucking time to play the martyr. Pull your head out of your fucking job and help look for him."

We burst through the first set of doors. I reach for my phone to try to call Lucie, but not a single call will go through with the number of people here. I manage to get a *Where are you?* text to go through, but I can't sit around and wait for her to answer.

We're getting closer to where it's going to get majorly crowded, and fans stopping us constantly is going to be a nightmare. I turn to Kate. "Did you at least talk to Lucie before finding me?"

She makes this hurt look on her face, but when she notices me not giving a fuck, she sighs. "Yeah, she knows. I thought Miles might have gone back to her, but he wasn't

there. She said she was going to start looking, and I came to
you."

Will pulls his ball cap off and adjusts it, pulling it lower
like that will help distract from the fact that he's in full
uniform. "Okay, you're not going to like what I'm about to
say, but listen before you freak out. We need to check
medical. Growing up, it's where I always told Lucie to go if
we ever got separated during games. I'm sure Lucie told
Miles the same thing."

"Let's go." Nodding, I follow Will but keep my head
on a fucking swivel looking for any glimpse of Miles or
Lucie.

When we reach the first aid and medical room, and I
don't see either, my heart sinks even deeper into my stomach.
A thousand scenarios have run through my head, and with
each passing minute, they just get worse and worse.

"Has anyone seen—" I start announcing to the room, but
a woman steps up to us immediately. She seems like the one
running the show with her clipboard handy and a badge
hanging from her neck.

"Mr. Larsen, while I want to say it's a pleasure to meet
you, I wish it were under different circumstances. Unfortunately, we haven't seen Miles. Your nanny—"

"My girlfriend." The correction comes out involuntarily.
Now isn't exactly the time to get all territorial, but hearing
"nanny" doesn't feel right.

"Right. Miss Anderson came by here and informed us of
the situation. We have a full description of Miles, and I sent
some volunteers out with her as well to help with the
search."

"Did Lucie say where she was going next?" Will asks.

The woman reaches for a walkie on her hip. "That girl

was determined. I'm sure she's been to five different places by now. Let me radio and see if anyone has her location."

Of course, Lucie's first instinct was to start looking and get all of Miles's info out. Kate came to me first and, while I needed to know, Miles was Lucie's priority.

God, I love her for it.

The woman clicks her radio back on her hip. "Okay, everyone is practically all over this stadium now. One of my volunteers said Lucie was headed back to the concessions area where he went missing, then was heading down to the dugouts after that."

"Great, thank you," Will replies because I started moving the moment she said where Lucie was going.

I could run around this fucking stadium, but I know Lucie—I know she has a plan and has sent people in twenty different directions already. I'm going to follow her damn lead because I have no doubt in my fucking mind that Lucie is going to be the reason we find Miles.

Kate and Will follow closely behind me. I know part of Will's concern in all of this is Lucie—I get it, and I hope he knows I want to acknowledge the whole "dad" situation, but I can't until I find my son.

With the concession stand in sight, I spot Lucie right away as she uses her hands to talk to four security guards in front of her.

She looks just as terrified as I feel, but she's organized a complete search party for Miles. My feet move to her immediately. Lucie places her hands over her head as the men walk off in different directions.

"Lucie!" I yell for her before she can get the chance to move. When I reach her, I pull her into my arms immediately. "Fuck, Luce."

"Dex?" Lucie lets out a small breath before wrapping her arms tightly around me. "I'm so sorry."

Pulling back, I cup her face and wipe away a stray tear. "Hey, it's okay—"

"I'm going to find him, Dex, I swear." Lucie swallows. "I'm sorry I didn't come and get you. I was about to, but I had to make sure everyone knew what to look out for first."

Still holding her face, I stare into her blue eyes as I say, "We're going to find him, Luce." Frankly, I needed to say it for myself too.

"Lucie," Will hollers, pulling Lucie's attention away.

Her eyes go wide. "Will? What are you doing here?"

Will pulls her away from me and into a hug. "Are you kidding? I'm here to fucking help, and to check on you! They said something about—"

"Lucie, I'm sorry, I came up short—" A man with dark hair races up to Lucie, but pauses when he sees Will. Pauses is too simple a word, actually—this man crumbles.

Will stumbles back from Lucie. He looks like he just took a punch to the gut.

"Will," Lucie speaks softly. "It's okay, he's sober and he wants to help."

Callie runs up out of nowhere. "Hey, Olsson told me what happened. I'm here to—Will?"

He pulls her close before speaking to his dad. "You need to go. I can't—"

"Son, I'm so sorry. If I could just explain—"

Will scoffs and looks like he's about to explode.

Shit, shit, shit. We don't have time for this right now.

Before I can even open my mouth, Lucie whistles.

"Everyone is going to shut up and swallow their pride right now. I don't care about the past twenty years at this moment. What I care about it finding Miles, so, everyone, listen up, so we can find my fucking kid."

Fuck, I love this girl so much.

Lucie steps to her brother. "Will, I love you, but I need you right now. *Miles* needs you right now. You and Callie, you guys go check the dugout and the Blues locker rooms. I already sent extra security to look on the Crimson side in case he got turned around."

Will gives her a nod, then meets the man's eyes one more time before Callie pulls him away slowly.

Lucie whips right around. "Dad, you go check our seats in the stadium. They're on the away side reserved seating closest to the dugout. Check anywhere in that section, really. I'm going to start checking suites."

When Lucie turns to me, I can see the emotional hell she's in. "Let me go with you."

She gives me a small nod, but then Kate cuts in. "I'm going wherever you're going, Dex."

Lucie exhales. "You two do the suites."

"Luce—"

"No." Lucie's voice comes out just as strong as it did a moment ago. "It's okay, really. We don't need three people searching one area, Dex. Pairs are fine for big spaces. You two check there first, and I'll start at the offices. I already have people searching the stands in general, and someone's staying here in case he comes back to this spot."

I know she's right, but damn it, I hate leaving her alone like this. "Okay, meet us back here in ten minutes if you can't find him."

Lucie nods before she goes one way, and Kate and I go the other.

Chapter 39
Lucie

So this is what pure terror feels like. Absolute utter terror.

It's been maybe ten minutes since Miles went missing, but it feels like an eternity. I've sent people in every single direction. I just need someone to find him. My chest physically aches, and I feel like I'm on the verge of throwing up, but I have to keep going.

I think I've run every horrible scenario through my head, and with each passing minute, they just get worse and worse. Today's crowd is thick; what if someone grabbed him in the shuffle? What if he got so turned around that he's found his way out in the city?

I know this kid knows stadiums, but he's only five years old, and this isn't our stadium. He could have easily gotten overwhelmed by this place with the number of people here. Then, add on the fact that he hasn't found anyone he knows. I know he has to be terrified.

I'm terrified.

Seeing Dex's face...Will's face. They both gutted me. I hate that I've put everyone in this situation.

Miles missing? My fault. I should never have let them walk away when we were in such a crowded area.

Dex having to learn his son is missing from someone who isn't me? My fault. I know he needed to know, but I couldn't physically take time out of getting this search started to tell him.

Will having to face our dad completely unprepared? Also my fault. My brother's done everything for our family. The slip of "son" from our dad's mouth, and I wanted to scream for Will.

The weight of everything threatens to make me crumble into nothing, but the pure adrenaline of finding Miles keeps me going.

I reach the halls on the far side where some of the onsite offices could be. I look up with closed eyes and take a deep breath. *Please be here.* I swear my next call is going to be the police if this comes up empty.

"Miles!" I call, swinging open doors and repeating his name louder with each room that shows up empty. I make it down three rooms, and my heart is sinking lower and lower.

Another room empty, and I'm dying.

"Lucie?" I hear from the end of the hall before there are footsteps charging toward me.

"Miles!" I fall to my knees as Miles launches himself in my arms. "Thank God, Miles. My heart couldn't take another second of you being missing."

"I didn't know where to go. The crowds were so scary, Lucie." Miles keeps his grip tight as he cries. "They don't usually feel so scary. Is this stadium bigger?"

Tears now streaming down my face in relief, I squeeze him tighter. "It does feel that way, doesn't it?"

I scoop him up, and he doesn't let go, and I really don't

want him to. Pulling out my phone, I send a text to Dex that I found him and to meet me back at the concession stand. "How about we go find your dad, buddy. I know he's going to be so happy to see you."

Miles sniffles. "Are him and Mommy mad? I didn't mean to, I just had to pee." *Sniffle.* "I thought I saw Callie, but it wasn't her." *Sniffle.* "Then I got confused and I ran into Shannon, but she just told me to find you. But I couldn't, Lucie, I couldn't." Miles cries so hard on my shoulder.

My feet slow as I process what he just said. "Miles, baby, did you say you talked to Shannon and she didn't help you?"

"Y-yes, she said to find you, but the crowds were scaring me, so I tried to find an office like Daddy's."

I'm going to kill her, I swear. Miles sniffles again, which gets my feet back in motion.

"Miles, I promise you, your dad and mom are not mad at all. They are going to be so happy you're okay."

I can feel Miles fiddling with my hair. "I didn't mean to get lost, Lucie. I thought it would be helpful if I went to the bathroom all by myself."

I run my hand up and down his back. "I know, baby. It's okay, we found you."

"You found me. Thank you, Lucie." Miles nestles his head in my neck.

Tears flow heavily as I carry him all the way back to the concession stand. The moment it comes into view, Dex is already racing to me with Kate not far behind.

Dex takes Miles from my arms, then reaches for me, but I step back as Kate rounds the front to look at Miles.

Miles's tears start falling in full force again, and I can see the grip Dex has on Miles tighten before Kate's arms come around Miles's back.

They need this moment. I can handle talking to the security and volunteers while they have it. I'll also be talking to Olsson as soon as possible.

I make my way over to the volunteer who stayed at the concession and have them radio to everyone that Miles has been found.

When I hear the girl repeat it out loud, I let out a shaky breath, and my knees wobble for a moment. But then I'm being turned around and engulfed in my brother's arms. Yep, here come my tears.

"It's okay, Luce. You found him." Will's grip tightens as he pulls me back to look in my eyes.

Will's face flashes in my mind when he realized our dad was here, and I yelled at him. "I'm so sorry, Will."

He lets out a small chuckle. "You managed to find the man who walked out on us two decades ago and then organized a twenty-plus person manhunt with a *semi*-cool head, just to find Miles yourself, and you're apologizing to me because?"

I can't laugh at the irony of his words, I can barely manage a smile. "My head wasn't cool at all."

Will pulls me back in for another hug. "Well, it looked like it was. Not to mention—you found him."

I sigh a breath of relief when my eyes find Dex over on the bench. Miles is moving his hands around—I'm sure recounting everything in heavy detail—while Dex and Kate sit on either side of him.

I think my panic attack is finally subsiding. I step back from Will and wipe my cheeks. "What are you doing here anyway? Aren't you supposed to be pitching right now?"

"Are you fucking kidding? I heard your name and a ghost's name in the same sentence. Miles missing upped my excuse to leave, but there was no way in hell I was pitching until I checked on you."

"Will...I didn't want you to have to face him like that, but he said he's sober. He said he comes to your games. It might be good for us to hear him out."

My brother deflates a bit in front of me. "I don't know if I can do it. Not alone at least."

Well, this is a rare occasion, Will needing someone else, not actually wanting to do something alone. I know he liked that Callie was independent, and he's backed off on the take-control front since she's been around, but asking for help...in an emotional situation? That's not something Will does.

"I can do it. You can come with me."

Will gives me a soft smile. "I can take Callie with me, if you want to stay with Dex."

I look back over to where they're sitting. Miles is still talking while a security guard waits close by, likely waiting for a moment to cut in and make sure everything is okay. I know today was scary for all of them. This isn't about swallowing my pride or even attached to any jealousy that they all need a moment together.

I know Dex wants to be with me, or well, I know he did before I lost his kid. Either way, I'm secure enough to know that this isn't about us right now.

"Let them have a minute." I look around and realize we're starting to get a lot of eyes and finger-pointing from fans. "You do realize you're in full uniform, right?"

Will shakes his head and pulls my shoulder. "Come on, let's go find...him and a quiet place to catch our breath."

I nod, letting Will drape his arm over my shoulder as we walk. We don't make it far before Callie comes up to my other side with a hug. "Thank goodness. I really wanted to let you guys have your sibling moment, but damn it, I want to hug you."

I chuckle softly, returning her embrace. It only lasts a second before I feel Will stiffen beside me. Looking over, I see our dad watching us from the side. Slipping out of Callie's hold, I nudge her to Will. If the people I love need me to be strong today, then that's what I'll be.

Walking up to our dad, I can see the deep breath he exhales. "I heard you found your kid."

My heart aches in my chest. "Yeah, he's with his parents, he's good now."

He glances from me to Will. "I can go now—"

I hold my arm out for a second, then pull it back. "Actually, do you have a minute?"

He nods, and when I look back at Will, he gives me a nod as well. I guess I'll be doing the initiating.

"Okay, let's go down to the family waiting room?" I lead our dad while Callie drags Will behind us.

On the way, I shoot Dex a text telling him to take his time and where I'll be. I don't want him to think I've abandoned him, but I respect that Miles needs his parents more.

As we walk into the room, I hold the door open for everyone. Will holds on to Callie like she's grounding him. She gives him a soft smile. "What is it with playing the Crimsons?"

Will manages a straggled laugh and mumbles, "They're fucking cursed."

When the door clicks behind me, I think over my words. I don't want to push anyone too far. I get why Will is struggling, and maybe I should be struggling more. I guess it's because I'm the youngest sibling—the person who had the least trauma with it, maybe.

I open my mouth to start with something simple—like, ya know, "So you said you were sober now." But surprisingly, he speaks first.

"I'm sorry. I didn't mean for any of you to know I check up on you guys. I have no right to anything you do, I know that. I'm so proud of the people you've become. With Reagan's floral shop...Will, your pitching career...and, Lucie, you may look like your mother, but it seems you got her incredible heart, too. I don't expect forgiveness—especially from you, Will. I want you to know I've been sober for five years. I will continue to be sober. I swear. I regret all of the moments I missed, but I know I'm not entitled to any new ones. I'm sorry for everything."

Will's sigh behind me sounds heavy. I wait to see if he wants to say anything, but he doesn't.

It might be gullible for us to completely believe him, but I like the idea that he means what he says. Doesn't mean I have to hold all my weight on it either.

"I'm glad you're sober. I can't speak for Will or Reagan, but I can speak for myself. I'm not against forming a relationship with you—taking it slow—but know that while you are my 'dad,' I don't need you to be. Will's my dad. He took care of me when you left—he took care of everyone. Reagan—in her own way—took on some of that role too. So...if you want to talk sometimes, that's great. You can earn my respect along the way. If you don't, that's on you. I'll be just fine with or without you."

"I believe that. Thank you." Our dad rocks on his feet and looks at Will. "Thank you for being the man I couldn't be."

Will whispers a string of curses. "I'm not quite where Lucie is yet, but...maybe one day."

I give Will a soft smile as Callie kisses his hand. Will looks at me and mouths a "thank you."

I didn't need him to say it. I halfway don't even feel like I deserve it, but Will deserves closure on this. When he's ready, that is, and it's nice I actually get to be there for him for a change.

I get his number, then slide my phone back in my pocket.

He doesn't push any further; he simply nods to Will and Callie, then offers me a slanted smile. "I'll find my way back."

"Okay, I'll reach out...soon."

"And I'll answer, no matter what." Our dad looks one last time at Will, but no words come from either of them. Callie folds her lips together, and I know words are on the tip of her tongue, but she leans her head on Will's arm as our dad walks out.

We all wait for the click of the door as he walks out. No one moves for another good five seconds after either, but then the door swings open and Dex steps in with Miles in his arms.

"Lucie!" Miles wiggles out of Dex's hold to run to me. "I didn't want you to leave again."

Oh, my heart. I scoop him up and he fiddles with my hair while he hugs me.

Will finally lets go of Callie and comes around behind me to talk to Miles. "That was my fault, Miles. I wasn't strong enough to do something on my own, and I needed Lucie's help. She's all yours now, though."

Tears prick at my eyes. "Will, I was doing so good."

Will kisses the top of my head. "I'll talk to you tomorrow. Go take some time for you, okay?"

I give him a thin-lipped smile because I know a nod isn't enough for him as a response right now.

Will takes Callie's hand, then stops in front of Dex. "I told you she'd find him."

Dex looks at me for a moment—he's got his stone walls back up, I can tell. "You did. I talked to Olsson. I'm taking Miles and Lucie back to the hotel, and I'll be talking to him again tomorrow. Considering he asked Callie to help search, I think you both know you're not in trouble for leaving, but I want you to know that it means a lot to me."

Will shakes his shoulder. "I told you—important people needed me. Now they need you."

Dex sighs with a slow nod. Oof, that's not a good sign.

When Will and Callie walk out, Dex finally meets my eyes as I continue to hold Miles.

"Dex, I'm—"

He holds up his hand, his tone clipped. "Lucie, are you okay?"

"I...um..." I'm not entirely sure how to answer that question. Physically, I am, but emotionally we've all been through the ringer and it's not even dinner time.

Miles fiddles with my hair again. "Can we go back to the hotel now?"

I tighten my hold on him. "Yeah, let's go."

Dex doesn't say anything as I walk past him. He doesn't reach for Miles either, but as I reach the door, he's there to pull it open. "Shuttle should be waiting for us out front. Heads-up, Kate's coming too."

"Okay," I say softly.

Dex presses his lips together. Man, he really threw his walls back up fast. No matter, I think I've finally figured myself out. I know I'm capable of breaking them back down again if I need to.

Chapter 40
Dex

I've had many adrenaline rushes throughout my life—throughout my career, but not a single one of them has ever felt like this. I can barely form words, I feel so drained.

But then I look at Lucie. This incredible woman is just taking this all in stride. She's, arguably, been through more emotional stress than any of us, and yet her light seems to shine even brighter.

Miles doesn't let go of her the entire shuttle ride back to the hotel, and I don't blame him. Hell, I want to hold on to her until I find my fucking bearings again. I want to comfort her about her dad. I want to kiss her for finding my son. I want to tell her I love her for every single moment of the day when she put Miles first. Over herself. Over me.

Fuck, I feel like I can barely breathe thinking back on it.

By the time we reach the hotel, Miles is out like a light. His crash hits him so hard he doesn't even wake up when I take him from Lucie and carry him up to our suite.

Lucie doesn't ask any questions when Kate follows us. When Kate asked if she could stay with Miles for a bit longer, I could tell she needed it, and I understood that, but I told her we needed to have a conversation before she left.

I couldn't really expand on it with Miles clinging to the both of us, but it's happening.

I lay Miles down in the bed and pull the blankets over him.

"Dex," Kate whispers. "Can I just lie here with him?"

I sigh, thinking over all my options. "Yeah, but you're not getting out of us having a conversation before you leave." I glance at Miles, still sound asleep. "I'm telling Miles about Lucie. I know we have a lot to figure out as co-parents, but Lucie is going to be a part of that. She deserves to be a part of it."

"I know." Kate gives me a thin-lipped smile. "I'm sorry for today."

I only nod before I back out of the room and quietly shut the door.

When I turn and don't see Lucie, my blood pressure goes through the fucking roof. Swinging her room door open, I find her in leggings and an oversized T-shirt, lying back on her bed like she's going to fucking sleep.

"What the hell do you think you're doing?"

Lucie shoots up. "Dex? I thought you were going to rest with Miles?"

"No, his mom's got him for a minute, Luce."

Her shoulders rest down. "Dex, if you want to be with Miles right now, I'm not—"

I cut her off by picking her up and throwing her over my damn shoulder. "Come with me."

"Wh-what? You're not giving me much choice now, are you?"

"You're right, I'm not." I carry her out of her room and

right out of our suite. When I told Olsson we needed to go back to the hotel, Beck caught me before I could leave the dugout.

"What are we doing?" Lucie huffs.

"Beck gave me his room key so we have a place to talk privately." I step across the hall and swipe the card.

"Can't yelling at me, wait until after we all get some rest?"

Oh, I'm about to yell at her alright.

I carry her inside, letting the door shut on its own before setting her down in front of the bed.

"No, it can't wait. Dammit, Lucie. After the day you've just had, you think I don't want to talk to you? That I don't want to have you next to me?"

Lucie's shoulders drop as she stares at her feet. "Dex, I'm so sorry for today, it was all my—"

I grab her face gently and thread my fingers through her hair. "Don't you dare say it was your fault. It was an accident, Lucie."

The corners of her mouth drop. "But I didn't even come tell you about it. Dex, I'm okay if you're upset with me right now. I told you I was patient."

Fuck, now I'm mad at her.

"Should I recount the whole afternoon for you? Luce, you organized a complete search party for Miles. Kate came and told me, and yes, I needed to know, but you kept Miles as your priority. Then, on top of that, you stepped to the fucking side because you thought it would be best for Miles to have his parents together in that moment.

"I say this in the best way possible, I'm fully convinced that you love my son more than me. It's what has made me fall so fucking in love with you so damn fast because I've never seen anyone—*anyone*, Lucie—take care of him the way you do. The way you take care of everyone! You fucking found your dad today. A man you haven't seen since you were a kid, but you took it in fucking stride during a crisis. And guess what? It doesn't stop there. You proceeded to take care of your older brother because you knew he couldn't face his father alone. Don't ask me how I know that. I know you. You think you don't know who you are, but that's bullshit. Your siblings are caretakers because they felt like they had to be, but not you. You're the most genuine, nurturing, self-sacrificing caretaker I've ever met. You find joy in other people's happiness and love being the reason it's there to begin with."

Lucie closes her eyes as she lets out a deep breath. Her hand holds on to my wrist. "Dex..."

I tilt her face so she can meet my eyes. "You've put everyone above yourself today. I know it's just who you are, baby, but damn it—I need you to be selfish for just one fucking minute. Yell every single stress at me, Lucie, I can take it. Speak unfiltered, because I know you've never felt like you could before. There's no one else here but me and you, baby, so *please*, be so fucking selfish."

I can see the fight in her eyes, then I see the moment it slips away. "Kiss me, Dex, then remind me how you don't want to stop."

That I can do. Pulling her to me, I kiss her with everything in me. She wants to be reminded of what she means to me, then I'll show her.

I pull her shirt over her head before reaching for mine. "Take your fucking clothes off, baby."

Lucie listens, ripping every stitch of clothing off while I do the same. Scooping her back up, Lucie's legs wrap around my waist and our kiss feels like a damn frenzy. All her tension, all her stress, and all her emotions are coming out in this kiss.

I lay her down on the bed. Her hips seek me out, lining us up. I can't tell if she's rushing because she wants to get back over to our suite or if it's because she needs it now. If it's the latter, I'll give it to her, but this isn't about anything other than her right now.

"You can be whatever you want to be with everyone else, but with me—baby, with me—I want you to be selfish. No other thoughts right now. No other wants but yours. Tell me what you *want*. Not need—I'll give you every fucking thing you need for the rest of your life. Here and now, tell me what you want."

Lucie's chest rises and falls. "I want to feel you. All of you. I never want your lips to leave mine—ever. Dex, I think I've wanted this for a *very* long time."

"I'm glad you think that, baby. I'll work on making you know that. I fucking know I want it."

I flip us around and then sit up against the headboard. I wrap my hand around the back of her neck, pulling her flush against me. "I want you, baby, for a fucking lifetime."

I don't wait for her to respond, I just give her what she wants. My lips find hers, then I bring her hips down on my cock. She slides on like a damn glove, because Lucie Anderson was fucking made for me. I could tell from the moment I laid my eyes on her.

Whether it was fate, some higher power intervention, whatever. My fucking gut instinct knew that she was more.

Lucie's hips slide back and forth as she works her clit against my pelvis while I fill her up. My mouth captures hers, kissing her like she asked. I understand why—kissing

Lucie is just as hot as anything else we do. I could get there from the taste of her mouth and feeling her pleasure around me alone.

Lucie's moans and whimpers drown out in our kiss. Her hips move faster and her muscles tense around me.

"You want that orgasm, baby?" I whisper against her mouth.

"I want it." Lucie lets out a long moan. She's right there. I can feel it. She pulls back from our kiss slightly, but doesn't stop her hips. "I want yours too."

My hand wraps back around her throat, pulling her back in. "Take it."

The moment my tongue tangles with hers again, her body sinks against mine as her climax takes over.

I slide down against the headboard, still holding her body tight against me, and thrust hard, quick strokes as her walls contract around me.

Lucie lets out a muffled scream of my name then a rush of her release soaks my cock. "That's my good girl, squirting for me."

My thrusts quicken, gliding even easier now. My hands tangle in her hair, pulling her lips back. She lets out another whimper as her walls squeeze me one more time, then I'm lost to her. Spilling into her with everything in me.

"Fuck yes, baby," I mumble into her mouth, biting at her lip as I fill her with my cum.

Lucie's body goes boneless against mine as our bodies slow. "That was—I've never—"

Her breathing is heavy, but that pure fucking light is shining so bright. I tuck her hair behind her ears. "You will now."

Chapter 41
Lucie

Dex slides away from me for only a moment to get a warm washcloth to clean us up, then climbs right back in next to me. I wrap myself back around him and trace the lines of his muscles with my fingers.

"I'm not sure Beck gave you his room key for this." I laugh.

Dex places a kiss on the top of my head. "It's Beck—I'm sure that's exactly what he gave us his key for. I'll call in room service before we leave, though."

I prop my head up on his chest. "We should probably head back over, shouldn't we?"

"Probably so. I can't say how long Miles will sleep. He stopped taking naps nearly two years ago. He'll be up till midnight as is. But before we go..." Dex flips us so he can hover over me and plants another kiss on my forehead. "I want you to be selfish more often for me, baby."

I roll my eyes with a chuckle. "Dex."

"Don't get me wrong, I won't complain if it's more sex, but I meant in general, Luce. You deserve it."

I trace a line with my finger between his biceps. "And what about you?"

"I'm plenty selfish." Dex leans down to give me a slow kiss. "I fell for my son's nanny." *Another kiss.* "I didn't even make it to you homeschooling Miles before I gave in." *This kiss a little deeper.* "And now I want everything from you, Lucie. I'm so fucking selfish that I want you in my bed every night and to wake up next to you every morning. I want Miles to see you as the woman I love, not just someone who's there to take care of him. I want your light, Lucie. I want all of it, and I don't ever want to let it go."

"I want all of that with you too, Dex," I whisper. "I know I said at the beginning of this that I felt like I didn't know who I was. A supporting character with no backstory, but being with you and Miles made me realize it doesn't really matter. I probably didn't need those guidelines, but they're what brought me to you." I place my hands lightly on his face. "Even if I'm technically the girlfriend now, can I still teach Miles?"

Dex's laugh comes immediately. "Whatever you want. I'll paint the classroom whatever color you say and you can move those damn turtles out of our living room."

"Our living room," I repeat with a crinkled smile. I love that—*our*.

Dex leans down again, his face just an inch away from mine. "Yes, Lucie, ours. Get ready to hear that for a very, *very* long time. And 'we' as well. So many fucking *we's*."

We lay in the hotel bed for another ten minutes just kissing. A slow, love-filled kiss that makes every single inch of my body feel alive.

So alive that it apparently remembers I did not get to eat

my lunch. My stomach growls, and our laughter fills the room again.

When we get back over to our suite, it's still quiet. Dex keeps his voice low. "I'll call us in some room service, then probably wake Miles up when it gets here. Do you want anything in particular?"

"A concession stand hotdog?" I joke as I raise my eyebrows with a sweet smile, but based on the look on Dex's face, he's already thinking of ways to get me the hotdog from the stadium. "I'm kidding. Just get me whatever you get. I'm so hungry, I could eat anything right now."

"Okay, baby." Dex kisses my temple, and while I think he'll get me food now, I'm sure one of the guys will be bringing back an assortment of concession stand food later.

I head out to the small balcony attached to the suite. The view of New York isn't as nice as the one from Dex's penthouse, but I guess I'm a little partial to Boston in general.

With a deep breath, I sit back in one of the chairs and let my eyes flutter shut for just a moment. The street noise might be crazy, but there's still peace in this moment because Miles is safe, Dex and I are strong, and food is on the way.

When the sliding door opens, Dex steps out. "Food's ordered."

"Okay, want to sit out here with me while we wait?"

I gesture to the other chair, but he walks right past it and picks me up out of my chair before sitting back down and pulling me in his lap.

"Well, this works too." I adjust, getting comfortable and resting my head back on his shoulder.

"It works so much better." Dex kisses the top of my head when the sliding door opens again.

Kate steps one foot on the balcony, leaving one foot still inside. "Hey, Miles is still asleep, but do you have a second?"

I look back to Dex, letting him handle this one. I know this isn't about them being together, Dex has made that so perfectly clear, but if he needs to handle this without me, he can.

"I can go—"

"No," both Dex and Kate speak at the same time.

"You deserve to be a part of this conversation, Luce." Dex adjusts me in his lap, pulling me tighter as he sits up, then holds out his hand toward the other chair for Kate to take a seat.

The metal of the chair legs scrapes against the balcony floor as she pulls out her chair. Getting a read on her is next to impossible. Her and Dex may have similar personality traits, but I don't know if my "we're a team" speech will work on her like it did him.

Kate settles into the seat then looks straight at me. "Thank you for today."

"Of course, you're welcome." I can't say I fully expected that to be the first thing she said.

"Listen, I know you want to have a talk about co-parenting, Dex, but I've been thinking..." Kate shuffles in her chair to look at the massive building in front of us. "I want you both to know that it's not that I don't love Miles. Because I do, and it's not that I regret my decision of having him...it's just that being a mother isn't what I wanted. Even though it may not always appear like it, I have tried."

Dex makes a small noise behind me, and I lightly smack at his chest. I saw the fear in her eyes today when Miles went missing. I know Kate cares—it's very different from the way Dex and I do, but I believe she does care on some level.

Kate cuts her eyes to us with a huff. "Just hear me out, Dex. You want to talk about co-parenting, and I agree. The idea of you and I getting pregnant seemed as if I could have *all the things*, all these things I thought I should want as a woman. This mom with a beautiful family and a great career, but Miles deserves more than what I can give him. I know it. You know it. Hell, it's the main reason I left, really. But then you go and hire this young blonde girl who my son goes on and on about...and I get in my head—like I failed at something I didn't even want to begin with."

I feel every muscle of Dex tense. His hand squeezes my thigh lightly for about ten seconds before he relaxes. I can see him mentally fighting off an argument, and I get it. I don't see how someone would not want Miles, but that's me.

Dex is right, I am a caretaker. I want to be a mom. Honestly, in an odd way, I already think I am. I want to nurture and care for each and every person around me, but that's not who Kate is.

I reach for Dex's hand, and he threads his fingers through mine with a sigh. "So, what are you saying, Kate? That you don't want to see Miles?"

Kate sinks in her chair. "Dex, you were meant to be a father, but this—this isn't meant for me. I love Miles, and I don't want to abandon him, but Lucie is the mother figure he needs. I know it might be hard to understand where I'm coming from, but it's my truth. As unfair and selfish as it seems to you both, I know I'm not capable of giving Miles my all."

I sit in silence for a minute, letting her words wash over me. I can see why she thinks I wouldn't understand, but flipping the perspective, Kate just seems to be giving a slightly different version of what my dad did.

Kate forms a thin line with her lips before looking at me. "I really can't thank you enough for finding Miles and letting Dex and I have that moment alone with him. I'm calm in courtrooms and on business calls, but this just isn't for me. I'm not about to step into your relationship; that's for you two to decide, but if you want to tell Miles about your relationship, then do it. I would still like to have my scheduled weekends because I know Miles deserves to have some of me, but he needs a mother and father more. I don't want to stand in the way of that."

I may not have needed a blessing from my brother or the support from my sister, but I think I needed this. Dex really needed this. I know this is the start of our relationship, but he's carried so much guilt about this divorce—this could be what he needed to let it go.

Dex squeezes my hand again. "I can't say I understand your decision, but if you're serious about this, then I can find a way to respect it. I don't want to take Miles away from you. That's not something I've ever thought of doing. If you want to stick to our original arrangement, then great. I can still be flexible if it benefits Miles."

Dex shuffles us in the chair again as he leans up to hold me close. "However, I am going to ask Lucie to marry me one day. One day, we might decide to grow this family. I need you to know now that our son isn't to be used as a weapon, bargaining chip, or an opportunity to one-up each other. He's also not a luxury you get to use when it benefits you. He's a child who doesn't deserve this bullshit. So we make an agreement and we respect each other's roles in that decision. No exceptions. I'm not your enemy, Kate."

This wave of emotion hits me like a ton of bricks. Being with Dex isn't something I ever anticipated, but being loved by him? Hearing that he sees this future with me? At the beginning of all this, I wouldn't have understood why he wanted all of these things with me. But now, it almost feels... right. I didn't find myself in Dex, but he gave me a safe place to see it on my own.

Kate lets out a sigh. "Agreed. We stick to our original agreement. And when that time comes, I'll have my lawyer draw up an addendum to add Lucie in, if that will make you feel better. I'm serious about this. Today made it abundantly clear to me that I need to be serious about it." Kate stands from her chair. "I'll wait till Miles gets up so I can say bye to him, but then I'll go."

Dex rests his head on my shoulder for just a second before speaking to Kate again. "We have plenty of food on the way, and I plan on waking him up when it gets here. You can stay to eat if you want, but if you don't, that's fine. We won't tell Miles about us until tomorrow—I think he's had enough happen today already."

Kate gives me a thin-lipped smile. "Lucie stepped aside earlier today to let me have my mom moment, and now it's my turn. I'll wait inside. I have some emails to answer anyway."

Dex simply nods, then settles back in the chair. When Kate steps back inside and the sliding door closes, Dex hauls me to his chest. "Fuck, was that the right thing to do? Should I have been angrier? I feel angry, but I don't know if it's at her, myself, or just the situation."

"I know...I'm sorry." I rest my head on his shoulder. "For what it's worth, I don't think you should be angry at yourself —you can be upset about the situation, but it doesn't change anything. You could be angry and try to force more out of Kate, but I don't think that will end up any better."

"You're right." Dex places a lingering kiss on my forehead. "I owe you an apology, though. I meant what I said about us, Luce. I see that future. But that probably wasn't the best way for me to go about it. I don't want to put pressure on you."

"Dex." There's a pain in my chest as I fully register what he's saying. I know the pressure that he felt he put on Kate was part of why he feels guilty about this whole situation, why he blames himself for it.

I lean back up so I can look at him. "Don't do that. I get it, we're still figuring this out, but I want that. I can see those things with you too. Don't confuse pressure with clear expectations of what you see in *our* relationship. This is a completely different situation. I know when I say this, you'll understand what I mean...I did fall in love with Miles first."

Dex chuckles softly. "I know you did. I think I love you more for it."

My smile comes with a blush on my cheeks. "You told me that you didn't need someone with one foot out the door to start. Dex, I would have never let you kiss me on your balcony if I couldn't see this future with you. For Miles's sake. For mine. And yours. You won't have to blame yourself over me, Dex. When you said you might not be able to stop, I knew what you meant."

Dex brushes my hair behind my ears before he cups my face. "You are remarkable, Lucie Anderson." Dex pulls me in for a small kiss, and then I nestle my head back on his shoulder.

Dex runs his hand lightly on my thigh. "I know you've probably had enough drama for today, but do you want to talk about your dad?"

"I don't know. I think I'm not as affected by it as Will is. I don't think I've ever really gotten to be the one to take care of him like that. I have zero clue how Reagan's going to handle it either."

"She hasn't reached out to you this week, right?"

The realization hits me harder than I would have liked. "No, she hasn't. She responded to Callie and Jensen a couple of times in the group chat over stupid stuff, but that's all I've heard from her."

Dex brushes his fingers through my hair. "She'll come around. I'll come with you if you want to talk to her when we get back."

A nervous laughter slips out. "She might try to scare you away."

"Eh, I'm not afraid of her. You, though. You still terrify me."

I sit up again with a scoff. "Dex! I'm like the least scary person ever. I think I can give you evidence of that, actually."

Dex lets out a laugh with this adorable smile on his face. "Please, don't. Luce, I fear how much I could love you with more evidence."

Chapter 42
Dex

The next morning, Miles sits at the small table in the suite. His legs are swinging back and forth as he inhales his waffle. Lucie would typically be sitting right next to him, but after finally getting food in her system yesterday, her adrenaline crash finally took her out. She passed out on the couch while Miles cuddled up next to her watching cartoons.

It's nearly nine in the morning and she's still out like a light. Miles has asked me at least five times if he can go wake her up and even though I'm just as tempted to, I tell him we should let her sleep.

Bringing my plate over to the table, I run my hand over his head as I take the seat next to him. "You ready for today's game, bud?"

Miles sends his bottom lip out. "Do I have to go? Can Lucie and I stay here?"

I sigh. Olsson offered me the day off and I considered it, but I don't want to let yesterday ruin game days for Miles. "I know yesterday was scary. I was scared too, but I don't want you to let what happened ruin the fun you usually have with the team and with Lucie."

Miles crinkles his nose. "You weren't really scared, though. You're a dad, I didn't think dad's get scared."

I humph a laugh. "Believe me, I was terrified yesterday."

"You were?" Miles hangs his head. "I didn't want to scare you."

Shit. "Miles, I'm not upset at you. I'm not upset at anyone." Well, except for Shannon, and that conversation will be happening today as well. "What happened yesterday was scary, but I want you to know that it's okay to be scared. If you really want to stay here with Lucie today, that's okay. But I'm going to the game because I don't want to let what happened ruin the fun I have with the Blues."

Miles picks his head back up, but his shoulders still sag. "I guess so. Can Lucie and I stay with you a lot today?"

I chuckle. "I would love nothing more." I plant a small kiss on his temple to which he immediately wipes off with a snicker. "Hey, while we're on the topic of Lucie, can I talk to you about big boy stuff?"

Miles shoves a big bite of waffles into his mouth and mumbles, "Okie."

When I give him a small look, he giggles as he mumbles an apology with his mouth still full of food. Well, not the point of today's talk, I guess.

"So, I know we talked about Lucie being your nanny and working for me, but—"

"Oh no, is Lucie leaving?" Miles cuts me off with a cry.

"No," I say immediately.

Fuck, I'm not handling this dad talk well this morning. Maybe we should have woken Lucie up.

"Lucie's not going anywhere, Miles, I promise. She still

wants to spend the days with you and teach you. None of that will change."

Miles tilts his head to the side. "Then what will change?"

I take a deep breath, let's try not fucking this one up. "Well, the thing is, I really like Lucie. I love her, actually."

I pause for a minute to think out my next words carefully, and Miles takes over. "Love her like I love Callie?"

I laugh. "Sort of, we've really got to talk about that a little more, but, essentially, yes. One day, I want to ask Lucie to marry me. I want her to be a part of our family. That doesn't mean you won't still have time with your mom, but our family is going to look a little different. Doesn't mean anyone loves you less, though."

Miles chews on his lip for a moment. Shit, I don't know if I've just fucked my kid up even more than I already have.

"Do you have any questions?"

I hold my breath until his little mouth opens. "So, does this mean you and Lucie will hug and kiss sometimes?"

"Yeah, probably sometimes." *Every second I have alone with her.*

Miles hums quietly for a moment, but then the floodgates open. "So, if you do marry Lucie, could we get more turtles? Or maybe a puppy! Oh, could I get a little brother? Or maybe a sister? Or we get both! I think I would be a really good big brother. Oh, if you do marry Lucie, does that mean you'll have a wedding? Could I be in it?!"

I swallow down my laugh, trying not to discourage any questions. "Um, good thoughts. Okay, no, we will not be getting any more animals in our house. The two turtles are the max, currently. I think you would be a great big brother, but maybe we just focus on it being us three for a little while.

And yes, whenever I do ask Lucie to marry me, you will be a part of the wedding."

Miles gives me a big grin. "Awesome."

I let out a deep breath. "Do you have any other questions? I want you to know you can ask me or Lucie any questions you think of, okay?"

Miles taps his chin with that smile still on his face. "Does this mean you can start playing baseball again? I know you were Lucie's favorite player. She might really like that, Daddy."

"I—" Shit. I know I told Lucie I would think about it, but it's been put on the back burner again. I'm not even sure if it's fully possible. There's absolutely no way I'm playing for any other team than the Blues, and we're stacked on this team already. "I don't think so, bud. I'm good with being one of the coaches for now."

Miles gives me a small shrug before going back to his breakfast. "Okay, but I think Lucie would like it. I would really like it too."

"What are we really liking?" Lucie's voice comes from behind us.

"Lucie!" Miles practically jumps up from the table, racing to her before she can even make it fully out of her room.

Lucie catches Miles as he launches himself at her with a huff, then a laugh. "Good morning, Miles."

Miles wraps his arms around her neck. "I wanted to wake you up a lot, but Daddy said to let you sleep. Daddy also said that he loves you, which is really cool because I was thinking I could be in the wedding and maybe the turtles too. Daddy said we can't get any more animals or a brother or sister yet, but maybe you could tell him we need one."

Oh, dear God.

Lucie looks at me with a laugh before setting Miles back down. She kneels in front of him, taking his hands in hers. "Ya know, Miles, I love your dad too, but I think I have to agree with him on waiting for more animals and babies."

"Oh." Miles pouts.

Lucie shakes her head with a smile. "You know who else I love? You. I really love you." She boops Miles's nose, and he giggles.

"I really love you too."

Lucie pulls Miles to her for another hug. I stand up from the table. "And I love you both, but someone's got waffles over here that he needs to eat."

Miles jumps back. "Oh yeah, I had Daddy put the berries on the waffles like you do, Lucie. I don't think he made it as good as you, but it's still good."

"Hey, I did the same thing she does."

Miles snickers a laugh. "I don't think so, it's just different."

"Yeah, it's a different hotel waffle."

Lucie's smile is wide as she winks at Miles. "I'll make you one tomorrow."

Miles snickers another evil laugh.

"Okay." I spin him around toward the table. "Go eat."

Holding my hand out, I help Lucie stand back up. "Thank you for letting me sleep in."

I brush her hair behind her shoulders. "You're no longer the nanny, and you're already taking advantage," I joke.

Lucie's eyes go wide. "Dex, you—"

"I'm kidding." I kiss her forehead. "You needed the sleep, baby. Go take a seat, let me get you some breakfast."

Lucie bites at her lip. I can feel her smartass remark

about her making the food better on the tip of her tongue, but she doesn't say it. Instead, she takes the seat I just left, next to Miles. "I think I'll just eat yours instead."

"Lucie, I was also thinking, should we get Daddy to play again?"

Lucie looks back to me for a moment, then to Miles. "I completely agree."

I shake my head, not bothering to put a damper on their morning. Walking around the island to the kitchen to make a new plate of food, my phone lights up with a ton of texts.

They're just baseball players

BECK

Life check on the peeps across the hall. I'm assuming it's good considering room service was remaking my bed when I got back from the game yesterday. 😏

WILL

Why? You know I'm in this chat. Why start my morning off like that?

ADAM

Welcome to it. Maybe you'll stop making out with my sister all the time now at games.

CALLIE

Magic eight ball says: Not likely.

ADAM

Shocked. How's Miles, Dex?

TRIPP

You guys want me to bring up breakfast? I'm downstairs now.

Fuck, this is why I could never play for any other team.

We're all good. Miles and Luce are eating breakfast together now. Thanks for checking in. I appreciate it.

The reply sits for about five seconds before I get a text from Will individually.

WILL

How's my sister doing?

She's good, we talked a bit about it yesterday. What's bothering her more is that Reagan still hasn't reached out to her since that day in my office.

Yeah, I'm working on that. Luce is coming to the game today, right?

Yeah, her and Miles both.

Alright, I'll check in with her on the shuttle. Enjoy the morning.

Setting my phone back on the counter, I throw together another plate of waffles. Before I can make it around the counter, there's a knock at our door.

Hell, I'm sure there's someone from this fucking chat on the other side of this door. When I swing it open, I'm taken aback to see Olsson standing on the other side.

"Morning, Dex. You all got a second to talk?"

I step back, opening the door wider. I had planned on talking to him later today, but now works too. "Sure, come on in."

"Hi, Mr. Owl-son," Miles says with a mouth full of waffles.

I let out a sigh, while my boss laughs. "Good morning, Miles. I'm happy to see you're in good spirits this morning. You planning on coming to the game today?"

Miles goes to talk while chewing again, but Lucie stops him. "Swallow first, please, then answer."

Miles scrunches his nose at her then swallows. "Yep, me and Lucie are going to hang out with Daddy today. I do *not* want to get lost again."

"Yeah, none of us want that." Olsson tips his head to the balcony. "Care to take this out there?"

"Yeah, come on." I hold out my arm to let him go first. Lucie sends me a look with furrowed brows, so I send her a wink in the hope that she'll relax. This conversation is going to be about Shannon. I don't plan on entertaining any other topics until that's discussed.

With the sliding door closed, Olsson doesn't miss a beat. "So, what actually happened yesterday? Shannon made it a point to follow up with me about it, but something isn't adding up. She said she heard about it from Callie, but you mentioned something about her being involved before you left, so hit me with it."

Why am I not surprised she tried to act as if she didn't know?

"Well, you were there when Kate explained how it all started. I could play the blame game all day, but it will really get me nowhere. Miles got turned around and couldn't find Lucie...but he said he did find Shannon. Look, I know Miles isn't her responsibility, but he's a child and he needed her help. That stadium was packed yesterday—I'm not sure if it's from the fights we had earlier this season that drew the crowd in, but it overwhelmed Miles. He may be comfortable being in a ball stadium, but he's only fucking five."

Olsson curses under his breath. "I was afraid you were going to say that. Between the complaints Will keeps making about the way she treats Callie and now this, I think it's time I bring someone else in."

I give him a curt nod. "I know that's a lot to put on someone mid-season, so if you need help, let me know."

"I'll make do. I think I have someone I can call in who's pretty comfortable with all this, but I'll keep your offer in mind." Olsson looks through the glass door at Miles and Lucie. "Seems like Lucie's working out. I knew she would be good for you, and I'm not talking about working for you."

I let out a chuckled curse. She's more than good for me. "Yeah, she's exactly what I needed."

Chapter 43
Lucie

Miles has pretty much been glued to my hip since we left the hotel. Not that I'm complaining—I did consider glue several times this morning while we got ready for today's game. Thankfully, he got the metaphorical sense of what I was going for.

Sitting on the benches to the side of the bullpen, we watch a couple of the guys throw some pitches. Dex stands close by, watching and correcting when needed. I'm not sure if he got the glue memo too, but he hasn't seemed to venture too far from us either.

Miles wiggles on the bench. His eyes narrow on Tripp and Beck in the outfield.

I nudge him with my shoulder. "You know, if you want to go catch some balls, you can."

Miles scrunches his nose. "Well, I kind of do..." He peers up at me, and I can practically see the hesitation to even finish the sentence in his eyes.

"I know yesterday was scary, but we shouldn't let it ruin doing something we love." I boop his nose. "Not to mention,

Miles, I think the entire team will be keeping a close eye on you today. You're a very loved boy."

Miles gives me a toothy grin. "You're right, I'm gonna go get my glove!"

He shoots off the bench, nearly colliding with Dex on the way out. Pulling myself from our seats with less enthusiasm, Dex pulls me to him when I get close to plant a kiss on my forehead. "He gonna go shag some balls?"

"Yeah, it took a little convincing, but not much. Something tells me we might be able to get today to replace what happened yesterday."

A smile tugs at Dex's lips. "I thought it might."

"I'm going to help him get his glove and go out there with him. You have fun coaching." I step around him, but turn back and send him a wink. "Maybe if you watch them throw enough, you'll change your mind about retirement."

Dex tilts his head back, that smile growing ever so slightly. "How long until you and Miles let that go?"

I shrug, walking backward toward the door Miles just went through. I don't want to give Dex too much opportunity to rebut, so I take a few more steps before I toss back, "I don't know...shall we find out?"

Dex tries to hide his laugh as he runs his hand over his face. When he looks at me, I can see the smart aleck remark on the tip of his tongue, but I turn around and step into the hall.

I'll give it until the end of the season. Miles and I will wear him down.

Before I can pull open the locker room door, Miles swings the door open. "I got my glove! Let's go!"

"Hold up, Hotshot." I catch him before he races around me. "Let's put on a little sunscreen first."

Miles's arms practically drop to the floor. "Ah, man."

"That's funny, Lucie used to make the same face when I'd tell her to put sunscreen on when we were kids," Will says, walking down the hall...with my sister. Will looks to Reagan. "You remember that pout, don't you, Rea?"

Reagan gives me a soft smile. "Lucie would pout, and I'd just run away from you."

Miles lifts his head with the thought. I might be a little taken aback with Reagan making a random appearance, but I don't miss that mischievous glint in his eyes.

"Don't even try it," I say before he can even attempt an escape. I turn back to my siblings now standing right in front of me. I want to ask what's going on, but I also don't want to freak Miles out again. I need my family members to stop ambushing me. "Miles, this is my sister Reagan. I don't think the two of you have officially met yet."

"Hi, Miles, I've heard a lot about you. Specifically, that you give Will a run for his money with Callie."

Miles tilts his head to the side. "I don't know about money, but I do love Callie."

Reagan laughs while Will whispers a curse. "I swear, Lucie, you were supposed to help with this."

I hold my hands up. "I made no such promise. You said it, I never acknowledged it."

Will pinches the bridge of his nose with a sigh. "Well, Casanova, let's get you sunscreen, and then, for some reason, I'm going to take you to see Callie in the outfield."

Miles jumps and bolts back to the locker room. "Yay! Hurry up, Will."

My brother goes to follow him, and I catch his arm. My brain feels like it's in slow motion. "I didn't plan on leaving him today."

Will's face softens. "You had my back yesterday. I think my pride can handle a five-year-old trying to steal my girlfriend for a bit. I've also already talked to Dex about it, so no arguments."

Reagan leans her head around the back of Will to meet my face. "Come on, Luce, I drove all the way down here for you to yell at me."

"I don't want to yell at you." Okay, maybe a little bit of a lie. I don't have the energy to yell at her.

Will opens the door to the locker room. "I've got Miles. You guys talk. My only request is that you don't burn the stadium down."

I barely get Will's name out in protest before he shuts the door. Dang it, I guess getting the last word in is an Anderson sibling thing.

"So, you want to yell at me in the hall or somewhere else?" Reagan twirls her finger at me. "You know you want to."

I smack at her hand. "I don't want to yell. I'm not exactly happy with you, but I don't need to yell at you to feel better."

Reagan's teasing smile turns down. "What if I need you to yell to make myself feel better?"

I want to laugh, but I bite it back. "Hate to break it to ya, but you're not going to get that from me. Did Will make you drive down here?"

"It didn't take too much convincing after I got all the details. It was just a four-hour drive. A little audiobook action, and it flew by."

I press my lips together. In a way, I'm happy to see Reagan. I miss her. Even before I started working for Dex she was standing me up. "Come on."

I step to the other side of the hall and go in the extra

equipment room Dex pulled me into yesterday. "So, Will told you about Dad too?"

The door clicks behind Reagan. "He did. I think I'm feeling somewhere in the middle of you two. Not afraid of a conversation, but not entirely sure how much of a relationship I want... That's not why Will wanted me to come down here, though. I know he told you about all the guys I've run off."

"He did." I swallow a bit of pride. "I'm not going to yell, and really it feels a little redundant to be angry at you considering I'm here now with someone who's actually good to me. That being said, I have a right to make my own choices, Reagan. I love you and Will both so much. I know what you did was with a good heart, and Will keeping it a secret until now—I get it. What's done is done, but I had a right to those bad choices. You deciding to tell those guys to leave me alone instead of telling me only leaves me to assume that you thought I was incapable of handling them myself. I can be a kind and caring person who doesn't want to yell, while still having a backbone and moral compass."

She hangs her head with a small nod, and I know my words land. "I know. I could use the excuse of just wanting to look out for you, but I'm not trying to undermine this. It wasn't my intention to make you feel that you couldn't handle it or doubt that you would make the right decision... It was more that I could just take care of it for you. It's still unfair—I know. I'm sorry."

"Thank you. I know that's what you were trying to do with Dex too, but this is different."

Reagan's mouth draws into a thin line. "You're right. Will told me that. I could see that in the office. I know I overstepped. We're usually together constantly, and with both of our moves...I don't think we've truly ever spent that much time apart, even through college. Then I saw how close you and Jensen had gotten...It's silly, I know, but the shift in our dynamic got in my head.

"I could practically feel what Will meant when he said you had the potential of a real relationship. I didn't want to run Dex off, but I needed to protect you in any way I could. I know I left you hanging with my own move. I thought I was overcompensating for it, but really I was just being a bitch. I'm sorry."

My nod comes slow as the weight of her words rolls off my back. This isn't about forgiving her. I'm not sure there's much my siblings could do that wouldn't come with my automatic forgiveness, but I want Reagan's respect.

"I'm not going to say it's okay. As my older sister, I appreciate that and accept the apology. I truly do. We were dealt a difficult hand when Dad left. I want a chance to play my own cards for once. Just me."

Reagan huffs an amused breath. "I like your metaphor. It feels very Reagan-themed. I'm sorry I cheated you a bit."

"Thank you."

A knock comes as Dex opens the door. "Hey," he says softly. He steps around to me, wrapping his arms around me, then pulling my back against his chest. "Will told me to check on you guys in five minutes for proof-of-life."

I tilt my head up to him. "Did he specify which sister he thought needed the life check?"

Dex places a kiss on my temple. "I'm not answering that."

Reagan hums. "I know it's for me, but alas, I think we've made our amends. Granted, I would have liked some yelling to see I've rubbed off on my sister even just a little bit."

Dex's arms squeeze around me. "Nah, Lucie doesn't need to yell when her calm reasoning hits a lot harder."

A baseball-sized ball of emotion forms in my throat.

"That it did." Reagan chuckles, then looks at me. "Mind if I hang out with you and Miles today?"

"Actually..." Dex starts before I can even open my mouth. "I think you interrupted something last time we met. Will could probably use your help with Miles for a minute."

My stomach does a little flip and I look up at him with my jaw dropped.

"Did you just tell me to leave so you could make out with my sister? In the equipment room?"

Dex looks at Reagan, not a single hint that he's joking shows on his face. "Yep."

The corners of Reagan's mouth tip up as she tries to bite back a smile. "Alright, fair. I'll go find Will on my own."

My jaw hangs until Reagan disappears behind the door. "Dex, did you really—"

My sentence dies off as Dex spins me around, and his lips find mine. His hands thread through my hair. "I did and I'll do it again."

He leans back in for one more slow kiss before pulling my hand against his chest and simply holding me to him. "Talk to me, Luce. Did seeing her help? I wasn't too sure about it, but Will said he knew what he was doing."

Of course he'd say that. "It was good. I had let all of her hurtful words go after yesterday. I know I wanted some space, but not like that."

"I get it. I'm glad that helped." Dex brushes his fingers through my hair. "You know...I have been meaning to bring something else up."

A pain comes straight to my chest. "I can't take any more drama, Dex. I don't have it in me."

I feel Dex's laugh vibrate against his chest. "Well, this is pretty serious."

When he pauses, I look up at him—my heart in my freaking stomach. Despite his playful tone, I don't know where he's taking this right now.

A sly smile plays at the corner of his mouth. "We've got to talk about your cursing. I mean, after yesterday's f-bomb—it's getting out of hand, baby."

I bury my face back in his chest. "Dex."

Dex tightens his hold around me. "I don't know if there's a place you can go for that. A class, maybe. I can't have my son's teacher cursing. It just won't work."

My laugh comes out easy now. "It's a good thing I'm not *just* his teacher then, I guess."

Dex leans back to cup my face. "No, you're definitely not. I think I want to hear you curse again, baby."

My eyes roll before locking with his. "Then earn it, Coach."

Chapter 44
Lucie

I scramble for the snooze button on my phone. Waking up in the penthouse in Boston instead of a hotel is a dream—waking up in Dex's bed with him wrapped around me is a heaven I never want to leave.

Two weeks ago, when Jensen made our nail appointments for nine in the morning, I didn't know it was going to be pulling me out of Dex's bed.

He pulls me back to him. His voice comes out all gruff and sleepy. "Morning, baby."

I roll into him. Between the warmth of his body and his hand making small strokes through my hair, I'm never getting up. Closing my eyes again, I mumble, "Good night, Dex."

Dex hums in amusement. "I would love nothing more than to stay here all day with you, but you've got to go meet Jensen." I let out a groan, which leads to another low hum from him. "We're also about to get ambushed in three...two..."

The bedroom door opens with a bang. "Daddy! Lucie! Wake up, we're decorating the classroom today!"

This time it's Dex who lets out a groan.

"Huh, now who's complaining?"

Miles jumps on the end of the bed. "Not me!"

I pull myself from Dex to sit up and smile at Miles. "No, never you."

I was worried about how all of this would go over with him. I know he was excited the morning Dex told him, but there's a difference between telling him and it actually happening.

For the final two nights in New York, Dex and I stayed in our separate rooms...well, mostly. Dex would sneak over to my room after Miles fell asleep.

I hadn't even anticipated being in Dex's bed last night, but when we walked inside, Dex took my suitcase straight to his room. He then proceeded to explain to Miles why my stuff was moving into his room, which somehow ended up with Dex agreeing to turn my room into a bigger classroom.

I wasn't even about to complain. I can teach with that view any day. I can also easily sleep in this bed every night.

Dex sits up next to me. "Alright, bud. Let's let Lucie get ready while we make breakfast, then we'll get to work after that."

"Could Lucie make breakfast? I don't know how to tell you this, but..." Miles tilts his head. "Lucie is the better cook."

I try so hard to swallow my laugh, but oh boy, do I fail. Miles joins me in a fit of giggles while poor Dex has to sit with that comment.

"I do the same exact thing she does."

Miles doesn't try to stop his laughter, but talks through it. "She just makes it better!"

Dex tosses his hands in the air, then reaches for Miles.

"That's it. Come here, I'll give you something to laugh about."

Dex pulls Miles to him, ticking until his laughter comes out in full force. "Lucie was...laughing...too!"

I practically jump off the bed. "Oh no, not me."

When Dex lets Miles go, he whips around and lunges for me. "Save me, Lucie!"

"Always, bud." I scoop him up off the bed before setting him back down on the floor. "Let's get our teeth brushed, then I'll help your dad make breakfast before I leave."

"Okie."

When Miles goes into the bathroom, Dex grumbles. "I make it the exact same."

I lean back on the mattress to kiss his cheek. "I'm sure you do, babe. You just don't have the sunshiny touch."

Dex gives me a cocky grin. "Nah, I lost that when I hit thirty. That's what I have you for."

"Oh, really? Needed someone younger to make you less grumpy?" I slide back off the bed, walking to meet Miles in the bathroom.

Dex huffs a laugh, meeting me at the end of the bed. His athletic shorts sit low on his hips. I'm tempted to start tracing the ink on his chest, but I know we're seconds away from walking in on a toothpaste explosion in the bathroom already.

Dex caresses my cheek. "I just needed you."

After brushing our teeth, I "help" Dex make some scrambled eggs. It only feeds into Dex's theory of favoritism when Miles tells him it's better when I help him.

While Dex gets Miles set up in the living room, I throw some of the eggs onto plates.

Dex walks back into the kitchen, shaking his head. "I told you I'm just as good a cook as you, baby."

"Hey, I never doubted you. Want me to go tell Miles that you did all the cooking?"

Dex comes around behind me, wrapping his arms around my waist. "No fucking way, I'll take the silent victory."

Dex gathers my hair to one side then places a small kiss on my neck. "We have the whole day off and you decide to leave me for hours, just to come back and drag me to a game night at your brother's place."

I giggle as he nips at my ear. "Listen, I'm already fighting off a small panic attack at the fact that the first time I'll be meeting your parents is when they're babysitting, even though *I'm* supposed to be the nanny."

Dex spins me around by my hips. "No, Luce, being the nanny was a detour. You were always supposed to be mine." Dex tilts my face up by my chin to give me a small kiss. "Take your breakfast and eat while you get ready, I don't want you to be late."

I hum softly, taking in the feel of him holding me close. "I'll be right back after."

"Take your time. I have a feeling Miles is going to hold us up in switching the rooms around for the entire day. I'd get out of it if I could."

I give him a playful shove. "It's your own doing. You just had to move my stuff into your room."

Dex pulls me back in. "Oh, it was a necessity."

It takes Jensen a total of five seconds for our butts to hit the salon chair to bring up Dex. "Seriously, just look at her. She's practically glowing, she's so in love."

Our nail girls give each other a look, while Jensen sends a smug one my way. "She entertained the fantasy, and look at her now."

Elle reaches for my hand to start. "So, tell us, how does his laugh sound now?"

"Yeah, yeah, so his laugh is great. I'm living a dream, and Jensen has a thing for one of his best friends. I'm working on that so we can round out the full fantasy."

Jensen's jaw drops. "Excuse me, I do not have a thing for Beck. You've lost your damn mind."

"Kylie, Elle, did I mention which best friend?"

Kylie taps her file on the desk with a smirk. "Nope, don't think you did."

If Jensen was in one of Miles's cartoons, I swear there would be steam coming out of her ears. "This was not the point of the conversation I started."

"Oh, come on, why not give Beck a chance?"

"What? No!" Jensen's cheeks start to turn red. "Beck has the energy level of a child, where I barely have enough energy to make it through the day as is."

"Ah, so it's a time thing—not that you're not attracted to him."

"Tell us about his laugh, Jensen," Elle teases.

"Okay, I'm done here." Jensen pulls her hand back from Kylie.

We all give her pointed looks as she sets her hands back in front of Kylie. "It's my turn for a topic shutdown. No Beck talk during the nail appointment."

"Fine. Fine. We'll drop it...for now."

"Thank you." Jensen sighs. "Let's go back to you. Are you still doing your list, or is that all null and void now?"

I thought about it, but then I kind of hated the idea that those guidelines would stop. Dex helped me see that who I am wasn't exactly about having my siblings' personalities, but more that I've been watching my brother and sister live their lives while I was simply letting mine pass me by.

I give Jensen a shrug. "They were never about anyone but me. If anything, I think the meaning behind them has changed. I have a clearer sense of who I am, but who's to say I shouldn't still do things that scare me or have a yes day every now and then? Refill my cup and all that good stuff."

"And the spicy side? What about those?" Jensen lowers her voice. "Daddy Dex make an appearance on those? Oh, is Daddy your kink?"

Oh, gracious. "Jen!"

Jensen looks at Kylie and Elle. "What? It's a fair question! Right?"

Elle pulls out my light pink nail polish with a huge grin. "Very fair."

Kylie laughs. "The jury is going to need an answer, Miss Anderson."

"Well, I plead the fifth." I feel my phone vibrate while Jensen boos me for not answering her.

They're just baseball players

Callie has added Emma Olsson to the chat.

CALLIE

Game night tonight, be there at 7!

BECK

Roger that Callie Bear.

TRIPP

Emma's riding with me, but we might be a little late. I'm helping them transfer over stuff since we have officially escaped bitchiness.

ADAM

Please tell me we're not playing Monopoly again.

WILL

As Miles would say, Adam is a sad loser.

FAV PLAYER

Luce and I will be there.

BECK

Aye, parent's night out. How romantic. You going to do it in the car or maybe sneak over to Adam's?

WILL

Can I uninvite Beck?

CALLIE

Lucie! You're with Jensen right? Ask her if she's coming!

BECK

If Jennie says she's coming then no I can't be uninvited. If she's not then… I'll still show up either way.

I snort a laugh. "Are you coming to Callie's game night tonight?"

Jensen scrunches her nose. "Are we playing Monopoly again?"

"No, I think after Adam nearly threw out the board after playing with Will, we're going to have to put that one off for a bit."

"Alright, I'll be there."

I bite back a smart remark about Beck. We're still at the nail appointment, so technically I can't bring it up, and mostly I don't want her to bail.

Jensen's coming!

BECK

Hell yeah.

"Great, you can also meet Emma. She's a year or so younger than us, I believe."

"She's the girl who replaced Shannon, right?"

Thank God. "Yeah, she's the GM's daughter. She seems really cool. Her and Tripp have this weird friendship. He doesn't even try to hit on her."

Jensen furrows her brows. "What?"

I switch hands. "I know, I asked Dex about it, but naturally—"

Jensen reads my mind. "He's a guy, so he has zero information."

"None! Mine and Callie's guess is that it's just the coach's daughter aspect. Then again, she's blonde, so part of me thinks she's just not his type."

Jensen rolls her eyes. "I'm not even going to attempt to understand any of those ball players."

I send a side eye to Kylie and Elle that Jensen does not miss.

"We're still in the middle of the appointment. The looks

fall into the acknowledgements of who we're not supposed to be talking about right now."

I hold my one painted hand up. "Alright, I'm sorry."

"Let's get back to you. What's your plan for the rest of the day? You could have yourself a yes day. You know...yes to nails, yes to game night..." Jensen tilts her head with a smirk. "Yes to Daddy Dex."

I tilt my head to match her smile. "Still not answering that. But I do have an idea. How much trouble would you get in for tattooing me?"

Jensen's eyes light up. "Shut up, this is the best day ever. Technically, I'm not allowed to tattoo outside of my apprenticeship, but I'd really hate to have you sit through a session with Hank hovering." Jensen's shoulders drop for a moment, then perk right back up with a wicked smile. "Then again, Hank is off today. One of the other artists, Blake, is the only one working. He'd probably supervise no problem."

"I don't want to get you in trouble, Jen."

"I'm still down to cut his balls off with my nail scissors," Kylie mumbles.

Jensen sends her a kissy face. "Man deserves it. Besides, he's been driving me nuts for a year and a half! It's not like you're going to get a sleeve, it's one session and done. He can consider it my one fuck you for the duration of this hell he's putting me through."

I really hate the idea of putting Jensen in this situation, but there's no way I would go to anyone else but her.

Jensen reaches out her hand. "Pleaseeeee, make it your yes day. Say yes to letting me give you a tattoo! Maybe a piercing too."

She's got me there. "Yes to the tattoo. No to the piercing."

Jensen lets out a girlish squeal that seems so far out of her character, but I love it.

Elle lets go of my hand. "Well, I hope you know you're not leaving here until we see what you're going to get."

Chapter 45
Dex

"Look, Daddy! Look! I'm painting!" Miles beams at me with a paintbrush in hand and the craziest lines of yellow on the wall in front of him.

"That's perfect, bud. Keep up the good work."

It took a total of three seconds after Lucie walked out the door this morning for Miles to insist on setting up his classroom. I didn't exactly plan on painting it, but it took an hour max to get the very few things Lucie had in this room to mine, then shove all the furniture into the office room down the hall.

With the room completely empty, the white walls looked so boring. I know Lucie loves the view, and I'd let her decorate it however she wants, but the all-white walls had to go.

After an hour at the hardware store, then another hour spent taping everything off, here we are—painting the main wall this sunrise yellow.

"Lucie's going to love this!" Miles squeals, tugging at the bandana tied around his face. "Can I take this thing off now?"

I turned on the fan in the room and the vent from the bathroom to help with the fumes, but I thought I'd go the extra step for Miles. He's definitely not a fan.

"Sorry...if you want to paint, you have to wear the bandana."

Miles groans as he slaps his brush back and forth aggressively on the wall.

Hell, the dramatics this kid has sometimes. I blame Callie. My phone dings in my pocket.

LUCE

Took a little detour with Jensen, now we're going to grab some lunch at Zenith with Reagan. Should be back after that.

Take your time. Just a heads-up, I might be taking this remodel thing a step too far.

That's okay, I also might have taken this day off a step too far.

Jensen didn't make you go running again, did she?

Ha ha, very funny.

Miles and I paint for another hour and manage to get the first coat on. I'm hoping the splotchy spots where Miles painted will even out with another coat, but if not, then I guess I'll figure that out later.

Miles helps me wrap the roller and clean off the brushes, all while complaining about having to stop. He continues to mope over it the entire way back to the living room.

"Careful, Miles, you might trip on that bottom lip if you're not careful."

Miles spins around with a huff. "I can't trip over my lip, Daddy. That's not possible."

I kneel in front of him, giving his shoulders a little wiggle. "It is when you're sad for no reason. I promise we'll paint again."

Miles hangs his head. "But what if Lucie doesn't like it since it's not done?"

"Kid, I assure you, Lucie's going to love it."

And just as if I speak her into existence, Lucie walks in the front door. "Hey, I'm home."

Miles's hanging shoulders go up, and his frown flips with bright eyes. "Lucie! You have to come see what we did!"

He barrels into her so fast that she nearly falls backward. "With this much excitement, I can't wait to see."

Lucie wraps her arms around Miles. *Wait...is that?* "Luce, did you get a tattoo?"

Miles steps back. "Like Daddy's tattoos? I wanna see!"

Lucie looks at me with a smirk. "I had a bit of a yes day. Any guesses on what it is?"

"You know I'm not good at this game."

Lucie scrunches her nose with a smile. "The deja-vu should be a hint itself." Lucie turns her arm, giving a clearer look at the two small turtles on the inside of her forearm. Tiny dots are sprinkled to give the illusion of wind blowing some clover and daisies around them.

"You got Pip and Pop!"

Lucie laughs. "I sure did. What do you think?"

"It's so cute!" Miles bounces around. "Little Pip and Pop stuffies. Pip and Pop tattoos. Can I get a tattoo?"

"No," Lucie and I say together.

Miles grumbles something under his breath, but I let it go.

"You've got growing to do before you can get tattoos, bud." I step around him to get a better look at Lucie's arm. "Jensen did a good job. It's very you, Luce."

"I thought so." A small blush comes to Lucie's cheeks, and she shrugs. "It was for me."

"Even better. I love when you're selfish." I wink.

Lucie gives me a little shove as her cheeks let out a full blush. "Hey, why does it smell like paint in here?"

"Ope!" Miles grabs Lucie's hand. "Come on, we have a surprise!"

While Miles drags Lucie down the hallway, she angles her head back. "What did you do?"

"Guess, baby."

Lucie scrunches her nose at me, then lets Miles drag her the rest of the way. When we reach the doorway, Miles lets go of Lucie's hand and jumps into the room, yelling "Ta-da!"

"Oh my goodness." Lucie looks back with wide eyes. "You painted a wall yellow?"

"I helped," Miles says with this proud grin.

"I can see that." Lucie flashes her eyes to me as she bites back a smile, then lets it go when she kneels in front of Miles. "It's perfect. I love it so much."

"I really wanted to keep painting, but Daddy said we had to take a break."

I shake my head. He might have tattled on me, but at least he didn't ask her to paint more.

Lucie boops his nose. "You know your dad has a point. We should let it dry then we can do another coat of paint. Maybe I can help this time too?"

"Yes! Yes!" Miles squeals. "Can we do it tomorrow morning?"

Lucie laughs. "We'll see. We also have some stuff to pick

out for school too. I promise we're going to have so much fun decorating this place together. We have plenty of time."

I know she didn't mean to, but Lucie's words hit me hard. *We have plenty of time.* It's a strange feeling. Everything over the past five years has felt like the only way I could operate was on a day-by-day basis.

Thinking of what my life would be over the years, I just saw Miles. I still do, but now I see Miles in little league practice with me, and whichever one of my teammates wants to help me make some kids' day by coaching. I see Lucie in the stands holding another member of our family, along with, I'm sure, the rest of Miles's fan club.

I see Lucie in my hat at every single game. I see our kids falling asleep with her on our couch, waiting for me to carry them to their beds. I see them all hating my food, but loving Lucie's. I see the fucking turtles in this classroom. I see Lucie and I on the balcony every chance we get.

Shit, all of that just because she slid me her coffee cup.

"Lucie." Miles fiddles in front of her. "Can we learn something today?"

Lucie stands back up. "Of course, we can. Why don't you go grab a box of crayons and some of the construction paper, and meet me at the counter?"

"Okie!" Miles takes off around me, then right out the door.

Lucie gets one shake of her head before I'm right there, pulling her in for a kiss. My hands caress her cheeks as her arms wrap around my back. I kiss her slow, because she's right—we have plenty of fucking time. Well, sort of.

"Lucie! Where are the crayons?" Miles yells all the way from the other side of the penthouse.

Despite her stress about meeting my parents, Luce was her usual ray of sunshine, which they adored. Not that anyone but Miles's opinion would change my mind about Lucie. I know it mattered more to her.

We barely make it to Callie and Will's place on time. Every glance at Lucie in that yellow dress I love had me seriously considering Beck's car sex text.

By the time we make it to the elevator, I can't stand not touching her for a second longer. I pull her to me by the jean jacket she threw on before we left.

"So, if we were to skip out on game night…"

Lucie rolls her eyes toward me. "Dex, can I not wear yellow ever?"

"I'm pretty sure I've begged you to never stop actually." I lean in, kissing her until the elevator dings. "It'll find its way to my floor later, I suppose."

Lucie sends me a mischievous little smirk. "It's almost as if I hoped that would happen."

Fuck. Lucie Anderson was never going to be the death of me—no, she's brought me back to life.

Lucie knocks on Will's door before walking in. Seems like almost everyone's here already, sitting at the kitchen table. Callie sits in the middle of Beck and Will, and Jensen is to Beck's right while Adam's on hers.

Callie stands up to greet us, then holds up a deck of cards. "Perfect timing. Tripp and Emma should be coming up now. Poker is tonight's game."

Lucie looks back at me. "Maybe we should bail, I have a terrible poker face."

"No," Jensen hollers all the way from her seat. "No bailing."

"Come on, baby. You can bet as much of my money as you want. No poker face required."

After Lucie and I grab our seats, Tripp and Emma file in, and Beck deals out the first hand. "So, who's watching Miles tonight?"

I wait to look at my cards until they're all passed out. "My parents. I'm sure he'll barely make it past eight tonight. He helped me paint a wall in Luce's old room today."

The moment the sentence leaves my mouth. I know I should have worded that differently.

"Oh, moving her in your room already?" Beck dances his eyebrows.

"Come on, really?" Will throws his hands up toward Beck.

But then Adam joins. "Dude, I helped move my sister into this very apartment to live with you two months ago."

Will sends a wink to Callie. "Touché."

Lucie reaches her hand over to my thigh. "Him and Miles are working to get that room turned into the new classroom. Seems the white walls were a little too boring, though."

Tripp picks up his cards and nudges Emma. "Ems could paint you something."

Emma's cheeks blush. "I could if you want, but if you don't—"

"No, I think that'd be great." I send a look to Lucie and she nods.

"That would be awesome actually. I love the yellow, but

Miles was a little heavy-handed in some places. I'm not too sure how many coats we need to make it even."

Emma sits up in her chair a bit. "Okay, we can talk about it later this week then."

Beck flips over the first three cards and Lucie leans over to show me her seven and two of clubs. "I don't know what to do with this."

Before I can reply, Will speaks. "Well, when you say that to the table, you fold."

Lucie sticks her tongue out at him, then sets her cards back down. "Fine, I'll just wing it."

Jensen perks up next. "Oh, Luce, did you show everyone what we did today?"

Lucie holds out her arm for everyone to *ooh* and *ahh* over. I mostly love watching Lucie as her face lights up when she talks about it. I hope she never stops this list of hers if it means she smiles like that when does things for herself.

Jensen tosses her card in the middle. "I tried to talk her into nipple piercings too, but she was being a big weeny about it."

My eyes cut to Lucie. Her mouth gapes open. "Hey, I let you stab my arm repeatedly with needles. I wasn't that big of a weeny."

Beck glances back at his cards, then shrugs. "Oh, don't worry, she'll be back. I didn't get my piercings until after a couple tattoos."

Callie whips her head to Beck. "Piercings? Tattoos? What do you mean? You have those?"

Beck fakes being offended. "Callie Bear, have you really spared me so little of your attention?"

The scrape of Callie's chair being pulled closer to Will fills the silence. "Obviously."

Beck tosses his cards to the middle. "They're all where you can't see anyway, Cals. I'd rather not catch a right hook from Will—I won't even offer to show you."

Jensen sends Beck a look. "Alright, I've seen your slutty thigh tattoo, but there's no fucking way you're pierced."

Beck gives her that cocky grin of his. "Want to find out, Jennie? I'll show all my slutty tattoos and piercings if you ask nicely."

I can see Jensen clench her jaw from here. "In your fucking dreams, Beckham."

Lucie leans over to me, but she keeps her eyes on Jensen's reaction. "Is he?"

"I'm not answering that, baby."

"Fair." Lucie sits back up with a chuckle. "Anyway! Miles and I have been trying to talk Dex into playing again."

Ah hell, not this again. Before I can even rebut, everyone piles in.

Beck takes the most offense first. "Why the hell have you not immediately agreed to this?"

Will surprisingly also joins in, even though I was a little worried he might hate this idea. "I second Beck. Actually, bring up the aggression. Why the fuck not?"

Tripp snaps his fingers. "Ems, get your dad on the phone."

"No, for fuck's sake, can you all chill out?" I shoot Lucie a look, and she just smiles back at me. She's lucky I love her so damn much. "I'm perfectly happy where I'm at. You all can drop it now."

The room sits in silence for five seconds max.

"Nah." Beck waves his hand. "Hate that. Next option."

Jensen nudges Adam. "Wait, can he even come out of retirement?"

Adam shrugs. "I mean, yeah. Olsson, I'm sure, would extend him a contract easily."

"I'm not above forgery," the love of my life adds.

Beck snaps at poor Emma this time. "Great. Emma, get your dad on the phone."

Callie pulls out her phone in a flash. "Quit snapping at her, this is her first game night. I'll do it."

Fucking hell. "Okay!" I yell, getting everyone's attention. "I'll tell you what, you guys win the World Series and I'll play again."

The room goes silent again before Beck extends his hand. "Alright, Dad, bet?"

I shake his hand, then murmurs of strategy and team meetings start.

I pull Lucie's chair closer. "You're going to pay for that one, baby."

She looks at me with this wicked smile. "You told me to be more selfish. I want to see my favorite player pitch again."

Chapter 46
Dex

A few months later – World Series final game

I gave these fuckers a common goal. I should have known they'd make it to the fucking end. For four months, everyone stepped up their game. They even had Emma draw up a poster like some damn affirmation reminding them of why they're playing.

Olsson asked me a time or two if I was serious about this bet. Granted, he prefaced the question that either way he's saying fucking nothing to the guys. The idea that this was everyone's motivation to play better was nice. However, I think it has shit to do with the fact that we're playing in this fucking game, though.

These guys busted their asses. Every game, they gave it their all. Even Jordan's pulled his head out of his ass...barely, but the progress is there. No one's schedules are getting looked over and hotels aren't being fucked up since Emma took over Shannon's job. Hell, Lucie and Callie love having her around.

Morale is up, and this team is damn strong from all angles. So, yeah, if these fuckers win this game I'll play again. Hell, I might even if they don't, but I only let Lucie in on that secret.

It's the top of the eighth, and Beck just stepped up to the plate. We don't have home-field advantage against the LA Rays, but it hasn't seemed to matter much. We're leading by two runs, but no one's dared to get too cocky yet.

With the perfect sound of Beck's bat connecting with the ball, he manages an incredible line drive to right field.

Beck points a finger my way with that stupid grin of his. Well, no one's been too cocky—except for Beck.

Will claps my back. "So, I'm not one to speak too quickly, but it seems like my sister might be getting her wish."

My eyes wander over to find my girl. She's been sitting on pins and needles the whole game. She has her arm wrapped around Miles's shoulder, and when we get another player on base, their arms go up in the air.

"It's possible." I may have made one bet with the guys, but I also made a deal with myself as well. I tilt my head back to him. "You said before that I didn't need your blessing. Did you mean that?"

Will chuckles. "No, you don't, so don't ask for it. No details. I won't ask questions. Just make my sister fucking happy."

"That I can do."

We watch as Adam sends a hit damn near out of the park, but unfortunately gets caught for the first out.

Will pitches his voice low. "Listen, heads-up for your little man. I have plans of my own at the start of next season.

I love Miles, but I plan on locking down my girl. I don't want it to break his heart in the process."

"Fuck. Only one of you with the last name Anderson gets emotions out of me, and I want to change her last name. Go away, you're making me feel bad for taking back the slot of best pitcher on the team."

Will laughs. "In your dreams, Larsen. I think you're slowing down in old age, or maybe my sister has made you lose your edge."

"Actually, your sister—"

"Alright, walking away now." Will steps back, but sends me the middle finger on his way.

Maybe someone should warn Olsson that he's about to have a bunch of brother-in-laws playing for him.

We make it through the eighth with no runs on either side. The dugout has done a complete shift. We're still 4–2, and while I like our odds, shit could still turn on us. Especially since we don't have last bat.

Miles and Lucie sit at the edge of their seats the entire top of the ninth. Through Beck's first out. Tripp's single. Adam's double. Then the following two outs.

Still 4–2. This is it, the Rays are up to bat. Two runs in an inning is far from impossible, but I'm confident in how these guys have played not only this game, but the whole damn season.

Our closing pitcher starts us off strong by striking out the first batter. One out.

The next batter makes it to first, but then the next hit is caught in the outfield. Out number two.

I look back at Lucie and Miles. They're hovering over their seats, I'm sure of it. Miles holds Lucie's hand, and she looks so nervous—almost a little pale.

The next batter makes contact and does us dirty by hitting a fucking ground ball. I swear we all hold our damn breath as Mateo scoops it up and sends it right to Beck.

Third out. That's the game.

I guess I'm signing a contract and getting down on one knee when we get back home.

Chapter 47
Lucie

Walking back into our home the next night feels so different this time. We have our World Series win, my man's going to pitch again, and, oh yeah, on the plane ride over here, I took two pregnancy tests in the bathroom. They were both positive.

It's the second time I've cursed this year.

With everyone taking last night to celebrate, Dex and I went back to the hotel, where I proceeded to throw up most of the night. I waved it off as a stomach bug, but then this morning another wave hit. It wasn't until I saw my period cup in my travel bag that it dawned on me I hadn't started.

I assumed I was late from stress and travel—that's not unheard of. Okay, I did miss a dose last month when I left my pills in the hotel bathroom in Houston. It was one pill missed before I got my prescription refilled...I thought it was no big deal. Granted, Miles was with Kate that weekend too.

I immediately messaged Emma and Callie begging them to pick me up a test. There was no way I was saying anything to Dex until I knew for sure.

I couldn't make it home, so I had to take them on the plane. So while all the guys thought I was sick, I was very much not.

Dex pulls me to him and plants a kiss on my forehead. "Go rest, baby. I've got bedtime tonight."

"No," Miles whines. "I want Lucie to help."

"I'm okay, Dex, really." Goodness knows it's not contagious.

Dex opens his mouth to argue, but Miles is quicker. "Pleaseeeee. It's more fun when we do family bedtimes."

My smile comes no matter how nauseous I'm feeling. "How do you say no to that?"

Dex sighs. "I'm pretty sure I'm incapable of it. Come on, let's go."

I let Dex man the teeth brushing and nightly routine while I stand close by, focusing on breathing in through my nose and out through my mouth. By the time we make it to his bed, I feel a bit like I'm fighting for my life as Miles asks me so sweetly to read him a story, but I manage to power through.

I caress Miles's cheek. "I love you, buddy. Get some sleep. No school work tomorrow."

Miles grumbles. I love how much he loves our class time, but I try to keep our weekends school-free.

I step back, letting Dex say his good nights, and slowly make my way to the living room. I have to tell Dex tonight, there's no way I'll be able to fall asleep if I don't.

Part of me knows deep down that Dex will be happy about it, but the other part is absolutely terrified. We're so different from how this happened before for him. I truly can't imagine my life without him, but I can't say how he's going to feel knowing that he's in another unplanned pregnancy.

I hear the click of Miles's door and the moment Dex steps into view, I blurt out, "Hey, want to join me on the balcony for a little bit?"

Dex narrows his eyes at me. I can see him fighting the urge to tell me to go lie down, but Dex has completely lost his prickliness. All it takes is me saying I want it, and he folds.

"Alright, Luce. Just for a little bit, then you've got to get some rest."

I give him a small nod. I don't understand why, but the idea of telling him on the balcony feels like the best advantage. A reminder of where we started—where he told me he may never stop.

Dex pulls me to him as we sit together on the lounge chair. A cool breeze hits my face and I exhale as nauseous waves roll through my body.

"Lucie, baby. Let's go inside."

"No, I'm good, I—" I spin around, kneeling in between his legs. I need to see his face. But for the first time, I think I might actually be afraid of Dex. "Okay, I'm going to tell you something, and you're just going to have to let me get it all out."

Dex chuckles. "You're scaring me a little bit, baby. Where's the guessing game I hate so much?"

I want to laugh. My smile wants to come, but all the anxiety and all the nausea stop me. "Dex, I love you. I'm so in love with you that I know what you meant now about being afraid of me."

Dex sits up to cup my face. "Lucie, baby, what's going on?"

I reach into the pocket of my sweats and pull out the positive tests. "I'm pregnant."

Dex's eyes go wide. He lets go of my face and takes the tests. "You're pregnant?"

Don't throw up. Do not throw up.

"You remember when I forgot my birth control...I didn't think it would mess it up too bad just missing a day...Well, I was very wrong. I'm sorry, I know this wasn't how we—"

Dex stands up abruptly. "Wait right here."

"Wait? What? Dex!"

He's through the sliding door in an instant. I watch as he walks into the living room, grabs something from his duffle bag, and walks right back out.

"Dex, what—"

Dex sits back down, grabs my face, and cuts me off with a deep, deep kiss. My breath is lost, it's consumed by this moment. My fears subside, and every part of my body relaxes at the demanding love I feel in this kiss.

"Lucie, baby. I love you so fucking much, but you're one-upping my move." Dex pulls out a velvet box. "I wanted to bring you out here tonight and ask you to make me the happiest man in the world by becoming my wife. I thought I'd put it off until tomorrow since you're sick, but—" Dex chuckles for a moment, then opens the box, revealing a gold-plated marquise diamond engagement ring.

"Lucie Anderson, you may have fallen in love with my son first, but I fell in love with you the moment I laid eyes on you. I didn't want to admit it—I couldn't understand it—but in that moment I felt it. I've continued to fall in love with you every single day. You and all your damn evidence has piled up."

A tear streams down my cheek as a laugh forces its way

out. "I love you too, Dex. I love Miles, and I love this baby. I just know this wasn't planned."

Dex's thumb glides across my cheek. "I'm so happy you're pregnant, Luce. I don't give a single fuck about a plan. You're already an incredible mother to Miles. I'm about to be so fucking annoying catering to you while you're pregnant. But I'm going to be selfish for one last time. Luce, please have my baby with my ring on your finger. Marry me?"

I let my happy tears fall. "Can I be selfish and say I need my husband to promise to still sign his contract?"

Dex's laugh fuels my soul. "Only if you say yes."

"Yes, I'll marry you, Dex Larsen." My smile grows as his thumb wipes at my cheeks. "I never imagined I'd marry my favorite player, let alone have his baby."

Dex hauls me to him. His forehead rests against mine. "I never imagined anything until you, Luce."

Epilogue — Lucie
Seven months later

"Okay, Miles, when you're done writing your vocabulary words of the week, we're done for today."

"Okie, Mommy." Miles picks up his pencil and scribbles away.

My heart grows a little every time Miles calls me "Mommy." It started soon after Dex and I had a very small wedding in the offseason. We really didn't want to do much of anything other than get married, but Miles had other ideas. Many compromises were made, but I have to admit—it was nice having everyone together to celebrate.

I watch Miles make every turn of his pencil when a loud bang comes from the other side of our house. Miles looks up to me. "What are they doing now?"

I shake my head. "I have no idea, want to go check it out?"

Miles jumps up from his seat. "Yes!"

He races down the hall, with a shout for me to follow, but there's no way I'm moving that fast. Imagine mine and Dex's surprise when we just had our shotgun wedding, then go to our first ultrasound to find out that we're having fraternal twins. I should have known when Miles said he wanted a brother and a sister, but I really didn't think I'd give him both at the same time.

There were a lot of emotions when we found that out. Dex tried saying that he'd just coach again and, for the third time, I cussed telling him *no fucking way*. I'm growing two babies—my man can throw some balls.

As I get closer, I can hear the bickering of men and then the squeal of Miles. I reach what used to be the office. After painting the alphabet and shapes all over the classroom, Dex started Emma on this room. One side is painted with a golden sunrise, and the other with a burnt orange sunset.

It's truly breathtaking every time I look at it, but right now, all I really see are pieces of wood on the floor and four men standing around them, staring.

"Okay, what's happening here?"

My brother points a piece of something at Dex. "Your husband bought the most complicated cribs I've ever seen. And we have two of them to put together."

Dex looks at Beck. "I'm not the one who unboxed both of them at the same time then threw away the boxes with the fucking instructions."

My dad covers Miles's ears. It's been a slow road for Will to come to terms with, but our dad continues to make an effort to make amends. He loves Miles, calls him specifically at least three times a week.

Beck continues to stare at the pile. "Okay, well, your father-in-law is in construction, so I'm pretty sure we can figure this out just fine."

I bite back my laugh. "Do I need to look through the trash to see if I can find them?"

I get a resounding "no" from every man in the room. Dex steps around the pile and kisses my head. "We'll figure it out. How are you feeling?"

"I'm fine, Dex. Babies are moving fine. Miles and I actually just finished up for the day."

Miles raises his hand high. "Can I stay here and help build?"

My dad doesn't miss a beat, like any grandparent would. "We'd love your help. Why don't you go get your tool kit that I got you for your birthday?"

"I'll be right back!" Miles squeals and then races back down the hall.

I huff a small laugh, but then one of the babies turns sideways and I'm pretty sure starts kicking the other.

I reach for Dex's hand and place it right where they're wiggling about.

Dex's eyes light up like they do every time he gets to feel them move. "Fuck, Luce." He leans down toward my belly to talk to the babies. "You guys take it easy on your momma."

Will steps up next. "Hey, let their favorite uncle feel."

"Hey, fuck off, that's my title." Beck tries to shove in the middle.

Dex blocks them both. "Back off. You can feel the babies after you assholes fix those cribs."

Will and Beck both mumble some more curses before backing off. My dad steps forward with his hands up. "I'm not asking to touch, just wanted to say you look beautiful, Luce."

"Thank you." I look down where Dex's hands still rest on my belly.

I have to admit, I like being pregnant. I also never want to do this again, but every time I get to my prenatal yoga class, they have a mirror set up and I just love seeing my belly.

"Have you guys decided on names yet?" Will asks.

It's been quite the debate. Miles has thrown out many suggestions, and while it's hard to say no to him, I did shoot down naming the babies Pip and Pop.

"Well, considering Dex has this whole sunshine thing going."

Dex kisses my temple. "You're my light, baby."

I grin up at him. "With light in mind, I looked up names with that meaning. We've picked Thea and Lucas. Specifically, Lucas William for the boy."

My poor brother, you'd think I'd put him through enough already. His hands rest on his knees for a moment before beelining right to me. He wraps me up tightly in a hug.

Beck tosses down a piece of wood. "Well, he can put these cribs together if he's the only one getting a namesake."

Epilogue — Dex
Three years later

I stand in the dugout of Blues Stadium as Miles tosses the ball in the air. "I don't know, Dad, Uncle Will says my two-seam fastball is better."

"Well, he's not wrong, but we're having an end-of-training scrimmage, why not throw the new changeup a couple times?"

It didn't take too long, but with Miles now nine, he has mastered the eye roll. My sweet Thea wiggles in my arms, reaching for her brother. "Trow fast, bubba. Weally fast."

Miles takes his sister while his team still bats. "See? Even Thea agrees."

These kids. I swear, they just want to fight me.

"How about throwing a few changeups for your mom, huh? Just show her some of the things you've learned this week, please?"

Miles looks to the stands for Lucie. It doesn't take him long because my beautiful wife shines everywhere she goes. Lucas has been stuck to her like Velcro since he was born.

Miles too, really. Both of my boys are obsessed with their mother. Not that I blame them, I'm obsessed with her too.

I, at least, got a little favoritism with my baby girl. Thea loves her momma, but if she's sticking to someone, it's me.

"Alright, just a couple. So Mom can see." Miles hands his sister back over with the final out.

"Thank you, I'm sure she'll love to see it."

"Can you make sure she's watching so I don't have to do it again?"

Yep, nine going on nineteen. "Yes, I'll gladly go talk to her. Now get out there."

Miles sends his eyes to the sky as he makes his way out to the field. When I meet Lucie's gaze, she's already shaking her head at me.

"Why do your sons do things for you and not me?"

Lucas bangs his little hands on the netting. "Daddy!"

Lucie scoops our littlest man up and brings him closer to the net so he can thread his hand through. "Look at that. See, they still love you."

"Yeah, I love them too." I play with Lucas's hand, then Thea joins in, giggling every time I pretend to move her hand away. "Miles has a new pitch, and he wants to make sure you're watching."

Lucie looks out to the field, raising her hand to block the sun.

"Baby, where is your hat?"

Lucie scrunches her nose. "I forgot. I have three kids to get ready, Dex. Hold on and watch Miles."

I turn to see him throw a perfect changeup that goes straight into the catcher's glove. The ump calls the strike, and Lucie cheers for Miles. Granted, the whole fan club cheers with her. Miles looks over with a hint of a smile. Yeah, I think he might throw a few more of those.

I look back at Lucie, her hand still on her forehead.

"Come here, baby." I walk over to the gap and wait for her to follow. I take my hat off and hand it over to Lucas. "Give this to Mommy."

"Okie." He grabs it from me, then holds it high for Luce.

She puts it on with a smirk. "Better, Coach?"

"Much better, baby."

Also by Mollie Goins

Thank you for reading Coach Me, I hope you enjoyed reading Dex and Lucie's story!

Find a bonus chapter for Dex and Lucie linked in the ebook version!

The Boston Blues aren't finished yet though, Beck and Jensen's story is up next in Stealing You.

Pitcher Us

Coach Me

Stealing You

Book Four TBA

Book Five TBA

Aster Creek - Small town series

Feel It All

Bring It All

Despite It All

Acknowledgments

Wow. What an actual trip! This series means the world to me and we're technically only on book 2! (Book 3 is in the works though.)

First thank you will always and forever go to my husband. I'm truly so grateful for all of your love and support. You are in fact a 9.5 on the man written by a woman scale. (Ten is reserved for the fictional, so sorry.) I love you and am so proud of all of the big goals we have achieved this year.

To Page. Holy shit. That escalated quick! I mean seriously, we hit the ground running and said who needs breaks?? I'm so happy that our paths crossed. Thank you for believing in me and essentially cleaning up the mess that is my brain. I love you big. Morale is high, how about you?

To Courtney. I can't believe this year I can't believe the insane growth my business has had since we started working together— I can't believe the friendship I found in a mom that I can lean on. To our endless voicememos for survival and pulse checks. Thank you for being a constant, a confidant, and a kickass marketing babe.

Thank you to each and every alpha and beta reader. Courtney, Page, Brittany, Kristen, Isabella, Jess, Bria, Kelsey, and Robyn. I appreciate each and every one of you and the time you took out of your day to read Dex and Lucie.

Thank you to everyone who had a hand in bringing Coach Me to it's final draft and building up the Mollieverse:

Cover design: Kimberly Sable - KBG Designs
Dev & Proof edits: Lauren Sakowski - Author's Best Friend
Line edits: Caroline Palmier: Love & Edits
Marketing/Publicist: Courtney + Page
Literary Agent: Amanda Wooden

Now, oddly, I kind of want to thank myself... Call it what you want, but I'm proud of me, so I'm going to thank myself for a minute. Damn. We've come a long way! This is has been the dream for the longest and now it's a reality. The mentality growth, the physical health growth, and everything in between.

To my readers. You are incredible. I'm pretty sure I say this in almost all of my acknowledgements, but who cares. If I could reach through this book and hug you, I WOULD. I hope you know how absolutely incredible you are.

From the bottom of my heart, thank you. Thank you for being you.

Love, Mollie.

About the Author

Mollie Goins is a contemporary romance author, with books in the sub genre of small town and sports. With swoon worthy men and strong women, each book delivers on all the sweet, spicy, and emotional moments that you can escape in.

Residing in a small town in Tennessee with her high school sweetheart, Mollie is also a mother to two adorable but wild kids who always keep her on her toes.

Mollie is a chronic out of order reader, so while her books are in a series, each book can be read as a standalone. However, Mollie also loves a good Easter egg, so be looking for callbacks from book to book.

For more information visit molliegoins.com